D0817801

The White Trilogy

3531138

DONATION

The White Trilogy

Ken Bruen

KATE'S MYSTERY BOOKS
JUSTIN, CHARLES & CO., PUBLISHERS
BOSTON

Copyright © 1998, 1999, 2000, 2003 by Ken Bruen

All rights reserved. No part of this publication may be reproduced, stored in a retrieval system, or transmitted in any form or by any means without the prior written permission of the publisher, nor be otherwise circulated in any form of binding or cover other than that in which it is published and without a similar condition being imposed on the subsequent publisher.

FIRST U.S. EDITION 2003

Originally published in Great Britain by The Do-Not Press Limited

This is a work of fiction. All characters and events portrayed in this work are either fictitious or are used fictitiously.

Library of Congress Cataloging-in-Publication Data

Bruen, Ken.
    The white trilogy / Ken Bruen.
        p. cm.
    Contents: A white arrest — Taming the alien — The McDead.
    ISBN 1-932112-02-2
    1. Detective and mystery stories, English. 2. Police — England — London — Fiction. 3. Police corruption — Fiction. 4. London (England) — Fiction. I. Title.

PR6052.R785 W53 2003
823'.914 — dc 21   2002038000

Published in the United States by Kate's Mystery Books, an imprint of Justin, Charles & Co., Publishers, 20 Park Plaza, Boston, Massachusetts 02116
www.justincharlesbooks.com

Distributed by National Book Network, Lanham, Maryland
www.nbnbooks.com

10 9 8 7 6 5 4 3 2

PRINTED IN THE UNITED STATES OF AMERICA

For Peg Amiston

and

To Matthew Zirak, a true literary outlaw

The White Trilogy

a white arrest

the pinnacle of a policeman's career
– Sir Robert Peel

the big one cancels all the previous shit
– Detective Sergeant Brant

R&B they were called. If Chief Inspector Roberts was like the Rhythm, then Brant was the darkest Blues. *Pig ignorant, more like*, was also said.

On Robert's desk was a phone, a family photo, a bronze and wood scroll, which read:

> On Easter Monday 1901, the Rev. James Charmers stepped ashore on Goaribari Island, off the Southern Coast of New Guinea, intent on converting the islanders. The Goas ran down to meet him, clubbed him senseless, then they cut him into small pieces, boiled him and ate him that afternoon.

It was all you needed to know for police work, he said.

WPC Falls contemplated the sugared doughnut. It sat like a fat reprimand next to her coffee. Another WPC joined her, said: "Now, that's temptation."

"Hiya, Rosie."

"Hiya – so, are you going to eat it?"

She didn't know, said: "I dunno."

Falls was the wet dream of the nick. Leastways, she hoped she was. A little over 5' 6", she was the loaded side of plump, but it suited her. Seeing her, the adjectives of ravishment sprang to mind: lush, ripe, buxom, available. The last in hopeful neon.

She gave a low laugh, lewd and knowing.

Rosie said: "What?"

"You know Andrews?"

"From Brixton nick?"

"Yeah, him. I gave him the old con last night – you know the shit men believe."

Rosie laughed, asked:

"Not the "Sex has to be spiritual for a woman, she can't just fuck and fly?"

Falls was laughing out loud, into it now, the story carrying her.

"Yeah, I explained how we have to be emotionally involved. The dim sod went for it completely."

She took another wedge of the doughnut, let her eyes dance with sugared delight and went for the kill:

"Worse – he believed me when I said size doesn't matter."

Rosie was trying not to laugh too loud. In a canteen full of men, women's laughter was a downright threat. She held up her thumb and index finger, measuring off a quarter inch, asked: "Look familiar?"

Falls shrieked.

"You had him too, wanton cow."

"Well, he was quick, I'll say that for him."

Falls shoved the remains of the doughnut to her, said: "Seeing as we've shared the little things..."

WPC Falls had curly hair, cut short in almost dyke style. It emphasised her dark eyes. A snub nose gave her an appearance of eagerness and a thin mouth saved her from outright prettiness. Her legs were her worst feature and a constant bane. Suddenly serious, she said:

"I was thirty-two years of age before I realised that when my dad said, "I'll kill myself and the girl with me," that it wasn't love – just drink talk."

"Is he still alive, your dad?"

"Some days, but never on weekends."

"Sounds like my Jack. Ever since he got laid off he's been legless."

"The stronger sex, eh?"

"So they think."

Rosie had what's termed grateful looks. She was grateful if anybody looked. Few did, not even Jack.

Leroy Baker was a poor example of strength. As he did the fifth line of coke he roared: "Ar...gh...rr. Fuck!"

Then stomped his unlaced LA sneaker, adding: "That shit's good."

He surveyed his flat. Awash in everything that money could buy. Leroy had a mountain of cash. The drug business was flourishing and he felt a little tasting of the product couldn't hurt, good for business in fact. That he was now hopelessly addicted got away from him.

He'd say: "Keeps me sharp – a man in de biz gotta stay focused."

A pounding on his door failed to register at first. The cocaine pounding of his heart had deafened him. As the hinges gave way and the door moved, he started to pay attention. Then the door came in and four men charged into his domain. He had a vague impression of boiler suits and balaclavas but fixed on the bats – baseball bats.

It was the last focus he had.

Twenty minutes later he was dangling from a lamppost, his neck broken. A white placard round his neck proclaimed:

E IS ENOUGH

Leroy was the first.

Down the street, a lone LA sneaker gave witness to the direction from which he'd been dragged. As the "E" story built, it would be alleged one of the gang whistled as he worked. The tune suggested was "Leaning on a Lamppost at the Corner of the Street."

Like so much to come it was shrouded in wish fulfilment and revulsion – the two essentials for maximum publicity.

"a blue collar soul"

Roberts picked up the phone, answered:
"Chief Inspector."
He never tired of the title.
"John. John, is that you?"
"Yes, dear."
"I must say you sound terribly formal, quite the man of importance."
He tried to hold his temper, stared at the receiver, took a deep breath and asked: "Was there something?"
"The dry-cleaning, can you pick it up?"
"Pick it up yourself!"
And he put the phone down, lifted it up again and punched a digit.
"Yes sir?"
"I've just had a call from my wife."
"Oh sorry sir, she said it was urgent."
"Never put her through. Was I vague in my last request?"
"Vague, sir?"
"Did I lack some air of command? Did I perhaps leave a loophole of doubt that said, "Sometimes it's OK to put the bitch through"?"
"No sir, sorry sir. won't happen again."
"Let's not make too much of it. If it happens again, you'll be bundling homeys on Railton Road for years to come. Now piss off."
He moved from behind his desk and contemplated his reflection in a half mirror. A photo of former England cricket captain Mike Atherton in one corner with the caption:

IT'S NOT CRICKET

Roberts was sixty-two and at full stance he looked imposing. Recently he found it more difficult to maintain. A sag whispered at his shoulders. It whispered "old."

His body was muscular but it took work. More than he wanted to give. A full head of hair was steel grey and he felt the lure of the Grecian alternative – but not yet. Brown eyes that were never gentle and a Roman nose. Daily he said, "I hate that fuckin' nose." A headbutt from a drunk had pushed it off-centre to give the effect of a botched nose job. According to his wife, his mouth was unremarkable till he spoke, then it was ugly. He got perverse joy from that.

Now he hit the intercom, barked: "Get me Falls."

"Ahm..."

"Are you deaf?"

"Sorry sir, I'm not sure where she's at."

"Where she's at! What is this? A bloody commune? You're a policeman, go and find her. Go and find her now and don't ever let me hear that hippy shit again."

"Yes, sir."

Five minutes later a knock and Falls entered, straightening her tunic, crumbs floating to the floor. They both watched the descent. He said:

"Picking from a rich man's platter perhaps?"

She smiled. "Hardly, sir."

"I have a job for you."

"Yes sir?"

He rummaged through his desk, produced a few pink tickets, flipped them towards her.

She said, "Dry-cleaning tickets?"

"Well identified; collect them on your lunch hour, eh?"

She let them lie, said: "Hardly, sir – I mean, it's not in my brief to be valet or something."

He gave her a look of pure indignation.

"Jeez, you don't think I'll collect then, do you? How would that look? Man of my rank poncing about a dry-cleaners?"

"With all due respect, sir, I–"

He cut her off.

"If you want to stay on my good side, love, don't bugger me about."

She considered standing on her dignity, making a gesture for the sisterhood, telling him, with respect, to shove it, then thought, yeah sure.

And picked up the tickets, said: "I'll need paying."

"Don't we all, love – where's Brant?"

Later: Roberts had just parked his car and was starting to walk when a man stepped out of the shadows. A big man. He bruised out of his track suit and all of it muscle.

He said: "I'm going to need your money, mate, and probably your watch if it's not a piece of shit."

Roberts, feeling so tired, said: "Would it help your decision to know I'm a copper?"

"A bit, but not enough. I've been asking people for money all day, asking nice and they treated me like dirt. So, now it's no more Mr. Nice Guy. Hand it over, pal."

"Okay, as you can see, I'm no spring chicken, and fit? I'm fit for nowt, but I've a real mean streak. No doubt you'll hurt me a lot but I promise you, I'll hurt you fucking back."

The man considered, stepped forward, then spat: "Ah bollocks, forget it. All right."

"Forget. No. I don't think so. Get off my manor, pal, you're too big to miss."

After Roberts moved away, the man considered putting a brick through his windshield, or slash the tyres or some fuck. But that bastard would come after him. Oh yes, a relentless cold fuck. Best leave well enough alone.

He said: "You were lucky, mate."

Who exactly he meant was unclear.

When Roberts got back home, he had to lean against the door. His legs turned to water and tiny tremors hit him. A voice asked: "Not having a turn are you, Dad?"

Sarah, his fifteen-year-old daughter, supposedly at boarding school, a very expensive one, in the coronary area. It didn't so much drain his resources as blast a hole through them – wide and unstoppable. He tried for composure.

"Whatcha doing home, not half term already?"

"No. I got suspended."

"What? What on earth for? Got to get me a drink."

He poured a sensible measure of Glenlivet, then added to it, took a heavy slug and glanced at his daughter. She was in that eternal moment of preciousness between girl and woman. She loved and loathed her dad in equal measure. He looked closer, said:

"Good grief, are those hooks in your lips?"

"It's fashion, Dad."

"Bloody painful, I'd say. Is that why you're home?"

"Course not. Mum says not to tell you, I didn't do nuff-ink."

Roberts sighed: an ever-constant cloud of financial ruin hung over his head, just to teach her how to pronounce "nothing". And she said it as if she'd submerged south of the river and never surfaced.

He picked up the phone while Sarah signalled "later" and headed upstairs.

"This is DI Roberts. Yeah, I'm home and a guy tried to mug me on my own doorstep. What? What is this? Did I apprehend him? Get me DS Brant and get a car over here to pick up this guy. He's a huge white fella in a dirty green tracksuit. Let Brant deal with him. My address? You better be bloody joking, son." And he slammed the phone down.

As an earthquake of music began to throb from the roof, he muttered: "Right."

Racing up the stairs, two at a time, like a demented thing: "Sarah! Sarah! What is that awful racket?"

"It's Encore Une Fois, Dad."

"Whatever it is, turn it down. Now!"

Sarah lay on her bed. Wondered, could she risk a toke? Better not, leastways till Mum got home.

"He who hits first gets promoted"

(Detective Sergeant Brant)

Brant leant over the suspect, asked: "Have you ever had a puck in the throat?"

The suspect, a young white male, didn't know the answer, but he knew the very question boded ill.

Brant put his hand to his forehead said: "Oh gosh, how unthinking of me. You probably don't know what a puck is. It's my Irish background, those words just hop in any old place. Let me enlighten you."

The police constable standing by the door of the interview room shifted nervously. Brant knew and ignored him, said: "A puck is—" and lashed out with his closed fist to the man's Adam's apple. He went over backwards in his chair, clutching his throat. No sound other than the chair hitting.

Brant said: "That's what it is. A demonstration is worth a hundred words, so my old mum always said – bless her."

The man writhed on the floor as he fought to catch his breath. The constable made a move forward, said, "Really, sir, I—"

"Shut the fuck up." Brant righted the chair, said: "Take your time son, no hurry, no hurry at all. A few more pucks you'll forget about time completely. But time out, let's have a nice cup o' tea, eh? Whatcha say to a brewski me oul' china?" Brant sat in the chair, took out a crumpled cigarette and lit it, said in a strangled voice: "Oh Jesus, these boys catch you in the throat – know what I mean?" He took another lethal pull then asked: "Do you want to tell me why you raped the girl before the tea, or wait till after?"

Before, the man said.

Brant was like a pit-bull. You saw him and the word "pugna-cious" leapt to mind. It fitted. His hair was in galloping recession and what remained was cut to the skull. Dark eyes over a nose that had been broken at least twice. A full, sensual mouth that hinted at gentility if not gentleness. Neither applied. He was 5' 8" and powerfully built. Not from the gym but rather from a smoul-dering rage. Over a drink he'd admit: "I was born angry and got worse."

He'd achieved the rank of detective sergeant through sheer bloody-mindedness. It seemed unlikely he'd progress in the Metropolitan Police. It was anxious to shed its bully-boy image.

Special Branch had wooed him but he'd told them in a memo-rable memo to "Get fucked". It made the Branch love him all the more. He was their kind of rough.

Outside the interview room the constable asked: "If I might have a word, sir."

"Make it snappy, boyo."

"I feel I must protest."

Brant shot his hand out, grabbing the man's testicles, growled: "Feel that! Get yourself a set of brass ones boyo, or you'll be patrolling the Peckham Estates."

Falls approached, said: "Ah, the hands-on approach."

"Whatcha want, Falls?"

"Mr. Roberts wants you."

He released the Constable, said: "Don't ever interrupt my interrogation again. Got that, laddie?"

The CA club had no connection to the clothing shop and they certainly didn't advertise. It stood for Certain Age, as in "women of a." The women were of the age where they were certain what they wanted. And what they wanted was sex.

No frills.

No hassle.

No complications.

Roberts' wife was forty-six. According to the new Hollywood chick-flicks, a woman of forty-six had more hope of being killed by a psychopath than finding a new partner.

Her friend Penelope had shared this gem with her and was now saying: "Fiona, don't you ever just want to get laid by a hunk and no complications?"

Fiona poured the coffee, laughed nervously. Emboldened, Penny urged: "Don't you want to know if black guys are bigger?"

"Good Lord, Penny!"

"Course you do, especially when the only prick in your life is a real prick."

"He's not so bad."

"He's a pompous bastard. C'mon, it's your birthday, let me treat you to the CA. You'll get laid like you always wanted and it won't even cost you money. It's my treat."

Fiona had already decided but wanted to be coaxed, even lured, and asked: "Is it safe?"

"Safe? You want safe, buy a vibrator. C'mon, live it up girl – men do it all the time, we're only catching up."

Fiona hesitated, then asked: "And the men, are they young?"

"None over twenty and pecs to die for."

"OK then – should I bring anything?"

"Your imagination. let's party!"

Brant didn't knock, just strode into Roberts' office.

"You don't knock?"

"Gee, Guv, I was so keen to answer your summons, I clean forgot."

"Keen!"

"Aye, keen as mustard, Guv."

"Don't call me Guv, this isn't *The Sweeney*."

"And you're no Reagan, eh? Here, I've another McBain for you."

He tossed a dog-eared book on to the desk. It looked like it had been chewed, laundered and beaten. Roberts didn't touch it, said: "You found this in the toilet, that's it?"

"It's his best yet. No one does the Police Procedural like Ed."

Roberts leaned over to see the title. A food stain had obliterated that. At least he hoped it was food. He said: "You should support the home side, read Bill James, get the humorous take on policing."

"For humour, sir, I have you – my humour cup overfloweth."

The relationship twixt R and B always seemed a beat away from beating. You felt like they'd like nothing better than to get down and kick the living shit out of each other. Which had happened. The tension between them was the chemistry that glued. Co-dependency was another word for it.

The phone rang, postponing further needling.

Roberts snapped it and Brant heard: "What, a lamppost? Where? When? Jesus! Don't friggin touch him. No! Don't cut him down. Keep the press away. Oh shit. We're on our way." And he put the phone down.

Brant smiled, asked: "Trouble, Guv?"

"A lynching. In Brixton."

"You're kidding!"

"Do I look like I'm bloody kidding? And they left a note."

"What? Like 'Back at two'?"

"How the hell do I know? Let's go."

"Right, Guv."

"What did I tell you Brant, eh? Did I tell you not to bloody call me that?"

Brant said: "Don't forget McBain, we'll need all the help we can get."

Roberts picked it up and with a fine overhead lob landed it in the dustbin and said: "Bingo."

"Homicide dicks"

By the time Brant and Roberts arrived in Brixton a crowd had already gathered. The yellow police lines were being ignored. Roberts called to a uniformed sergeant, said: "Get those people back behind the lines."

"They won't move, sir."

"Jesus, are you deaf? Make 'em."

The medical examiner had arrived and was gazing up at the dangling corpse with a look of near admiration.

Roberts asked: "Whatcha think, doc?"

"Drowning, I'd say."

Brant laughed out loud and got a dig from Roberts.

The doctor said: "Unless you've got a ladder handy, I suggest you cut him down."

Roberts gave a grim smile, turned to Brant, said: "Your department, I think."

Brant grunted and summoned two constables. With complete awkwardness and much noise, they lifted him level with the corpse. A loud "Boo" came from the crowd, plus calls of:

"Watch your wallet, mate."

"Give 'im a kiss, darling."

"What's your game then?"

When Brant finally got the noose free, the corpse sagged and took him down in a heap atop the constables. More roars from the crowd and a string of obscenities from Brant.

Roberts said: "I think you've got him, men."

As Brant struggled to his feet, Roberts asked: "Any comments?"

"Yeah, the fucker forgot to brush his teeth and I can guarantee he didn't floss."

❖❦

The cricket captain was tending his garden when Pandy came by. A local character, he was so called because of the amount of times he'd ridden in a police car. His shout had been: "It's the police, gis a spin in de pandy." They did.

Booze hadn't as much turned his brain to mush as let it slowly erode. Norman had always been good to him, with cash, clothes, patience.

When Pandy told the drinking school he knew the famous captain, they'd given him a good kicking. Years of Jack, meths, surgical spirit had bloated his face into a ruin that would have startled Richard Harris.

He said: "Mornin' Cap!"

"Morning Pandy, need anything?"

"I've an urge for the surge, a few bob for a can if you could?"

Once, Norman had seen him produce a startling white handkerchief for a crying woman. It was the gentleness, the almost shyness of how he'd offered it. Norman slipped the money over and Pandy, his eyes in a nine-yard stare, said:

"I wasn't always like this, Cap."

"I know, I know that."

"Went to AA once, real nice crowd, but the Jack had me then, they said, "Get a sponsor.'"

"A what?"

"Sponsor, like a friend, you know, who'd look out for you."

"And did you get one?"

Pandy gave a huge laugh, said in a cultured voice: "Whatcha fink, take a wild bloody guess."

Norman, fearful of further revelations, said: "I better get on."

"Cap?"

"Yes?"

"Will... will youse be me sponsor?"

"Ahm..."

"Won't be a pest, Cap, it'll be like before but just so I'd have one. I'd like to be able to say it, just once."

"Sure, I'd be privileged."

"Shake."

And he held out a hand ingrained with dirt beyond

redemption. Norman didn't hesitate, he took it.

When Pandy had gone, Norman didn't rush to the kitchen in search of carbolic soap. He continued to work in the garden, his heart a mix of wonder, pain and compassion.

He'd be dead for weeks before his sponsor learnt the news.

"You can't just go round killing people, whenever the notion strikes you. It's not feasible."

Elisha Cook to Lawrence Tierney in
Born to Kill

Kevin, without knowing it, used an Ed McBain title. As he greeted the "E" crew with "Hail, hail, the gang's all here." He was tripping out, had sampled some crack cocaine and gone into orbit, shouting: "I can see fucking Indians. And they're all bus conductors."

He trailed off in a line of giggles. When the crew had taken their first victim, they had also "confiscated": a) a mountain of dope; b) weapons; c) heavy cash.

Kevin, sampling all these like a vulture on assignment, roared: "I love LA!"

Albert, worried, had asked: "Is it dangerous?" Meaning the drugs, and got a nasty clip round the earhole.

"Dope is risky for those who're fucked up to start. See me, it's recreational. Like, that's why they call them that."

"Call them what?"

He dealt Albert another clip and answered: "Recreational drugs, you moron. What is it, you gone deaf? Listen to that monkey's shit. Wake up fella, it's the nineties ending."

He set up another line of the white.

❖❦

Patrick Hamilton wrote: "Those whom God deserted are given a room and a gas fire in Earls Court."

If homelessness is the final rung of the downward spiral, then a bedsit may be the rehearsal for desperation. In a bedsit in Balham, a man carefully pinned a large poster of the England cricket team to his wall. He stood back and surveyed it, said:

"To you about to die – here is my salute."

And he swallowed deep, then spat at the poster. As the saliva dribbled down the team, he half turned, then in one motion launched a knife with ferocity. It clattered against the wall, didn't hold, fell into the line. He took a wild kick at it, screaming:

"You useless piece of shit."

The knife had come from *Man of War* magazine. Monthly, it catered for would-be mercenaries, tories and psychos. Their mail-order section featured all the weapons necessary for a minor bloodbath. The "throwing knife" was guaranteed to hit and pierce with "deadly accuracy." The man dropped to the floor and began his morning regime of harsh exercises, shouted:

"Gimme one hundred, Mister."

As he pumped, the letters on his right arm, burned tattoo-blue against the skin: SHANNON. Not his real name, but the character from Frederick Forsyth's *Dogs of War*. Unlike the fictional character, he didn't smoke, drink, drug. The demons in his mind provided all the stimulation he would ever need. Words hammered through his head as he pounded the floor:

Gimmie a little country or gimmie rock 'n' roll but launch me to Armageddon I will smote the heathers upon the playing fields of Eton and low I will lay their false Gods of sporting legend I will I will I am I am the fucking wrath of the nineties. The new age of devastation.

"Setting a Tone"

Brant and Roberts were sitting in the canteen.
Not saying a whole lot. Both had newspapers, both tabloids. None on the *Guardian* liberal pose in here. In his office, Roberts kept the *Telegraph* on top, lest the brass look in.

They were comfortable, at odd times sometimes were. Grunts of approval, decision, amazement. Of course the obligatory male cry had to be uttered periodically to emphasise there were no pooftahs here:

"Fwor, look at the knockers on 'er."

"See this wanker, he ate the vicar's dog."

Emboldened by the reassuring bonding of the sports page, Brant put his page down, had a look around, then took out his cigs, asked: "Mind if I do, Guv?"

Roberts raised his eyebrows, said: "And what? You'll refrain if I do?"

Brant lit up, asked: "You packed 'em in, Guv. How long now?" "Five years, four weeks, two days and..." Roberts looked at his watch, "...Nine hours. More or less."

"Don't miss 'em at all, eh?"

"Never give 'em a moment's thought."

Brant's chest gave a rumble, phlegm screaming "OUT" and he said: "You heard about the new kid. Tome?"

"It's Tone, but what?"

"He answered a mugging call. An old-age pensioner was set upon by four kids. Took his pension. The usual shit. So, along comes the bold Tone, says: "Why didn't you fight back?"

Roberts laughed out loud, said: "He never!"

"Straight up, Guv, the old boy says, "I'm eighty-six fugging

years old, what am I gonna do, bite then with my false teeth?"
Then, Tone asks if he got a description and the old boy says:
"Yeah, they were in their teens with baseball caps and them
hooded tops, like half a million other young thugs. But they used
offensive language. Might that be a clue?"

Roberts went and got some more tea and two chocolate snack
biscuits.

Brant said: "Don't wanna be funny, Guv, but I'd prefer
coffee."

"Who can tell the difference? So, are you going to watch out
for young Tone?"

"You think I should?"

"Yes. Yes I do."

"All righty then, we'll make a fascist of him yet."

"That I don't doubt."

"The King of thieves has come, call it stealing if you will but I say, it's justice done. You have had your way, The Ragged Army's calling time."

After Brant had left Roberts returned to his paper. He wanted to read an interview with John Malkovich. He'd seen him give Clint Eastwood the run around in the late night movie, *In the Line of Duty*.

And here's what he read:

"'What the public perceives is shit and what they think is vomit for the best part. The public doesn't read Faulkner, it reads Danielle Steele. The movies they think are good I couldn't even watch.' – actor John Malkovich."

"Good Lord", said Roberts, "The man has the soul of a copper, pure brass." There was a photo of the actor, shaved skull, predatory eyes, and Roberts thought: "You ugly bastard." Yet, as is the way of a loaded world, woman adored him. Unconsciously, Roberts' hand ran over his head. The gesture brought no comfort. He remembered when he first courted Fiona – the sheer adrenaline rush of just being in her presence. He missed two people: a) the girl she was; b) the person she'd made him feel he might have been. A deep sigh escaped him.

❖⃰ℰ̃

Back at the station, Roberts was summoned to the Chief Super's office. Chief Superintendent Brown resembled a poor man's Neil Kinnock. For a time he'd cultivated the image but as the winds of political change blew, and blew cold, he'd tried to bury it. His thinning black hair was dyed – and very badly. Men believe they can pop into Boots, buy the gear and do the job at home: presto! A fresh colour of youth and no one the wiser. Oh boy, even the postman knows. Women go to a salon, pay the odds and get it done professionally. The Chief's latest colour was darker than a tory soul. Roberts knocked, heard: "Enter." Thought: "Wanker."

Brown was gazing at his framed photos of famous batsmen, said: "Time-wasting by batsmen – like to explain that to me, laddie?"

"Excuse me?"

"Very well, I'll tell you: other than in exceptional circumstances, the batsman should always be ready to strike when the bowler is ready to start his run."

Then he waited. Roberts wasn't sure if he required an "Oh, well done, sir!" or not. He settled for not.

Brown ummed and ah'd, then said: "The newspaper chappies have been on to me."

"About the hanging?"

"What hanging?"

Roberts explained and Brown shouted: "Hard not to approve eh, but hardly p.c."

"No. I'm referring to some crackpot called 'The Umpire,' who threatened to kill the cricket team."

Roberts smiled, said: "Then the bugger will have to stand in line."

Brown gave him the Kinnock look, all insulted dignity.

"Really Chief Inspector, that's in appalling bad taste. Probably some nut case, eh?"

"Or a Paki more like."

"Get on it Roberts, toot-sweet."

Outside, Roberts muttered: "get on bloody what?"

Brant was mid-joke: "So I asked her, can I have the last dance. She said: 'You're having it, mate.'"

Loud guffaws from the assembled constabulary. Roberts barked: "Get me the current file on nutters."

As he strode past, Brant clicked his heels and gave a crisp Hitler salute. More guffaws.

The CA Club was situated in Lower Belgravia. Vice thrives best in the centre. Ask Mark Thatcher. Inside it looked like a Heals catalogue. All soft furnishings, pastel colours. A woman approached Penny and Fiona. Dressed in what used to be optimistically called a pants suit, she was a healthy sixty. Everything had been lifted but was holding. It gave her face the immobile rictus of a death mask. She gushed:

"My dears, welcome to Cora's. To the CA."

Penny handed her a card, which she discreetly put away before suggesting: "Drinkees?"

Fiona had an overpowering urge to shout: "Get real." Being married to a policeman did that. Penny said: "Pina Coladas."

"Oh dear yes. Bravo." And she took off. Fiona said: "Where is everybody?"

"Fucking."

Cora reappeared, followed by two young men. They looked like Boyzone wannabies. Cora placed the drinks on a table with a catalogue, said:

"Enjoy, mon cheries."

The men stood smiling. Fiona looked at Penny, said: "Oh God, I hope they're not going to sing."

Penny was flicking through the catalogues. Page on page of guys, all nationalities and all young.

Fiona lifted her drink, said: "I never know, do you eat or drink these?"

Penny said to the men: "I'd like to book Sandy," then nudged Fiona: "C'mon girl. Pick."

Fiona tried to concentrate. An entry looked like this:

Photo: (some gorgeous hunk)

Name:

Vital Stats:

Age: (all 19/20)

Hobbies: (they all hang-glided, skied and squashed)

Fiona had a vision of the sky over Westminster, near black with gliding Sandys and all with the killer smile. She said: "Jeez, I can't decide, I mean… are they real?"

Penny, impatient, said: "I'm getting itchy, twitchy, and bitchy – here, take Jason, he's a good hors d'oeuvre."

"Will I have to talk to him?"

Penny touched her hand: "Honey, we ain't here to talk."

Basic survival
"Never trust anyone who puts Very before Beautiful"

Phyl Kennedy

The England wicket-keeper, Anthony Heaton, was a rarity in sport. A classical scholar, he believed he had the ear of the common people. In private moments, he'd listen to "Working Class Hero" and smile smugly.

As part of his public bonding, he frequently rode the tube. But the Northern Line will test the very best of men. As he headed down the non-functional Oval escalator, he whispered:

"*Rudis indegestaque moles*" – "I'd hoped for something better."

On the platform, he watched a nun pacing. Steeped in the mystique of *Brideshead Revisited*, he was fascinated by Catholicism. At college he had been described as "Anthony Blythe with focus". He thought their rituals very beautiful. Now the nun made a second sweep of the platform, not glancing at the destinations board, which read:

MORDEN 3 MIN   KENNINGTON 4 MIN

Then he saw what she was casing, the chocolate machine. Anthony could quote: "Oh sweet temptation" and "Thrice you shall betray me."

Now the nun stopped and rooted in her habit, her face flushed with expectation. Coins were "thunked" in and a calculated selection made. Cadbury's Turkish Delight. A classic. The handle was pulled and the nun moved in for the kill. Anthony watched her face, "un-lined, unblemished". She could be sixteen or sixty. Definitely from the Philippines, who were producing a bumper crop of nuns for the nineties.

One of Anthony's team-mates had said recently: "Hell is Imelda Marcos singing 'Amazing Grace.'"

No chocolate: *nada*, zip, *tipota*. The nun looked round in dismay. As the Americans say: "Who you gonna call?"

The train could be heard approaching and Anthony could see tears in the nun's eyes. He moved with the grace he kept for Lords, and one, two, open-palmed he hit the machine.

The Turkish Delight popped out. With a flourish, he presented her with her prize. The nun was beaming, her face aglow, and she said: "God be praised."

He nodded gravely, added: "Veritas."

After Anthony Heaton's murder, the nun would gaze at his photo in the paper and hope they'd given him the last rites. In her breviary, beside his snap, was a neatly folded chocolate wrapper, smooth as a silent prayer.

David Eddings was one of the England batsmen. He was having a bad morning. His wife had issued an ultimatum.

"You go on tour and I'm history."

He hadn't handled it well, his reply being: "I'll help you pack."

The toaster had short-circuited and there was no bloody orange. Losing it, he shouted: "Where's my juice?"

From upstairs the sound of slamming doors, suitcases, and: "That's what the *Daily Express* asked too."

Said paper had been sniping at his age. The doorbell rang and he shouted again: "Are you going to get that?"

"Well I doubt it will answer itself, darling."

A hiss underlined the endearment. A yeah, he'd definitely heard a sss… Striding to the door, muttering: "This flaming better be good."

He pulled it open. A postman, not their usual. Postbag held in front of his chest, he said: "Batsman leaving the field."

"What?"

And coming out of the bag was a barrel of a gun. Now the

postman intoned: "I am the Umpire. When a batsman has left the field or retired and is unable to return owing to illness or injury, he is to be recorded as 'retired not out.'"

And he shot David Eddings in the face.

Weights...

When the call on the shooting came through, Brant was, as usual, missing. He'd left his bleeper on the desk. There it shrilled till a passing sergeant dropped it in the bin.

Brant was in the canteen, smoking a Player's Weight. These were only available in a tobacconist off Bond Street, on a shelf with Sobranies, Woodbines and Snuff: the forgotten stimulants of a Jack the Ripper in London. Brant had an arrangement with the owner – "I'll keep an eye on the premises." There had been five break-ins since his pledge. Unfazed, he asked: "Did they get my Weights?"

"No."

"See: no taste no worries."

He took a deep drag now. As the powerful nicotine blasted across his lungs, he gasped: "Jaysus."

A radio was blaring Michael Bolton and he muttered: "Shut up yah whining wanker – put a bloody sock in it." And chanced another draw of the cigarette. In unison, if not in harmony, a WPC gave a series of short, sharp coughs. Brant's head came up like a setter.

"Hello," he said.

"S-sorry sarge, the WPC stammered, "I've got a strep throat – nothing will shift it."

He gave a professional smile. It's in the manual and has absolutely no relation to warmth. He said: "There is one sure cure."

The WPC was surprised. New to the force, she'd heard he was an animal but maybe she'd be the very person to bring out his feminine side. Show he was gentle, caring and compassionate and hey – he wasn't at all bad looking – a bit rough but she could change that. Encouraged, she asked: "What's it called?"

"C-men."

"C-what?"

"C-men. It's got to be delivered orally. I'm off at four, I could come round, let you have it."

A moment before it clicked. As the words took shape on her lips, she felt bile in her stomach. Jumping to her feet she said: "You... animal!" And ran out, leaving three-quarters of her apple Danish. He reached over, broke a wedge off and popped it in his mouth, went "mmm," and muttered: "Women? Go figure."

The duty sergeant put his head round the door and said: "Brant, all hell's broken loose, better get outta here."

"Another hanging, I hope." He snatched up the remains of the Danish and between bites managed to hum a bar of Michael Bolton.

The fucking rooms at the CA were a rampage of luxury: Wet bar, silk sheets, soft to softest furnishings. Jason was twelve, or so it seemed to Fiona. But the body was a healthy twentysomething. He'd lightly oiled his torso and it made his tan glow. He was dressed in only black shiny briefs. Fiona couldn't keep her eyes off it. She had a variety of witty lines to break the ice but they translated as "ah." Jason smiled – teeth that shouted "capped glory." He said: "What's your pleasure?"

Alas, he tried for husky, but Peckham and tight undies played havoc. Fiona went up to him, said: "Shush. Shh..." She put her hand in his knickers, gasped: "Oh God!", fell to her knees and took him in her mouth. Then, breaking off, she said: "Jason, I want you to fuck me till I can't walk but I don't want you to speak, not now – not ever. Can you do that?"

He could and he did.

Her husband, meanwhile, was also being fucked, but over, by the Chief Super, the press and Mrs. David Eddings.

By the time Brant reached him, he was in the coronary zone, barked: "Been on vacation, have you?"

"Sorry Guv, was chasing down leads on the 'E.'"

"The what?"

"'E,' sir – E for enough. The hanging job, or did it slip your mind? You've a lot on, I suppose."

Through a barrage of obscenities, Roberts outlined the cricket murder. Brant looked thoughtful, then said: "Bit of a sticky wicket what?"

"You know cricket?"

"That's it, Guv – only the one expression, I have to ration it."

"Well, you're about to get an education. In shall personally ensure you get a crash course. Don't the Irish play?"

Brant tried to look deprived. It made him satanic.

"Just hurling I'm afraid."

"What's that then?"

"A cross between hockey and murder."

"Wonderful, I've a thick Paddy to help me. Get down to the incident room, it should be set up by now."

"And... er, where's that, Guv?"

"How the bloody hell do I know. Ask a policeman. If you can find one."

"Righty ho... I'm on it, fret not. McBain has me wise to procedural."

"Fuck McBain."

"As you wish, Guv."

Doggone!

The Umpire had returned to Balham. Back and forth across his bedsit he roared: "Yes yes yes – we have begun!" and punched the air. The gun was held tightly in his left hand. An impulse to blast holes in the wall was near overwhelming. He marched to the poster of the England team, stabbed his finger in Dave Edding's face, asked: "Were you surprised, Batman? Were you fuckin' stunned?"

Looking around he found the knife on the floor and began to gouge out the face in the picture. Then he stood back, examined his handiwork, and in a singsong voice, trilled:

"Eeny meeny miney mo
Catch a cricketer by the toe,
If he repents, let him go
Or else The Umpire cuts him so."

He went to his bed and from underneath pulled a battered suitcase. Opening it he leafed through yellowing newspaper. Fragments of headlines registered briefly:

- SCHOOLBOY CRICKET SENSATION
- YOUNGEST EVER INTERNATIONAL
- BITTER END TO SCHOOLBOY'S DREAM

He threw his head back and emitted a long cry of pure anguish. Unknowing, he shredded the frail papers as he lamented. Pieces of the articles fluttered briefly round his legs then settled in a mess about him. It appeared as if he'd been marooned in the remnants of an old wedding. The party had moved on but he'd become lost in the primary celebration. Not that he wouldn't get to the feast, it was more, he didn't realise he could have moved on.

❖❦

WPC Falls, by one of those meaningless coincidences, also lived in Balham. Not in a bedsit though. The house had been left to her by her mother. Her father, a perpetual drunk, made hazard raids on her time and decency. Both were running thin.

She'd had a long day. It seemed a convention of lunatics had invaded their manor.

Vigilantes, cricket executioners, and God only knew how many copycats plus false confessors. She went to the hi-fi, put the Cowboy Junkies on loud. *The Trinity Session* had been literally worn out. Now she was wearing out the Canadian live album. As she ran a bath, Mango Tameness' enchanting voice began "The song's about a fucked-up world, but hey – a girl ain't giving in." *Oprah* material, but when Mango sang it, just maybe there was a chance. In a weak moment she'd told a cop about her passion for the group. True to form, he zeroed in on prejudice: "Junkies! You're listening to bloody dopers. Try Coldharbour Lane or Railton Road on Friday night."

And he'd ranted till she lied and said Dire Straits were what got her hot. It blew him off.

Now as she sank into the bath, Mango was telling of the hunted. Out loud Falls said: "Sing it, sister."

The immediacy of the day began to fade. She'd had a call to a tower block near the Oval. Surname Point: the top of the building had come off in a big storm that snuck past Michael Fish – "no storm tonight," he forecasted, as the worst one in a hundred years came thundering down the pike. The call was to the thirteenth floor. Did the lifts work? Not that time. An irritated Falls finally made it to the scene. A crowd was gathered outside an open door. A huge black woman approached, asked: "Couldn't they send a bloke then?"

"I'm it."

"Should've sent a fella."

"Can we get to it?"

"Blimey... 'ere look, they've sent a woman!"

And a chorus of "Should've been a bloke" rose from the

Ken Bruen

"'Ere, don't you get shifty with me, sis... blokes don't get like that."

Falls forced her way through the crowd. Someone goosed her but she had to let it go. She strongly suspected the black woman.

A neighbour's dog had been a constant barker. Open all hours. Now the occupant, a white male in his fifties, had snatched the animal and was holding it over the balcony.

Falls had eventually elicited his name: "Mr. Prentiss. You don't want to do this."

"Oh yes I do."

The assembly pitches in: "Drop the fucker, see if he bloody flies. Go on then, let 'im go."

Falls shouted: "Be quiet!"

And was answered by: "Show us yer knickers." And quieter observations, such as: "She's got the hump – throw her off 'n' all."

Now Prentiss spoke again: "See, he's not barking now. See? First time in six months he's bloody shut it."

Falls had taken Psychology One and had done some classes in hostage negotiation. But not enough. She said: "We can work this out."

"Bollocks." And he let the dog go. The animal got in one last bark on his descent.

After Falls had marched Prentiss down the stairs, all thirteen stories, someone said: "You know what I fink, love?"

"Yeah, yeah. They should have sent a bloke."

"No, you should've took the lift – it come back on while you were on the balcony."

Prentiss, wiping sweat from his face, said: "You sure you're in the right career, darlin'?"

Falls was too knackered to reply.

Hand job

When Roberts got to his home it was clocking midnight and he was clocking zero.

The house was in Dulwich, the Knightsbridge of south-east London. This was always said with a straight face. Else how could you say it? Dulwichians liked to think they were but temporarily out of geographic whack. Others said out of their tree. Dulwichians felt they gave the rest of the south-east something to aspire to. And they did. The aspiration to break into their homes and hopefully kick the shit outta them as bonus.

Hope is the drug. The mortgage was the payment from hell and Roberts carried it badly. In the sitting room, he sank into a leather chair that was designed for show. You moved – it cracked and ran friction on the arse. Course it cost a bundle, which was why he felt obliged to use it. Fiona Roberts wasn't long home but she showered, put on a worn housecoat and hoped she looked... well, housewifey. Jason had done as instructed and she could hardly walk. Composing herself, she got the expression fixed, the bored look of feigned interest. Looking as if she couldn't quite remember his name and jeez, how much did she care? All this went right out the window when he said:

"You look shagged."

Guilt cascaded over her and she floundered, tried: "What a thing to say to your wife, good Lord!"

But he wasn't even looking at her now, asked: "Pour us a scotch, love – I'm too whacked to wank."

Indignation rose, as did her voice: "How dare you use such language."

"What? What did I say?"

"That you're too tired to to masturbate."

He laughed out loud, said: "Jeez, get a grip. *Wag*, I said, too tired to wag. You've bloody sex on the brain."

She sloshed whisky into a tumbler and pushed it to him. He said: "Thanks dear, so kind – like to hear about my day?"

"I'm rather tired. If it's all the same to you, I'll turn in. Good night." And she was outta there. For a few moments he just sat, the whisky untouched in his hand. Then he chanced a large sip, let it settle and said: "A hand job would have been nice."

On his way home Brant stopped at an off-licence and picked up half a dozen specials. The owner knew him and, not with affection, asked: "You want them on the slate, Mr. Brant?"

Brant gave his malevolent smile, tapped his pockets, said: "I find myself without the readies Mr. Patel. Wanna take a cheque?"

They both had an insecure chuckle at the ludicrousness of such a gesture. As if on afterthought, Brant said: "Chuck some readies in there, I'll get back to you on Friday – how would that be?"

Patel turned to the cash register, raised his eyes to heaven and rang no sale. The continuing story with Brant, who'd planned it for his tombstone. Patel handed over the carrier bag: "A pony all right, Mr. Brant?"

"Lovely job and you're a lovely fella."

"No further trouble with the NF, I trust?"

"No Mr. Brant, all is rosy."

Brant nodded and turned to go, then: "By Jove Patel, I must say you've mastered the Queen's tongue rather well, eh? They'd be impressed back in Calcutta."

Patel couldn't quite let it go, said: "Mr. Brant, Calcutta is in India. I am from Rawalpindi."

"Whatever." And he let his eyes flick across the price list, adding: "Thing is boyo, you keep charging like that you'll be able to bring the cousins over from both places eh? You keep it in yer pants now, hear?"

After he'd gone Patel slammed the counter in frustration. He considered again making the call to Scotland Yard.

Brant lived in a council flat in Kennington. On the third floor, it was a one-bedroom basic unit. He kept it tidy in case he scored. One marriage behind him, he was out to nail anything that moved. Roberts' wife was his current obsession. As a trophy fuck she couldn't be bettered. Plus, as he said: "A pair of knockers on her like gazooms."

One wall was devoted entirely to books. All of Ed McBain, the 87th Precinct stories. Two shelves were given to the Matthew Hope series – a less successful enterprise for the said writer. The lower shelf was Evan Hunter, including *The Blackboard Jungle*.

Brant liked to think he had thus the three faces of the author. The 87th's went all the way back to the original Penguin editions. Brant kicked off his shoes, opened a special and drank deep, gasped: "Bloody lovely, worth every penny." He settled in an armchair and begun to muse on a White Arrest. First he picked up the phone – get the priorities right.

"Yo, Pizza Express account number 936. Yeah, that's it, bring me the pepperoni special. Sure, family size." And then he thought – go for it, do the line they use in every movie: "And hold the anchovies. Sure, before Tuesday. OK."

Back to his musing. There were no two ways about it:

One: Roberts was fucked. Two: The station was fucked and he was poised to be the worst fucked of all. All his little perks, minor scams, interrogation techniques, his attitude, guaranteed he'd be shafted before the year was out. A grand sweep of the Met was coming and they were top of the list. Unless… Unless they pulled off the big one, the legendary White Arrest that every copper dreamed about. The veritable Oscar, the Nobel Prize of criminology. Like nailing the Yorkshire Ripper or finding shit-head Lucan. It would clear the books, put you on page one, get you on them chat shows. Have Little John kiss yer arse, ah!

He crushed the can in excitement. Jeez, even his missus would want back.

The doorbell went, crushing his fantasy. A young kid with the pizza. He checked his order form: "Brant, right? Family size pepperoni?"

"That's it, boyo."

The list was rechecked and then the kid said: "It's to go on a slab?"

"Slate, son, but hey, I was all ready to pay. However, I will if they insist!"

He took possession of the pizza. "Oh yeah, you deserve a tip don't you?"

"If you wish, mister."

"Don't do it without condoms."

And he shut the door, waited. Moments later, a half-hearted kick hit the door. He was delighted. "Good lad, that's the spirit – now clear off before I put my boot in yer hole."

After eating most of the meal, he had to open his trousers to breathe and could hardly get the beer down. He hit the remote just in time for *The Simpsons*. Later he'd catch *Beavis and Butthead*. He thought: "Top of the world, Ma."

"All of us that started the
game with a crooked cue
that wanted so much and
got so little that meant
so good and did so bad.
All of us."

Jim Thompson

Jacko Mary was living proof of the adage "Never trust a man with two first names." He was a snitch. Not a very good one. But the vast machinery of policing needs a few key ingredients:

a) Ignorance, b) Complicity, c) Poor wages, d) Snitches.

Or so the received wisdom goes. He was what the Americans call "of challenged stature." He was short. And he fuckin' hated that. Roberts met him at the Hole in the Wall at Waterloo. The very walls here testified to serious, no-shit drinking. A toasted sandwich and a milk stout on the table before Jacko. He said: "Afternoon, Guv."

"Whatever."

"You want anything, Guv?"

"Information."

Jacko looked hurt, said: "Can't we be civil?"

"You're a snitch, I'm a policemen, ain't no civility there." Roberts spoke more harshly than he felt, as he had affection for Jacko, not a huge liking, but in the ballpark. The snitch seemed different but Roberts couldn't quite identify the reason, then he noticed a badge on his coat, two ribbons intertwined, one gold one pink.

"What's that?"

"Oh, it's for people who've had cancer."

Too late, Roberts realised what was different. Jacko was renowned for his head of jet black hair. So dark it looked dyed. Now huge clumps were missing and Roberts wondered if he was losing his grip. Now he didn't know what to say, said: "I dunno what to say."

Jacko touched the top of his head. "It's coming out in clumps. Every time I comb it there's more on the bleeding brush than on the head. It's the chemo what does it."

"Ahm... lemmie get you a drink."

"Naw, won't help me hair. The doctors say it's non-invasive, know what it means?"

"I don't."

"Not spreading. It's a nice expression, though, don't you fink? Like cancer with a bit o' manners."

Roberts wanted to go, screw the chance of information, but he felt he should at least make an effort. So he said: "Don't suppose you can tell me where to find the lunatic who's wasting the cricket team?"

"Naw, don't really do nutters. Mind you, there's two crazy brothers in Brixton might be worth a roust."

"Who are they, then?"

"The Lee brothers, Kevin and Albert. Word on the street is they've come into heavy action."

Roberts tried not to scoff. But a note of condescension crept into his voice. "Small time, Jacko. I know their form. Strictly nickel and dime."

"I dunno Guv, there's -"

But Roberts cut him off. "Sorry Jacko, when you've been at this game as long as I have, you develop a nose."

Then he rooted in his jacket and produced a few notes, apologising: "It's a bit short, Jacko."

Jacko Mary gave a huge laugh. "You're talking to me about short?"

Clue like

Penny was losing it. Tried not to scream at Fiona Roberts as she asked: "You're saying you won't come to the CA with me?"

"Not today Pen, I'm up to my eyes."

"I need you, Fiona."

"I can't, honestly. Let me call you tomorrow, we'll arrange coffee."

"Jeez, I can't wait. Thanks a bunch, girlfriend!"

And she slammed the phone down and thought: I could hate that cow. Well OK then, I'll go shoplifting."

Thing was, she was a very bad shoplifter. But if she resented Fiona, she out-and-out loathed Jane Fonda. She had admired Jane as the American Bardot and heavily envied her. Then she'd held her breath during the hard Jane bit. Had been in awe during the years of "serious" actress. Had the hots for her when she was fit and forty. Began to resent a tad how fabulous she was at fifty. Screamed "bitch" when she sold out at sixty to a billionaire and became one more trophy wife in the Trump tradition.

Penny had been in Hatchards of Piccadilly when a hot flash hit and she'd fled in search of cool air. Outside the Trocadero, she realised she'd stolen a book. There was Jane on the cover. A cookbook. Oh shame! And worse. She hadn't even written it but borrowed recipes from her THREE chefs. THREE! Count 'em and weep. She'd slung the book at a *Big Issue* vendor. The man had taken it well, shouted: "Saw the movie."

Restless, irritated, pacing, she tried to watch breakfast TV. A gaggle of gorgeous blonde bimbos were discussing the merits of being "childfree."

"Hold the bloody phones," she screeched. "When did we go from being childless to this hip shit?"

A child, the woe of her aching heart and the biological clock hadn't so much stopped as simply run into nothingness.

Upstairs she had a wardrobe full of baby clothes. These weren't stolen. She'd bought each item slow and pained, and paid a lot of money.

"E" is not for Ecstasy

In a house on Coldharbour Lane, four men sat round a coffee table. Open cans of Heineken, Fosters and Colt 45 crowded a batch of black and white photos.

Two of the men were brothers, Kevin and Albert. The others were Doug and Fenton. All were white. Kevin said: "I don't think they take us serious."

Albert sighed: "It's early days, and besides, the cricket thing had got priority."

Doug joined in: "Yeah, c'mon Kev, who's gonna get the six o'clock news – a batsman or a dope dealer?"

Kevin slammed the table.

"You think this isn't important?"

Fenton got his oar in: "Take it easy, Kev."

Kevin rounded on him, slight traces of spittle at the corners of his mouth. "Was I talking to you Fen? Did I say one fuckin' word to you, mate?"

"I was only -'

"You were only bollocks – this is my plan, my show."

"You don't tell me shit, mate."

Fenton knew the danger signs: up ahead was the twilight zone. He shut up. Kevin grabbed a beer, drained it in a large, loud swallow. The others watched his Adam's apple move like a horrible yo-yo. Finished, he flicked the can away, then:

"Now, as I was saying, before I got interrupted, they ain't taking us serious. Think we're just a one-off. I'll show 'em – the next hanging I'll also torch the bastard. Eh? Whatcha fink o' that? Be like a beacon in the Brixton night sky."

The others thought it was madness. What they said was:

"Good one, Kev – yeah, torch 'em, that'll do it."

Kevin sifted through the photos. "Who's next then? Here's an ugly looking bastard – who's he?" Turned over the photo, read out the details: "Brian Short, twenty-eight years old, dope dealer, rapist, and lives on Railton."

"Shit, he's practically next door."

Albert looked at the others, then said: "Kev, there's a problem."

"What, he's moved, that's it?"

"No. He's… I mean…"

"What? Spit it out."

"He's white."

"He's scum and what's more, he's gonna burn, and tonight."

"Kev…"

"Don't start whining, go get some petrol – get a lotta petrol."

Policing, like cricket, has hard and fast rules. Play fast, play hard.

Picture this. Brant is seven years old. The Peckham estate he lives on is already turning to shit. A Labour legacy of cheap contemporary housing is exactly that; Brant has been fighting. But he's learning, learning not to cry and NEVER to back down. At home his mother is bathing his cuts and beatings. He doesn't hear her. *Dixon of Dock Green* is on the telly: "Evening all," and Brant whispers a reply. *Z Cars* flames the call and ten years later he answers it fully. Through the years he'll wade through *Hill Street Blues* right along with homicide. But they don't give him the rush. His is an English version of the bobby and for some perverse reason he finds that Ed McBain in the police procedural comes closest to the way it should "have been." Long after he'd dismissed Dixon as a wanker, his heart still bore the imprint of Dock Green. In Brant's words, television had gone the way of Peckham. Right down the shitter.

Brant was mid-quiz, deliberately misquoting: "and the herring shall follow the fleet."

A constable sneered: "That's too easy – it's that wanker, the kick-boxer Cantona."

Brant tried not to show his dismay. He'd been sure it was a winner. A clutch of uniforms was gathered round in the canteen. He said: "OK wise-arse, try this: 'Do you care now?'"

The group laughed, shouted: "De Niro to Wesley Snipes in *The Fan.*"

Free tickets had been left at the station. Brant stood up in disgust. "You bastards have been studying. It's meant to be off the cuff."

He marched away resolving never to play again. Near collided with a galloping Roberts who shouted: "Another one, they've gone and done it again."

"The Umpire?"

"No, the other lunatics – the lamppost outfit. C'mon, c'mon, let's roll."

Outside the library in Brixton, the dangling corpse was still smouldering. Brant asked: "Got a light?"

Roberts gave a deep sigh: "This will hang us too."

Brant nudged him, asked: "Did you read McBain yet?"

"Oh sure, like I've had time for that."

Unfazed, Brant launched: "The 87th Precinct, there's two homicide dicks, Monaghan and Monroe. At the murder scenes they crack a graveyard humour. In *Black Horses* the -"

"Shut up! Jeez, are you completely nuts? Anyone know who this victim might be?"

The duty sergeant said: "Brian Short, twenty-eight years old, dope dealer, rapist, lives on Railton Road."

Both Roberts and Brant gaped, gave a collective "what?"

The sergeant repeated it. Roberts said: "Now that's what I call impressive police work. In fact it's miraculous."

Brant looked at the corpse, asked: "Fuckin' hell, you can tell all that from here?"

The sergeant indicated the item he held, said: "It says so here."

"Here?"

"Yeah, on the back of this photo."

"Hey, gimme that." Brant looked at it and smiled." How did you get his snappy, Sarge?"

"It was pinned to this notice."

"E is for EXTREME measures."

The police had come prepared this time and two ladders were used to bring the body down. The medical examiner arrived, hummed and hawed, then whipped off his glasses and said: "This was not a boating accident."

Brant laughed out loud. Roberts said: "Wanna share the joke fellas or shall I just continue with my thumb up my arse?"

Intriguing as the picture was, Brant decided not to elaborate and said: "It's from *Jaws*, sir. Richard Dreyfus said it."

A press photographer grabbed a series of shots before Roberts cried: "Get him outta here!"

The evening paper ran a full photo of them apparently laughing delightedly over the body. The caption read: WHAT'S THE JOKE, OFFICERS?

And the accompanying article gave them a bollocking of ferocity. Burned them, so to speak.

Loyalty

Durham, a rising CID star, had been sent to Roberts' station to conduct a full assessment. Now, in front of the whole force, he berated WPC Falls, his voice laden with syrup.

"Ladies and Gentleman, we have here a policewoman who demonstrated yesterday how NOT to handle a case. She went alone to a potentially explosive situation, near invoked a riot and did uncalculated harm to community relations."

His voice was rising progressively as he built to his finale. He knew his punchline would be hilarious and it showed that tough, stern, he was not without humour. Leadership qualities on display, he got ready.

"But worst of all – to quote the poet, "The dog it was that died."

Silence. Rattled, he figured the morons didn't get the reference and repeated it. Nope. Nada. Angry, he tore further into Falls and lost it a bit. Murmurs from the ranks finally halted him. A crushed Falls felt the tears blind her, groped her way out of the room. Durham shouted: "I don't recall dismissing you, WPC."

To work on an egg

The Umpire raised himself from the floor and stretching, folded away the killer.

Blinked, opened wide his eyes and was SHANNON, not exactly ordinary citizen, but he had done some of the moves. Even psychos have to eat. He showered and then carefully shaved, using a pearl-handled open razor from his dad. In truth, he'd bought it at a car boot sale but now believed the former. With long, slow sweeps he cut the bristles, and as he reached the Adam's apple he paused. The eyes reflected and for a minute the Umpire had control, whispered: "gut him like." Then he was gone and Shannon began to whistle. All spruced up, he said: "let's get booted and suited."

For breakfast he boiled two eggs and buttered three slices of bread. Then he cut the slices into thin wedges and lined them up neatly: "Stand easy, men."

When the eggs were done, he took a felt marker and did this:

to the eggs. Wrote Jack 'n' Jill on the tips. Ready to nosh down, he sat and crossed himself. He'd seen this on *The Waltons* and felt it was really cool. Evenly, he removed the tops from the eggs, saying: "Hats off at the table, kids."

Taking one bread soldier, he dipped it in Jack and ate. To and fro, Jack through Jill, he ate with gusto.

It was DHSS day. Standing quietly in line, Shannon replayed *The Dogs of War* movie in his mind. The window lady looked at his card, said: "Mr. Noble wants to see you – desk number three. Next!"

Shannon waited for two hours before Noble got him. Time for the Umpire to uncoil, begin to flex. Noble had a thin moustache, like a wipe of soot, and he fingered it constantly. With a degree from one of the new polys, Noble had notions. Scanning through the file, he clicked his tongue, said: "Mr. Shannon, we seem to have had you for rather a long time."

Shannon nodded.

"And... Mmm... you completed the Jobclub, I see."

Nod.

"No prospects on the horizon – no hopeful leads from there?"

A giggle.

Noble's head came up: "I said something amusing?"

Shannon spoke, huge merriment bubbling beneath the words: "I'm seeking a rather specialised position."

"Oh, and what would that be, Mr. Shannon, pray tell?"

The Umpire looked right into Noble's eyes, and the man felt a cold chill hit his very soul.

"I'd like to participate in cricket – a position of influence, ideally."

And now the laughter burst. A harsh, mocking sound like a knife on glass. Shannon stood up and leaned across the desk, whispered: "I expect there to be vacancies soon."

And he was gone.

An ashen Noble sat rigid for several minutes until the tea-lady arrived. "One or two biccies, Mr. N?"

Later in the day, Noble contemplated a call to the police. The loony definitely had a fix on cricket. But what if they laughed at him? It would be round the office in jig-time. Worse, he might have to shave his tash, total horror, resign and sign on. Probably here in his very own domain. A shudder ran through him. No, best leave well enough alone. He'd just put it out of his mind. Right! That's what he'd do. See how decisive he was. Let his tash reign supreme.

Falls was twixt laughter and tears, hysteria fomenting. She said: "You know what the ambulance guy said when he saw how Dad was lying?"

Rosie didn't know, answered: "I dunno."

"I do love a man ON a uniform."

Pause.

Then they cracked up.

BASIC SURVIVAL

"How much more can they not talk to me?"
(d.B)

Kev's brother Albert had a grand passion, the idea fixed almost – The Monkees – as they'd been. And due to syndication, in fifty-eight episodes, they would forever be condemned by celluloid to Monkee around – with shit-eating grins for all eternity. A hell of mammoth proportions, proof indeed that God was deep pissed. To Albert, it was bliss. He knew all the lyrics and worse, lines from the TV series, and horror, repeated them.

When the "guys," in their fifties and looking old, had a reunion tour, he was appalled. Peter Pan can't grow up, and seeing Davy Jones at fifty-three you knew why. Albert could do the Monkee walk, but had learned the hard way that it's a kink best kept private. When he'd first shown it to Kev, he got a merciless beating. Albert's dream was to visit that beach house where the Monkees had such adventures. When he was nervous, which was often, he'd hum "Daydream Believer" and believe the fans were fainting outside. The "E" crew could be like the guys, he thought. He coiled a cog and lit it with a Zippo.

"Hand jobs" Kev called them. He'd go: "Suckin' on yer hand job. I don't see Mickey Dolenz smokin, eh?"

Not a lot.

In truth, Albert didn't like Mickey all that much. He reminded him of their father and that was the pinnacle of mean. The full down-in-the-gutter vicious bastard. Kev was forever sliding in anti-Monkee propaganda, to rattle the cage. As if he researched it! Like: "Hey Albert, you dozy fuck, that Mike Nesmith, the one with the nigger hat, he's not hurtin. His old lady invented Liquid Paper which crafty Mike sold the patent for. Yeah, the old lovable chimp got forty-seven million from Gillette. How about that for bucks, just a carefree guy, eh? No bloody wonder."

And cloud city when Peter Tork went to jail for drug possession; Kev was delighted. Kept needling. Kept singing:

"We're just goofin' around."

When *The Simpsons* began to replace the TV show on major networks, Albert hated them double. 'Cos too, they were so ignorant. Homer Simpson was like Kev's role model. Go figure. Albert had been down Brixton Market and – ye gods, hold the phones – he saw Mike Nesmith's woolly hat on a stall, told the stall owner who said: "Mike who? I don't know the geezer!"

"From The Monkees!"

The guy took a hard look at Albert to see if it was a wind-up, then had a quick scan around, said: "Yeah, yeah, this is Mike Neville's hat, the actual one."

Albert got suspicious, said: "It's Nesmith's?"

"Course it is son, but he uses Neville as a cover. Know what I mean, to avoid the fans like."

"Oh."

"Straight up, son. Any road, I couldn't let it go."

Albert had to have it, pleaded: "I have to have it."

"Mmmm. I suppose I could let you have it for twelve."

"I've only got this, a fiver."

Which was fast snapped up, with: "It's yours son, much as I hate to let it go."

Later, the guy wondered if it was that tea commercial with the chimps, but he didn't remember a hat. As if he gave a fuck anyway. He got out another dozen of them. Kev burnt it the same evening.

To die for

Falls said to Rosie: "You know how much it's gonna cost to bury Dad?"

"Uh-uh. A lot?"

"Two and a half grand."

"What? You could get married for that."

"And that doesn't even include flowers or the vicar's address."

"You have savings, right? You do have savings?"

"Ahm..."

"Oh Lord, you're skint!"

Falls nodded. Rosie searched for alternatives, then: "Could you burn him?"

"What?"

"Sorry, I mean, cremate him."

"He was against that."

Rosie gave a bitter laugh. "C'mon girl, I don't think old Arthur has really got a shout in this. He couldn't give a toss what happens now, eh?"

"I can't. I'd feel haunted."

"Typical. Even in death, men stick to you. What about the Police Benevolent Fund?"

"I've been. They'll cough up part of the dosh, but seeing as he wasn't one of the force..."

Rosie knew another way but didn't wish to open that can of worms. Or worm. She said: "There is one last resort."

"Anything. Oh God Rosie, I just want him planted so I can move on."

"Brant."

"Oh no."

"You're a desperate girl. He does have the readies."

Then Rosie, to change the subject, patted her new hairstyle. It was de rigueur dyke. Brushed severely back, right scraped from her hairline to flourish in a bun. She asked: "So what do you think of my new style? I know you have to have some face to take such exposure."

Falls gave it the full glare. She couldn't even say it highlighted the eyes, a feature that should be deep hid, along with the rest. The eyes were usually a reliable cop-out. To the ugliest dog you could safely say: "You have lovely eyes."

Not Rosie.

Falls blurted: "You have to have some bloody cheek."

But Rosie took it as a compliment, gushed: "I'll let you have the address of the salon, they'll see you on short notice."

Falls wanted to say: "Saw you coming all right." But instead: "That'd be lovely."

Brant came swaggering in and Rosie said: "Oh, speak of the devil, sergeant."

And over he came, the satanic smile forming: "Ladies?"

"WPC Falls has a request. I'll leave you to it."

And she legged it. Brant watched her, then said to Falls: "What the Jaysus happened to her hair?"

Shannon was in a café on the Walworth Road, not a spit from the old Carter Street Station. He'd ordered a large tea. As it came, an old man asked: "Is this seat taken?"

"No, sir."

The man was surprised, manners were as rare as tories on that patch. He sat down and was about to say so when the young man said: "No umpire should be changed during a match without the consent of both captains."

"Eh?"

"Before the toss the umpire shall agree with both captains on any special conditions affecting the conduct of the match."

"Ah, bit of a cricket buff are you?"

"Before and during a match, the umpires shall ensure that the conduct of the game and the implements used are strictly in accordance with the laws."

The old man wondered if he should move but there were no other seats. Plus he was gasping for a brew. He tried: "Day off work, 'ave you?"

The Umpire smiled, reached over and with his index finger, touched the man's lips, said: "Time to listen, little man, lest those very lips be removed."

Before the man could react, the Umpire stood up and came round the table, put his arm over the old man's shoulders, whispered: "The umpire shall be the sole judge of fair and unfair play."

The waitress, watching, thought ahh, it's his old dad, isn't that lovely? You just don't see that sort of affection any more. It quite made her day.

As Brant sat with Falls, the canteen radio kicked in, Sting with "Every Move You Make." Brant grimaced, said: "The stalker's anthem."

Falls listened a bit, said: "Good Lord, you're right."

He gave a nod, indicative of nothing. She got antsy, didn't know where to begin, said: "I dunno where to begin."

He took out his Weights. Asked: "D'ya mind?"

"Personally no, but it is a no smoking zone."

He lit up, said: "Fuck 'em." And waited.

Falls wanted to leave. A silent Brant was like a loaded weapon, primed. But she had no alternative. In a small voice, she said: "I'm in a spot of bother."

"Money or sex?"

"What?"

"It's always one or the other, always."

"Oh, right, it's money."

"How much?"

"Don't you want to know what for?"

"Why, what difference does that make? I'll either give it to you or I won't, a story won't help."

"It's a lot."

He waited.

"It's three thou."

She never knew why she went the extra. Called it nerves, but didn't believe it.

"OK."

She couldn't believe it, said: "Just like that?"

"Sure, I'm not a bank, you don't have to bleed."

"Oh God, that's wonderful, I'm in your debt."

"Exactly."

"Excuse me?"

"In my debt, like you said, you owe me."

"Oh."

He got up to leave, asked: "Was there anything else?"

"No."

"I'll have the money by close of business – that OK with you?"

"Of course. I —'

But he was gone.

Precarious the pose

Brant was in the "E" room. Expecting a long run. Someone had hooked up a microwave. He looked through the goodies and found a Cornish pasty, muttered "Mmm," and put it in the micro. Zapped it twice and had it out. Took an experimental bite and stomped his foot, tears running from his eyes. The pasty, blazing, had fastened to the roof of his mouth. He grabbed a coke bottle and swallowed. Finally the burning eased and he said: "Jay-sus."

A passing WPC said: "Don't touch the Cornish, Sarge, they're way past their date."

The phone rang and he snatched it: "Incident room 'E'."

"Are you investigating the hangings?"

"Yes, that's right."

"I have some information."

"Good, that's good. And your name, sir?"

"To prove I'm legit, check the last victim's fingers."

"Might be a tad difficult mate – sir."

"Because of the torching? I doubt that would disguise broken fingers. I'll call back in an hour." And the caller hung up.

Brant was electric, got on to Roberts and the coroner. When Roberts arrived, he told him of the call and of the coroner's confirmation: "The bugger was right, and what's more, I've set up for a trace, he was ringing from a mobile, it kept breaking up. We'll have him if he calls back."

Roberts was impressed, said: "I'm impressed."

Brant could feel his adrenaline building. It felt like a hit. Roberts took a seat. A picture of calm, he said: "Could be the one, the White Arrest."

Brant had already raced to the same conclusion, was feeling generous in his victory: "For us both, Guv."

"No, this is all your own, another Rilke, maybe."

The phone rang. Brant signalled to the technicians, who gave him the green light, and he picked up: "Incident room 'E.'"

"You checked the fingers?"

"We're just waiting for confirmation."

"We're not criminals, we're only doing what the courts are failing to do."

Roberts made an S motion in the air. Stall.

"Why don't you come in, we'll have a chat, work something out."

But the caller was on a different track. "It wasn't meant to be like this, you know, not white people. Not that I'm a racist."

Brant tried it on. "Course you're not, I mean you live in Brixton, right?"

Roberts shook his head, signalling U-turn. The caller continued: "I don't think he'll stop now, he likes it."

"But you're different, I can tell. I mean why don't you and I have a meet?"

There was static on the line, then a note of panic. "Shit, I've got to go. I'll call again."

And then the line died. Brant swore, looked pleadingly to the techs. They were engrossed for a moment, then gave the thumbs up, shouted: "Got him!"

Brant punched the air: "Yes!" And a cheer came from the room.

A technician listened, wrote something down, then handed a piece of paper to Brant. He read aloud: "'Leroy Baker." Got yer ass, fucker." And reached for a phone.

Roberts was up, saying: "Wait, wait – what's the name?"

"Leroy Baker, we have him."

Roberts took his arm, pulled him to the other side of the room, saying: "Listen, Tom."

"Fuck listen, let's go – we're on him."

"Tom, the name. It's the first victim."

"What?"

"Yeah, he's using the guy's mobile."

Brant sank into a chair, muttering: "The thieving scumbag, of all the low-down nasty bastards, I'd like five minutes..." and he trailed off into silence.

The room had gone quiet. Roberts said: "What's this, you've finished for the day? Get bloody on it!"

A half-hearted hum began to return, with furtive looks to Brant. Roberts touched his shoulder. "C'mon sergeant, I'm going to buy you a drink."

Madness more like

Nineteen-sixty-five. The Umpire had been a cricket sensation. As a schoolboy, he'd already been watched by the England selectors. Provision was made to ensure his talent was nurtured and developed. But...

If Albert of the "E" crew was missing some vital pieces of human connection and born with a lack, then the Umpire was born with an extra dimension – a dimension of destruction. He liked to watch it burn. On the day of his first schoolboy accomplishments, he set fire to the pavilion. And got caught. His father beat him to a pulp and they put him away in a home for the seriously disturbed. They got that right. What they got wrong was releasing him. His first night home, his father took out all the press cuttings. All the stories of hope and triumph, then proceeded to whip him, ranting: "There'll be no madness in this family."

Could you beat insanity? It only drives it underground. Teaches the art of stealth. The first time the Umpire burned a dog, he couldn't believe the rush, enhanced by such discovery. In his mind the words were etched: "See it burn."

As the years passed, he began to look on the England team. The fame, publicity, accolades he felt were rightly his. It began to foment in his mind: if he couldn't have the prizes, why should they? When he read *Day of The Jackal* he was elated. Then on to *The Dogs of War*, and as his psychosis came to full bloom he imagined himself to be Shannon, the hero of the book. Later, he thought, Frederick Forsyth would base a book on him.

❖

Roberts studied the growing pile of paper on the Umpire, said: "I'll get the murderer sooner or later. It's always simpler when they're insane."

Brant said: "That's a hell of a positive attitude. Way to go, Guv."

A self-conscious Roberts blustered: "It's a quote."

"Oh yeah?"

"Thomas Gomez in *Phantom Lady*."

"Those old movies again Guv, eh? It's black-and-white, it's a classic."

"Don't be a daft bugger, sergeant. It's film noir, never better than in the forties and fifties."

Brant, already losing interest, answered: "You know, Guv."

It wasn't that Brant was an ignoramus, Roberts thought, but that he revelled in ignorance. His sole passion was to win. In his mind he played Robert Mitchum talking to Jane Greer in *Out of The Past*:

"That's not the way to play it."

"Why not?"

"'Cause it isn't the way to win."

"Is there a way to win?"

"Well, there's a way to lose more slowly."

"Ahhh."

"Guv. Guv!" Brant's harsh tone cut through his movie.

"What?"

"You're muttering to yourself. Doesn't look good."

"A privilege of rank."

Brant was tempted to add: "Madness, more like." But he'd tested his cheek enough. For now.

Slag?

Fiona had arranged a "coffee meet" with Penny, her treat. She'd selected Claridges, to reach for the class she so desperately craved. It would have amused her to learn she shared a musical preference with WPC Falls. As she ordered a double cappuccino with cream, the words of "Misguided Angel" ran through her head. The waiter was in his twenties and had the essential blend of surliness and servility. In short, a London lad. She admired his ass in the tight black pants and felt a flush creep across her chest. Since Jason, she was drenched in heat. He'd fit perfectly into the CA catalogue. The coffee came with all the prerequisites of the hotel. A mountain of serviettes with the Claridges logo, lest you lost your bearings, a bowl of artery-clogging cream and one slim biscuit in an unopenable wrapper. Penny arrived looking downright dowdy. Not a leg away from a bag lady. They exchanged air kisses. No skin was actually touched. Not so much consciousness of the age of AIDS as the fact that they were steeped in pretension.

Fiona led: "Are you all right?"

"Don't I look all right?"

"Well, no... no you don't."

Penny turned her head, shouted: "Waiter, espresso before Tuesday, OK?"

Fiona cringed. "They're not big on shouting in Claridges. Discretion is such a form that they'd really appreciate you not showing at all. But if you must, then quiet, eh?"

Penny took a Silk Cut from her purse, said: "I'm smoking again, so shoot me."

The waiter brought the coffee. No perks with this, just the basic cup and saucer. He waited and Penny snapped: "Take a hike, Pedro."

He did. Then, no preamble, she launched: "The bastard's leaving after twenty-six years of marriage. He's off."

"But why?"

"He needs space. Can you believe it, that he'd use that line of crap to me? Everyone's in therapy and no one's responsible anymore."

"You'll have the house?"

"I'll have his balls, that's what I'll have."

Then she rooted in her handbag, produced a boxed Chanel No. 5 and flung it on the table, said: "I got you a present."

"Oh."

"Sorry it's not wrapped. Well, it's not paid for either."

"I don't follow."

"I nicked it. That's what I'm doing these days, roaming the big stores and stealing things I don't even want. On Monday I took a set of pipes. You wouldn't prefer a nice briar, would you?"

"No. Oh, Pen, if you need help -'

"Go into therapy is it? Find my inner child and thrash it?" She jumped up. "I'll have to go. I'll call you."

And she was gone. It was a few moments before Fiona realised that Penny had pocketed the espresso cup. She gave a deep sigh, thinking: "It's nothing to do with me."

But it was. Penny had a major effect on her life. She opened the Chanel, put a bit behind her ears, said: "Mmm, that's class."

The leader of the "E" crew, Kevin, was singing at the top of his voice: "Tom Traubert's Blues," aka "Waltzing Matilda." He was well pissed, empty Thunderbirds strewn at his feet. As the high point of the song touched crescendo, so did Kev. He was right moved to tears at the strength, nay, the majesty of the voice. For Christmas his brother Albert had given him Rod Stewart's *Greatest Hit Ballads*, and now aloud he roared: "I love this fuckin' album!" And cranked open another Thunderbird, near drained it in one gulp. He'd followed Rod from the Small Faces all the way through "Killing of Georgie" parts one and two, and fuck, never mind that Rod was an arrogant arsehole, the fucker could sing like a nicotinized Angel. Now Kev began to dance, to waltz, one two oops three with an imaginary Matilda. She was a combination of all the women he'd never had. Then as is wont with the booze, it metamorphosed fuckin' bliss to viciousness in the click of a beat. He stumbled and then pushed the dancing partner away, shouting: "Slag!" Spittle lined his lips as hate fuelled by alcohol propelled him to a dimension where few would wish to be. Kev had done time, hard time. But he'd discovered books and found they provided a brief escape. His all-time hero was Andrew Vachss with the Burke novels. They were Kev's speed, chock full of righteousness brutality, total vengeance. It never occurred to Kev that the very people Burke pursued were Kevin's own. Not that he didn't identify with the pure villains, the twenty-four carat psychos that scared even Burke. Wesley, the monster who signed his suicide note with a threat: "I don't know where I'm going but they better not send anyone after me."

Class act. Kev had copied it down, carried it like a prayer of the damned. Damnation was romantic as long as it didn't hurt. When his brother Albert was born, they left something out, some essential connection that kept him two beats behind. Kevin was his brother and bully. The other two crew members were ciphers, their sole purpose being to fill prisons or football stadiums, and they were partial to both. Go in any bookie's after the big race, they're the guys picking up the discarded tickets, the human wallpaper. When God chose the cast, he made them spear carriers. Rage began early in Kev. A series of homes through Borstal to the one where the big boys play. Prison. In Wormwood Scrubs, he was made to bend over by a drug dealer and thus began his lock on their trade. Discovering Burke gave a hint of crusade to his vision and the seeds of vigilantism were sown. The Michael Winner *Death Wish* series was a revelation. When Bronson eliminated a guy, the audience stood up and cheered. Kev began to see how he could become famous, heroic and use a gun. If he got to settle personal scores, well hell, that was just how the cookie crumbled. The first weapon he got was a replica Colt and he spent hours in front of the mirror striking poses. Mouthing defiance: "Bend over! You fucking bend over now... Hey, arsehole... Yeah, you!" He got *Taxi Driver* on vid and finally came home. Here was destiny, and in his movie he'd insist George Clooney played him. Get the chicks hot. At times, standing by Brixton tube station, he's see black guys come past in cars whose names he couldn't even pronounce. Rap music pouring from the speakers and arrogance on the breeze. He'd grit his teeth and mutter: "You're going down, bad-ass." When he got the crew together, he laid it out as a blend of Robin Hood meets Tarantino and how they'd be front page of the *Sun*. Doug and Fenton didn't care either way and, if it provided cash, why not? Albert did what Kevin said, as always. The "E" was born and ready to rock 'n' roll.

Band aid

As Brant and Roberts headed for the pub, they passed a urinating wino. Delirium tremens hit him mid-piss and his body did a passable jig. Brant said: "A riverdancer."

The pub was police-friendly. Meaning if you were a cop, they were friendly, if you weren't, you got shafted. A blowsy barmaid greeted them: "Two officers."

Brant smiled and said: "My kind of woman."

"Friendly?" said Roberts.

"No, big tits."

Roberts ordered two pints of best and Brant added: "Two chasers, Glenfiddich preferably."

Roberts said: "Cheers."

"Whatever."

"You know, Tom, we should do this more often."

"We've never done it before."

"Oh, are you sure?"

"I'm positive, Guv."

"Hey, Tom, no need for that here, we're not standing on rank."

But he did not offer an alternative. Brant sank the short, said to the barmaid: "Maisie, same again."

"That's her name?"

"Is now."

Four drinks passed. Roberts offered: "You're a single man now."

"That's me."

"No kids."

"None that I've admitted to."

Six drinks later, Brant's turn: "You and yer missus, Guv, doing all right?"

"Well, she's doing something, not that she tells me, mind."

Eight drinks later, Roberts: "I think I'm pissed."

"Naw, it's early yet."

Closing time. Roberts: "Fancy a curry? I could murder a chapati."

"Yeah, let's get a carryout. Molly!"

"I thought she was Maisie."

"Naw, it's Molly, they're always Mollies."

Midnight.

Sitting outside the pub attempting red hot curry, Brant said: "D'ya want to kip at my place?"

A passing bobby stopped, said: "What's all this then?"

It took Roberts a few moments to focus, then he slurred: "Yer bloody nicked, son."

When Brant finally got home he was beginning to sober up. A foul taste on his mouth, he blamed it on the early Cornish pasty. He never blamed whisky. His sobriety was sealed when he saw the door of his flat off its hinges. He roared: "Bastards! Not to me, not ever!"

The living room was destroyed. Ripped and gutted photos. But his beloved book collection: the McBains were shredded, the delicate Penguin covers torn to pieces. Piled on top were remnants of Matthew Hope and Ewan Hunters. To cap it, urine had been sprayed all over. Tears blinded him and a sob-whisper: "Yah fuckin' animals."

He ran to the bedroom, tried to ignore the used condom on his pillow, went deep into his dirty laundry, extracted a bundle of undies, roared in triumph: "Ah, yah stupid bastards," extracted a Browning automatic, fully loaded, shoved it in the waistband of his trousers and stalked out. Left the door as it was, said: "Daddy's gone a-hunting."

Brant's shoulder took the door off the basement flat. He felt that was poetic justice at the very least. Inside, the occupant began to rise from bed. But Brant was over and kneeling on his chest within seconds, saying: "Sorry to disrupt your sleep, Rodney."

"Mr. Brant, oh God. Mr. Brant, what's going on?"

"Someone turned my gaff, Rodders, someone very bloody

stupid, and by lunch today you'll have their names for me, else I'll move in with you."

"Your gaff, Mr. Brant? No one would have the bottle, unless it were junkies, yes, has to be, they don't know from shit."

"The names, Rod, by lunchtime. Am I clear?"

He let his full weight settle and Rodders gasped, then managed: "OK Mr. Brant, OK."

Brant got up, asked: "Got any aspirin? My head is splittin'."

As he left, Rodney asked: "My door, Mr. Brant, who's gonna see about that?"

Brant looked at it with apparently huge interest, then said: "Don't leave it like this, it's a bloody open invitation, know what I mean?"

Rodney rang Brant at 11:50, said: "I found the geezers who done yer, Guv."

"Yeah?"

"They're junkies, like I said. A guy and his girlfriend. Yer own crowd as it happens."

"What, they're coppers you mean?"

Rodney didn't know if this required a polite laugh. Brant's humour was more lethal than his temper. He decided to play it straight, said: "Ahm, like Micks, you know, Oirish. But they've been here a bit so they speak a mix of Dublin and London."

"So where do I find these cultural ambassadors?"

"They have a pitch at the Elephant and Castle, in the tunnels there. He sits and she begs."

"How Job Centre-ish, eh?"

Rodney felt sweat gather on his brow. Any dealings with Brant had this effect. He hoped to terminate the call with: "They're easily recognisable as they wear a Band-Aid under the left eye."

"Why?"

"Fuck knows."

"OK Rodders, you done good. Stay in touch."

"Definitely."

And he put the phone down. His heart was whacking in his

chest. However bad he felt, he knew it was way beyond what a set of junkies would soon be experiencing. But he shrugged it off, saying: "For all I know, they're Ben Elton fans."

Brant found them in jig time. Sure enough they were in the tunnels, begging and Band-Aided.

Unlikely lad

The man was sitting on a blanket and the woman was pacing. They had the uniform intimidation: combat jackets, Doc Martens and an air of menace. No dog, surprisingly. Brant looked up and down. Nobody about. He kept his head down and walked up to them, giving the London look of cowardly expectation. He saw the woman smile as she moved to block his path, whining: "Few bob for a cup o' tea, mistah?"

As he drew level, he swung round and smashed his shoe into the man's face, then whirled and ran her into the wall. Checking again for onlookers, he then pushed her down beside the man. A symphony of shocked groans came from them: "Whatcha do dat for ya cunt?"

"Ah..."

Brant hunkered down. Grabbed the man by the hair, said: "What's with the bandages, dudes?"

The man was hurt but still managed to look amazed: "What?"

"The Band-Aids Bros., what's the deal?"

"'Cos if I'm cut, she bleeds."

Brant smiled and lashed out with his open palm into the woman's face, said: "Hey, pay attention."

She tried to spit, then asked: "Whatcha pickin' on us for, mistah? We dun nothing to youse."

He banged their heads together as a man entered the tunnel. Brant said: "You turned over a gaff, the wrong one, believe me. Now you have two days to compensate me for the damage, or I am talking major hurt. I'll leave it to you guys to figure out how much it should be. Else... well, I'll come looking for you."

The man drew level and asked: "Anything wrong here?"

Brant stood up, said: "Naw, I'm doing a survey on urban deprivation."

The man peered at the battered couple, said: "Good Lord, they're bleeding."

"Yeah, but see, they have band aids, that should do it."

As Brant strolled off, he calculated the pair's collective age at about sixty. They had the air of a hundred and sixty. Never-nomind, he thought. Like all junkies, they'd been dead for years, the news just hadn't reached their fried brains yet.

Shannon watched the cricket story fade from page one to back towards the horoscopes. His story! But unlike the "E" outfit, he didn't get angry. Time was on his side and he knew how to instantly pull it back. He'd been to military shops on the Strand and quite openly bought a crossbow.

The proprietor had said: "Alas, I've only three arrows."

The Umpire smiled, said: "Then thrice shall I smite them."

The proprietor couldn't give a toss if he answered in Arabic, said: "Whatever." And he put the goods in a M&S bag, warning: "Careful how you handle 'em," and pocketed the money.

Now the Umpire dry-tested the bow and found it slack. He tightened and tested for over an hour till it gave a taut *zing*. He couldn't believe how easy it had been to kill his second cricketer. At the very least, he'd expected a uniform on the beat. But zip, *nada, tipota.*

When he'd begun his crusade, he found most of the team addresses in the phone book. That strengthened his conviction and zeal. Three of them with south-east London homes. Better and better. The sheer power of the arrows enthralled him. As he saw the wicket-keeper stumble down the steps, he felt exhilaration. But cunning ruled. He quickly put the weapon in the M&S bag and simply walked away. Shannon began to reemerge as the two personalities roared: "Cry havoc and let loose the dogs of war."

PC Tone was what used to be called a raw youth. He didn't have acne but it was close. At twenty-three years of age, he looked seventeen. Not a big advantage in south-east London. But he had four O-levels and one A-level. The changing Met looked at exams, not faces. When Brant first clapped eyes on him, he'd said: "For fucksake."

Tone worshipped the Sergeant. The rep of violence, rebellion and fecklessness was irresistible. That Brant despised him didn't cool his devotion since Brant seemed to despise everyone. Tone figured if he could attach himself to Brant, he'd learn the real method of policing. Not an easy task, as most times he was told: "Piss off boy." Until this morning.

He'd been summoned, so to speak. Brant was in the canteen, wolfing down a glazed doughnut. The only person to have his own drinking vessel, even the brass got plastic cups. His was a large chipped mug with Rambo on the side. A logo read: *I'm a gas*. But the *g* had faded. Brant gave a big smile, particles of sugar in his teeth, said: "Have a seat, boyo."

Tone was 6'1" and awkward. Roger McGough might have used him for the PC Plod poems. He had his hair cut short and gelled. His face was made up of regular features and his whole demeanour suggested "unlikely lad."

He sat.

Brant gave him a full look, then asked: "Tea or coffee, boyo?"

"Ahm, tea, I think."

Brant snorted: "Well, it won't come to you lad, hop up there and gis a refill, two sugars."

The canteen lady, named Doris, gave Tone a wink, said: "Watch'im."

When he returned, Brant said: "Lovely job," and took a gulp, went: "Jaysus you never stirred it."

Which was true. Then he took out his Weights, said: "I'd offer you one but it's a smoke-free zone," and lit up. Tone tasted his tea. It was like coffee or turpentine or a cunning blend of both. Brant leaned over, asked: "Do you want to get on boyo, eh? Are you ambitious?"

"Yes, sir."

"Good, that's good. I have a little job for you."

"I'm ready, sir."

"Course you are, a fine strappin' youth like you. You'll sire legions."

"Sir?"

"Now, there's two dossers, male and female. In their late twenties. They have their pitch in the Elephant and Castle tunnels. They wear Band-Aids on their faces. I want their names, their squat, who they run with, any previous. Got that?"

"Yes sir."

"Well don't hang about lad, get crackin'."

Tone stood up, perplexed, then: "But sir... Why? Have they done owt? What's the reason?"

Brant held up a hand, palm outward: "Whoah, Sherlock, hold yer water. The reason is I asked you – d'ya follow?"

"Yes sir."

"That's the job, and oh, Tome..."

"Tone, sir. It's an 'n.'"

"Whatever. Mum's the word, eh?"

When the constable had gone, Brant said, and not quietly: "Fuckin' maggot."

Room mate?

A hammering likely to wake the very dead

Falls was dreaming of her father when the hammering began at her door. Awakening, she checked the time, 3:30am, and heard in disbelief: "Open up, this is the police."

Throwing on a robe, she went to the door and opened it on the safety chain. Brant.

"What the—?"

"I bring you greetings."

She could smell the wave of liquor and he looked demented. She said: "Sergeant, this is hardly an appropriate hour."

"I need a kip."

And she figured: "Pay up time."

Before she could protest, he said: "Don't be a cow. I've been turned over. I'll sleep on the couch."

Reluctantly, she opened the door. He slouched in, muttering: "McBain, Hunter, all done in."

"Your friends?"

And he gave what she could only describe as a cackle and said: "Friends? Yes, yes. I believe they were, and better than most." He flopped down on the couch, said: "Jay-sus, I need some sleep. Get the light would you?" And within minutes he was snoring. She got a blanket from her bed and as she put it over him she saw the gun in his waistband. Afraid he'd do damage, she reached for it, only to have her wrist seized. He said: "Don't handle my weapon."

As she tried to regain her sleep, she wished: "Hope he shoots his balls off."

❖❦

Falls prided herself on the flat being a "smoke free zone." Even her old dad, no matter how pissed, never had the bottle to light his "home-mades" there. Now she woke to the stench of nicotine, clouds of it hung in the air. Storming out to the living room, she found Brant wrapped in her best towel, a cigarette dangling on his lips. He said: "Breakfast's made. Well, sort of. I've boiled the water. Whatcha fancy, coffee all right?"

"No thank you, I'm a tea drinker."

As she went into the kitchen, he observed: "Jay-sus, you've got a big arse, haven't you?"

The kitchen was a ruin. Used cups, stained teatowels, opened jars left everywhere. He strolled in after her, asked: "How'd it go then?"

"What?"

"The funeral."

"Oh. Great. No, I mean OK, it was small."

"He was a small man, eh?"

She glared at him: "Is that supposed to be funny?"

"Did Roberts go?"

"Yes, him and Mrs. Roberts."

"Ah, the lovely Fiona. I could ride that."

She slammed a cup on the sink, said:

"Really, sergeant. Are you trying to be deliberately offensive?" He gave a look of near-innocence.

"Me? Listen babe, don't get yer knickers in a twist, this is my good side."

She looked at him with distaste, said: "Your chin is bleeding."

He wiped at it with an end of the towel, her favourite white fluffy one, said: "Them lady razors, near tore the face offa me."

Another item for the bin, she sighed. He stood up, said: "I need to ask your... co-operation."

"Oh?"

"If certain items – shall we say information – about the big cases, arrive, I'd appreciate a nod before it gets to Roberts."

"I don't know, Sarge, I mean..."

"C'mon Falls. I'm not asking much. He'll be informed. Eventually." Without another word, he went into the sitting room, dressed, and presented himself, asking: "How do I look?"

"Er..."

"Yeah, I thought so. I've got to go chat to a junkie."

She felt she'd been a tad cold, nay harsh, and tried to pull back a bit. In the hall, she said in a soft voice: "Sarge, thanks for not, you know, trying it on."

"Hey, I don't jump the help, OK."

Roberts had watched a documentary on Francis Bacon. He especially liked Bacon's cry when he entered a club in Soho: "Champagne for my real friends. Real pain for my sham friends." He was about to experience some major pain himself. The Chief Super was having more than a piece of Roberts' hide and kept repeating: "I'm not the type to say 'I told you so'."

He was crowing over the "solution" to the cricket murder. Roberts was seething, said quietly: "Oh, it's been solved?"

"Don't take that tone with me, laddie. It's solved as far as we're concerned."

Roberts wanted to shout: "Fuck you, sir, fuck the brass and the chain of command and the politicians." But he said: "If you say so, sir."

"I do say so. Our American cousins talk about bottom feeders. Are you cognizant with it?"

"Bottom of the shit pile, sir, would that be close?"

"Brant, now he's a good example. Look here." And he threw a document across the desk, said: "The yard have been on to me. Your precious Detective Sergeant is accused of bribe-taking by a Mr. Patel, of intimidation by a tobacconist in the West End, of brutality by an accused rapist, of freebies by a pizza company... the list goes on."

Roberts barely glanced at it, said: "Nickel and dime. He's a good copper."

"He's finished, that's what he is. I doubt even a cream arrest could save him."

"That's white, sir. A White Arrest."

"Are you sure? Well, I want to ensure he doesn't pull off one of those. So you're back in charge of the vigilante business. See it's put to bed quickly."

"Put to bed, sir?"

"Get on with it, and I'll remind you of thin ice yourself, questions have been asked before."

With that he was dismissed. Outside he ran his finger along the rim of his ear. A passing WPC asked: "All right sir, your ear I mean?"

"Oh yeah, I've just had a flea put in it."

The law of holes: when you're in one, don't dig

All hell erupted at the station as the news of the murder broke. The Super charged down the corridor, barged into Roberts' office, roared: "You're in for it now, laddy, there's been another one."

Roberts wanted to say, "I told you so," but instead came running, said: "Someone surprise me, tell me Brant is here and reachable." Nobody surprised him.

The down-scaled "U" incident room was activated and Roberts was given the details of the killing. He asked: "Any witnesses?"

"No, sir."

"The weapon?"

"A crossbow, Guv."

"Bloody hell. Wait until the press get wind of this."

Silence.

"What, they're on to it already?"

"Sorry, Guv."

"Holy shit, we're fucked. So no chance of containment, the ol' damage limitation?"

Many heads shook. Negative all the way.

Roberts sat, said: "Isn't there any good news?"

Falls tried to lighten the mood, said: "Well, we've got a shoplifter in an interview room."

He turned his full gaze to her. He spoke slowly: "That's some sort of levity, I gather. How about this WPC! Hop lightly to yer plod feet, go interview them and get out of my bloody sight!"

Roberts had thus made two mistakes. The first was not seeing the shoplifter. The second one was alienating the hitherto loyal Falls.

"Ashen was the way I felt
when shunned by people I
had justified. Didn't all
that much really warrant
grief."

The Umpire

The Umpire's father had adorned the house with framed portraits of cricket's greatest. A who's-who of the best. He'd point to them and shout: "You could have been better than any of them, but oh no, you're a namby pamby, a mummy's boy. You'll never hold a light to these, these giants." Light, a light to light. He looked on it like a mantra of darkness.

His father's pride was a three-year-old setter named Fred Truman. Sleek and arrogant, it ruled with ease. The day of the Umpire's transformation, he recalls it like a vision.

The Dogs of War was showing on BBC1. The screen's image flicking back and forth across Fred Truman as he dozed. The Umpire had removed his father's bat from the glass case and said: "Here boy, come and get it." As the dog's head reared, the Umpire batted. He heard the crowds leap to their feet at Lords, the applause crescendoed at the Oval and the dog lay stunned. The Umpire laid the bat beside Fred and doused both with petrol. On the TV Christopher Walker loaded up as the match ignited, the words rose: "Cry havoc and let loose the dogs of..."

Falls sat opposite her, put the file on the table and decided to
"Brant" it. Said: "Well, Penny or Penelope, which?"

No answer.

"Okey-dokey, let's settle for Penny, shall we?"

No answer.

"You're going to jail, Penny."

Gasp!

"Oh yes. I see you've been up twice before but got off on
probation. Says here you agreed to have therapy. I hate to tell
you, it isn't working."

"I can't. I can't go to prison."

"I'm afraid so, Pen. The courts are sick of rich middle-aged
women wasting their valuable time. You'll do six months in
Holloway. The girls there, they'll appreciate a bit o' class. Get
yerself a nice lez, knit away the winter."

Penny began to smile, said: "Oh, I don't think so, you see, I
have something to trade."

"This isn't the bloody market, we don't barter."

"Don't be so sure. I need to see someone in authority." Here
she gave extra dimension to the smile as she added: "I don't think
it's really a decision for the Indians. Go get the chief, there's a
good girl."

Falls came close to clouting her, and realised that Brant might
have the right idea. She rose and left the room, still wondering
whether or not to go to Roberts. Two factors determined her next
move: one, her anger at Roberts; two, almost colliding with Brant.

He said: "Whoa, little lady, don't lose yer knickers."

She told him, watched his face and calculated. He said: "I'll
have a word, shall I? You keep watch outside."

"Shouldn't I be present?"

"Outta yer league darlin'." Tell you what though, I could
murder a cuppa." And he opened the door, looked back and said:
"Two sugars, love."

Brant sat down slowly, his eyes on Penny. She said: "You're a
senior officer?"

He gave the satanic smile, asked in his best south-east London
voice: "Whatcha fink, darlin'?"

"I think you look like a thug."

"That too! So, honey — "

She snapped. "Don't you dare call me that. I'm not your honey."

"Leastways not yet. Whatcha got?"

She got foolish and attempted to slap him. He caught her wrist and with the other hand double palmed her. The marks of his hand ran vivid on her cheeks. He asked: "Have I got your attention now?"

She nodded.

"Okey-dokey, babe. What's cooking?"

She told him about the CA, about Fiona. The whole shooting match. He listened without interruption until: "You pay for sex?"

"Yes."

"Fuck me."

"Actually, it's to avoid that very possibility that we do pay."

He liked it, said approvingly: "Cheeky." Then: "Run it all by me again, hon." She did.

He thought for a while, took out his Weights and absentmindedly offered her one. She took it and waited for a light. He finally noticed, said: "Jaysus, do you want me to smoke it for you too?" A knock at the door. Falls peered in, said: "The Chief Inspector is due this way."

"Shut the door." She did.

Brant drew on the last of his cigarette, sucked it till his cheekbones hit his eyes, leaned over close, said: "Here's the deal. It's not negotiable."

'When the first side has completed its innings, the other side starts its own. A match may consist of one or two innings by each side. If the match is not played out to a finish, it is regarded as a draw."

The blues

The funeral for the first cricketer was a massive affair. The coffin was carried by his team mates and they'd donned the blazing whites. Even the Devon Malcolm racism storm was temporarily shelved. David Syd Lawrence had called for Ray Illingworth to be banned from every TV and radio in the country. The former chairman of selectors was alleged to have called the Derbyshire paceman a "nig-nog." Officers at Lords prayed the funeral would distract from the whole sordid affair. It did.

A huge police presence blocked off most of south-east London. It was feared the Umpire might try to annihilate the remaining nine in one fell swoop. Sky had obtained exclusive rights and was considering a whole series devoted to dead cricketers. It was rumoured that Sting was composing a song for the occasion, but this was proved to be only scaremongering. It scared a lot of people.

Brant and Roberts were positioned on the roof of St. Mark's Cathedral, a tactical position according to the Super.

"Out in the bloody cold," snapped Roberts.

Brant, lowering his binoculars, said: "Good view, though. The *Big Issue* is selling nicely."

"We're out of it Tom, the big boys are running the show. The game is a total media event now. See, we'd be on our arses altogether if they didn't need local background."

Brant didn't care. The more the investigation built, the less notice he attracted. He asked: "Think they'll get him?"

"They have as much chance as you do of understanding cricket."

"I know a bit."

Roberts opened a thermos, refilled their cups and asked: "Oh yeah? Who's Allan Donald?"

"Um?"

"Like I thought."

"Tell us, Guv, go on."

"The South African paceman offered mega bucks by Warwickshire to break the hundred-wicket barrier."

"He's good then, is he?"

"Good good? He claimed eighty-nine first class victims for the country in '95. In '96, in a summer off from country cricket, he took a hundred and six wickets to help Rishton retain a League title."

Roberts' voice had risen and he self-consciously pulled back, said apologetically: "I get a bit carried away."

Brant found a sandwich, took a bite and said: "Don't mean shit to me, Guv."

Roberts went quiet, watched the funeral halt briefly, and he imagined all went still, a suspended moment when past glories, the sound of bat against ball and the hush of the crowd are recalled.

Brant said: "At a guess Guv, I'd say you haven't suffered from the Paradise Syndrome."

"The what?"

"You remember the Eurythmics, thin chick who looked like a faded Bowie and a hippy guy named Dave Stewart. Made fuckin' shitpiles of money, that's yer Paradise Syndrome right there."

"Lucky sod, I could do with a blast of such depression."

They watched the huge line of cars and Brant said: "Me, I'd have to put one song to that funeral."

"What's that then?"

"'Brothers in Arms,' no contest."

Brant began to scratch at his chest and Roberts watched, then said: "That's it, you're wearing a Met Vest. I thought you'd got fat."

They were knife- and bullet-proof items issued to 30,000 officers. Needless to say, they hadn't come cheap and they didn't fit under the regulation shirts. Every officer had an issue of shirts and all of them had to be replaced.

It amused Roberts no end and he slipped into a near-pleasant mood. He reminisced: "The other night, Tom, when we had a few drinks, it was a bit of an eye opener."

A now surly Brant tore at the vest, saying: "Bloody things. What? Oh, the other night, yes, I suppose. Me, though, when I go for a few bevvies, I hope it's going to be a leg opener. I'm never wearing these vests again."

A TV helicopter hovered above and the cameraman zoomed in on Roberts and Brant. The pilot asked: "Anything?"

"Naw, just a couple of wankers."

The discarded Met Vest lay on the roof of the cathedral, like a prayer that wasn't said.

The notice read: *Annual Met Dance. Fancy Dress Preferred. Tickets £10.Buffet & Bar Till Late, '60s Band. All Ranks Expected To Attend.* Roberts was staring at it when Brant came up alongside and said: "Sixties? Does it mean they've been around since then, which would mean they've got to be knackered."

"You sure have some odd thought processes sergeant. I dunno if that's because yer Irish, a policeman or a weird bastard."

A light hit Brant's eyes. "Jeez Guv, I've had a brainwave."

"Yeah? You know who the Umpire is?"

"Now listen, see that fancy dress? Here's something..." Roberts listened to Brant's idea then exchanged:

"I couldn't... good Lord, sergeant, I mean, they'd think we were taking the piss."

"Ahm, c'mon Guv, it's a wicked notion, you know it is, it's downright – what's the word you like – Nora?"

"Noir. Yeah, it is a bit, lemme have a think on it."

"Nice one, Guv. You'll see, it'll be a gas."

"Mmm."

Law 42: Unfair Play. The Umpires are the sole judges of fair and unfair play

Nobody listens to Mantovani, I mean, get real. Not even Mantovani listens much anymore. He's been consigned to the fifties rack and labelled miscellaneous.

But Graham Norman did, and all the time. His wife had given up joking about it and his kids just prayed the bastard never made it to CD. As captain of the England cricket team, Graham could indulge his whims.

He'd attended an indifferent public school, but ambition burned like the old values. He had a small talent and an unending thirst for practice, plus he knew how to please, especially the press. Early on, he sought them out, and when his ascent began, he took them along. He took up golf to cash in on his name link with Greg Norman. One of his proudest moments was immortalised in a framed photo of them together, with the caption "Two greats."

He glanced round his study and felt near satisfied. For a southeast London boy, he'd come all the way. As the strains of Mantovani reached a feeble peak, his wife peered round the door, said: "For heaven's sake, turn it down. I declare they'll be playing him at your funeral."

Words that would all too soon come to taunt and torment her.

❖

As Brant left the station, a TV reporter approached: "DS Brant?"
"Who's askin'?"

"I'm Mr. Mulligan, from Channel 5. I've been an admirer since you solved the Rilke case."

Brant guffawed and the reporter stepped back. His hand behind his back, he signalled the cameraman to roll it.

"I said something funny, DS?"

"Mr. Mulligan. No relation to "The Gold Cup Winner," I suppose?"

"I'd like to ask your views on the cricket killings."

"No comment, boyo, not my case."

But off the record, what sort of man do you think is behind this?"

"A nutter. One of those bed wetters. Hey, are you filming?"
"Thank you, Detective Sergeant Brant."

It aired at prime time and among the viewers was the Umpire. The very next day he began to follow Brant. It wasn't in his plan yet to kill policemen, but his rage was such that he felt compelled. Two days later he was at vigil outside Brant's flat when the sergeant emerged with a very mangy dog on a battered leash.

Watching them, he could see the mutual affection. It looked as if someone had attempted to shear the animal. But even the Umpire could sense they made a pair, odd and bizarre but suited. He knew then how to hurt the policeman. Down the street, the dog's heart leapt as his idol said: "C'mon Meyer, I think it's saveloy and chips for two, eh? Whatcha fink, extra portions? Yeah, me 'n' all."

Brant had parked his car on the double yellow. A traffic warden materialised out of the sewer. Had the book open, was already writing.

Brant flashed his warrant card, said: "Get a real job, Adolf."

As the warden slunk back to his yellow lair, Brant headed for his flat. A howl of pure anguish pierced his skull and he whirled round, muttering: "Jesus, Mary and Joseph, what is that?"

An alley beside Brant's building seemed to be the source. There as another howl of such pain that he felt the hairs stand up on the back of his neck. He moved faster.

A man with a pick-axe was beating a dog with slow, measured intent. Brant shouted: "Oi, you!"

The man turned, a smile on his face. Well dressed in a casual way, a knock-down Armani jacket, subdesigned jeans, Nikes. About fifty, he looked like your friendly uncle. Well, your friendly uncle with a pick-axe handle. He said: "You want some of this, is that it?"

"Yes please," said Brant, and pushed him.

The pick-axe handle went high and to the right. Brant flinched, stepped to the left and dealt two rapid power punches to the kidney. That's all she wrote.

Brant bent down, rummaged in the man's jacket, extracted a wallet, flipped it open. Read: "Swan," looked at the man, then added, "Sorry, MISTER fuckin' Swan. Says so right here. See me boyo I've a white shirt, but I've a blue collar soul. That means I like dogs."

As the man's pain eased, his attitude returned and he smirked: "I'll have the police on you mate."

"I am the bloody police, and this – he took a wedge of notes from the wallet – is for the RSPCA."

Brant went over to the dog and said gently: "Can you walk boy?" Clumps of hair had been torn from the creature, and there was a large bald patch. Brant stroked him softly, said: "You're the spit of Meyer Mayer, as bald as an egg."

Brant was chewing on a slice of pizza, the rest he'd hand fed to Meyer. He was saying: "I'm a man in his eens. No, not teens, listen up fella, it's caff-eine, nicot-ine, non-prot-een that's made a man of me. You only need to remember one thing about pizza: bite the delivery boy's ankles. Yeah, like Norman Hunter in his day. There was a card, none of yer Ryan Giggs preciousness. Or here, Dave Prouse, a London boy. Played Darth Vader. Didn't know that, eh? Want some beer?" Meyer hadn't known, and yes to the drink. He liked how it made him dizzy. And shit, he could bite ankles, would welcome the chance.

Brant, lost in wonder, said: "Jeez, old Dave didn't know what

Star Wars was gonna do, so he took a flat fee. Three large. But Alec Guinness, he opted for a percentage, has got over a hundred million so far. Make you bloody howl, eh?"

Silence descended as man and dog chewed, pondering the sheer awfulness of chance.

Outside, the Umpire kept vigil, his mind in flames.

Brant was washing Meyer in the bath, said: "You're a babe magnet." He'd heard that walking a dog was a sure way to meet women. You exchange phone numbers over leashes and later you did it over the doggy bowl. The other way was supermarkets. Jeez, even Falls had scored there. So OK, she got a security guard, which was kinda rolling yer own, but what the hell. Who's keeping score? The bath didn't alter Meyer radically. Now he was a clean balding animal, like a *Time Out* reader. Meyer stared at Brant with a look of "it ain't gonna work."

And Brant said: "Hold the phones buddy, you gotta have magnetism, draw them in with scent," and blasted Meyer with Old Spice. He could almost hear the Beach Boys" "Surfin Safari," and began to hum it. Not the easiest tune to solo.

As the smell of spice wafted forth, Brant said: "Hey, not bad," and gave himself more than a generous dollop. When they hit the common you could have smelled them coming. If dogs could strut, then Meyer tried. And sure, the women were out en masse, both dogged and dog-less.

Alas, the boyos didn't score. In fact, one woman said: "You barbarian, ought to be arrested for mistreating that animal." But Brant took it well, almost waxed philosophical, said: "Might have over done after-shave a tad."

Babe-less, they headed for the chip shop. The Umpire clocked their progress. Brant might have noticed but he'd already decided it was best they didn't score. Now he could focus on Fiona Roberts. She might have a dog. She already had a husband.

The eyes of a dog

Brant sat down to his breakfast. He'd prepared a mega pot of tea, a mountain of toast, four sausages, black pudding and a badly fried egg. He'd got a wok from cigarette coupons and used it for everything. All the fry had been blasted together and as he studied the mess, he said: "Lookin' good!"

The dog sat looking at him. William James once said if you want to know about spirituality, look into a dog's eyes. Alas, William never tried to outrun the Rotweillers in Peckham or stare down the Railton Road pit bulls. What was in the dog's eyes was love and gratitude. This man had saved his sorry ass, he knew that. Now if he could only train him, and eating from the wok direct would be a great beginning. He tried to communicate this to the man.

Brant forked a wedge of sausage and said: "Tell you something, Meyer. I've had some dogs in this gaff, but you're the first bald one." In McBain's 87th Precinct mysteries, Meyer Meyer is a Jewish detective with not a hair on his head.

Meyer Meyer was already a little legend in the nick. It was even suggested Brant had gone soft. True, he'd felt enormous emotions he'd thought were tight locked away. But it was fun, he got a buzz out of it. The ribbing and piss-taking didn't bother him. Of course it was held in check, since with Brant you never knew. Even Roberts got wind and asked: "So, Sarge, what's the story with the Rin-Tin-Tin?"

"Meyer Meyer."

"What?"

"See, you'd know if you'd read yer McBain. But oh no, not Nora enough, eh?"

"That's noire, N-O-I-R-E!"

"Whatever."

"Where is it then, I mean during the day?"

"Out, he goes out, but he's always waiting when I get home."

Roberts was quiet and then added wistfully: "It must be good to have someone waiting."

When Brant got home that evening, there was no dog.

Brant was mid pie-man's lunch when Roberts called him. "Can't it wait Guv, I'm in the middle of me dinner here."

"No."

"Ah, shit."

When they got outside Brant asked: "Where's the bloody fire then?" Roberts gave him a startled look, then said: "There's been an... incident, one of your neighbours called in. The uniforms are at the scene."

When they got there Brant pushed ahead up the stairs. The stench was appalling. What remained of the dog was barely recognisable, smoke still trailing slowly up. Brant turned back, said: "Ah... Jesus!"

Roberts bundled him outside, got him the car, rummaged in the back, produced a thermos, poured a cup, said: "Take this."

"Don't want it."

"It's brandy."

"OK." And he let it down. After a moment, Brant produced his Weights, but the tremor in his hand prevented him lighting.

"Give it 'ere Tom." Roberts lit the cigarette in Brant's mouth, then said: "The dog. I mean your dog... he was covered in a white coat."

"So?"

"A knee-length white coat. It was singed but not burned."

"Yeah?"

"Well, like we were meant to see it."

"Jeez, Guv, so bloody big deal."

"Tom, it's an umpire's coat."

A house is not a home

PC Tone was also "encore une fois-ing." But like Roberts' daughter, it wasn't doing a whole lot for him. He was determined to be cool. But already, even Oasis were on the slide. Never-no-mind, he put on "Champagne Supernova" and felt connected. On the door of his flat was a full-length poster of Claire Danes, his ideal woman. He'd first stumbled upon her in the defunct series, My So-called Life, and he was lost, smitten, entranced. Her part as Juliet in her first full-length movie sealed his fate. Once being interviewed, she'd admitted to listening to "Wonderwall," "Like one hundred times." And he'd shouted: "Me too!"

Then he got dressed, imitating the words of Brant: "Let's rock 'n' roil." Like that.

A pair of tan Farah slacks, tight in the ass and crotch so the babes could ogle. But his courage faltered and he pulled on a Nike long sweat, then a shirt loosely buttoned to highlight the sweat's logo: No. 1. All right!

Then a pair of market trainers designer-soiled so he wouldn't appear an asshole, like the new kid on the block or something. Shades of cool. A short denim jacket, black lest he appear obvious. Final touch, the Marlboro Lights in the top right-hand pocket. Looked again in the mirror, said: "My man," and headed out. Then sheepishly, he had to return a few minutes later to check the gas was off. Worry and cool didn't blend. Shit, he knew that. If Brant didn't check the gas, he'd say: "Let it blow." Tone hadn't reached that plateau of recklessness yet. Deeply suspected he never would.

He went to the Cricketers on Thursday, it was darts night. Maybe Falls would show and he felt his heart palpitate. A wino waylaid him outside the Oval, whining: "Gis a pound."

"I'm the heat fella."

"Gis two pounds, Mr. Heat."

Tone checked round, then handed over 70p. The wino, indignant, said: "What am I supposed to do wif this, yah wanker?"

"Call someone who gives a toss."

He left near dizzy with the macho-ness, but quickened his pace lest the wino follow.

The pub was jammed. Trade was "aided and abetted" by the "blue hour." A police version of the happy one. Two drinks for the price of a single, drink them blues away. It was working.Tone had to elbow to the bar. Tried in vain to get noticed and served. The staff knew rank and knew he hadn't. So he could wait.

Till: "What ya want, son?"

Chief Inspector Roberts.

He wanted a tall shandy to motor his arid mouth. "A scotch, sir."

And hey, jig time, he'd got it. Roberts nodded, then said: "Park it over here, son."

The blue sea parted to reveal a vacant stool. He climbed on, took a slug of the scotch, thought: "God!" as it burned. Did it ever. Roberts eyed him, asked: "Got some new clobber there?"

"Oh no, sir, just old stuff."

The Farahs were so new they sparkled, and no way would they lighten up that crease. Tone had a horrible thought: would the Guvnor think he was on the take? He asked: "Is Sergeant Brant about, sir?"

Roberts sighed, signalled the barman, and in a terse voice, told of the Meyer Meyer incident.

"Good grief," said Tone.

If Roberts thought that cut it, he said nothing. Falls and Rosie brushed past, said: "'Night, Guv."

He didn't answer. Tone shouted: "'Night," and tried not to look after them.

Roberts said: "She's getting hers, eh?"

Tone prayed, crossed his fingers, then said: "Rosie?"

"Naw. Falls, some security guard's putting it to her." Tone died.

In this world, you turn the other cheek, you get hit with a wrench.

Brian Donlevy, Impact

Roberts saw the young man's face in tatters. He felt a sense of such loss that he could almost no longer recall what power a yearning could be. He touched the bar, said: "Whatcha say to a double?"

"Ahm, no, sir, I mean... I thought I might call on Sergeant Brant."

"Mmm."

"Just to see if he needed anything."

"I dunno son, he's a man best left to sort himself."

Tone got off the stool, said, near defiant: "All the same, sir."

"Yeah, well, don't expect a warm welcome."

After Tone had gone, Roberts thought he should have offered some advice on the woman. But what could he tell him? That everything would be fine? Whatever else things turned out to be, fine was almost never one of them. As he left the bar later, brown-nosers called "Goodnight." He neither acknowledged nor quite ignored them. It just didn't matter, not when you'd lost the magic of yearning.

PC Tone was more than a touch apprehensive about calling on Brant, but he composed himself, said: "How bad can it be?"

He heard the music from the street, as if all the cruising cars in Brixton had a Rap convention. That loud. That annoying. When he reached Brant's door, the noise was massive, and he thought: it sounds like house. It was.

Earlier, Brant had gone into HMV, said: "Gimmie all the hits of house."

The assistant, in ponytail and zeiss bifocals, joked: "Bit of a rave, eh?"

"Bit o' minding yer own bloody business."

The assistant, who in kinder days would have gravitated from mellow hippy, was now on job release from DHSS in Clapham. He shut it.

Tone had to hammer at the door till eventually it was flung open. A demented Brant before him. Dressed only in maroon Adidas shorts and trainers, sweat cascading down the grey hair of his chest, he sang: "C'mon ye Reds."

Tone asked: "Are you OK, sir?"

"Whatcha want? See if I've a dog licence? Well cop this, I've no bleeding dog, not never more."

"Sir, sir, could you lower the music?"

"Whats-a-matter boyo? Not *tone* deaf are yer?" Brant laughed wildly at his joke. Tone was lost, didn't know how to leave or stay, tried: "We'll get him, sergeant." And Brant lunged forth, grabbing him by his shirt front, the fabric tearing, and roared: "Oh will you? Didn't I already ask you to find them Dublin fucks with the Band-Aids. Didn't I?"

"Yes."

"And did you?"

"Not yet."

"Ah, you couldn't catch a child's cold. Go on, hoppit, fuck off out of it ya cissy!"

And slammed the door.

As the young copper crept away, he fingered the ripped clothing, saying: "Didn't have to do that, cost me a tenner in the market that did." He wanted to bawl.

He who laughs last usually didn't get the joke

Inside, Brant returned to his evening. He'd busted enough raves to get the gist. You stripped to your shorts, took the E and bopped till you dropped. What Brant had felt was, they didn't feel. No one hurting at all.

And that's what he wanted. Because of the dehydration factor, he'd a line of Evians along the wall, and for lubrication, a bottle of Tequila.

New to drugs, he had the booze as insurance. The E he'd bounced from a dealer in Kennington Tube Station.

Letting back his head he howled: "Had us a time, Meyer."

Towards the close of the night's festivities, the sergeant, way down on the other side of the ecstasy moon, began to munch the doggie treats, intended as a surprise for Meyer, whispering: "Bit salty, but not bad, no."

Albert was miming before the mirror: "I'm a believer…" and occasionally he'd give what he believed to be an impish grin like Davy Jones. Till a shadow fell across him.

Kevin.

"What the fuck are you doing, and turn off that shit."

He aimed a kick at the hi-fi and The Monkees screeched to a halt. Albert rushed across to rescue the album. Sure enough, it was deeply scratched. He wailed: "Whatcha want to do that for?"

Kevin gave a nasty laugh. "Don't be so bleedin' wet. It can only improve those wankers, give 'em that unplugged feel. Now pay attention, I want to show you somefin'."

He bent down and pulled out a long box from under the couch. He flipped the lid off and took out a rifle, said: "Feast yer eyes on this, isn't it a beauty?"

"Is it real?"

"Real? You friggin' moron. It's a Winchester 460 Magnum. See that 'scope? Pick the hair outta yer nose from a rooftop."

He pulled the bolt all the way back. A cartridge in the chamber slid home and he swung the barrel round into Albert's face, said: "Grab some sky, pilgrim."

"What?"

"Put yer bleedin' hands up."

Albert slowly did so and Kev leaned closer, whispering: "Make yer peace, Mister."

"Kev!"

The gun went up an inch above Albert's head, then the trigger was pulled. The impact slammed the stock into his shoulder and knocked him back. The bullet tore into the wall, decanting a plastic duck. Albert stood in open-mouthed shock, and Kev, on his ass, on the floor, exclaimed: "Fuck me, now that's fire power. What a rush."

> "Like a bad actor, memory
> always goes for effect."

James Sallis, Black Hornet

B rant comes to and hears the most awful screeching, like someone is tearing the skin off a cat. Someone is indeed tearing the skin off a cat, on *The Simpsons*, in the "Itchy and Scratchy" cartoon. The noise is deafening and Brant reaches up to turn it off. Pain in the major league as his body moves. His arse naked and he shudders to think why. But thank fuck he didn't go out... did he? His mind was careering in every direction. From one side surfaced a recent documentary he'd seen on the American Marine Corps. No matter what shit went down, they'd up, kick ass and shout: "Semper Fi!"

He gave a weak attempt at it now, but it came out like a piss – flat and narrow. Then he rolled onto his stomach and visualised a harsh five military push-ups, and tried.

"Semp-"

And collapsed, muttering: "Bollocks."

Brant finally got to his feet, limped to the shower, caught sight of himself in the mirror.

Bad idea.

Pot belly. No, worse, a drooping one. Grey hair on his chest like sad brillo pads. He thought of the word "bedraggled," said: "I'm bedraggled."

Too kind. It just didn't cut it. Call it fucked, more like. The shower was all he knew of heaven and hell, then to the medicine cabinet and two, no, fuck it, three Alka Seltzer. Ahh. Oh shit oh sweet Mary and Joseph, stay down. Nope. Up comes a technicolour yawn. Sweat pouring down his body, he couldn't pull his head up and so saw the multicoloured spread. Yup, there's the Seltzer. Useless fuckers, and be-gods, is that an E? Gimmie an E... gimme an... oomph-ah Paul McGrath. Now he tried again, with Andrews Liver Salt, and popped two soluble aspirin in the milk. Here we go.

Oh yes, there is a God, it stayed. Took one more shower. He knew a sharp belt of booze would fix him right up for an hour or less, and from there, it's flake city.

True, he'd managed to get Sally back for a time. Had sworn all the promises. Would have done it on the bible if needed. But alas, he couldn't make the pledge in his heart, where it most counted. Through work, booze and the sulking silences, he'd lost her all over again.

Then, as the caffeine danced along his nerve endings, he vaguely remembered young Tone. Oh shit, the kid had come to the door. Brant lit a shaky Weight, and tried to change mental tack. He couldn't recall what he'd said to the lad, but oh, oh he knew it was rough. Was it ever otherwise?

He turned to shout for Meyer Meyer, then remembered that too.

Atonement in white

"I like Jamiroquai," said Tone.
"Yeah? Me, I like Tricky."
"Yeah."
He knew if he said yeah a bit, it gave him cool. Not ice or brain-dead, but hip without pushing it. Like he had attitude without having to work at it. He badly wished he'd brought his Bans, just let those shades sit easy on his face. As it was, the smoke was killing his eyes. He'd decided to get a lead on the Band-Aid duo, prove to Brant that HE was the bollocks. To his surprise, he'd gained entrance to the club on Railton without any hassle. True, they'd charged him "instant membership," a straight twenty-five and then admission. But hey, he was in – this was the place – the happening, he was Serpico, undercover, he was cookin'.

Clubs in Brixton change overnight. What's hot on Tuesday is vacant city on Thursday. So it goes, they let Tone in 'cos he had cash, he was yer punter, yer John, yer actual Jimmy Wanker.

Shortly after he sat down, the girl put chat on him. Then he casually mentioned the Band-Aid people and she asked: "Whatcha want them for?"

"Oh nothing bad. In fact, I've a few quid owing them."

She gave a mischievous laugh, said: "Give it here. I'll see they get it."

He laughed too. One of those clued-in jobs. Like he could dig it, yeah, go with the flow. She said: "See the new weapon of choice?"

"What?"

"Yer baseball bat, it's passé. It's clubs now, like golf clubs."

"Yeah?"

"Sure, since the black kid won that big golf thing."

"The Masters."

"What?"

"Nothing. Go on."

"Yeah, well, that's what they're bouncing off skulls now."
"Tee-off."

"What?"

He ordered two more drinks and felt he was really blending.
She said: "Back in a sec."

Which she wasn't. More like an hour. During which a huge
black guy took her seat and her drink, eye-balling Tone all the
while. Finally he asked: "Now who I be?"

"Ahm."

"I be the Archangel Tuafer."

Tone tried to think of what Brant would say, something like:
"Hot enough for yer?" like that. What he said was: "Uh. Uh."

Then the girl appeared, slapped the guy on the back, said:
"Move on, big ass."

He did. Tone said: "He thinks he's an Archangel."

"He's a divil all right."

He tried to place her accent. I sounded like Dublin, but only
sometimes. Then she said: "C'mon, I can show you where those
people are squatting."

When they found Tone's body, he was naked, he'd been stabbed
repeatedly and his head was bashed in. Roberts said: "Jeez, if I
had to guess, I'd say someone put a golf club to him."

Brant was too ill to be outright sick, but he sure wanted to be.
He said nothing.

Roberts continued: "I saw him you know, that evening."

"Yeah?"

"He was thinking of going to see you."

"Was he?"

"Yeah. So did he?"

"Did he what, Guv?"

"Jeez, wake up man. Come to see you!"

"I dunno."

"What?"

"I was out of it."

"Christ, keep that to yourself."

"Okay."

Roberts knelt down, stared at the battered face, said: "He'd a pair of Farahs, you know."

"What?"

"Those smart pants, Jeez, I hope they didn't do him for a bloody pair of trousers."

"Round here, Guv, they'd do you for a hankie."

"Too bloody right."

Brant thought, what a slogan for a company: *Would you kill for a pair of Farahs?*

But said nowt, he didn't think Roberts would appreciate it. He did half want to tell him about the wreath. How, when he opened his door that morning, there it was. A poor excuse of a wreath, but plainly recognisable. The flowers were withered, wilted and wan. In fact it seemed as if someone had first trampled on them. Even the ribbon was dirty. And get this, someone had bitten it.

Was it for him or Meyer, or both, or fuck? No big leap of detection to deduce, it was from the Umpire. Roberts would ask, if he'd been told: "How do you know it was him? Mebbe kids took it from the cemetery, decided to wind you up."

Then Brant would pause, look crestfallen, humbly take his hand from behind his back, and dah-dah! A cricket ball. Say "'Cos this was nestling smack in the centre. Deduce that, ya prick."

> "That is not dead which can eternal lie. And with strange aeons even death may die."
>
> H.P. Lovecraft, The Necronomicon

How the Umpire giggled as he laid the wreath at Brant's door. He'd had to bite down on his hand to stop, lest he be heard.

The Euro-hit from a few years back, "Hey Magdalene," was jammed in his head and he hummed with forced repetition. Had he known the wild abandon the ordained had danced with in hordes on Ibiza to this song, he might have taken pause.

Deliriously oblivious to past trends, he hummed as if he meant it. He couldn't believe the rush it was to tease, torment and outright taunt the police. When the cricket mob were done, he'd have to have a serious look at the Met. So much work, so little time.

He hummed on. Shannon felt so wired, he couldn't stop walking. He saw sparks light up his steps and found himself in the middle of Westminster Bridge. On impulse, he threw the Marks & Spencer bag over. It contained the crossbow.

Then he decided to suddenly cross the road. Without pause, he walked out into the traffic and a 159 bus lifted him about six feet and he fell back onto the pavement. As if the bus had said: "Get back there, asshole."

Passers-by gathered round, and a buzz of observations danced above him.

"Did you see that?"

"Walked right out in front of it."

"Pissed as a parrot."

"What a wanker."

An ambulance was eventually called, but it got caught in the rush. Its siren wailed uselessly, but loud enough to irritate the shit out of the stalled motorists.

And speaking of wreaths

They buried Jacko Mary on a cold November morning long after *A White Arrest* was concluded. There was the grave-digger, Roberts and a shabby woman. When the coffin was down, she said: "Rough enough to die alone."

"You're here."

"I'm not a friend. He owed me money."

Roberts tried to temper his anger. "Thought you might still get it, eh?"

"'Ere, don't be sarky. You must be that copper."

Roberts looked round, said: "Yeah. Keep it down, OK?"

"He liked you, he did."

"Really?"

"Oh yeah. Were he any good as a snitch, like?"

Roberts considered. Jacko Mary had cracked the "E" case, sort of, but he said: "No."

"Didn't fink so."

As a cop, Roberts had to do lots of dodgy things, came with the territory. But this denial was to be one act he felt forever ashamed about.

At a squat in Coldharbour Lane, a woman was stirring. "Tony."

She raised her voice. "Tony!"

"What? What's going on?"

"Brew us a cup o' tea, two sugars."

"Fock off."

She got up and gave him a smack on the head with an old copy of the *Big Issue*. If she'd checked, Tricky was on the cover. He got up and moved over to the gas ring. Near tripped on a number nine club. The grip was worn, well used. The woman watched him as he tried to get it together to light the gas, said:

"Jaysus, yer arse looks great in them Farahs."

"They're a bit tight, cut into the crack of my hole."

And he moved his right leg to demonstrate. She said: "Naw, I like 'em."

"D'ya think I'm sexy?"

"Yeah, dead sexy."

In Coldharbour Lane, Kevin had called a meet. He was dressed in combat gear, and wired to the moon. Doug and Fenton exchanged wary glances. Albert arrived late and got a bollocking. "What is it, Albert, yer getting tired of our crusade, that it?"

"I had to sign on, Kev I was up the DHSS."

"Yer head is up yer ass, is what. Time to get yer attention, fella. Time to get everybody's attention."

He threw three black-and-white photos on the coffee table, said: "We're moving up."

Albert felt his heart thump, tried: "Like another area?"

Kevin crossed to him, began to jab his chest with his fingers, jabbed hard, spitting: "No shithead, we're staying put, no scum's running me outta my manor. We're gonna off three fucks at once."

Fenton was on his feet: "What? C'mon Kevin, how the hell are we gonna pull that off?"

Kevin didn't look at him, but continued to jab at his brother, said: "See these three, yeah in the photies, they've set up shop together. Got a co-op in Electric Avenue and that's where we're gonna take 'em."

Doug sighed, asked:

"And the three guys, they're just gonna say, 'Hey OK, we'll come with youse – oh, nice rope.'"

Kevin's eyes gleamed, his moment, said: "That's it Douggie, we'll do them in their gaff."

A week later...

At the CA Club, Cora was gushing energetically.

"But Penelope, are you sure you won't let one of the boys pamper you?"

"No! Is there something you can't grasp? Try this: N-O!"

"Oh golly, we seem a trifle tense today. Perhaps a drinkipoos?"

"Ah, for heaven's sake!" And she snapped to her feet, began to pace. Cora fussed on: "Your friend seemed keenish, I do believe she has a minor crush on our Jason."

Penny glared at her, said: "Get bloody real!"

The door chimes went. Today they played "Uno Paloma Blanca," it added to Penny's bile. Cora said: "Excuse me lambikins, but I must see to that. Don't you just die with those chimes?"

Cora lightly patted her frosted hair before answering the door. The hair was rigid and today resembled an off-kilter meringue mess. She opened the door.

Brant said: "Yo Cora, how they hanging?"

A fraction later, she tried to slam it. He gave it a push, knocking her back inside. Falls followed behind, like the biblical pale rider. Cora tried for indignation: "How dare you? I trust you have a warrant?"

Brant stepped right up to her, said, "It's bloody Maggie Johnson... I wondered where you'd legged it to. My, my, come up in the world, 'aven't you? Here constable, this is Maggie, the cheapest ride this side of the Elephant 'n' Castle."

Cora raised her voice. "Damn impertinence, you've overstepped your brief, sonny. We're protected."

Brant drew an almighty kick to Cora's knee and she dropped

like a stone. He hunkered down, tried unsuccessfully to grasp her hair, and settled for her neck, said, "What the fuck kind of shit you got in yer hair? Now listen up, don't back-talk me, ever, or I'll break yer nose... OK?"

She nodded. He caught her shoulder and hoisted her up, said: "Let's hobble inside, see what's cookin'."

On seeing Penny, Falls nearly spoke, but settled for a look; one of pure malice. Brant pushed Cora into a chair, asked Penny:

"Room number?"

"It's not numbers, it's names."

"So gimme the bloody name."

"The Cherise Room, upstairs, first on the right."

"OK, now hop it."

"I can go?"

"Yeah, fuck off."

Cora wanted to shout abuse, to tear at Penny's eyes, but Brant said: "Don't ever think about it."

When the door had closed, Brant turned to Falls, said, "Keep yer eyes on this cow. If she even twitches, give her a clout round the ear-hole."

Fiona was over an orgasmic rainbow. Jason, between her legs working like a bastard. Moans and cries punctuated the seizures of her body. The door crashed open and Brant said:

"Tasty."

Jason turned his head, confusion, shock, writ large. His brain whispered "husband."

Fiona tried to sit up, pushed against Jason and grabbed for a sheet. Brant closed the door and leant against it, began to light a Weight as the pair fumbled on the bed.

He said, "Hey, don't stop on my account."

Eventually, Jason got his briefs on, and Fiona pulled the sheet up to her chin.

Brant smiled, then reached back to open the door. "Off yah go, cocker."

As Jason edged past to get out, Brant gave him a hefty slap on the arse and shut the door behind him. He turned to Fiona. "Get dressed then."

Fiona was trying to calm her roaring mind, said: "How can I, with you standing there?"

He gave a hearty laugh. "Jaysus, I've seen what you've got. Now move it or I'll dress you."

She did. Shame and bewilderment crowded down as she pulled her clothes on. Brant's eyes never left her.

Then she said, "I'm ready."

"Whoo-kay, I'll drive you home."

"What?"

"You don't wanna walk, Fiona. Not after the exertion you've been putting in. Naw, the motor's outside."

Fiona gave a last shot at comprehension. "You're not taking me to my husband?"

"What? Naw, whatcha think I am, some kind of animal?" Brant put Fiona in the front of a battered Volkswagen Golf, said to Falls:

"You'll be all right from here, there's a tube down the road."

Falls didn't like any of this, said: "Shouldn't I be along as a witness?" He gave a snide chuckle, a dangerous sound. "Wise up, babe."

She put her hand on the door, insisting. "I'm sorry, Sarge, but I feel I should..."

He pushed her hand away, losing it a little.

"Piss off Falls, you're drawing attention. Don't ever do that to me."

She backed off. He moved in close, anger leaking through his eyes. "You want to worry about something Falls? Worry about paying me back."

He slammed the door, causing Falls to shudder. Then he moved to the driver's side, got in and slammed the door, burnt rubber leaving. Falls watched them go and gritted her teeth.

"OK, I'll pay you back you bastard, and BIG TIME."

Brant looked at Fiona and winked.

She asked: "Where are you taking me?"

"Hey, relax, go along for the ride." A pause. "Whoops, sorry! As they say, you've been there, done that, and did you ever. That Jason, eh? For a half-wog he was hung."

If there was a reply, she didn't have it, and tried to crawl way within herself. There wasn't a place that far away. Brant pulled up on the Walworth Road, parked carelessly on a double yellow.

"I thought Carter Street nick had closed?"

"Tut-tut, restless girls get spanked. C'mon, get out."

He escorted her to a transport caff near Marks & Spencers, pushed her inside, found a back table. The table was alight with dead chips, rasher rinds and toast crumbs. Brant seemed delighted, said: "If it's not on the table, it's not on the menu."

"It's disgusting."

"You'd know."

A waitress in her fifties came over. She'd obviously had disappointing news in her teens and wasn't yet recovered. Her face seemed unfinished without a tired cigarette. She said:

"Yeah?"

Brant knew the risk of towing Fiona round his own manor but it gave a kick.

He said: "Two sausages, egg, bacon, puddin', and two rounds of buttered toast."

He looked at Fiona.

"You've got to be kiddin'."

Brant smiled at the waitress, said, "She'll have the same, and throw in a family pot of tea." As the waitress turned to go, he added, "The smile needs some work, OK?"

The waitress ignored him.

Fiona stared at him and asked, "You don't seriously think I'll eat that garbage?"

"Oh you will, *and* like it."

He didn't move, but she felt the physical presence of him. It rolled across the table to taunt and threaten her.

He touched the once-white tablecloth.

"Gingham would have worked."

"Excuse me?"

"For the table; you know, a woman's touch. I like the touch of a woman." He took out the Weights. "Do you?"

She shook her head and knew the "no smoking" edict hadn't penetrated here. The food came, and after the plates were set down, Brant asked, "Where's that smile?"

But his attention was diverted as two people entered the caff. He recognised the Band-Aids, and they clocked him. Turned right about and legged it. He thought, "Later," and pared a wedge of sausage, nodded to Fiona.

"Eat."

She tried.

He poured scalding tea into mugs, raised his, said: "Get that down yah, girl."

She tasted it and nearly threw up. It was greasy, seemingly heavily sugared and tasted of tobacco. She put the mug down, said: "OK, you've had your fun."

"What? I'm having me grub, but no, I've not had me fun. Not yet."

"What is it you want, exactly?"

He took out a surprisingly clean handkerchief, dabbed delicately at the corners of his mouth, said:

"I'd like to be your suitor."

Maybe my future starts right now.

John Garfield: Voice over, The Postman Always Rings Twice.

A s Falls prepared her shopping list, she fantasised being a Goth. Just for one outing. She couldn't stand The Cure, and if that was music... yeah. But the gear, all those black dresses and the death white make-up. Ah, dream on...

They'd love it down the nick. She could just hear Brant's war cry: "I could ride that."

The man would get up on a cat. She was dressed for shopping. Reeboks (off white) Tracksuit (one white).

And a large carrier bag. Black. Daren't be seen to "Accessorise," very ungothic. She'd been reading an article head-lined "SO, WHAT KIND OF SHOPPER ARE YOU?"

Retail analysts divide shoppers into six types, they use this information to attract the shoppers they want, and deter others. Supermarkets will tempt the Comfortable and Contented with displays of minor luxuries. Mainstream Mercenaries will be deterred by supermarkets offering either lack of choice, or too much.

Falls was a sucker for quizzes. Forever completing *News of the World* magazine questions like "What kind of lover are you?"

She read aloud the first three types of shopper:

1. Mainstream Merchant: The retailer's least favourite group – low budget shoppers who buy only the cheapest goods on sale. Impervious to the siren-call of exotic foods.

2. Struggling idealist: scrutinise every label for contents, buy only eco-sensitive soap powder. Ozone friendliness very important.

3. Self Indulgent: self-explanatory. Very welcome in super-markets.

"Mmmm," she thought. "Alas, that first rings a bell. Then, the final three:

4. Comfortable and Contented: favourite with the retailer because these happy bunnies like to reward themselves with that extra tin of tuna ("Well, we do use a lot of it, and it is very healthy.") Delia Smith is their icon.

5. Frenzied Coper: fastest shopper in the west. Knows what she wants and where to get it, homes in on target sections at speed. Will not even spot the most seductive gondola or special-offer basket.

6. Habit-Bound Die-hard: frugal but loyal; the mostly male section. Meat and two veg man, spuds and sprouts only, never mange tout. Buys six days' worth of food for £20. This (surprise, surprise) is the type the analysts have also dubbed the "Victor Meldrew"

As she scanned No. 6, she thought, "Oh God, I'll end up married to one of those."

Crumpling the article, she threw it in the bin. On a T-shirt she'd seen once, the logo was: "When the going gets tough, the tough go shopping."

It seemed about right.

She strapped on her Walkman and was ready to roll, Sheryl Crow blasting loud.

At the entrance to the supermarket, she bought the *Big Issue* and the vendor said:

"Have a good one."

She'd tried.

A gaggle of girls brushed past her, nearly knocking her over. One of them petulantly crying: "Oh... ex-cuse me!" in *that* tone. What John L. Williams describes as an "Angela," a particular drawl that upper-class junkies seem to have patented: One part frightfully, frightfully; two parts frightfully fucked up. The type who insist on slimline tonic as they swill buckets of gin.

Falls got a trolley and turned off her Walkman. The supermarket had a loop tape, the same song 100 times. Today it was U2 with "You're So Cruel."

Killer tune, but over and over.

Reach for them razor blades or mainline Valium.

Falls knew the very next track should be "The Fly."

Sounds like Bauhaus on speed. But course, due to the bloody loop, it never gets there.

She headed for the frozen veg.

If he was a colour, he'd be beige.

Past toiletries and disinfectants to see a kicking. A man was on the ground and three teenagers were putting the boot in. And kicking like they meant it. Steel caps on the toes flashed like treacherous zips of empty hope.

"Oi!" she roared.

Reaching for a tin (it was marrowfats) she lobbed it high and fast. It bounced off the first kid like whiplash. He dropped like a sack of thin flower, and the others legged it.

People were shouting and coming up behind her. She got to the man on the ground and saw he was in uniform. Security. Blood was pouring down his face. He said: "I showed them, eh?" She smiled and helped him up. His brown hair was falling into his eyes and she clocked startling blue eyes, big as neon. She felt her heart lurch and reprimanded herself mentally: "Don't be daft, it couldn't be."

She said: "We'd better get you seen to."

"Like a cat is it?"

As he stood up she saw he was just the right height, a hazy six foot, and that they'd look good together. A man came striding up, all shit, piss and wind: the manager. He barked: "What on earth is going on?" and glanced at the teenager who was stirring and moaning. Falls said: "The apprentice thug there was apprehended by your security, at great physical cost."

The manager barked louder: "But he's just a boy, what's wrong with him?"

"He got canned."

Falls accompanied the security guard for aid. To the pub. He ordered a double brandy and she a Britvic orange, slimline. She put out her hand, said: "I'm glad to meet you. And you are?"

"Beige. That's how I feel, but put me on the other side of that drink, I'll be, as Stephanie Nicks sang, 'A Priest of Nothingness'."

His Irish brogue surfaced haphazardly as he lilted on some of the words, then he added: "I'm Eddie Dillon."

"Dylan?"

"Naw, the other one, the Irish fella."

"He's famous?"

"Not yet, but he's game."

She laughed, said: "I haven't one clue to what you're on about."

He gave a shy smile, answered: "Ah, there's no sense in it, but it has a grand ring!" He looked at her hands, added: "And speaking of rings, can I hope yer not wed?"

She was filled with warmth, not to mention a hint of lust. She said: "Are you long in security?"

He drained his glass and she clocked his even white teeth. He said: "I was with the Social Security for longer than either of us admit, but yes, it's what I do. I like minding things. I used to do it back home, but that's a long time ago. Thank Jaysus... and no, it's not what I do while I'm waiting to be an actor. I'm with Woody Allen who said he was an actor till he got an opening as a waiter."

She laughed again, then said: "I've got shopping to do, so are you going to ask me out?"

"I might."

Roberts looked at his wife across the breakfast table. Deep lines were etched around her eyes, and he thought: "Good Lord, she's aging." But said: "England went under with barely a whimper, losing their final match by twenty-eight runs today."

"That's hardly surprising dear, surely?"

"Oh?"

"Well, I mean the poor lambs have a maniac stalking them. It's not conducive to good cricket, is it?"

He felt his voice rising: "All they had to chase was a perfectly manageable victory target of 229."

"Says you. And darling, I'm sure they feel you should be chasing a maniac instead of criticising."

Falls was surprised that Eddie Dillon had a car. She felt he'd have a lot of surprises. The motor was a beat-up Datsun, faded maroon. He said:

"I won it off a guy in a card game."

"What?"

"Just kidding. It's the kind of line guys adore to use."

"Why?"

"Good question, and one I have no answer to."

He was dressed in a thin suit; everything about it was skinny, from the labels to the crease. A startling white shirt cried: "Clean, oh yes." Falls had her sedate hooker ensemble. Black low-cut dress, short, and black tights. Slingback heels that almost promised comfort, but not quite. He said: "You look gorgeous."

She knew she looked good. In fact, before he arrived, she'd almost turned herself on. He'd brought a box of Dairy Milk. The big motherfucker that'd feed a flock of nuns.

She asked: "Won them in a card game?"

"Yup, two aces over five, does it every third hand."

"Where are we going?"

"To Ireland."

And in a sense, they did.

"I was a small time crook
until this very minute,
and now I'm a big-time
crook!"

Clifton Young in Dark Passage

Fenton, of the "E" gang, was becoming less wallpaperish. He was beginning, for the first time in his life, to follow the plot. Not completely, but definitely in there. Now, coming off a football high, he challenged Kevin, said: "See that young copper got done?"

"Yeah."

"The papers are saying we done it."

Kev was dressed in urban guerrilla gear. Tan combat pants with all the pockets, tan singlet and those dogtags they sell in the arcade. Desert storm via Brixton. He sensed Fen's attitude and squared off. A Browning automatic peaking from the pocket on his left thigh. He smiled, said: "Fuck 'em."

Fenton, less sure, wanted to back off, but had to hold. Asked: "Did ya, Kev? Did ya do him?"

Kev was well pleased. It kept the troops in line if they believed the boss was totally not to be fucked with. He said: "Whatcha fink Fen, eh… what do ya reckon, matey?" Now Albert and Doug were on their feet and the air was crackling. Fen fell back into a chair, saying: "Aw Jeez, Kev, you never said nuffing about doing the old bill. Jeez, it's not on. It's not…" And he groped in desperation for a word to convey his feeling. "It's not British."

Kev gave a wild laugh, then pulled the Browning out, got into shooter stance, legs apart, two-handed grip, swung the barrel back and forth across his gang, shouted: "Incoming!" and watched the fucks dive for cover.

He could hear hueys fly low over the Mekong Delta, and vowed to re-rent *Apocalypse Now*.

"What a place. I can feel the rats in the wall."

Phantom Lady

The Galtimore Ballroom confirms the English nightmare. That the Irish are: One, tribal. Two, ferocious. Three, stone mad.

To see a heaving mass of hibernians "dancing" to a showband with an abandon of insecurity, is truly awesome. Like a rave with intent. When Falls saw the entrance and felt the vibes, she asked: "Are we here to dance or to raid?"

Eddie took her hand, laughed: "They're only warming up."

She could only hope this was a joke.

It wasn't. Two bouncers at the door said in unison: "How ya, Eddie."

Falls didn't know: was this good or bad? Good that he was known, but how regular was he? Was she just another in a line of Saturday Night Specials, cheap and over the counter?

Eddie said: "They're Connemara men. Never mess with them. When penance is required, they think true suffering is to drink sherry."

Inside it was sweltering, and seemed like all of humanity had converged. Eddie said: "Wait here, I'll get some minerals," and was gone.

Falls panicked, felt she'd never see him again. The sheer mass of the crowd moved her along and into the ballroom. She thought: "So this is hell."

A stout man, reeking of stout in a sweat stained shirt asked her: "D'yer want a turn?"

"No thank you, I'm -" but he shouted: "Stick it, yer black bitch!"

A band, consisting of at least fifty or so it seemed, were doing a loud version of "I Shot the Sheriff." Mainly it was loud, and they sure hated the sheriff. And here was Eddie, big smile, two large iced drinks, saying: "So, did you miss me?"

"Yeah."

Then they were dancing, despite the crowd, the heat and the band. They were cookin'. He could jive like an eel. Falls had never met a man who could dance. In fact most of them could barely speak. It deeply delighted her. Then a slow number: "Miss You Nights."

And she drew him close, enfolded him tight. She asked: "Is that a poem or are you real pleased with me?"

"It's poetry all right."

And later, it would be.

The Beauty of Balham

Falls was in love with love. She yearned to feel the mix of sickness, nausea and exhilaration that came with it. So in love you couldn't eat, sleep or function. The telephone ruled your life and ruined it. Would he phone, and when, if, oh God...

You bastard. She wanted to do crazy shit like write their married name and buy him shirts he'd never wear. Cut his hair and hang out with his family, prattle on about him until her friends roared: "Enough!"

Lie awake all night and stare at his face, trace his lips gently with two fingers and half hope he'd wake. Kiss him before he shaved and wear the beard rash like a trophy. Mess his hair just after he'd carefully styled it, and iron his laundry, or even iron his face. She giggled. Publicly, on matters musical, she'd drop the name of cool like Alanis Morissette. Sing the lyrics of mild obscenity and mouth the words of kick ass. At home, if it wasn't the Cowboy Junkies, she'd tie her hair in a severe bun and put Evita on the turntable. Her window had a flower box, and with the tiniest push of imagination – open that window full – she was on the balcony of the Casa Rosada in Buenos Aires. A couple of dry sherries fuelled the process and she'd sing along with "Don't Cry for me, Argentina."

The track on total repeat till tears formed in her eyes, her heart near burnt from tenderness for her "shirtless ones'. Till a passer-by shouted: "Put a bloody sock in it!"

It's not beyond the bounds of possibility that, at odd times, her voice carried to the Umpire, and eased the dreams of carnage he'd envisaged. Reluctantly, like a sad Peronist, she shut Evita down and considered her situation. If she told Roberts about Brant and

Mrs. Roberts, she was in deep shit. If she didn't tell him and he found out, she was in deeper mire. If she said nowt to nobody, she'd probably survive. It stuck in her gut like the benign cowardice it was. Falls could vividly remember the day her friends ran up to her in the street saying: "Come quick, look at the man on the common."

When she got there, her heart sank. The object of their curiosity was her dad. Staggering home from the pub after a day's drinking. She tried to help him. She was four years old. As long as she could remember, her life had been overshadowed by his drinking. He was never violent, but it cast a huge cloud over the family. She felt she was born onto a battlefield. His booze destroyed the family. With it came with the four horsemen: Poverty, Fear, Frustration, Despair.

Dad was anaesthetised from all that. There was never money for schoolbooks or food. Nights were spent trying to block out her parents' raised voices. Or curled up, too terrified to sleep because her father hadn't come home. Wishing he was dead and praying he wasn't. Never inviting her friends home as her father's moods were unpredictable. Most of her childhood spent covering up for his drinking. Once, asking him: "Can I have two shillings for an English book?"

"Sure, don't you speak it already?"

Whispering, lest his sleep be disturbed. All of this destroyed her mother. Being of Jamaican descent, she developed the "tyrant syndrome," and tried to enlist young Falls on her side. Early she learned to "run with the hare and savage with the hound." Oh yes! Then she became convinced that mass would help. If she went to church enough, he'd stop.

He didn't.

She stopped church. Slowly, she realised the terrible dilemma for such a child as she. They have to recover from the alcoholic parent they had, and suffer for the one they didn't have. When she was nineteen she had a choice: go mad or get a career. Thus she'd joined the police and often felt it was indeed a mobile madness.

"Love makes the world go round"

Falls, looking in the mirror, said: "I am gorgeous." She sure felt it. Eddie told her all the time, and wow, she never got tired of it. For no reason at all, he'd touched her cheek, saying: "I can't believe I found you." Jesus!

A woman dreams her whole life of such a man. If all his lines were just lines, so what? It was magic. She was sprinkled in stardust. True, she'd tried the clichés, the mush on toast of trying out his name to see how it fit: "Susan Dillon."

Mmm. How about Susan Falls Dillon?

Needed work.

Eddie Dillon rolled off Falls, lay on his back and exhaled. "The Irishman's Dream."

"What's that, then?"

"To fuck a policeman."

After the dance, she'd asked him for a drink. He'd had her. In the hall, the kitchen, the sitting room and finally, panting, he'd said: "I give up – where have you hidden the bed?"

As they lay on the floor, knackered, the age-old divide between the sexes was full frontal. She wanted him to hold her and tell her he loved her, to luxuriate in the afterglow. He wanted to sleep. But new-mannish educated as he partly was, he compromised. Held her hand and dozed. She had to bite her tongue not to say "I love you." Then he stirred, said: "I've a thirst on me to tempt the Pope. I'll give you a fiver to spit in me mouth."

She laughed and, victim of the new emancipation, rose and got him a pint of water. After he'd drunk deep, he gave a huge burp, rested the glass on his chest, said: "Jaysus, a man could love a woman like you."

Ah! The perennial bait, the never-fail, tantalising lure of the big one. Her heart pounding, she knew she was in the relationship minefield. One foot wrong and boom, back to Tesco's pre-frozen for one. She said: "I hope you were careful." He tilted the glass slightly, said: "Oh yes, I didn't spill a drop."

When finally they went to bed, he slept immediately. Falls hated how much she wanted to be held. Later, she was woken by him thrashing and screaming, and then he sat bolt upright. She said: "Oh God, are you OK?"

"Man, the flashbacks."

"What?"

"Isn't that what the guys always say in the movies?"

"Oh."

"Jesus, it was some movie."

As Falls settled back to uneasy sleep, she ran Tony Braxton's song in her head – "Unbreak My Heart."

Eddie had all the moves. After he'd spent a night at her flat, next day she'd discover little notes, tucked in the fridge, under the pillow, the pocket of her coat. All of the ilk: "I miss you already," or "You are the light in my darkness," and other gems. Mills and Boon would have battled for him. Walking together, he'd say: "Can I take yer hand, it makes me feel total warmth."

A God.

And what a kisser. Finally, a man born to lip service. She could have come with kissing alone and did often.

"If your dead father comes
to you in a dream, he
comes with bad news. If
your dead mother comes,
she brings good news."

Rosie couldn't decide which coffee. She and Falls had met at one of the new specialty coffee cafés. The menu contained over thirty types of brew. Falls said: "Good Lord, I suppose instant is out of the question."

"Shh, don't think such heresy, the windows will crack in protest."

Falls took another pan of the list, then said: "OK, I'll have the double latté."

"What?"

"I know the names from the movies."

"Mmm, sounds weak. I'll have the Seattle Slam." They laughed.

Rosie said: "So, girl. Tell all, can you?"

Falls giggled, said: "If I tell you he kisses the neck…"

"Uh-huh."

"…right below the hairline."

"Oh God, a prince."

"And holds you after."

"He is unique, beyond Prince."

The coffee came and Falls sampled it, said: "Yeah, it's instant with froth." Then she leaned closer, added: "You know why I did, like, on the first date?"

"'Cos you're a wanton cow."

"That too. But when we came out of the dance, I felt faint."

"Lust, girl."

"And I sat on the pavement."

Rosie made a face as she tasted her drink, telling Falls to continue.

"Before I could, he whipped off his jacket and laid it on the path."

"So you sat on it and later you sat on his face."

They roared, shamefully delighted, warmly scandalised. Rosie said: "Taste this,' and pushed the slam across. Falls did, said: "It's got booze in there, check the menu."

Sure enough, in the small print, near illegible, was: "Pure Colombian beans, double hit of espresso, hint of Cointreau." Falls said: "I know what the Cointreau's hinting."

"What's that, then?"

"Get bladdered. Did I tell you I dreamed of my dad?"

Later, wired on slammers, hopping on espresso, Falls showed her Eddie Dillon's poem.

"He wrote a poem for you?"

"Yes." (shyly)

"Is it any good?"

"Who cares? 'Cos it's for me, it's brilliant."

"Give it here, girl!"

She did.

Benediction

Never believed
in such as blessings
were
you threw
a make
un-helped, upon the day
and help available
was how you helped
yourself – A crying
down
to but a look in caution – stayed alert
reducing always towards
the basic front
in pain
– never
– never the once
to once admit
you floundering had to be

Such Gods as crossed
your mind – if God
as such it
might have been
you never took
to vital introspection

Such it was from you
did feel
the very first in love's belief
form feaming every smile
you ever freely
gave

Rosie's lips moved as she read. For some reason, this touched Falls and she had to look away. Finally: "Wow, it's deep."

"'Tis. that's what he says, ''tis'."

"Do you understand it?"

"Course not. What's that got to do with anything?"

"Oh, you lucky cow, I think I hate you!"

Virgin? What's your problem. Where? What's your number.

Naomi Wolf (Rocking Years)

Sent flowers every other day, she said: "I am blessed full."
Not a cloud to be seen... almost. One or two tiny niggles,
hardly worth consideration: one, he couldn't take her to his
flat; two, she couldn't phone him. Weighted against the other
gold, these were nothing – right?

Rightish! No point even sharing those with Rosie. Why
bother? But: "Rosie, whatcha think about..?" And Rosie: "Oh
God, that's very ominous."

Falls was raging: "Ominous? When did you swallow a dictionary?" That's it, no more input from Ms. Know-it-all.

The doorbell went and she felt her heart fly. At a guess, more
roses. With a grin, she opened the door.

Not Interflora.

A bag lady. Well, next best thing. A middle-aged woman who
could be kindest described as "frumpy," and you'd be reaching.
Her hair was dirt grey, and whatever shade it had been, that was
long ago. Falls sighed. The homeless situation was even worse
than the *Big Issue*'s warnings. Now they were making house calls.
She geared herself for action: arm lock, a few pounds and the
address of the Sally... she'd be history.

The woman said: "Are you WPC Falls, the policewoman?"

Surprisingly soft voice. The new Irish cultured one of soft
vowels and easy lilt, riddled with education.

"Yes."

"I'm Nora."

Falls tried not to be testy, said: "I don't wish to be rude, but you say it as if it should mean something. It doesn't mean anything to me."

The woman stepped forward, not menacingly, but more as if she didn't want the world to hear, said: "Nora Dillon, Eddie's wife."

Falls had dressed for confrontation. The requisite Reeboks, sweatshirt and pants. She sat primly on her couch, letting Eddie hang himself. First, she'd considered sitting like Ellen DeGeneres. That sitcom laid-back deal, legs tucked under your butt, yoga-esque. Mainly cool, like très. But it hurt like a son-of-a-bitch. Since Dyke City, when Ellen had come out of the closet, was she a role model? "We think not,' said Middle America. So, Eddie arrived with red roses, Black Magic and a shit-eating grin. He's even quoting some of his poetry. Like this:

I gave you then
a cold hello
and you
being poorer
gave me nothing
nothing at all.

He was dressed in a tan linen suit with a pair of Bally loafers. His face looked carbolic-shined. He looked like a boy. It tore at her heart. Jesus. Now he was repeating the line for effect: "Gave me nothing." Lingering, slow-lidded look, then: "...nothing at all."

Eddie looked up, awaiting praise. Falls got to her feet, said, "Come here."

He smiled, answered, "I love it when you're dominant."

He moved right to her, turned his head to kiss her and she kneed him in the balls, said, "Rhyme that, you bastard."

Dropped to the floor like a bad review. She thought of Brant and what he'd say.

"Finish it off with a kick to the head."

Part of her was sorely tempted, but the other half wanted to hug him. Summoning all her resolve, she bent down and grabbed hold of the linen jacket and began to drag him. One of his tan loafers came off. Got him to the door and with the last of her strength, flung him out. Then she gathered up the flowers, the chocolates and the loose shoe, threw them after him. Then she slammed the door, stood with her back against it for a while, then slumped down to a sitting position.

After a time she could hear him. He tapped on the door and his voice,

"Honey... sweetheart... let me explain..."

Like a child, she put her fingers in her ears. It didn't fully work: she could still hear his voice but not the sense of the words. It continued for a time then gradually died away. Eventually she moved and got to her feet, said, "I'm not going to cry anymore."

She had a shower and had it scalding, till her skin screamed SURRENDER. Then she found a grubby track suit and climbed into it. It made her look fat.

She said, "This makes me look fat... good!"

Opened the door cautiously. No Eddie. Some of the flowers still strewn around clutched at her heart.

Falls had seen all sorts of things in her police career, but these few flowers appeared to be the very essence of lost hope.

At the off-licence, she ordered a bottle of vodka and debated a mixer. But no, she'd take it bitter, it was fitting.

Back home, she drank the vodka from a mug. A logo on the side said: *I'm too sexy for my age.*

Bit later she put on Joan Armatrading and wallowed in total delicious torment.

Near the end of the bottle, she threw the music out of the window.

End of the evening, she took a hammer to the mug and bust it to smithereens.

Brant was booted and suited. The flat had been cleaned by a professional firm. They hadn't actually been paid yet, but assured of "police protection." He was well pleased with their work. The suit was genuine Jermyn Street bespoke. A burglary there had brought Brant to investigate... and pillage. If a look can speak columns, then this suit spoke like royalty. You could sleep in it and have it shout: "Hey, is this class or what?"

It was. The shoes were hand-made Italian loafers and whispered of effortless arrogance. He wore a Police Federation tie, a blotch on any landscape, and a muted shirt. He gazed at himself in the new full-length mirror and was delighted, said: "I ain't half delighted." The whole outfit was clarion call to Muggers United till they saw his face, and rethought: "Maybe not."

He took his bleeper in case the "E" rang. He needed access. A genuine Rolex completed the picture. Alas, it was so real it appeared a knock-off and supplied a badly needed irony to his whole appearance. He said aloud: "Son, you are hot." As he left he slammed his new steel-reinforced door with gusto.

It's been heard in south-east London that "a copper's lot is a Volvo." Brant was no exception. He found it a distinct advantage to have a recognisable cop issue. Saved it from being nicked. Others said: "Who'd bloody want it?" As he unlocked his car, a few drops of rain fell. He said: "Shit." And remembered his old man one time, saying: "Ah! Soft Irish rain." His mother's reply: "Soft Irish men, more like."

A woman approached, dressed respectably, which revealed absolutely nothing. Not to Brant. She said: "Excuse me?"

"What?"

"I hate to trouble you, but my car's broken down and I'm without change. I need three, perhaps four pounds to get a cab."

"You need a new line, lady."

And he got into the Volvo. She watched him, astonishment writ large, and as he pulled away, she said clearly: "Cunt."

He laughed out loud. The night had begun well.

"Tooling up"

"Tonight… Tonight… Tonight… we go… oh yeah."
On the floor, he'd spread a tarpaulin, and now began to lay weapons down: two sawn-offs, one canister of CS gas, three baseball bats and a mess of handguns.

He looked to his brother first, said: "OK, Albert, pick yer poison." Al took a handgun, tested it for weight, and then jammed it in the back of his jeans. Kev whistled: "Very fucking cool. Mind how you sit down."

He snatched the sawn-offs and chucked them to Doug and Fenton, said: "'Cos you guys are a blast."

He too the handguns and, holding them down by his sides, added: "No need for the bats, eh? This is purely a shooting party." Albert smiled, thought of the gun he'd looted. Now he'd be truly loaded.

Fiona Roberts knew her marriage was bad, and often woesome. But she was determined to keep it. If it meant lying down with the dogs… or dog, then she'd suffer the fleas. She wasn't sure how to dress for a blackmail date. Did you go mainline hooker or bag lady? A blend of the two perhaps. When Brant had said he wished to "woo' her, she'd nearly laughed in his pig face. But instinct had held her tongue and she knew she could maybe turn everything round. So she agreed, he was to pick her up at Marble Arch. Ruefully she reflected it was a hooker's landmark. A cab took her there and as she paid the fare, the driver said: "Bit cold for it, luv."
"How dare you!"
"What?"

"Your implication. I don't think I know what you are saying."
"Get a grip, darlin'. I didn't mean nuffink unless civility has been outlawed."
"Hmmph!"

She slammed the door and he took off with her tenner.

Brant was turning into the Arch with the radio blaring. Chris Rea was doing "Road to Hell" and Brant hoped it wasn't an omen. He stopped, flung open the door, shouted: "Hiya, ducks!"

She'd been expecting the Volkswagen Golf, but realised he'd keep her on the hop. As she got in she saw him eying her legs but refrained from comment. Without a word he did a U-turn and swung back towards Bayswater. A highly dangerous move.

She said: "Illegal, surely?"

"That's part of the rush."

She smoothed her dress over her legs and he asked: "Hungry?"

"Why, have you another greasy spoon to slum in?"

"Hey!" And he gave her a look. She could have sworn he appeared hurt and she thought: "Good."

He swerved to avoid a cyclist and said quietly: "I've booked for Bonetti's."

She didn't say anything, and he added: "Well?"

"Well what? I have never heard of it."

"It's in the Egon Ronnie."

"Ronnie? That's Ronay."

"Whatever, I thought you'd be pleased."

And she was, kind of.

Roberts got the call before six. "Chief Inspector Roberts, is that you?"

"Yeah."

This is Governor Brady, over Pentonville."

"Oh yeah?"

"I have a chappie on B wing, might be of interest to you."

"Why?"

"You are still in charge of the Umpire investigation, aren't you?" A note of petulance crept in as he added: "I mean you are interested in solving the cricket business?"

"Of course, absolutely. I'm sorry, it's been a long day."

"Try a day in the Ville sometime."

Roberts wanted to shout: "Get on with it, fuckhead," but he knew the butter approach was vital, and with a trowel, said: "You do a terrific job there, Governor, it can't be easy."

"That's for sure."

"So, this man you've got, you think he might be our boy?"

"He says he is."

"Oh."

"Came in yesterday on a GBH. We had to stick him on B because of his psychotic behaviour."

"Might I come see?"

"I'll be waiting."

When Roberts put down the phone, he didn't feel any hope. They were up to their asses in Umpires, all nutters and all bogus. But he'd have to check it out.

As Brant parked the car, he said: "This Volvo is like my ex."

"Yes?"

"Too big and too heavy."

"Gosh, I wonder why she left you."

The maître d' made a fuss of them, placed them at the best table, said: "Always glad to be of service to our police."

Fiona sighed. The restaurant was near full and a hum of conversation carried. Two huge menus were brought. She said: "You order."

"Okey-dokey."

A young waiter danced over and gave them a smile of dazzling fellowship. Brant asked: "What's the joke, pal?"

"Scusi?"

"Jeez, another wop. Give us a minute, will yer?" A less hearty withdrawal from the waiter. Fiona said: "You have such magnetism."

"That's me all right." Then he clicked his fingers, said: "Yo, Placedo!" And ordered thus: starters, prawn cocktails; main, marinated Tweed salmon with cucumber salad and a pepper steak, roast and jacket potatoes; dessert, pecan sponge pie with marmalade ice-cream; wine, three bottles of Chardonnay.

The waiter looked astonished and Brant said: "Hey, wake up Guiseppe, it won't come on its own."

Fiona didn't know what to say, said: "I dunno what to say."

"Yer man, light on his feet I'd say."

"Excuse me?"

"An arse bandit, one of them pillow biters."

"Oh God."

The food began to arrive, and the first bottle of wine. Brant poured freely, raised his glass, said: "A toast."

"Good heavens."

"That too."

She was glad of the alcohol and drank full, asked: "Do you hate my husband so much?"

"What?"

"You must do. I mean, all this."

"He's a good copper and straight. This isn't to do with him."

"Why, then? Surely it's not just a fuck."

He winced at her obscenity, put his glass down slowly, then said: "It's about class. I never had none. You have it. I thought it might rub off."

"You can't be serious."

```
"You wouldn't kill me in
cold blood, would you?"
"No, I'll let you warm up
a little."
```

Paul Guilfoyle and James Cagney, White Heart

He spooned the prawn cocktail as if it contained secrets, then looked her straight in the eye, began: "I think I was born angry and there was plenty to be pissed about. We had nowt. Then I became a copper and guess what?" She hadn't a clue but he wasn't expecting an answer, continued: "I mellowed 'cos I got respect at last. It felt like I was somebody. Me and Mike Johnson. He was me best mate, Mickey, bought the act even more than I did. Believed yer public could give a toss about us. One night he went to sort out a domestic, usual shit, old man beating the bejaysus out of his missus. Mickey got him up against the wall, we were putting the cuffs on him, when the wife laid him out with a rolling pin." Brant laughed out loud, heads turned, he repeated: "A bloody rolling pin, like a bad joke."

"Was he hurt?"

"He was after they castrated him."

Fiona dropped her spoon, said: "Oh, good grief."

"Good don't come into it. See, you gotta let 'em see you're the most brutal fuckin' thing they've ever seen. They come quiet then." Brant was deep in memory, even his wine was neglected.

"My missus. I loved her but I couldn't let 'er know. Couldn't go soft, know what I mean? Else I'd end up singing soprano like old Mickey."

Whatever Fiona might have said, could have said, was averted. Brant's bleeper went off, he said: "Fuck," and went to use the phone. A few moments later, he was back. "There's heat going on in Brixton, I gotta go."

"Oh."

He rummaged in his pockets, dumped a pile of notes on the table, said: "I've called a cab for you, you stay, finish the grub,' and then he was gone. Fiona wanted to weep. For whom or why, she wasn't sure, but a sadness of infinity had shrouded her heart.

As Brant approached the car, his mind was in a swirl of pain through memory. He'd let his guard down, and now he struggled to regain the level of aggression that was habitual. As a mantra, he mouthed Jack Nicholson's line from *A Few Good Men*: "The truth, you can't handle the truth – I eat breakfast every day, four hundred yards from Cubans who want to kill me." For a moment he was Jack Nicholson, shoving it loud into the face of Tom Cruise.

It worked. The area of vulnerability began to freeze over, and the smile, slick in its satanic knowledge, began to form. He said: "I'm cookin' now, mister." And he was. As the Volvo lurched towards south-east London, Nicholson's lines fired on: "You come down here in your faggoty white uniforms, flash a badge and expect me to salute."

Last train to Clarkesville

As Roberts was resigning himself to a haul to Pentonville, the phone rung again. He considered ignoring it, but finally said: "Damn and blast,' and picked it up. "Yes?"

"Is that the police?"

"Yes." (very testy)

"This is the nursing sister at St. Thomas'."

"And?"

"Well, I don't know if I'm being fanciful, but we have a man here who... I don't know how to say this."

Roberts exhaled loudly and said: "You have the cricket murderer, am I right?" He could hear her amazement and it was a moment before she could say: "Yes. Yes, at least it might be."

Roberts couldn't contain his sarcasm, said: "Confessed, did he?"

"Not exactly, no. A man was brought in after being hit by a bus, and in his sleep, he was shouting things that were peculiar."

Roberts felt he had been hit by a bus himself, said wearily: "I'll get someone over there toot sweet."

"Toot what?"

"Soon, sister, OK?"

"All right, I'll expect you."

"Yeah, yeah."

And he rung off. He rooted in his pocket, took out a coin, said: "Heads the 'Ville, tails the other monkey."

Flipped it high.

It was heads.

Officers had blocked off Electric Avenue. Brant could see armed officers lining up along the roofs. Falls came running, said: "You got my call?"

"I owe you, babe. Is this what I think it is?"

"Someone reported a barrage of shots and the local PC went to investigate. He narrowly escaped having his head shot off." Brant approached the officer in charge, said: "I think I know who's inside. What's the status?"

"A bloody shambles. We know it's a dope pad, and four white men were seen going in. Then the shooting started. Nobody's come out. We have a negotiator on the way and we are trying to set up a phone link."

Brant turned and said to Falls: "Watch this."

Before anyone could react, he walked across the street and into the building. The scene-of-crime guy exclaimed: "What the hell?"

Brant made no effort to sneak up the stairs, but walked loudly, turned into a dimly lit corridor. The smell of cordite was thick, and something else, the smell of blood.

Kev was slouched against a wall, his legs spread out. He held a gun in each hand, not aimed but lying loosely on his chest. He was covered in blood.

Brant said: "Shop!"

A lazy smile from Kev, then: "You should've seen it, mate. We got in and told the fucks not to move. You know what they did?"

"They moved?"

"Started bleedin' shouting. At me brother, he got it in the neck. And Doug, well, he got it everywhere. I dunno about Fenton, I kinda lost him in the excitement."

"Are you hurt bad?"

"I dunno, I don't feel nuffin'... bit tired I suppose."

"You are the 'E' mob, right?"

"Yeah, that's us."

"Tell you son, you done good, had us going a bit."

"We did, didn't we?"

Brant edged closer, said: "Thing is, whatcha gonna do now?"

"I dunno, mate."

A little nearer. "If you give it up boyo, you'll be famous. Lots of press, movie rights, mini-series, books. Jeez, you'll be on T-shirts."

Very close now.

Kev began to move the gun in his right hand, and Brant smashed his foot into Kev's face. Then bounced his head against the wall a few times, pulled the guns away, said: "That's all she wrote."

He straightened up and slowly approached the flat, took a peek inside, muttered: "Jesus!"

Moved in and stepped carefully over bodies. Saw a heavy wedge of banded cash and said: "I'll be 'aving that."

He pushed open the window, let himself be clearly seen, and shouted: "All clear!"

After the clean-up process had begun, Brant was sitting in a police van, sipping tea from a styrofoam beaker. Falls walked over, said: "Hear the buzz?"

"What? No, is it sirens?"

"No, sarge, it's a White Arrest."

Brant said: "I've been accused of all sorts of stuff. Some of it stuck, some of it's even true and none I'll admit to. But, hand on my heart, I've never been a racist. So, I can honestly say, you're the first nigger I ever liked."

Falls didn't know whether to assault him or plain ignore him. Instead: "Well, sergeant, perhaps you're not as black as you're painted." It was the closest they'd come to camaraderie.

Roberts emerged from Pentonville spitting anger. The suspect was a complete wash out. So loaded on Thorazine he confessed to being Lord Lucan.

It took all of Roberts' patience not to wallop him. Worse, he had had to brown-nose the Governor, who said: "Can't be too careful, eh?"

"Exactly."

As he got in his car, he thought he'd have time to swing by St. Thomas', then said: "Fuck that for a game of soldiers."

❖

Fiona answered the phone, wondered if it was Brant, said: "Yes?"

"Fiona, this is Penny."

"What do you want?"

"Oh Fiona, I'm so sorry, but I had no choice."

"That's not quite right, you chose, but you chose to save yourself."

"Can you ever forgive me?"

"I shouldn't think so."

"What can I do to make up for it? Anything. I'll do anything."

"Would you?"

"Oh yes."

"Then go fuck yourself, you've done it to everybody else."

Two weeks later

A t St Thomas' Hospital, the doctor was releasing his patient. "Now Mr. Shannon, will you take it easy?"
"Is sport OK?"
"Purely as a spectator, is that clear?"
"Crystal," and the Umpire smiled.

The furore of the Brixton shoot-out was ebbing. Commendations, awards, lavish praise, expected promotion: all followed Brant's way. The George Medal was being mentioned.

Brant was coming home after yet another evening of liquid congratulation. Outside his building, he let back his head and muttered: "Ain't life grand?"

A woman approached and asked: "Change for tea, mistah?"

Too late he registered the Band-Aid, and a knife went deep into his lower back.

As he fell to his knees, he thought: "Ahh... bollocks."

Roberts checked again in the full-length mirror. He was dressed in a tight black shirt, homburg on his head, and dark shades. Oh yeah, and white socks, meeting the too-short pants. Brant had finally talked him into the idea for the fancy dress at the Met dance. When Fiona saw him, she gasped: "What on earth?"

"I'm a Blues Brother!"

"You look like a spiv."

And she'd retreated in gales of laughter. When Brant had explained, it seemed more feasable. How they'd burst into the hall, light shining behind them. Before anyone could recover,

they'd launched into an improvised version of a) "Rawhide' or:
b) "Stand By Your Man" ("As long as it's loud, Guv").
Roberts readjusted the shades and said tentatively: "We're…"
No!
"We're on…"
Better. And finally, out loud and proud:
"We're on a mission from God."

taming
the alien

To Fall
falling
have fallen   in love

Falls knew the guy would hit on her. With such a short mini, it was nigh mandatory. She sat, tasted her drink, waited. Yeah... here he was.

"Mind if I join you?"

"Not yet."

He gave a quizzical look. "Not yet you don't mind, or not yet to joining you?"

Falls shrugged and tried to look at home in the bar. Not easy to carry off when you're:

a) English

b) Female

c) Black.

He sat.

She asked, "Do you swim?"

"What?"

"It's just that you have a swimmer's shape."

"Yeah? Well, no... no I don't, not since *Jaws*, anyway."

She gave a laugh. "There's no sharks in England."

He gave a tolerant smile. Nice teeth. Asked, "How long since you shopped on the Walworth Road?"

She laughed again, thought, Good Lord, if I'm not careful I'll be having me a time.

He then proceeded to lay a line of chat on her. Not great or new, but *in there*.

She held up a finger, said, "Stop."

"What?"

"Look, you're an attractive man. But you already know that. We'd date, get excited, probably have hot sex." He nodded, if uncertainly, and she continued. "I know you'd have a good time – shit, you'd have a wonderful time – and I'd probably like it too. But then the lies, the fights the bitterness...

Why bother?"

He thought, then said, "I like the first part best."

"Anyway, you're too old." And it crushed him. One fell swoop and he was out of the ballpark. No stamina and they hadn't even started. It didn't feel good.

"Oh hell," she thought. "Revenge is supposed to be sweet."

Her father, in a rare moment of sobriety, had said: "If you're planning revenge, dig two graves."

He sure as Shooters Hill was in one, and she was contemplating the second. All because Eddie Dillon had smashed her heart, her trust into smithereens. The married bastard.

Roy Fenton tasted the tea, went, "Euck... argh..." and called to the waitress.

"Yo, Sheila, how can you fuck-up a tea bag?"

Sheila didn't answer. The Alien was known in the Walworth Road cafe and most of south-east London. What was known was his reputation, and that said people got hurt round him.

His cousin had been part of the "E Gang". A group of vigilantes who'd hanged drug dealers from Brixton lamp-posts until they'd been slaughtered in a crack house on Coldharbour Lane. Smoke that!

No one called Fenton "The Alien" to his face. At least not twice. He read his poem, chewed the tea:

UNTITLED
And he had his books,
second-hand
and nearly twenty, neatly stacked
A tape recorder, German made, some

prison posters
Same old ties, some photos too
And the camera, convincing lies.

For the booze
a Snoopy mug,
two shoes too tight
And English jeans
A silly grin with still,
the cheapest jacket
off the rack during some sales.

A belt
its buckle made of tin... and clean
with undies, unmatched songs
and a hangover
God bless the mark
the usual London cover.
A watch
Timex, on plastic strap.

He stopped. Remembering... When Stell had come to the 'Ville, him six months into the three years, and said: "Ron, I got pregnant."

And he didn't know what to say. "I dunno what to say."

And she'd begun to weep, him asking, "What... what's the matter, darlin'?"

And her head lifting, the eyes awash in grief.

"Ron... I had an abortion."

And he was up. Remembered that. Head-butting the first screw, taking down a second without even trying and then: the clubs, the batons. Raining down on him, like the purest Galway weather. Harsh and unyielding.

Did three months on the block, lost all remission and got an extra year. Not hard time, hate time. Fuelled and driven by a rage that never abated. The head screw, a guy named Potter. Not the worst; in many ways a decent sort. Still some humanity lingering. He gave a hesitant smile, almost put his hand out. No chance.

But tried anyway.

"Give it up Ron, she's not worth it."

Fenton spat on his tunic.

The other screws moving forward but Potter, waving them back, said, "Have this one on me, Ron."

He'd searched every pub in north London. Should have known better than to step outside the south-east in the first place. Jeez... North! Highbury and shite talk.

Word was, she was in San Francisco. OK. He could do that... but he would need a wedge, a real buffer. He was working on it...

During lock-down he'd begun to write the poem. One toilet roll, with a midget William Hill biro. Gouging it down.

One of the nick fortune tellers saying: "I can see yer future, Ron."

"Yeah? See a double scotch anytime soon?"

The tier sissy who'd blown him then saw the poem, said, "You should send that to a magazine."

Gave him a fist up the side of the head, said, "Don't touch my stuff."

But got to thinking...

One lazy Saturday, Millwall were two down, he'd idled through a magazine and these words hit him like a pool cue:

POETRY

FREE APPRAISAL

CASH PRIZES

PUBLICATION

So he sent it off.

"Fuck 'em if they can't take a joke." The psycho Dex used to say it all the time. Dex, they found him in a bin liner on a heap in Walworth. An old copy of *The Big Issue* down his Y-fronts. Liked to read, did old Dex. And talk. But talked too much. A black chick took his throat from ear to mouthy ear.

She was dead 'n' all.

Since Derek Raymond died, so did all the characters.

He sent the poem.

They replied:

> Dear Ronald, If we may be permitted
> the liberty of addressing you thus...

Fenton thought, "Uh-huh, watch your wallet,' but read on:

> Our panel of specially selected
> judges have chosen your poem to go
> forward to the Grand Final. The
> winner receives a thousand guineas.
> All entries will be published in a
> lavish volume that all good book
> stores must have. As you'll appreci-
> ate, the cost of printing is high for
> a book of such quality. For a stipend
> of fifty pounds, we can reserve your
> own engraved copy. Please hurry as
> demand is limited.
> Of course, your donation in no way
> affects the outcome of the Grand
> Final which, as we stated, is for ONE
> THOUSAND GUINEAS!
> We eagerly await your prompt reply.
> Yours,
> P Smith, Co-ordinator
> The World of Poetry Inc.

He wrote back:

> Dear P. Smith,
> Take my end outta the thousand
> large.
> Yours,
> R.Fenton
> Convict.

If you turned right on the Clapham Road, you could walk along Lorn to the Brixton side.

Few do.

Brant had his new place here. The irony didn't escape him.

Lorn... forlorn.

Oh yeah.

Since he'd been knifed in the back, he'd been assigned to desk duty, said: "Fuck that for a game of soldiers."

His day off, he'd go to the cemetery, put flowers on PC Tone's grave. Never missed a week. Each time he'd say, "Sorry son. I didn't watch for you and the fucks killed you for a pair of pants."

What a slogan – *Trousers to die for.*

The Band-Aid couple had gone to ground or Ireland. No proof it was them. Just a hunch. Some day, yeah... some day he'd track 'em.

Only Chief Inspector Roberts knew of Brant's hand in the murder of the boy. He wouldn't say owt. Brant's own near death had somehow evened it out for Roberts.

Odd barter but hey, they were cops, not brain surgeons.

Chief Inspector Roberts was aging badly. As he shaved, he looked in the mirror, muttered: "Yer aging badly."

Deep creases lined his forehead. The once impressive steel grey hair was snow white and long. Clint Eastwood ridges ran down his cheeks. Even Clint tried to hide them. Wincing is cool... sure... maybe till yer dodgy forties, but after that it comes across as bowel trouble.

Roberts loved the sun, nay, worshipped it – and cricket. Too many summers under long hours of UV rays had wreaked havoc. Worse, melanomas had appeared on his chest and legs. When he'd noticed them he gasped, "What the bloody hell?"

He knew... oh sweet Jesus did he ever... that if them suckers turned black, you were fucked. They turned black.

The doctor said, "I won't beat around the bush."

Roberts thought: Oh, do... if necessary, lie to me – lie *big* – beat long around any bush.

"It's skin cancer."

"Fuck!"

After he thought, I took it well.

Was ill as a pig when he heard about the treatment.

Like this: "Once a week we'll have radiation."

"We? You'll be in there with me?"

The doctor gave a tolerant smile, halfways pity to building smirk, continued: "Let's see how you progress with the 'rad,' and if it's not doing the business we'll switch to laser."

Roberts wanted to shout, "Beam me up Scottie! Signpost ahead... The Twilight Zone."

He let the doctor wind down. "Later on, we'll whip some of those growths away. A minor surgical procedure."

"Minor for you, mate."

The doctor was finished now, probably get in nine holes before ops, said: "We'll pencil you in for Mondays, and I'd best prepare you for two after effects:

1. You'll suffer extreme fatigue, so easy does it.

2. It leaves you parched – a huge thirst is common."

He had a mega thirst now.

Right after, he went to the Bricklayers. The barman, a balding git with a pony-tail and stained waistcoat, chirped, "What will it be, Guv?"

"Large Dewars, please."

"Ice... water?"

"What, you don't think I'd have thought of them?"

"Touchy."

Roberts didn't answer, wondering how the git would respond to rad. As if abbreviation could minimise the trauma. Oh would it were so. Dream on.

Robert's other passion was Film Noir of the forties and fifties. Hot to trot. Now, as he nursed the scotch, he tried to find a line of comfort from the movies. What he got was Dick Powell in Farewell My Lovely:

> *I caught the blackjack right behind my ear.*
> *A black pool opened up at my feet.*
> *I dived in. It had no bottom.*

Yeah.

He'd given the git behind the bar a tenner, and now he eyed the change. "Hey buddy, we're a little light here."

"Wha…? Oh… took one for me. I hate to see anyone drink alone."

Roberts let it go. Londoners… you gotta love them. Bit later the git leans on the bar, asks, "You like videos?"

"Excuse me?"

"Fillums, mate. Yer latest blockbuster – see it tonight in the privacy of yer own gaff. Be like 'aving the West End in yer living room."

"Pirates, you mean."

"Whoa, John, keep it down, eh?"

Roberts sighed, laid his warrant card on the counter.

"Whoops…"

Roberts put the card away, said, "I thought in your game you could spot a copper."

"Usually yeah, but two things threw me."

"Yeah, what's those then?"

"First, you have manners."

"And…?"

"You actually paid."

Fenton got his nickname thus: During the movie *Alien* he killed a guy – the scene where the creature crashes outta John Hurt's chest. He'd used a baseball bat. Near most, it was his weapon of choice. The guy, Bob Harris, had stitched up his mates. They were doing life-plus on the not so sunny Isle of Wight. Mind you, the ferry over had been scenic. Fenton was offered two large to payback. He did it gratis. What are mates for?

Oh, Bob liked his horror flicks and was a particular aficionado of Ridley Scott's work on *Alien*. Could wax lyrical about the used hardware look of the scenes. Shite talk.

Fenton had called round, six pack of Special and some wacky-backy. They'd done a tote, got munchies and cracked the brewskis. Fenton asked, "Yo, mate, still got *Alien*, have you?"

"Oh yeah, good one. Wanna see it now?"

"Why wait?"

Indeed.

Fenton said he'd grab some cold ones from the fridge as they got into the flick. Bob was on the couch, glued to the screen, yelping about the "vision" of Allen Dean Foster. Fenton unzipped the Adidas hold-all and took out the Louisville slugger. It had black tape wound tight on the handle, tight as cruelty. He gave the bat a test swing, and yeah, it gave the familiar whoosh of long and comfortable use.

The crew of *The Nostradome* were sitting down to their meal and John Hurt was getting terminal indigestion.

Bob shouted, "Yo... Fen! You don't wanna miss this bit!"

Fen came in, put his weight on the ball of his right foot, pivoted, and swung with all he had, saying, "I won't miss, buddy."

And wallop – right outta the ball park.

The crew on the TV screen gave shouts of horror and disgust at the carnage. Fenton let the movie run, he hated to leave things unfinished.

Fenton had a meet with Bill in The Greyhound near the Oval. It's always hopping, but no matter how tight, Bill gets to sit on his tod down the end. All the surrounding seats are vacant. Not free but empty, like McDonalds cola. A time back, a pissed Paddy decided to have a seat right up close to Bill, said, "Howya."

Bill didn't look, said, "You don't wanna perch there, pal."

"Pal? Jaysus, I don't know you. Buy us a double, though."

A muscle man outta the crowd slammed Paddy's ears in a simultaneous clatter. Then had him up and frog marched out to the alley. There, his arm was broken and his nose moved to the right. After, sitting against the wall, he asked, "What?... What did I say?"

Bill and Fenton went way back. Lots of cross referenced villainy. Masters of their respective crafts. Bill asked, "Drink?"

"Rum 'n' coke."

"Bacardi or...?"

Fen smiled, "Navy up."

An old joke. Just not a very good one. Bill was drinking mineral water – Ballygowan Sparkling.

The drinks came and Fen said. "I dunno Bill, I must be getting old, but I could never get me head round paying for water."

Bill took a sip and winced. "What makes you think I pay?"

"Nice one."

They sat a bit in silence. You could nigh hear the bubbles zip, like pleasant times, like fairy tales.

Then, "We found her."

"Great."

"You're not going to like it."

"Gee, what a surprise."

"She's in America, like you thought – San Francisco – living with a teacher, name of Davis."

"A teacher... wow."

Bill said, "Let it be, Fen," and got the look, boundaries being breached. He sighed. "Sorry... you'll need a wedge."

"Big time."

Bill rooted in his jacket, took out a fat manila envelope, said "There's a cop, name of Brant, needs sorting."

"When?"

"Soon as."

"How far in?"

"Not fatal but educational."

"Can do."

Fen got up and Bill said, "Oi, you didn't touch yer rum."

"Hate that shit."

And he was gone.

Brant had taken Falls with him to interview a suspected arsonist.

No proof had surfaced but the Croydon cops swore he was the man. Now he'd moved to Kennington and, hey, coincidence, a warehouse was gutted on the Walworth Road. He was in his early thirties with the eyes of a small snake. He'd answered his door dressed in a denim shirt, cutoffs, bare feet.

Brant said, "If you'll pardon the pun, we're the heat."

The guy smiled, let them know he could be a fun person, asked, "Got a warrant?"

"Why? You done somefing?"

And everybody smiled. The guy was enjoying it, said, "What the hell, c'mon in."

The flat was a shithole. The guy said, "It's a shithole, right, but I just moved in and..."

Brant said, "From Croydon."

"Yeah!"

"We heard."

He stretched out on a sofa, waved his hand. "Park it wherever."

Brant parked it right next to the guy's head, still smiling.

The guy sat up, decided to pull the "blokes" routine and nodded towards Falls. "You didn't need to bring a cunt with yah."

And got an almighty wallop on the side of his head.

Brant said, "Here's how it works, boyo – you call her names, I'll wallop you... OK?"

Too stunned to reply, the guy looked at Falls, thus failing to see the second sledgehammer punch to the back of his head. It knocked him out on his face and he whinged, "I didn't say nuffink that time."

Brant hunkered down, said "I hadn't finished explaining the rules. See, if you even *look* like you're going to call her a name, I hammer you. Get it now?"

The guy nodded.

Falls had long since despaired of Brant's methods. She owed him three large for her father's funeral and was obliged to suffer in silence.

When they were leaving, Brant said to the guy, "They think you're an arsonist. Me?... I dunno, but if there's another fire soon, I'll put you in it."

Back on the street, Falls said in exasperation, "I need a holiday."

"Yeah? Anywhere nice?"

"Some place far, like America."

"And you need money, is it? How much?"

She was too enraged to answer.

Brant was humming a Mavericks tune as he put his key in the door. He felt fucked and looked forward to a cold one – lots of cold ones – and maybe a sneak peek again at *Beavis And Butthead Do America*.

Stepping inside his flat, his inner alarm began.

Too late.

The baseball bat tapped him smartly on the base of his skull and two thoughts burned as the carpet rushed to meet him.

a) Not this shit again

b) The carpet sure is worn

When he came to, many pains jostled for supremacy – his head... the rope round his neck... the ache in his lower back...

The Alien said, "I wouldn't move if I were you. See, what I've done is tie a rope round your neck and connected it to yer feet. You move either, you slow strangle. But, don't sweat it – you'll catch on quick."

Brant tried to move and the strangle hold tightened. He went: "Urgh...uh..."

And Fenton said, "Exactly! I think you've got it."

Brant's pants and Y-fronts were around his ankles and he felt a baseball bat lightly tap his bum. For a horrific moment, he envisaged rape of an American variety.

Fen said, "I hear you're a hard ass. Time to change that. For the next few weeks when you try to sit, remember: keep yer bloody nose outta people's business."

A whistle began to scream from the kitchen and Fen said, "I put the kettle on. Handy, those whistle tops, eh? No boiling over. Excuse me a mo!"

Brant was awash in cold sweat. Rivers of it coursing down his torso. Fear was roaring in his head.

Then, "Okey-dokey... here we go. I'll pour..."

And white hot pain electrified Brant's brain.

Fiona Roberts was stalled in traffic. Cars were blocked all the way down to the Elephant. Her husband had many proclamations, most of a police bent. Among them was, "If you're caught in traffic, keep the windows shut."

Yeah, yeah.

She could hear a blast of rap from a nearby car and glanced over. A man with dreadlocks was giving large to a mobile. How he could hear anything above the music would be nothing short of miraculous. He caught her eye and gave a huge dazzling gold capped smile. Not too sure about her response, she looked away. Didn't do to encourage the game. A woman's head appeared at her elbow and a distinctly Irish accent whined, "Gis the price of a cuppa tea, missus, and I'll say a prayer for ya."

Fiona had never mastered the art of street encounters. As a cop's wife she'd learned zero except the response of confusion.

Like now. She muttered, "I've no change."

And the woman spat in her face.

The shock was enormous. As the spittle slid down her cheek, a symphony of horns began and shouts: "Eh, get a bloody move on!" "Shift yer knickers darlin'!"

She did. As the Americans say – "Who ya gonna call?"

Her husband would crow, "What did I say? ... Didn't I tell you about windows, eh? Didn't I say?"

The Ford Anglia 205E saloon is a classic. You gaze at it, you can almost believe the fifties and sixties had some worth. See your reflection in the chromed wing mirrors, you can almost imagine you have a quiff stuck in Brylcreem heaven with sleek brushed sideburns. The wheels are a collectors wet dream – rubber tyres with separate chrome hubcaps. Note that word "separate." The difference twixt class and mediocrity. Ask Honda as you whisper British Leyland. Throw in Harley Davidson and you've got one pissed off Jap. Roberts called his Anglia "Betsy." In the fifties, it was easier to name the car than the child. Roberts was financially strapped. A mortgage in Dulwich, a daughter in boarding school. And he was hurting big time. Now that he'd been diagnosed with skin cancer, he'd flung the lot – caution, care, budget – to the cancerous wind.

The car was a bust. It didn't overstretch his finances so much as shout BLITZKRIEG.

He wasn't sorry, not one little bit. He loved – nay, adored – it. Kept it in a lock-up at Victoria. The garage belonged to a mate of Brant's and he was glad to oblige the police. Well glad-ish. Come a pale rider. In the nineties in London. Come joy riders. Bringing anything but joy.

Patience isn't high on their list of characteristics. They opened the lock-up no problem, but couldn't get the Anglia to start. So... so they burned it where it was. The fire took out three other garages.

When Roberts arrived, the blaze had been brought under control, but too late to save anything. The fire chief asked, "That your motor in there?"

"Was."

"You'll be insured?"

Roberts gave him the look. "I'm a cop – what do you think?"

"Uh-oh."

"Yeah."

They watched the flames for a bit and then the chief said, "There's a cup o' tea going... fancy one?"

"I don't think tea will do it."

"You could be right. Me, I take comfort where I find it."

"Gee, how philosophical... maybe I should be glad the fire gives heat to the neighbours."

"See – you're sounding better already."

Before Roberts could respond to this gem, his bleeper went and the Chief said, "Could be a long night."

"It's been a long fuckin' life, I tell you."

But the Chief already knew that.

As Roberts sighed and turned away he ran a turn through his favourite noir movies. Always from the forties and fifties. What surfaced was Barbara Stanwyck to Keith Andes in *Clash By Night*:

"What do you want, Joe, my life history? Here it is in four words:

BIG IDEAS, SMALL RESULTS.

Yeah, the story of it all.

Brant had passed out from shock. Now, as he came to, he curled up in anticipation of horrendous pain.

Curled up?

He thought – *What?* – and rolled easily onto his side. No pain. No rope.

Trembling, he moved his hand to his ass... wet and cold.

Cold water.

He'd been suckered with the oldest psych trick in the book.

Rage and relief fought for supremacy as he got shakily to his feet. Stumbled to the cupboard and got a bottle of Black Bushmills. He'd been keeping it for a four star moment like getting the knickers off Fiona Roberts. Twisted the top savagely, let the cap fall and chugged direct. Did this bastard burn... oh yeah!

He leaned against the cupboard and waited for the four stars to kick in. They did. Fast. And he muttered, "Jaysus."

After a few more slugs, he moved to the armchair and with a steady hand, lit a Weight. He knew who his assailant was. The so called "Alien," the legendary fuck. Only one person would have the balls to set him loose. With Fenton it was just a job, but to the one calling the shots, it was personal.

Brant began to savour how he'd boil the two of 'em together. Not with bloody cold water either.

L eigh Richards was a snitch. What's more, he was Falls' snitch, passed on by Brant who said, "The most vital tool for police work is a grass. One of their own who'll turn for revenge, spite or money. But mainly money. Fear, too, that helps. I'm giving you this piece of garbage, 'cos I can no longer stomach 'im."

After meeting Leigh, Falls could understand why. Years ago, Edward Woodward made his name playing a character called Callan. He had a sidekick named Lonely. Leigh was the Lonely of the turn of the century. No specific reason that made him distasteful. Everything about him was ordinary. So much so that he looked like a photo-kit. Everybody and nobody. If there's such a thing as auras, then his spelt "repellent."

He said to Falls, "This is a new departure for me."

"What?"

"Working with a woman."

Falls had a constant urge to lash out at him. Ordinarily, she was no testier than your average Northern Line commuter, but once in Leigh's presence, she felt murderous. She said slowly, "Listen, shithead, we're not working together. We never have, never will – am I getting this across?"

He had his hair cut in a French crop. This is a crew-cut with notions. His eyes never met yours, and yet, he never ceased watching you. That's what Falls felt – she felt watched.

He put up his hands in mock surrender, said, "Whoa, little lady! No offence meant.

I like niggers, anyone will tell you Leigh Richards isn't a bigot. Go on, ask anybody... you'll see. Live and let live is my motto."

If Falls had sought Roberts' advice, he'd have said, "Never trust a grass." He knew from bitter experience. More, he could have recounted the lines from *The Thin Man*:

"*I don't like crooks.*
And If I did like them, I wouldn't like crooks who are stool pigeons.
And if I did like crooks who are stool pigeons, I still wouldn't like you."

Roberts would have liked to rattle off the lines anyway because he liked to. Plus, he'd love to have been Nora Charles' husband. But she didn't ask and the lines stayed on celluloid – unwatched and unused.

Instead, Falls counted to ten and then she smacked Leigh in the mouth. His feelings, not to mention his mouth, were hurt.

He said, "My feelings are hurt," and he figured it was time to rein Falls in. Let her see a little of his knowledge, know who she was dealing with. He said, "I know you. I know yer Dad died recent, and more, you couldn't cough up the readies to plant him." He had her attention and continued, "My old Dad snuffed it too. See this belt?"

In spite of herself, she looked. It appeared to be a boy scout one, right down to the odd buckle.

"When I went to the morgue, the guy said: 'It's all he left, shall I sling it?' *Oi!* I said, *that's my estate!*"

Falls didn't smile, but Leigh could go with that. He'd smacked her right back and never even had to raise his hand or his voice.

She asked, "There's a moral in there?"

"Like the great man said – 'Be prepared!'"

"Who?"

"Baden Powell, founder of the scouts."

Falls gave a harsh chuckle, said, "They weren't real popular in Brixton."

"Oh…"

"But let me give you a little story."

Leigh didn't care for the light in her eye. He'd heard blacks got funny when they mentioned Brixton. Shit – when *anybody* mentioned it. He said: "There's no need."

"I insist. The cat asked: 'Do you purr?' 'No,' said the ugly duckling. 'Then you'll have to go'." She let Leigh digest this then, "So, you're a snitch... then *snitch*."

"I'll need paying."

"After."

"It's good information."

"Mr. Brant was anxious to locate two Irish people, a man and a woman."

"So?"

"He believes they can help with his... ahm... recent accident."

"Do you know where they are?"

"I know where they went."

"Yeah."

"One of them was wearing a nice pair of Farahs as he boarded the plane – a plane for Amer-i-kay."

In spite of herself, she uttered, "Jesus."

Leigh was excited, babbled on, "According to my sources, a certain young copper was wearing said pants on the night of his demise."

Falls grabbed both his wrists and, Brant-style, leant right into his face, said, "Their names?"

"Josie... and Mick... that's all I know."

She squeezed harder.

"Belton... OK! Mick Belton – you're hurting me!"

She let go, then reached in her purse and began to gather loose notes. He said in alarm, "For Godsake, don't do it like that – palm it!"

She did and he squeezed her fingers during the move, said, "I have a good feeling about us."

"Yeah?" She sounded near warm.

Emboldened, he risked, "You'll find me more than satisfactory in the... ahm..." And here he winked.

She whispered, "And you ever talk to me like that, you'll find it in Brixton among the used condoms and other garbage."

Then she was up and moving. He waited till she was a distance, then said, "Yah lesbian!"

The Alien was sitting in The Greyhound, in Bill's private corner.

He was drinking a mineral water, slowly savouring the sparkle. Bill arrived with two minders. They branched off to man both ends of the bar. Fenton said, "Impressive."

Bill looked back at them. "Yeah?"

"Oh definitely, real menace."

Bill sat down and nodded to the barman. A bowl of soup was brought and two dry crackers. They were encased in that impossible to open plastic. Bill nodded at them, said, "Get those, eh?"

"Why don't you call the muscle, give em a chance to flex."

Bill smiled, "You wouldn't be trying to wind me up would you Fen?"

"Naw, would I do that?"

Bill was quiet for a bit, then, "You did the biz?"

"Course."

"Didn't overdo it, did yah?"

"Naw, just put a frightener to him – he's mobile but dampened. You'll have no more strife."

"I wouldn't want any of this coming back on me, Fen."

"It's done, you've no worries. He's tamed – nowt for him now but nickel and dime till he gets his shitty pension. He's bottled out."

Bill passed over a fat package. "A little bonus, help you find yer feet in America... you'll be off soon."

"Soon as shootin'."

They both gave a professional laugh at this, not that either thought it as funny or even appropriate.

This is how the call came in.

"Hello, is that the police?"

The desk sergeant, weary after an all-nighter, answered, "Yeah, can I help?" Not that he had a notion of so doing.

"I'm about to eat my breakfast."

"How fascinating."

"When I've finished, I'll wash up, and then I'm going to kill my old man."

"Why's that then?"

"He molested me till I was twelve. Now I think he's going to start on my little brother…"

The sergeant was distracted by a drunk being manhandled by two young coppers. At the pitch of his lungs, he was singing: "The sash my father wore…" No big deal in that, unless you noted the man was black. Thus perhaps giving credence to the expression "a black protestant" or not.

When the sergeant got back to the call, he couldn't hear anyone on the line. Testily he repeated, "Hello… yello?"

Then two shots rang clearly down the receiver and he knew, without thinking:

Shot gun – 12 gauge – double o cartridges and muttered, "*Jesus*!"

A homeless person with a grubby T-shirt proclaimed, "Jesus loves black and white but prefers Johnny Walker," and touched Fiona Roberts on the arm. She jumped a foot off the ground thinking:

"They've even reached Dulwich."

He said, "Chill out, babe." Even the displaced were going mid-Atlantic.

She ran. No dignity. No finesse. Out 'n' out legged it.

Inside her home she said aloud, "I know! I'll never go out again – that'll do it." And received a second jump when her daughter Sharon approached suddenly. "Christ, Sharon, don't do that – sneaking up on a person."

"Get real, Mom."

Fiona thought: "A nice cup o' tea, that will restore me," and went to prepare it. She glanced in at the blaring TV. Regis and Kathy Lee were discussing manicures for dogs.

"*Sharon... Sharon!* Why is the telly so loud?... Why do you always need noise?"

The girl threw her eyes to heaven and sighed, "You wouldn't understand."

"What?... What's to understand? Tell me!"

Chewing on her bottom lip, the girl said, "'Cos yer old, Mum."

Fiona scratched the tea and headed upstairs for a Valium – a whole shitpile of mother's little helpers... sorry, old mother's little helpers.

When Charlie Kray, brother of the twins, tried to flog cocaine, three of his customers turned out to be undercover cops. A true sting. Over seventy, Charlie was found guilty, despite his own lawyer calling him a pathetic case. Who Charlie called was Bill. Like this.

"Bill?"

"Yeah."

"It's Charlie."

"Hi, son, I'm sorry about yer bit o' grief."

"They set me up Bill."

"I know, they put you right in the frame."

"You know me, Bill – I 'ate drugs."

"We wouldn't be 'aving this chat if it were otherwise."

"Thanks, Bill. Reggie always said you were the bollocks."

"Was there somefing, Charlie?"

"Is there owt you can do for us, mate? I go in, it's life... at my age."

"Wish I could, son but it's solid. You're going down, but I can 'ave a word, make it cushy as possible."

A pause. Defeat hanging full, then resignation.

"Yeah, righto Bill... Will you look out for my old girl?"

"'Course, you don't 'ave to ask."

"Maybe you'll get up my way, bring us in a bit o' cheer."

"Course I will, soon as."

But he never did. Bill wasn't a visitor and in this case he didn't even send the help.

That book was writ.

When Roberts had proposed to Fiona, her family had raised huge objections. Roberts had told his own father of their view. His father, a man of few words, said, "They're right."

"What – you think I'm not good enough for her?"

"I wasn't thinking about you. As usual you've got it backwards."

Roberts was pleased, then said, "They've money."

"Ah!... Well, perhaps you have class. Now it's possible we'll get money, whereas..."

He figured he'd call on Brant, maybe even talk about Fiona. But probably not. Brant's door was open and Roberts thought "Uh-oh."

Brant was sitting on the couch watching TV. Two bananas were coming down the stairs and singing.

Roberts said, "What the hell are yah watching?"

"It's *Bananas in Pyjamas*, quite a catchy little tune."

He turned round to stare at Roberts, who said, "The door was open... I..."

"Hey, no sweat. Everybody else just walks in."

"You had a visit?"

"Yeah, a villain with a message. Next, he'll have a chat show."

Roberts moved in closer. "Are you all right? Any damage?"

"Any damage. Hmm... he wanted to boil me bollocks and I speak not metaphorically here."

"Jesus."

"Yeah."

"Can I get you anyfin'?"

Brant looked at the mug he was holding, said, "It's tea."

"Another?"

"Two sugs, Guv. It's them triangle jobs – and you know what? – they *do* taste better; like yer old Mum used to make."

Roberts went to the kitchen and marvelled at the mess. Like squatters had staged a demo there. Brant shouted, "Heat the cups."

"Yeah, right."

Once the tea was squared away, Roberts sat. "You want to tell me what's going down?"

"Bill Preston."

"Tell me you're winding me up. You haven't been sniffin' round in *his* biz... the order came from on high – hands off."

"Let 'im run riot, that it?"

"They're building a case, it takes time."

"Bollocks."

"C'mon, Tom, the softly-softly approach will bring him in finally."

"So meanwhile, we sit back and play with ourselves."

"Shit! You started pushing him!"

"A bit."

"And you got a visit. Who'd he send?"

"Fenton, last of the fuckin' Mohicans."

"The Alien. You should be flattered – means you got their attention."

"Yeah, that's what I am. Flattered."

Roberts drained his tea and wondered if he'd have another. Thing was, you always regretted it.

Brant asked, "Want 'nother brewski?"

"Love one."

They did, and sure enough it had that stewed taste which British Rail have raised to an art. A sour tang of metal and over-indulgence.

Roberts said, "You're going to leave it alone now."

"Mm... phh!"

"C'mon Tom, walk away."

Brant looked like he was seriously considering this as an option. They both knew otherwise, but as Roberts was the senior officer, he at least had to dance the charade.

Then Brant said, "I was watching a documentary on the New York cops, it was on BBC2."

"Yeah, any good?"

"When a drug dealer gets killed, the detectives say 'Condition Corrected'."

Roberts smiled in spite of himself, stood and asked, "Can we expect you at work any time, son?"

"Absolutely, soon as Regis and Kathy Lee finish."

"Like them, do you?"

"Naw, it's just I can't distinguish one cunt from the other."

Black as he's painted

When Falls had joined the force, she had near perfected a neutral accent. If the situation demanded, she could "street' with ease, or float the Brixton patois... *and* twist her vowels to blend into south-east London like a good un.

Early on she'd fallen in love with a bloke from CID. He said he adored her blackness and appeared to have no hangup of being seen with her. There were no derisory comments, as he had the "cop face." The one which says: "Fuck with me and you'll fuckin rue the day." Like that.

Finally, the time came when she had to know how he felt, and she asked, "Jeff, how do you feel about me?"

Risky, risky, risky.

He said, "Honey (sic), I really like you. And if I was going to settle down it would definitely be with you."

Yeah. Sayonara sucker.

After Roberts' departure, Brant remained in front of the TV, schemes of mayhem and destruction flicking fast through his head.

Dennis The Menace came on, an episode where the Menace was camping in the woods. A wild gorilla was loose and Dennis' father asked: "Who'll warn the gorilla?"

Brant smiled. If he'd believed in omens he'd have called it a metaphor of fine timing.

Next up was Barney. Brant said aloud, "I can't friggin' believe I'm watching an eight foot purple dinosaur with green polka dots... *singing*. And worse, *tap dancing*."

Then, as if a cartoon light bulb went on over his head, Brant said, "Wait a mo!" And knew how to proceed.

Over the past few years, he'd begun to acknowledge his Irish heritage. He'd begun to collect a motley pile of Irish paraphernalia, including ugly leprechauns, bent shillellighs, horrendous bodhrans and – yes, he still had it – a hurley.

Hurling is the Irish National game. A cross between hockey and murder. Now he pulled out the stick from beneath a mess of shamrocked T-shirts. Made from ash, it fits like a baseball bat. He gave it a trial swing and relished the *swoosh* as it sliced the air.

He shouted, "Cul agus culini for Gaillimh!"

And added, "Way to fuckin go, boyo!"

Exporting aliens

The Alien had one last look round his gaff, saw nothing he'd particularly miss. When you do hard time, it's nigh impossible to ever make a home. You get it all comfy, the screws come and move you or toss it or piss all over the floor.

Keep it simple. Keep it mobile.

He'd packed two pairs of black 501s – they were the old full-faded jobs he'd got in Kensington Market. In the days when people still spoke English in that part of London. Four Ben Sherman knock-offs and two white T-shirts. A pair of near new Bally loafers he'd found in Oxfam at Camden Lock. Did they fit like a glove? Put them on and they whispered, "Is this heaven or what?" They were.

For travel, he'd a pair of non-iron khaki chinos and a blazer. Slide one of the white T-shirts inside, you were the Gap ideal.

Casual

Smart

Hip

He thought, "Asshole!... Right."

At the airport he bought a walkman and The Travelling Willburys. It reminded him of a mellowness he might have achieved. In Duty Free there was a promotion for Malibu. Caribbean rum with coconut.

Yeah.

Plus, he kinda liked the bottle. The sales assistant said, "Boarding card?"

"We can do that."

"Cash or charge?"

He smiled – this was not a south-east London girl – and

produced a flush of crisp readies. "Just made 'em."

"I beg your pardon?"

"Hey, no need to beg, these are the jokes."

She produced a garish T-shirt. "It's free with purchases over twenty pounds."

"Tell you what, hon, you wear it – help yah to loosen up, get the bug outta yer ass."

The flight was delayed and Fenton said, "Fuck." Sat on a couch-type seat and unscrewed the Malibu.

He was about to sample when a voice said, "I sincerely hope you're not thinking of drinking that."

"What?"

He turned to see a yuppie guy of about thirty. Dressed in a spanking new Adidas tracksuit, he had a fifty quid haircut and cheap eyes. Said, "One is not permitted to open Duty-Free before departure."

Fenton put the cap back on the bottle, asked, "If I drank it – just supposing I went ahead and took a swig – what exactly is it you'd do, then?"

The guy pursed his lips. Fenton had always thought it was only an expression, but no, the guy was doing just that. Then he gave a tight smile. "Alas, one would feel it obligatory to inform someone of authority."

"Ah!"

"If every chap flouted the rules, where would we be?"

Fenton didn't think it required an answer so he said nowt. Eventually the guy pushed off and Fen tracked him with his eyes. Sooner or later, the guy had to piss, right?

Right.

"You know the law isn't for people like us."

"What is?"

"That's another thing I've been trying to figure out for years."

(Lola Lane to Bette Davis in *Marked Woman*).

As Roberts walked towards The Greyhound, a holy-roller pressed a leaflet into his hand. He glanced at it, read:

"The God We Worship Carves His Name On Our Faces."

He figured it might be true, especially as it was said that Brant had the devil's own face. The light in the pub was dark and it took a minute for his eyes to adjust. The barman asked, "What can I do for you, John?"

"Eh?"

"A drink. You want one or not?"

"Is Bill here?"

"Who's asking?"

Roberts leant over the counter, not sure he'd heard it right, then decided to go for it. "Tell him it's the *Old* Bill."

He wasn't sure but he thought he heard a malicious laugh. Bill was in his usual place and if not master of all he saw, he certainly had its attention. A novel lay opened in front of him, one of the Charlie Resnick series by John Harvey. Roberts glanced at the title – *Rough Treatment*.

Bill said, "My kind of copper."

Roberts didn't think he meant him. "Mind if I join you?"

"No, I don't mind. Get you somefin'?"

"Nice toasted sarnie I reckon, I missed breakfast."

"They do a good un here, cheese, tomato… shoot the works."

"Course."

That done, they sat in silence a bit. Their relationship went back a long way, almost the old code. When villains kept villainy internal and cops kept some other agenda. More a show of respect than any actual feel for it.

The sandwich came and Roberts got right to it. As he finished the first half Bill said, "Jeez, you did miss brekkie."

"Yeah, we had a son kill his old man – phoned it in himself."

"Funny old world, eh?"

Roberts pushed the plate away. "How's Chelsea?"

Bill had a daughter with Down's syndrome. Now seven years old, she was the true joy of his life, his one vulnerability.

"She's doing good, full o' verbals."

Thus the pleasantries, time for biz.

Roberts tried to inject hard into his voice, not too much, but there. "My sergeant got a call."

"Yeah?"

"That's Detective Sergeant Brant."

"A man of reckless inclination."

"He'll want to see the messenger."

"Ah!"

"Keep up appearances on every side, can't have some laddie shoutin' the odds in his local."

"No fear."

"Why's that then?"

"Took a trip, to America."

"Sudden."

"A mad desire to see his missus."

"I wouldn't want to have this chat again... *Bill*." It sounded like what it was – a threat.

Bill said tightly, "I'm a bit confused over yer concern for the said Sergeant."

"We've got mileage."

Bill considered then went for the cut. "You're a big hearted bloke, Mr. Roberts."

"Eh?"

"Well, if one of my lads was putting it to me missus, I'd be more than a tad miffed."

Roberts was taken aback, near lost it, but rallied. "Low shot, Bill, I'd have figured you for a more mature angle."

Bill didn't answer. Roberts stood, put some money on the table and walked away.

At the door he heard, "Hey Old Bill, Brant likes maturity. You ask down the nick – he likes 'em downright middle aged."

Falls had the golden oldies show playing. Playing loud.

Jennifer Rush with "The Power of Love."

A sucker song.

As she belted out the lyrics, Falls threw in the obligatory *Ohs... Uhs...* and hot *Ahs...* Being black helped cos she felt the music.

Reluctantly, she turned the radio off. Being hot at nine in the morning was wasted heat. She put on a light khaki Tshirt, loose and blousey. Then white needle cords, very washed, very faded. A dream to wear, like skin that didn't cling. At the dentist, she'd flicked through a copy of *Ebony* and read that needle cord was coming back.

Where had they been?

She thought: "Not this pair. One more wash and it's disintegration city."

Checking the date of the magazine, it was February '88.

Oh.

Falls felt lucky wearing these pants. Plus, she felt hip, not big time or to the point of wearing sunglasses on her hair, but a player. She was wearing a black pair of Keds. They made her feet look tiny and she wished she could wear them in bed. And might yet do so.

Opening her front door, she felt downright optimistic.

Always a bad start.

A skinhead was spraying her wall, it read:

NAZZI RULES? OK.

He was a young fifteen with badly applied tattoos, the usual Doc Martens and black combat trousers. The spraying stopped and his eyes said *run*. But even a junior skin couldn't be seen to run from a woman, especially a black one. He fingered the aerosol nervously and pushed out his chest.

Falls asked, "Who's Nazzi?"

"What, doncha know?"

"No."

"Like Gestapo and shit, ya know."

"Oh, *Nazi*."

"Yeah."

"Then you've spelt it wrong."

"Ya what?"

"One 'z'."

He looked at his handiwork, unsure as to what she meant. But hey, if confused, attack. The first rule of the urban warrior. "So what? Wogs can't read."

Falls did the very worst thing. She laughed. The boy didn't know which was next:

fight

or

flight.

Fighting required the pack and flight was... available.

Just.

To add to his turmoil, she smiled, said, "Nice chattin' to you but I've got to go."

"You gonna report me?"

"Naw."

"Don't you mind, then, me doin' yer wall?"

"Oh I mind, I just don't mind a whole lot."

As she headed off, he shouted, "Don't suppose ya got the price of a cup o' tea?"

And stunned him by giving over some coins. Before he could think he said, "Jeez, thanks a lot missus."

She said, "Why not skip the tea and buy a dictionary?"

Part of him wanted to roar, "I can spell cunt."

But he couldn't bring himself to. As he watched her go, he had his first mature observation.

"She's got some moves."

Ticket to ride

As Fenton's flight levelled out over Heathrow, he unbuckled the seat belt and stretched his legs. A flight for New York was further delayed due to a missing passenger. Later, he'd be found in the toilet booth, both halves of his torn ticket protruding from his arse.

The passenger next to Fenton reached out his hand, said, "Hi guy, I'm Skip."

Fenton said,"You're kidding!" and thought, "Lemme see... like, nine hours beside this wanker... Jesus!"

Unperturbed, the man said, "I'm in software out of Illinois. How do you guys stick that damp climate?"

Fenton straightened up, looked the man in both eyes, said, "Skip it."

Barney is a dinosaur from our imagination

Bill remembered his old man. The last time he saw him he'd gone to meet him in a pub at Stockwell. The old man was a cap in hand merchant. Sitting at the counter, the cap on the stool beside him, he was nursing a small whiskey.

Bill was on his uppers, flush with the takings from a series of post offices. He said, "Dad, what can I get you?"

"I'm drinking on the clock, son."

Bill knew about "drinking on the slate." You didn't grow up in Peckham without learning that and fast. "What?"

"I've enough for three drinks – if I make each last an hour, I'll be up to lunchtime."

"Jeez, here…" Bill laid a wedge on the bar. The old man never even glanced at it said, "Give it to yer Mother."

"Fuck her."

And his father turned, eyes flashing, hand raised. Not clenched, but definitely ready. "Don't you curse her. Mum, she had it hard."

"She legged it, didn't she?"

His father sighed. "Go away son, I can't watch right with you here."

Yeah.

When his old man was being planted, Bill was standing over the grave and threw a wrist watch in after the box.
"Clock that."

Bill was musing on this as his daughter played along the

Embankment. Every Thursday they came there, he'd sit on the bench and she'd stand watching the cruise boats.

Nothing gave her as much joy.

When he'd asked why, she said, "'Cos boats make people happy."

Argue that.

Her having Down's syndrome meant she had an extra chromosome. Or, as he now believed, *normal* people had one missing. Whatever. She meant so much to him it hurt. He'd always said: "Hope I never have a daughter," because he knew she'd make him vulnerable and that was the one thing he couldn't be. Now here she was, and left him with an Achilles heel. But it was worth it for all his worry – she lit up his life like nothing ever had. And lit it more every passing day. If having a child changes you, having a child with Down's syndrome changes you entirely.

Thus preoccupied he'd taken his eyes off his daughter. Then snapped back and turned to see her.

No Chelsea.

Heart pounding, he jumped to his feet, heard, "Hey asshole, this way."

Turned to see Brant holding the girl in his arms, dangerously close to the high bar of the Embankment.

Brant held out one hand, a furry toy hanging loose. "I got Barney for her, seems to work." Bill took a step forward and Brant cautioned, "I wouldn't do that boyo; you don't want to startle a dinosaur – they're unpredictable."

Bill tried to keep calm. Brant was one crazy fucker, built a rep on it. Looked round, not a sign of his bloody minders, asked, "What do you want, Brant?"

"Fenton."

"He's gone to San Francisco."

"Bit of a holiday, is it?"

"He's tracking his ex-wife."

Brant swung the little girl up above the railing, the dinosaur held against her. "See Bill, I want you to know how easy it is to touch you. You stay the hell away from me, everything's hunky-dory."

"I hear what you're saying."

"I wonder, Bill. I wonder if you do. Perhaps a demonstration..."

And he let go. The purple dinosaur tumbled down, its small head bounced off the bottom bar, then it rolled on the concrete before it slid into the water.

It sank quickly.

"Jesus," breathed Bill.

Brant let the girl down and nodded towards the water.

"Just wasn't getting the ratings anymore."

The girl ran to her father and wrapped her arms round him, cried, "Dad, Barney's gone."

"It's OK, sweetheart, it's OK..."

Brant started to move away, not hurried but measured. "See how it goes, Bill? Dinos are past their sell-by date."

On break the 12th lament

Falls read the words aloud.
   "Her evocation then of all that mystery allures"
   She hadn't one clue what it meant but never-no-mind – she adored it.
In the canteen with her friend Rosie, she asked, "Do you know what it means?"

"Not a clue."

"Me neither."

"But it sounds kinda, I dunno... sexy."

Falls looked down then said, "I always wished I'd have them boobs that jiggle, you know – if you're running, they'd hop up 'n' down."

Rosie, who was more than endowed, shook her head.

"No you don't... believe me."

"Men prefer big boobs."

"Men are pigs."

And they laughed. Falls got serious and said, "Rosie, I'm worried."

"What, that men are pigs?"

"No...I've been sick three mornings..."

Rosie shrieked, "Oh God, are you...?"

Falls shushed her quick, said, "Jeez, keep it down!"

"You're telling the wrong person, me girl."

And they got the serial giggles. Lots of the cops glared. If there was laughing to be done, the men would do it.

Rosie lowered her voice. "You've got to find out."

"Oh God, I can't!"

"Get one of those do-it-yourself tests from Boots."

Further speculation was halted as the duty sergeant put his head round the door and shouted: "We've got a would-be rapist shot!" A cheer went up. "Oi, that's enough of that. I need two WPCs... c'mon, snap to it."

As they headed out Falls said, "Leastways if I am I'll get decent boobs."
Rosie laughed. "You'll be jiggling more than them!"

The shooting had taken place off Camberwell Green. A man had attacked a woman in her kitchen, but she broke away and somehow managed to shoot him.

The flat was packed with cops. Falls was directed to the woman. She was sitting on a kitchen chair, her face white with shock. A loud moaning could be heard from the sitting room. Falls closed the door.

The woman asked, "Is that him?"

"I think so."

"I thought I'd killed him."

Falls patted her shoulder, asked "Like a cup o' tea love?"

"I'm sick of tea."

"Do you want to talk about what happened?"

"I was washing up and next thing I was grabbed... but I've been taking classes... in self defence. So I stomped on his instep and bit his arm."

"Good girl."

The woman was animated, into it. "He let go and I hit him with the saucepan – here." She indicated her chin. "And I heard a crack. He started roaring and I walked out to the sitting room. Got my Dad's gun and then... I shot him. I missed a few times, I think."

When everything was being wrapped, the woman touched Falls' hand. "What will they do to me?"

"Well, I think you'll get off, but I believe you should get a medal."

The man had been shot once in the upper leg. Once on the stretcher, Falls managed to get near him. He said, "The bitch tried to kill me... I'll sue..."

Falls leant over, asked in a soft voice, "Does it hurt?"

He gave a macho smile. "No, it's not so bad."

Falls shot out her hand, pounded once on the wound.

"Any better?"

Lies are the oil of social machinery

(Proust)

When Brant heard of Falls' treatment of the rapist, he was well delighted, thought: "Yer coming along, lassie."

He'd been to see the Super and been granted a period of leave. Twixt sickdays and holidays, he'd a block of time owing.

The Super, keen to be rid of him, suggested, "Might be time to consider getting out."

Brant gave a police manual smile, a mix of servility, spite and animal cunning, and said, "We'd miss you, sir."

He headed to the canteen and met Roberts en route, said, "Lemme get you a tea, Guv."

"And you'll pay for it."

"Course."

"It would be a first."

In the canteen, Brant got two Club Milks and two sweetened coffees, then said to the cashier, "Bung it on the Chief Inspector's tab."

"We don't 'ave one."

"Time to start, boyo."

Roberts couldn't get Bill's accusation out of his head, that Brant had been with his wife. He said, "I went to see Bill."

"Oh yeah."

"Tried to wind me up."

"How's that?"

"Said you'd been jumping my missus."

Brant's heart jumped, but said smoothly, "Jeez, would I be so stupid?... I mean... apart from everything, I'd like to think we were mates."

They both tasted the lie, let it roll around a bit and decided it would suffice. Not great or even satisfactory but almost sufficient... it would do.

Brant ate his Club Milk. First he nibbled the chocolate round the edge, then chomped the biscuit loudly. Roberts had a horrible picture of him nibbling his wife.

Brant gestured to the second biscuit. "Going to have it, Guv?"

Roberts wasn't, but no way could he stomach Brant eating it. "I'll get to it later." He slipped it into his pocket.

Days later, after his first radiation treatment, he'd find it congealed in his hankie, latched to his keys like a tumour.

Brant said, "I watched *The Missouri Breaks* last night."

"Yeah?"

"I love that boyo, Harry Dean Stanton. He's one of a battered outlaw gang led by Jack Nicholson. He tells a great yarn." Brant stopped and Roberts didn't say anything. A tad testy, Brant asked, "You want to hear this story or not?"

"Oh... yeah, of course."

"He says when he was a kid, he had a favourite dog. One day his father came home and found the dog with its nose in the butter, so he shot it. Later on, a guy says to Harry Dean: 'You don't like people much' – and Harry says – 'Not since the dog put his nose in the butter'."

Roberts wasn't sure how to respond and finally said lamely, "Must see that."

Brant was agitated, asked, "Don't you get it?"

"Course I do." But he didn't. Worse, they both understood that. A moment comes, a friendship can move up a notch or is lost.

The moment was lost irretrievably.

They have to get you in the end Otherwise there'd be no end to the pointlessness

(Derek Raymond)

"Yo, fool..."

This was Fenton's introduction. He'd arrived at SFIP (San Francisco International Passport) and breezed through Immigration. Manners and a British accent being a passport all their own. The official had even said, "Y'all have a good day now."

He was having one... sort of... ish.

Until:

Waiting on his luggage a black guy had shouted the above. Fenton turned, saw the guy dressed in an impoverished Mr. T style. Lots of gold bracelets, medallions, but of a distinctly tin quality.

Fenton asked, "Are you talking to me fella?"

"Whatcha think? Y'o be a fool, then I talking to you, mother fuckah."

If this had been the Oval, he'd probably have dropkicked him for exercise. Instead he smiled and got, "Wha'cha smiling fo' bro'? Yo be laughin at de brother?"

Fenton got his case, turned and said, "Get me a taxi – sorry – a *cab*... OK?"

This stopped the guy dead. While he was figuring it, Fenton

breezed past him. "Jeez, before Tuesday, OK?"

On the other side of the United States, the Band-Aiders were finding that the BIG APPLE was not exactly the good apple.

Still wearing the Farah pants, the guy said to the woman, "This place's a hole."

"Was your idea to come."

"Was not."

"Was too."

They seethed a while, then the woman said, "Let's mug some fuck and go to California."

He liked that, said, "I like that. Yeah. Let's kick the bejaysus outta a Yank."

"Yeah... and tell 'em to have a nice day."

In my last darkness there
might not be the same need
of understanding anything
so far away as the world
any more.

(Robin Cook)

Roberts was an hour early for his radiation treatment. Got
to wait three more. Eventually his time. He said, "Does it
hurt?"

"Huh?"

"The radiation, you know, during the... ahm... process..."

The technician, with a distracted air seemed to have trouble
concentrating. Roberts wanted to grab him, roar, "For fucksake,
focus!"

The guy wasn't actually wearing a walkman but he might as
well have been. Worse, he was humming... and humming
"Vienna." Not an easy task, but definitely irritating.

He said, "Imagine yer on a sun bed, topping up for yer hols."

Roberts felt this was in particular bad taste in light of his
complaint, but said nothing. It wouldn't do to antagonise the
hand on the machine.

It didn't take long. Roberts asked, "Is that it?"

"Yup, yer toast."

Roberts felt a rush of elation and wanted to hug the fuck, but
the guy was already humming a new tune. Sounded like the

Eagles' "Lying Eyes," or was it "Dancing Queen"?

Roberts said, "I'll be off then."

"Whatever."

Roberts had been a cop so long, it was difficult to surprise him. But every now and again...

Outside, three winos were sitting against the wall. All were shoeless. A pair of black shoes sat in front of them. Mid-way polished, they stood in near dignity and in reasonable condition A hand-written sign said,

FOR SALE
Only one owner.
£5 or nearest offer.
Full MOT.

He smiled from way down. One of the winos copped him, said, "Size 9, Guv?"

Reaching in his pocket, he encountered a melted Club Milk latched to his keys. Finally, he located some coins and handed them over. One of them said "God bless you, Guv."

Further along, a young woman pushed a collection box in his face, demanded, "Buy a flag."

"What's it for?"

"Racquet Club in Hampstead."

"Well that's badly needed – another sports club in bleeding Hampstead." He gave her the remains of the Club Milk.

At the Oval, to complete his trilogy of street encounters, he bought a copy of *The Big Issue*. The vendor said, "Fair cop," and Roberts wondered what it was that proclaimed him to the world as a copper. He wasn't sure he wanted to know.

Castro

The Castro in San Francisco has been called "The gayest place on earth."

Fenton was headed there. He knew it would be the centre for activists. Now that Stell, his ex-wife was with a teacher, she'd be politically active. A dormant radical, she'd blossom in the Castro.

He had the cab cruise through Market and Castro Streets.

It reminded him of Camden Lock on a pink Saturday. Same sex couples strolling openly. The cabbie turned and drove along Church, 22nd, and Duboce.

"You figger on stayin' here, buddy?"

"Naw, I just wanted to see it."

The driver checked him in the mirror, ventured, "You gotta get down here in the evenings, catch the action then."

He let the question hang in the air – *Are you gay or what?*

Fenton didn't help and kept staring out the window. He half believed he'd see her on the street. Just like that! After all the years, all the hate, there she'd be. She wasn't. He got a mental grip and said, "I've seen enough, take me to the El Drisco."

"Say again?"

Fenton consulted his guide book, nodded and said, "It's 2901 Pacific Avenue."

"Gonna cost you, buddy."

"Did I ask you for a financial opinion?"

The cabbie took another look and decided to let it slide. "You're the man."

"So they tell me."

❖

The constables had organised a knees-up in The Greyhound for Brant's departure. They had the back room and the booze was flowing. Word had got to Bill about the function so he'd relinquished his usual place. He could wait.

Sometimes, it was what he did best.

Brant was top of his shit list yet again but he wanted something major. For now, he simmered.

Brant was mid-pint and mid-story. "So, the guy had tried to pay the hooker with a stolen credit card. The pimp was kicking the bejaysus outta him and the guy's shouting: 'Be fair mate!'"

Falls arrived, and went, "Uh-oh, boys at play."

Someone shoved a drink at her and a plate of cocktail sausages. That made her smile. Brant swaggered over, said, "Memories, eh?"

She put the plate aside, thinking: "They never rose to that length!" She said, "I have a going away pressie for you."

"I'll be back."

"Of that I've no doubt." She handed him an envelope. He shook it loose and found two photos. They were from those platform machines, the quick-snap jobs that ensure you look like Myra Hindley, regardless of sex. A sheet of paper was clipped to them.

"What's this?"

"It's the Band-Aiders, the two who stabbed you and maybe killed Tone. They've gone to America."

"Nice one, Falls."

Her bleeper went and she headed for the phone. On her return, Brant hadn't moved. She said, "A fire in East Lane... and deliberate. You think it's our man?"

"Want me to come visit him with you again?"

"No Sarge, no need, you enjoy the party."

She was wrong. There was ample need for Brant. Then and later. Especially later.

Roberts arrived late at the party. Brant, his face flushed from drink, said, "We started without you."

"Oh really?" And got two mangled sausages handed to him, plus a pint of flat Guinness. "What a feast."

"Ah, we didn't forget you Guv."

Roberts let the sausages slip to the floor and said, "You're off, then."

"Yeah, I'm going via Ireland from Shannon, so I'm going up to Galway for a night. I've a distant cousin there name of Paddy Joyce."

"Related to James, no doubt."

Brant gave him a puzzled, befuddled look. "No... related to me, I said."

"Whatever. Here."

And he too produced a slip of paper. Brant said, "Jaysus, I've more notes than Rymans."

"It's the number of an American cop. He was over here on a course a few years back. He might be useful."

Brant was slipping from the booze high to a mid-plateau of surliness, just before sentimentality. "Don't need no Yank, I've got me hurley."

"Yer what?"

But a sing-song had started and Brant was moving away.

Roberts felt a bone exhaustion begin and a raging thirst. As he made his exit, he could hear Brant, loudest of all with "If you ever go across the sea to Ireland..."

When Falls had applied to the police force, she'd had to wait six months. *The Bill* was hot then and they were flooded with applications, even wannabe actresses who believed they'd be doing the method.

During that period, Falls worked in a department store. She was assigned to Customer Services and dealt with returned items. It was the ideal training for police work.

Here came the scum of the earth, the true dissatisfied. The more respectable the customer, the more brazen the lie. They'd bring back blouses, the collar soiled, lipstick on the front, creased to infinity, and claim: Never Worn!

Receipts years out of date and frequently from other stores were produced in apparent innocence. A week on this front made her a cynic for life. And of course she got the full dose of bigotry.

Like, "I demand to see someone in authority. Someone white in authority."

The up-side was Falls could spot a liar at close range. The downside, apart from insults, aggression and bile, was that she could never again return goods. No matter how pressing the urge. The girls thus employed went two ways – became immune or became traffic wardens, which amounted to the same thing.

Falls broke the cardinal rule of visiting a suspect alone. She hoped she might wrap the deal in one evening.

She was wrong.

Calling on the suspected arsonist, she was pumped with adrenalin.

For nowt.

A woman answered the door. In her early twenties, she was barefoot in shorts and Spice Girls top, said, "Yeah?"

"I'm WPC Falls and..."

The woman put up a hand, signalling *don't bother* and said, "He's not here. Dunno when he'll be back. I've no idea where he is." Said this to the tune of "Mary had a little lamb." Said it with world weariness. Like, how many times have I to repeat this shit?

Her eyes were deep blue and deeper stoned. If she'd recently touched planet earth, she hadn't much liked it. Her expression moved to:

You know I'm lying.

I know you know I'm lying.

So whatcha gonna do about it, bitch?

Not a whole lot, save: "And you are...?"

"Oprah Winfrey, can't you tell?"

Falls shook her head. "Gee, that's an amusing line. Well Oprah, I'll be back. Often. See how that helps the ratings."

The woman slammed the door and Falls figured that whatever else the woman was, intimidated wasn't part of it.

She knew if Brant had been with her, the result would be completely different. Not legal, maybe not even satisfactory, but definitely radical. And thinking of results, she had an appointment in the morning with her GP. Find out if she was pregnant /

with child / knocked up / in the family way. As the various expressions ran through her head, she felt both exhilarated and terrified.

Two feelings not unknown to the man across the street.

Standing in a doorway, he watched her walk away. When he usually got these feelings, it was immediately after he'd tossed the match to his work.

Excitement gripped him now as he wondered how the black woman would burn.

Americana

The Alien was well pleased with his hotel. The El Drisco, on Pacific Avenue is one of those open secrets. Owned and operated by the same family since the twenties; Eisenhower and Truman had made visits. It sure looked presidential – deep pile carpets, green leather banquettes, crystal chandeliers... Like that. For a moderate arm and leg it's worth getting the hillside view. The receptionist had told Fenton the guest rooms were much more reasonable; but Fenton said, "I'm only doing it one time. Best to do it right, eh?"

The receptionist agreed that this was indeed a fine method of reasoning. Back in London a similar response would have been dangerously close to taking the piss. Here it was the American way.

In his room, Fenton stretched out on the bed, thought: *One or two days to find Stell and kill her... and maybe grab a few days rest and recreation in Tijuana...* "Yeah," he said aloud. "I like the sound of that R & R..."

Fenton liked San Francisco. He was beginning to like it a whole lot. That it's very much a walking city didn't hurt, didn't hurt at all. Twixt cabs, trolley and foot, he got to Fisherman's Wharf.

The cabbie had said, "Yo buddy, a real native is a guy who's never had eats at The Wharf. You hear what I'm saying?"

The Alien hadn't quite got into the sheer *in yer face* dialogue, as if they'd known you always. He answered, "'Course I hear you... I'm not deaf."

The cabbie took a look back. "English, right?"

"How perceptive."

Unfazed. "I love the way you guys talk, like Masterpiece Theatre. Everyone talks like that in England, am I right?"

Jesus! "Yeah... except for the taxis – they shut it."

"That's like the cabs, right?"

Getting out at the Wharf, Fenton paid, and sure enough the cabbie said, "You have a good day."

"Whatever."

Fenton went straight for a bar. He was wearing thin on American goodwill. The barman welcomed him effusively.

Fenton said, "Give us a beer, OK?"

"Domestic or imported?"

"Fuck."

Fenton was the other side of three bottles of Bud. Not outta it or even floating, but feeling them, a nice buzz building. He figured he'd do three more then go buy the baseball bat.

An exaggerated English accent cut through: "I say old chap, might I trouble you for a light?"

Fenton turned. On the stool beside him was a guy in his bad sixties. Liver spots on his hands and brown shorts, top to accessorise. He had eyes that Fenton could only think of as stupid, i.e. eager, friendly and open.

Fenton shrugged. He was definitely feeling those beers. "I don't smoke."

"Actually, neither do I – I heard you order your drink and thought I'd give my skills a try. Was I convincing?"

"As what?"

"Oh yes, the English humour! I have all of Monty Python, would you like to see my Ministry of Funny Walks?"

"You're serious... Jesus!"

"You might have caught me on Seinfeld, I was the English cab driver."

Fenton was suddenly tired, the beers wilted, the show winding down. He asked, "You're an actor... act scared."

"Scared?"

"Yeah, as if I'm going to put this bottle up yer arse."

The man looked full into Fenton's face and got a hearty slap on the shoulder, with, "Hey, that's not bad, you look like you could shit yerself...I'm impressed."

After Fenton left the bar, he was entranced by the traffic lights, blinking:

WALK

DON'T WALK

No frills, yer straight command. He kinda appreciated it – reminded him of prison.

A black guy in a combat jacket was handing out pamphlets, shouting, "Yo', homies, see what de fat cats be doin' wit' yo' tax dollars!"

Fen took the booklet. "Ain't my tax dollars, mate."

"Say what, homey?"

He was about to sling it as the guy shouted, "Yo' all gots de right to know they be killin' folk."

Fenton looked at the pamphlet.

A Study of Assassination.

(A training manual written by the CIA for distribution to agents and operatives)

He said aloud, "No shit!"

And as he flicked through it, he gave intermittent "Wow's, "Jeez', and an outright, "I'll be fucked!"

Under the heading *Justification* was:

Murder is not morally justifiable. Assassination can seldom be employed with a clear conscience. Persons who are morally squeamish should not attempt it.

Fenton said: "You got that right, guys."

More: *It is desirable that the assassin be transient.*

Then: *Techniques.*

A human being may be killed in many ways...

Fenton muttered, "Oh really?"

The assassin should always be cognisant of one point – "death' must be absolutely certain.

Call it serendipity or chance, but when Fenton stopped to take his bearings he was outside a sporting goods shop.

Went in.

The music was deafening and he had to recheck it wasn't a

disco. No, a sports shop. He asked an assistant, "What's that noise?"

"It's Heavy D."

"What?"

"Waterbed Hev."

"I'm going to have to take yer word for that. Why is it so loud?"

"Most of our clientele are Afro-Americans."

"You mean black."

The assistant ignored this and asked what he could do to help. Fenton said, "I want an old style baseball bat. Not metal or some brilliant new plastic or low fat – the basic slugger. Can you do that?"

Four hundred bucks later, he could.

Lond♦n

Roberts was determined to tell his wife about the skin cancer. At the very least he'd get laid. So... so it would be a sympathy fuck, but who was counting? All the other ails:

dead bank balance

burnt car

nervous job prospects

he'd leave a bit. No need to tip the balance. He was almost looking forward to dropping his health bombshell. Move him centre stage for a few days.

A *Big Issue* vendor was sporting a spotlessly white Tshirt which declared:

70% of Prostitutes are Convent Educated.

Roberts said, "What about the other 30%?"

The vendor smiled. "They're the education." Argue that.

When he got home he checked quickly to see if his daughter was home.

Nope.

He muttered, "Thank Christ for that." Recently she'd been treating him as if he were invisible... no, scratch that –invisible and annoying.

His wife said, "You're home."

He was going to congratulate her powers of observation, but it wouldn't be a loving start. Instead: "I have something to tell you."

She hmphed and said, "Well, I certainly have something to tell *you.*"

Testily, he snapped, "Can't it wait?"

"Oh, if your daughter being pregnant isn't a priority then of course it can wait."

"Jeez… what? I mean, how…?"

"Well darling, I know it's been a while, but if you can't remember how it happens…" And she shrugged her shoulders.

He couldn't believe it. Worse, she walked off.

He thought: "Skin cancer *that*."

To roost

Stella Davis – Fenton's ex-wife – was loading her washing machine. If she could have known it was the last day of her life, she might have done the wash regardless. It's highly doubtful she'd have added fabric softener.

Her new husband was a teacher and the most stable person she'd ever met. Even his name – Jack Davis – rang of security. A no frills, no shit kinda guy. Jack was yer buddy, the sort of stand up guy who'd have a few beers and slip you a few bucks if you were hurting. When they devised the "Buddy" system, it was the likes of Jack they envisaged.

Stella didn't love him but, as they say at The Oval, she had a fondness for him. Plus, he was her Green Card, worth a whole shitpile of love and roses.

The love of her life had been The Alien. She came from a family of part time villains:

part of the time they were doing villainy
part of the time they were doing time.

So Fenton's rep was known and admired in her street. It was a mystery to her why it was described as a working class neighbourhood, as few worked. Fenton appeared glamorous and dangerous and all that other good shit that causes fatal love. The biggest hook of all, he was gentle – to, with and about her.

When she got pregnant, he got three years and she woke up. That would be the pattern. He'd be banged up or killed and she decided to start over. Then she miscarried and the loss unhinged her. Near insane with grief and rage, she'd gone to the prison. As he walked into the visiting room, she saw the macho swagger, the hard-eyed hard man and she wanted to wound him.

So, she told him. "I aborted."

And he'd gone berserk. Across the table at her and it took six guards to beat him into a stupor if not submission. Perhaps the worst horror was him never uttering a sound.

When Jack Davis showed up, she took him. She'd received one call before she left London from Bill who said, "Run... for all you're worth."

She did.

As the machine kicked into overdrive, Stella made some decaff. It was the state of low fat living. She'd been starting to talk American, eg "carbohydrated."

The washing was in mega spin and she turned on the radio, it had Star Wars speakers and come-on hyper. It was nostalgia hour and she heard Steeler's Wheel with "Stuck In The Middle With You." Oh yeah. With Gerry Rafferty in the line up, they'd been touted as Scotland's answer to Crosby, Stills and Nash, which was pushing the envelope; and then Vince Gill with "Go Rest High on that Mountain"...

As she'd boarded the plane at Heathrow, a song was playing. Elton John's homage to Princess Diana. Then and now, Stella felt the song that sang it best, that sang it heartkicked was Vince Gill.

When she heard it, she saw the photo of Di that would wound the soul of the devil himself. It shows her running in a school race at her boys' school. Her face is that of a young girl, trying and eager, and mischievous.

Full of fun.

This whole thing Stella had told to Jack and then played the Gill song.

In a rare moment of insight, he'd said, "Down those mean streets, a decent song must sometimes go."

She'd said, "That's beautiful Jack."

"No, it's Chandler pastiche."

"Oh..."

Which bridge to cross and which bridge to burn.

(Vince Gill)

Brant had to change flights at Dublin. There are no direct flights to Galway in the West of Ireland. He had contacted a long neglected cousin who said he'd meet him on arrival. Brant asked, "How will you know me?"

"Aren't you a police man?"

"Ahm... yes."

"Then I'll know you."

Brant wanted this crypticism explained but thought it best to leave it alone. Instead, he said, "So, you're Pat de Brun."

"Most of the time."

Brant concluded he was headed for a meet with a comedian or a moron. Probably both.

Brant was already confused by Ireland. At Dublin Airport the first thing he saw was a billboard, proclaiming:

"Costa l'amore per il caffe'

Unless he'd boarded the wrong flight and was now in Rome, it didn't make sense. Shouldn't they be touting tea, or jeez, at the very least, whisky?

His cousin, Pat de Brun, was smiling and Brant's old responses kicked in. "What's the joke, boyo?"

"Tis that you look bewildered."

And more bewildered he'd get. Pat said, "You'll be wantin' a drink, or, by the look of ye, the hair of the dog."

Brant let it go and followed him to the bar. A middle aged woman was tending and declared, "Isn't the weather fierce?"

Pat ignored the weather report and said, "Two large Paddies."

Brant half expected two big navvies to hop on the counter. The drinks came and Pat said, "Slainte."

"Whatever."

They took it neat, like men or idiots. It burned a hole in Brant's guts and he went, "Jesus."

"Good man, there's a drop of Irish in yah after all."

"There is now."

Brant's travel plans were:
1. London to Dublin
2. Dublin to Galway
3. Overnight stay
4. Shannon to America
So far so something.

A tape deck was playing "Search for the Hero Inside Yourself." Both men were quietly humming. Brant said, "Not very Irish is it?"

Pat finished his drink and answered, "Nothing is anymore. My name is Padraig but there's no way a Brit like yourself could pronounce it."

The drink was sufficiently potent for Brant to try. He said, "Pawdrag."

"Good on yah, that's not bad; but lest I be living on me nerves, let's stick to Pat."

Brant swallowed. "Or Paddy."

Pat de Brun was a distant cousin of Brant. Migration, emigration and sheer poor pronunciation had mutated de *Brun to Brant*. Go figure.

Brant was to find Pat a mix of pig ignorance, slyness and humour. If he'd been English, he'd be credited with irony. Apart from sporadic Christmas cards, they were strangers but neither seemed uncomfortable. Course, being half=pissed helped. Brant took out his Weights and offered. It was taken and the bar woman said, "I could do with a fag myself."

They ignored her. As Pat blew out his first smoke, he coughed and said, "Jaysus... coffin nails."

"Like 'em?"

"I do."

"Good."

Envious glances from the woman. But she didn't mind. Men and manners rarely met.

Brant said, "I better get a move on."

Pat was truly surprised, asked, "What's your hurry, where are you going?"

"Well... America... but I better check into a hotel."

Pat got red in the face... or redder; near shouted, "There'll be no hotels for the de Bruns! The missus is in Dublin for a few days so you'll be stoppin' with me."

Brant was tempted, answered, "If it's no trouble."

"But of course it's trouble, what's that ever had to do with anything?"

A point Brant felt couldn't be bettered. When the bar woman put them out, she pocketed the cigarettes.

Felicitations

Falls held her breath as the Doctor began to speak. "Well, Miz… or Miss – I never know the PC term."

And he looked at her. The expression of the misunderstood male run ragged by women's demands.

She wanted to shout, "Get on with it you moron," but said tightly, "Miz is fine."

"All right, Miz…" And he looked at his notes.

She supplied: "Falls."

"Quite so. Well, Miz Falls, you are pregnant. Three months, in fact."

She was speechless. Now that it was confirmed she felt a burst of happiness and finally said, "Good!"

If the doctor was expecting this response, he hid it well. "Ah… when there's, ahm… no *Mr.* Falls, one isn't always… pleased."

"I'm delighted."

"So I see. Of course, there are alternatives, once the initial euphoria has abated, one might wish for… other options."

She wanted to smack him in the mouth but said, "I'm keeping my baby. I am not euphoric, I am, as I said, delighted."

He waved his hand dismissively like he'd heard this nonsense a hundred times, and said, "My secretary will advise you of all the details. Good day Miz Falls." As she was leaving, he said, "I suppose one ought to say felicitations!"

"You what?"

"It's French for congratulations."

"Oh, I know what it means, doctor, but I doubt that you do… in any language."

The secretary typed out all the data and as she handed it over, said, "Pay no heed to him, he's a toss-pot."

"Aren't they all?"

A mugging we will go

"Wild, Wild Angels" by Smokie was pouring from a gay bar in the lower reaches of the East Village. A near perfect pop song, it contains all the torch a fading queen could ask for.

The Band-Aiders wanted out of New York and they wanted out now. Josie and Sean O'Brien were the names they were currently using. Their brains were so fucked from chemicals, they weren't sure of anything save their Irish nationality, but years of squatting in south-east London had added a Brixton patois to their accents. Their one surety was they wanted to hit California, and hopefully hit it fucking hard. Sunshine and cults – what could be better?

And wow, had their luck ever held out? First, they broke into Brant's flat and though he'd found and threatened them, they got him first. Next, they murdered a young cop named Tone for his new pants – a pair of smart Farahs. Beaten him to death with a nine wood, not that they were golfers. Golf clubs had replaced baseball bats as the weapon of choice for a brief time in Brixton. Things had returned to normal, though, and bats had now reemerged for walloping the bejaysus outta punters.

That Brant would come a-hunting never occurred to them.

Josie had once been pretty, a colleen near most, blue eyes, pert nose and dirty blonde hair.

But that was well fucked now.

Brixton

squats

sheer viciousness

and of course, every chemical known to boogie had wrought havoc.

Her hair was now a peroxided yellow, as once touted by Robbie Williams. Her skin was a riot of spots and sores. Crack cocaine had given her the perpetual sniffles.

And if *she* was rough, Sean was gone entirely like Sid Vicious... two years after his death.

They'd got into America as part of a punk band entourage. They'd then ripped off the band and pawned the instruments. Now broke, they resorted to what they were – urban predators. Prey was best from gay bars.

But their amazing run of luck was about to dive.

From the shadows, they watched a group of men on the sidewalk. Obviously stewed, they were saying goodbyes with laughter and hugs.

Sean said, "I'd kill for a cuppa tea."

"Yeah, gis two sugars wif mine, yah cunt!"

They giggled.

Sean watched as one man broke away, and muttered, "I'll give him a good kickin', I will."

"Yeah, we'll do the bollocks!" Josie felt the rush of adrenalin, the juice kicking into override. She gasped, "*Crank it up muttah-fuckah!*" Even the boys in the hood would have admired her accent, not to mention her sentiments.

As the man moved off alone, Sean said, "Show-time!"

Julian Asche was thirty-five years old. A successful architect, it had taken him a long time to accept his homosexuality. But New York is a good place to come out. To hear the women tell it, try finding a guy who *wasn't*:

gay
married
lying
OR
all three.

As a seasoned Manhattanite, he'd paid his city dues. Found a way to cohabit with cockroaches, ignore the homeless and be mugged twice. He'd declared, "Enough already!" and, "This shit ain't happening to me again!"

Thus, he was left with two choices:

1. Leave

2. Get a gun

He got a gun. Finally, he was a fully fledged commuter. Right down to his Reeboks and war stories. To complete the picture he ate sushi and liked Ingmar Bergman.

The weapon was a Glock. It came to prominence as a terrorist accessory – made mostly of plastic, it got through metal detectors without a bleep. Lightweight, easy to carry and conceal; even the cops took to it. As their no-mention second gun, the true back-up.

Now Josie nudged Sean, said, "Rock 'n' roll."

He grunted, added, "Roadkill."

They moved.

Their tried and tested method was for Josie to approach the vic and whine, "Gis a few quid, mate." Sean then did the biz from the rear. Simple, deadly, effective. It got them Brant, the young copper and one per cent of the Borough of Lambeth. Why change? Indeed.

But Sean did.

Perhaps it was the Rolex. Julian was wearing the Real McCoy. A present from his first lover. So genuine, it looked fake.

Josie did her part, only altering the currency to suit the geography. The song now coming from the bar was Lou Reed's "Perfect Day." If fate had a sense of the dramatic, "Walk On The Wild Side" would have been apt; but it has an agenda, which rarely includes humour, and almost never timing.

The dance began as before. Josie strode up to Julian, whining, "Gis a few bucks, Mistah."

Sean, if not exactly the pale rider, pulled rear. For one hilarious moment, Josie's accent confused Julian. He thought she was saying, "Gis a few fucks Mistah." He was about to tell her that – "Gee sister, you sure dialled the wrong number," when Sean, breaking their routine, went for the Rolex like a magpie on speed. Grabbed for the wrist.

Julian shrugged him off, crying, "What the…?" Then reached for the Glock in the small of his back. He was a child of the movies, he knew you carried it *above* yer bum. Thus explaining perhaps "*cover yer ass.*" A homophobic would interpret it differently and more crudely. Whatever…

The gun was out, held two handed in Sean's direction.

Sean, who'd expected a drunken vic, was enraged, shouted, "Gimme the watch, yah bollocks!"

Julian shot him in the face. Then the Glock swivelled to Josie and she dropped to her knees, pleading, "Aw, don't kill me mistah, he made me do it, I swear."

The CIA responses are hard to beat, that is:

Catholic

Irish

Appalling.

Julian felt the power, the deer kicking the leopard in the nuts. Adrenalined to a new dimension, he asked, "Tell me, bitch. Tell me why I shouldn't off you. You deserve to be wasted. Go on – *beg* me. Beg me not to squeeze the trigger."

She begged.

Full frontal

When Brant came too, he'd no idea where he was. What he did know was he was in pain. Ferocious pain. He stirred and realised he was half on the floor, half on the sofa. Still half in the bag. Gradually, it came back:

Ireland
Pat's house
Pub crawling
Quay Street
Dancing Irish jigs.

Dancing! He prayed – "Please Jesus let me be wrong about the dancing!"

He wasn't.

He was clad in his grey Y-fronts. Not grey by choice but cos he'd washed them white with a blue shirt. Sweat cascaded off his face and he said, "I'm dying."

The door opened and Pat breezed in bearing two steaming mugs of tea. "Howyah, you're wanted on the phone."

"What?"

"An English fella and by the sound of him a policeman. Likes giving orders."

"Roberts?"

"That's the lad."

Lawrence Block in *Even the Wicked*:
"It's a terrible thing,' he said, "when a man develops a taste for killing."
"You have a taste for it."
"I have found joy in it," he allowed. "It's like the drink, you

know. It stirs the blood and quickens the heart. Before you know it, you're dancing."
"That's an interesting way to put it."

Brant gulped the tea and roared, "Jesus, I'm scalded."
"Aye, it's hot as Protestants."
But something else, something that kicked. Pat smiled, said, "That'll be the hair of the dog."
"Bloody Rottweiler, was it?"
A moment, as the liquid fought his insides, near lost and Brant got ready to puke. Then lo, it crashed through and began to spread ease.
Pat said, "Yah better get to the phone."
Brant said, "OK," and thought: "Ye Gods, I do feel better."
Roberts said, "Got you outta bed, did I?"
"Naw, I was playing golf, had to rush in from the ninth."
"Eh?"
Brant scratched his balls, couldn't believe how better by the minute he was feeling. Maybe he'd never leave Ireland.
Roberts said, "I had a hell of a job to locate you."
"I'm undercover."
"Under the weather, it sounds like. You're not pissed now are you? I mean it's not even ten in the morning."
"Haven't touched a drop."
Roberts took a deep breath. He had startling news and he wanted to be startling with it. The plan was to meander, dawdle, and plain procrastinate.
Get to it e...v...e...n...t...u...a...l...l...y.
Like that.
What he said was, "They've caught the Band-Aiders."
"Jesus!"
"Yeah."
Brant wanted to roar:
Where?
When?
Who?
Why?
But instead repeated, "Jesus!"

Roberts figured that counted as "startled." so he said, "The deadly duo tried to mug a punter in New York, but guess what?"

Brant had no idea. "I've no idea."

"He was carrying a nine millimetre Glock. He must have been influenced by the subway vigilante... what's his name?"

Brant didn't know or care. The healer in the tea had done its job. In fact, he wanted more, more of everything, especially information. "He killed them?"

"Naw, just the man – the girl begged for her life, and by the time the cops arrived she coughed up everything – stabbing you, killing young Tone... I think she even copped to Lord Lucan and Shergar."

Brant laughed, this was great. He was truly delighted and thought: "I love Ireland!" Which, if not logical, was definitely sincere.

Roberts said, "Now, here's the thing. She's waived extradition and wants to come back. There's one condition though."

"What? She wants a seat on Concorde or to meet Michael Jackson?"

"Worse. She wants *you* to bring her back."

Brant couldn't believe it, shouted, "No, Fuck that! I've plans... I'm going to San Francisco... that's where Fenton is."

Pat heard the shouting and did the Irish thing. He got Brant more tea and a cigarette. Roberts felt it was time to pull rank and kick some subordinate butt. "Sergeant, it's not a request. Those on high aren't asking you politely for a favour. It's an order."

"Shite!"

"That too, but look on the bright side – they're springing for it, won't cost you nowt."

Brant took a hefty slug of the tea, better and bitter, but he wanted to sulk and as he crushed out the cigarette, he whined, "It's not about the money."

Roberts laughed out loud. "Gimme an Irish break. With you it's always about the money."

It was... *always*.

Brant could hear the shower running and... yes, the sound of Pat singing. Sure enough – "Search for the Hero Inside Yourself."

Roberts said, "Go to the local Garda station in Galway and all the details will be faxed."

"Fucked, more like. They'll welcome an English policeman, I suppose."

Roberts was beginning to enjoy this. How often did you get to mess Brant about? His skin cancer was itching like a Hare Krishna and he felt the dehydration beginning. "Why were they called Band-Aiders? Musicians, were they?"

Brant snorted. "The only tune they played was from an Oliver Stone film. The guy had a cut on his face and said, "When I'm cut, she bleeds." They both sported snazzy bandages.

Cute, eh?"

Roberts couldn't resist it. "They'll need some bloody bandage to cover what's left of his face." He wanted suddenly to share his pain about his illness. Brant was the nearest to a friend he had. He began, "I've been in some pain, Sergeant."

"Jaysus, who hasn't boyo?"

And he hung up.

Trying to recapture the great moments of the past.

Pat had prepared breakfast as if Man United were expected.
Two plates on the table with:
    sausages (2)
eggs (2)
tomatoes (2.5)
fried bread (1)
black pudding (1)
The plates were ample enough for a labour party manifesto.
Brant said, "Holy shit!"
Pat was already tucking in. "Get that inside you, man, soak up the booze."
Odd thing was, Brant was hungry. He sat down, lifted a fork and indicated the black pudding. "What kind of accident is that?"
"Would you prefer white?"
"White what... eh?"
"It's pudding, the Pope loves it."
Brant pushed it aside, speared a sausage and said, "Which tells me what exactly? I mean, the *Pope*... is that a recommendation or a warning?"
Pat laughed, had a wedge of fried bread, said, "The Pope's a grand maneen."
"A what?"
"Man-een. In Ireland we put 'een' onto names to make them smaller. By diminishing, we make them accessible. It can be affectionate or mocking, sometimes both."
Brant found the sausage was good, said, "This sausage is good... or rather, sausageen."

"Now you have it. Pour us a drop of tea like a good man."

They demolished the food and sat back belching. Brant said, "Lemme get my cigarettes."

"Don't stir... try an Irish lad."

He shoved across a green packet with "MAJOR" in white letters on the front. Brant had to ask. "Not connected to the bould John I suppose?"

It took a moment to register, then "Be-god no, these have balls."

Pat produced a worn Zippo lighter and fired them up. Brant drew deep and near asphyxiated. "What the fuck?"

"Mighty, eh?"

"Jesus, now I know what they make that pudding from."

Pat excused himself, saying, "Gum a less school." At least that's how it sounded to Brant. It means simply, "Excuse me."

Like that.

He came back with the inevitable tea pot and a large white sweater. "This ganzy is for you. It's an Aran jumper and if you treat it right, it will outlive yer boss."

Brant never, like *never* got presents; thus he was confused, embarrassed and delighted. "That's... Jesus... I mean... it's so generous."

"Tis."

After Brant had showered, he donned a pair of faded Levis and then the Aran. He loved it, the fit was like poetry. He said, "I'll never take it off." Put on a pair of tested Reeboks and he was Action Man.

Pat eyed him carefully, then said, "Be-god, you're like a Yank."

"Is that good?"

"Mostly! Mind you, it can also mean, 'Give us a tenner'."

Pat volunteered to show him how to find the Gardai. Before leaving, he asked, "Who's Meyer Meyer?"

Brant was stunned. "What?"

"Meyer Meyer. You were roaring the name like a banshee last night."

Brant sat down. "Gimme one of those coffin nails." He lit it and felt the tremor in his hand. "A time back, I had a dog named

Meyer Meyer... after a character by Ed McBain."

Pat didn't have a clue as to who McBain was, but he was Irish and learnt from the cradle not to stop a story with minor quibbles, so said nowt.

Brant was into it, back there, his eyes holding the nine yard stare. "We had a psycho loose called the Umpire, he was killing the English Cricket Team."

If Pat had a comment on this, he didn't make it.

"I called him names on TV and he burned my dog, just lit him all to blazes, the dirty bastard." Brant stopped, afraid his voice would crack.

Pat asked, "When you caught him, you beat the bejaysus outta him?"

"No." Very quiet.

"You didn't?" Puzzled.

"We didn't catch him."

"Pat was truly amazed, muttered, "I see." But he didn't.

Brant physically shook himself as if doing so would do the same to his mind. It didn't. "I loved that dog – he was the mangiest thing you ever saw." Is it possible to have a smile in a voice? Brant had it now. "I used to take him for walks up Clapham Common, thought we'd score some women."

"Did ye?"

"Naw, I was the ugly mutt." And they both laughed. The tension was easing down, beginning to leak away.

Pat, being Irish, was attuned to loss, pain and bittersweet melancholia. "Lemme tell you a story and then we'll talk no more of sad things. Tell me, did you ever hear of the word "bronach"?"

"Bron... what?"

"You didn't. OK, it's the Gaelic for sadness, but be-god, it's more than that, it's a wound in the very soul." Pat paused to light a cigarette and sip some tea. He knew all about timing. "Our eldest lad, Sean... a wild devil. He'd build a nest in yer ear and charge you rent. I loved him more than sunlight. When he was eight he caught a fever and died. There isn't a day goes by I don't talk to him. I miss him every minute I take breath. Worst, odd times I forget him, but I don't beat myself up for that – it's life... in all its granite hardness. The point I'm hoping to make – and eventually I'll get there – is life is terrible, and the trick is not to let it make you a terror. Now, there's an end to it. C'mon, I'll bring you to the Garda."

Brant couldn't decide if it was the wisest thing he'd ever heard or just a crock. As he rose he decided he'd probably never be sure; said, "Pat, you're a maneen."

Cast(e)

Falls was in the canteen eating dry toast, no butter; drinking milk, no taste. Rosie, her friend, breezed in. As much as you can breeze if your arm's in a sling and your face is bruised.

"Hiya Rosie."

"Hiya hon."

Like that.

Rosie said, "Yer wondering what happened to me, right?"

"Ahm…"

"Falls – look at me! I'm a wreck."

Falls put the toast down. "Oh my God! What have you been doing, girl?"

"Didn't you know I was on holiday? Jack and I've been saving to go to India, and we went."

Falls couldn't resist. "And they didn't like you much."

Rosie reached over, touched her friend's arm. "Wake up and smell the coffee honey, OK? I've always wanted to go to Goa cos of the old hippy trail and those beaches…" Her arms and face were tan; what's known as a cowboy tan – the body stays soap-white.

Falls tried to focus. "Did you have a terrific time?"

"I can't believe you don't know! We flew to Delhi and got a cab at the airport. The taxis, they drive like the worst night in Brixton… sorry… I mean…"

Falls being black, didn't take it personally. When white Londoners reached for adjectives, metaphors for chaos, they used Brixton. If hardly commendable, it was vague times comprehensible. So it goes, an urban blues.

Rosie, less fired, said, "A transit van hit us, driven by

Australians. The taxi driver was killed and I was unconscious for five days."

Falls, for an instant, near forgot the child she carried and touched her friend's face. "Ah darlin', are you all right?"

"I am now. They pinned my arm, and do you know, they don't bind broken ribs? They hurt like a son-of-a-bitch. Jack, the rascal…"

"Rascal? Have you been watching Sean Bean in Sharpe?"

Rosie laughed. She had a reach down in your gut laugh with her heart – and screw the face lines. "He never got a scratch. I had concussion and the doctor said, 'Your head won't be right for some time.' The wanker. I'm a WPC – my head will never be right! But enough about me, fascinating though it is. What's with you, girl? You're distant."

Falls let her eyes drop to her stomach and edged a tiny smile lit with mischief, wonder, delight.

Rosie stared, eyes like saucers, and then, "*Oh my word*! Oh… oh… oh!" And jumped up, trying to hug Falls with her good arm. The various cops in the canteen turned round, their look proclaiming: *What the hell is it with these women*?

Rosie touched her head, looked bashful as well as bashed, said, "Sorry,' then whispered, "Congratulations… oh, I love you."

So all in all, it has to be said, Rosie sure received the news a whole lot better than the doctor. Trying to keep her voice low, she asked, "How does it feel? Are you having morning sickness?"

"No, nothing; but I think I'm going to get my wish."

"What?"

"Huge boobs."

Their attempts to stifle the laughter only made it worse. Then Falls told her of the arsonist and how Brant was away. "Don't you see? It's my chance. If I catch the guy I'll get promotion and be able to afford the baby bills."

Rosie shook her head. "Don't be crazy, the guy could be dangerous."

"He's all mouth, no danger."

But she was wrong.

The duty sergeant appeared, said, "If comedy hour is over, I have a case that requires female tact." Which told them exactly zero.

On the way, Falls said "If it's a girl, I'll call her Rosie."

An elderly woman was sitting in the interview room. Falls sat and checked the charge sheet. The woman leant over, peered and said, "Good Lord, you're a black person!"

Falls geared up. "Is that a problem?"

"Oh no dear. It's nice they're letting you people in. I love Ray Charles."

The charge sheet was, as usual, unhelpful, so Falls said, "Mrs. Clark... Why don't you tell me in your own words what happened?"

She was happy to.

"I was sitting in Kennington Park – so nice there – and a man walked up to me and just stood there. So I said, 'Can I help you?' and he said, 'Look, look – I'm exposing myself!' He sounded very agitated."

"Was he?"

"Was he what, my dear?"

"Flashing... I mean, did he... take out his privates?"

"His John Thomas, you mean? I said – 'You'll have to move closer as my eyesight is poorly'."

Falls tried to contain herself, asked, "What happened?"

"He moved closer and I stabbed it with my Papermate. That's when he started screaming and the police came."

Falls wanted to hug her. "Would you like some tea?"

"Oh yes please, dear. Two sugars and a Marietta. Just one, I don't want to spoil my dinner." As Falls stood up, the woman added, "You're so kind, dear. Might I ask you a question?"

"Of course."

"Your tribe, the coloureds – why do they wear those caps the wrong way round?"

"It's fashion, Ma'am."

"I think it's rather silly, but... if it keeps you happy..."

Then she added, "I hate to be a nuisance but will I be able to get my Papermate back?"

The American way

The Alien walked into a Seattle coffee place. He'd always wanted to say, "Hi, how you doin'? My usual… half-caff decaff triple Grande caramel cappuccino with wings…"
And of course, the chick'd say, "You're British, right?"
Instead he said, "Espresso please." Got that and a wedge of Danish, went to check the phone directory.
Bingo .
There she was, under the name Bill had given him. Jotted down the address and bit into the Danish. Too sweet. The sports bag was at his feet and the shape of the bat was barely discernible.

Stella, the Alien's ex-wife, had snuck a cigarette. In America now they don't frown on smoking they just out and out shoot you. Her last trip home, unbeknownst to Jack, she'd bought a carton. Rothmans. In all their deadly glory. They'd come with a free T-shirt which shrunk in the wash. Size XL, a few more spins, it would fit a person.
Cracking the cellophane, she opened a fresh pack and lit up with the kitchen matches.
Ah… Dinner was in the oven and she'd have time to use air fresheners before Jack got home, add a splash of Patchouli.
Who's smoking?
Her mother regularly sent Liptons tea and the South London Press. Jack would say, "You English and your tea!"
Loving it, loving she was English and stressed it. When Jack got home she made him a dry martini, very dry and with two olives. It was a ritual. He'd say, "Two?"
"Cos I love you too much."

Like that.

Then, "Something smells good."

"It's your favourite."

"Meatloaf?"

"You betcha."

When he'd first asked for it, she thought he meant "Bat Out Of Hell." She was still English then. Now she had to work at it. It wasn't that she ever felt American, but she had the moves.

Then he hugged her and she got a blast of Tommy Hilfiger. For one fleeting moment she remembered Brut and Fenton, but let it slide, not even linger… just keep on moving, like a song you can't recall.

So that was how it was when Jack got home. After the meatloaf, the doorbell went and Jack moved to answer.

A voice said, "Package for Stella."

As he opened the door, he was still half turned to her, a huge smile making him look boyish. Fenton said, "One!"

And slammed the bat into Jack's stomach.

"Two!"

Upended it and drove the top against Jack's chin, the bone splintering into his brain.

"Chun!"

And he beamed at Stella, asked, "Howzat, darlin'?"

She was holding the dinner plates, too frozen to drop them.

Fenton kicked the door shut.

"Guess Who's Coming to Dinner…? And blacker than you can begin to imagine."

"We were somewhere around Barstow on the edge of the desert when the drugs began to take hold."

(Opening lines of 'Fear and Loathing in Las Vegas')

"You're a cute hoor,' said Pat.
'What?"
'The way you handled them cops at the station. Jaysus, they were eating outta yer hand. When did a policeman ever offer a cup o' tea? I'll never get over the bate of that ... As I said, *glic*."

"Click?"

"It's the same as cute hoor, but slyer."

"But it's a compliment?"

"Is it?"

They were in The Quays pub on Quay Street. Lest you forgot, it said so above the door. Pat had told Brant that Brad Pitt had been in and that, "No more than Geldof, he was a bit shy of the soap 'n' water."

Brant exclaimed, "You can be one vicious bastard, you know!"

"Ary, I'm only coddin'."

Brant had come to Ireland for all sorts of reasons and curiosity was probably the best he'd articulated. Getting laid never came into it, but lo and behold, he was about to. They were drinking slow bottles of Guinness and Pat said, "There's a wan over there has an eye for you."

"What?"

"She has a mighty chest on her and a bit o' mileage, but for all that..."

"What are you on about?"

Pat moved back from the bar, gave Brant the full Irish appraisal, then said, "I'd say you're a holy terror for the women." And then he stepped over to the woman, had a few words and returned. "She thanks you kindly and a glass of sweet sherry would be grand."

Brant took a look, not bad at all. A touch of the Margo Kidders... well, OK – Margo's mother, but in prime shape. Course, the fact that she fancied Brant gave her bonus points all over the shop.

As Brant ordered, Pat said, "Tis what Connemara men do for penance."

Yet again, Brant had no idea what he meant and dreaded trotting out, "What?" yet again. What he'd do, he'd get two small cards printed,

1. Yellow

2. Red

Write in small letters "What?" on the first, then "WOT?" on the second. Jaysus, they'd think he was deaf. Scratch that. So he said, "What?" And threw in, "Excuse me?" for colour.

"Connamara men, they drink sherry as penance." The sherry was placed on the counter and Pat said, "Well, go on, man, she can hardly whistle for it."

He brought it over, said wittily, "Hi."

She laughed and said, "I can see I'm not going to get a word in edgeways."

"What?"

"Sit down there, you big lump – I'm Sheila."

A while later, Pat came over, said, "I've lost me friggin' lighter."

"The Zippo?"

"Aye, blast it to hell, it had '1968' on the front."

Sheila said, "Ask St Anthony."

And Brant said, "Ask him what?"

Pat and Sheila loved that.

"I have long known that it is part of God's plan for me to spend a little time with each of the most stupid people on earth."

(Bill Bryson)

When Falls met the snitch in the place he'd selected, she remembered a description from Karon Hall's "Dark Debts."
*"If you didn't have a gun going in,
they'd provide one at the door."*
At the rear of the Cricketers, near The Oval, it was a dive. Falls arrived first and nodded to the barman. A big guy with
red shirt
red jeans
red face
She resisted the impulse to say, "Hi, Red."
He said, "You sure you got the right place?"
"I'm sure."
"We don't get many chicks, is all."
Chicks!
"Well I'm sure once the word on the ambiance gets out, you'll be stampeded."
Leigh came in, immediately looked angry and pushed her to a back table demanding, "Why were you talking to him?"

"It's against the rules?"

"You're not supposed to draw attention."

"Well, there was me 'n' him – did you expect me to hide?"

"People talk, you know."

He then jumped up, had a word with Red and came back with two glasses of a greenish tint, pushed one at her, said, "It's lime cordial."

"And I'm supposed to do what with it exactly?"

Leigh was getting seriously upset. "It's for cover."

"Oh I see, we lurk behind them."

"Mr. Brant was never like this."

Falls felt they'd done enough pleasantries, time to jerk the leash. "You're a stupid person, but that's OK. What I need is fairly simple. You tell me and I'm outta here. There's an arsonist, recent of Croydon, and I need to know where he hangs."

Leigh began moving his glass, the colour didn't improve. "You don't want to be messing with that piece of work."

Falls sighed then clamped her hand on his knee. "Where?"

"You're not playing by the rules, it has to be drawn out."

She pinched hard and he jumped. She hissed, "Leigh, there are no rules... *where?*"

"The snooker hall at The Elephant. Thinks he's Paul Newman in *The Hustler*... He's there all day."

She released her grip, rooted in her bag and then palmed him a twenty. He was indignant. "This is supposed to buy me what? It wouldn't pay me light bill for a week!"

Now she smiled, said, "I dunno, you could always hop up there, get us a few more of these drinks... oh, sorry – *disguises.*"

On her way out, she ignored Red and it seemed to be what he expected.

'The best the white world offered was not enough ecstasy for me. Not enough life, joy, kicks, darkness, music; not enough night.

(Jack Kerouac)

As Fenton tried not to run, he felt the adrenalin build to a point beyond mere rush. His mind roared: *You did it, you did it, you bloody did it!* — Then his arm was grabbed. Disbelief pounded through his body.

Caught! Already!

And turned to see a black guy, something familiar about him, the guy saying, "Yo, fool, you owes me a buck and a half!"

"What?"

"The other day, dude. I be giving yo' sorry ass a pamphlet 'bout dem CIA…"

"Oh right… I thought it was free."

"Where yo' been, dude? Ain't nothing free on the street."

Fenton reached for change, handed over a five. The guy wailin', "What cha thinkin', like I'm gonna make change?"

Fenton laughed, said, "Keep it, knock yourself out mate."

"Yo dissin' me man, dat what cha thinkin'?"

Now the Alien laughed out loud, asked, "Is that what they're calling it? Dissin'. What will you guys think of next?"

Close call

The Super had summoned Roberts.

These meetings were never warm; it usually meant a bollocking. When Roberts came in the Super was dunking a biscuit in tea, said, "Hurry up, man, shut the door."

He didn't offer tea or a seat; got to it. "I've had a call from across the water."

Roberts wondered – from Ireland? ... Brant? ... No. Even he couldn't be that drunk – and said neutrally, "Yes, sir?"

"From Noo Yawk."

Pronounced it thus to demonstrate he could be a kidder or simply an asshole; continued: "There's been a murder – two murders – in San Francisco."

Roberts wanted to say, *only two?*

The Super brushed crumbs from his splendid uniform, noisily finished the tea. Can tea be chewed? He was giving it a good try.

"Reason they called us is the woman is a Londoner." He consulted his notes. "A Stella Davis, but originally Stella Fenton. Ring any bells?"

"Uh-oh."

"Is that an answer?"

"Reg Fenton, 'The Alien'... Did he use a bat?"

The Super was impressed, if a tiny bit miffed. Had to check the notes, then confirmed, "By Jove, you're right. They expect he'll head for home, so notify the airport chappies."

"Yes, sir... How did they know it was him...I mean... so quickly?"

"He left the bat."

❖

Falls was a touch surprised that Leigh's information was correct. She went to the snooker hall in the late afternoon. Round three, in there.

She'd been expecting a tide of looks and remarks.

Lone woman in the last male bastion.

Lone black woman.

But there wasn't, as the place was empty.

It was situated above a tailors with the sign "ESPOKE."

It puzzled her till she realised the "B' had done a Burton, so to speak. Up two flights of badly lit stairs and she knew, in her condition, it wouldn't be long till she wouldn't be able to do that. The baby was beyond joy, it was up there in the realm of ecstasy.

A toilet flushed and out emerged the suspect. He didn't seem surprised to see her, asked, "Fancy a quick game?"

"Some other time."

He was smiling. "On yer lonesome this trip?"

"Am I going to need help?" She kept it light – let's all stay nice 'n' loose – relaxed, even.

He spread both hands on the table, said, "No way, babe."

Falls moved a little closer. "If you could spare me a short time to come to the station, clear up a small situation."

He was running his hand idly over the snooker balls, exclaimed, "What? Now?"

"If you wouldn't mind, it would be a great help."

Now he had the black ball in his right hand, fisting it. "You speak well for a nigger, almost like a white bitch. That what you want, to be white, eh?"

She took a deep breath.

He shouted, "Black in right centre pocket!" and flung it in her face. Caught her full impact on the forehead and she staggered back, felt her knees buckle. Then he was dragging her by the hair, saying, "I keep telling them, put-out-the-trash."

And he dragged her through the doors, paused, then slung her, roaring, "Black on the way out!"

"Yada Yada" or some such

(Melanie)

B rant was sitting in the GBC – a restaurant right in the centre of Galway. It had the mentality and kudos of a transport caff, ie lashings of food, *good* food, cheap and friendly. Brant liked it a lot.

A waitress asked, "By yourself, are you?"

"What?… Oh yeah… No. My cousin's coming."

And caught himself, thought — "What am I doing? Jeez, I'll be telling her the size of me socks next."

He gave a mortified smile and she said, "T'will be nice for ye."

Argue that.

Brant recalled the night before and Sheila. She had a small flat along the canal, and no sooner there, than she hopped on him. Gave him a ferocious ride. He'd lain back on the floor, exclaimed, "Wow, that was Trojan!"

"You mean you're done?"

"Jeez, woman – one shag and I'm for a kip!"

She'd given him an elbow in the ribs, said, "Ary go on outta that! Two squirts and you're calling it a night! I'll get you roaring till the small hours."

She did and did, till them small hours. Finally he cried, "I'll give you serious money not to touch me dick again."

She laughed out loud and climbed on. When finally she'd nodded off, he'd limped to his feet and hobbled outta there as fast as he could manage.

Pat arrived in. "There you are… Sheila's looking for you."

When he saw Brant's alarm, he added, "Only coddin'yah! Isn't she a gas woman?"

"Gas?"

"She's a widow, you know."

"Christ, I believe it! I'm only surprised she's at large."

Pat shouted across the tables, "Mary, bring us a nice cuppa tea and a currant bun, there's a good girl." He sat down, said, "So you'll be going now?"

"Yeah, the local boyos are running me down to Shannon... see me off the premises, I suppose."

Pat looked sad. "I'll be sorry to see you go."

Brant reached in his pocket, produced a fancy bag with "WILLIAM FALLER" written in gold across it. "I didn't know what else to get."

Pat opened it fast and out fell a shining gold Zippo. He turned it over, the inscription: "PATEEN." Pat said, "I'll mind it like laughter."

"In south-east London we're not big on hugs or that, so I'll..."

Pat got up and grabbed him in a hug that Sheila would have admired, said, "You be careful now, young Brant."

On the way to Shannon, Brant reached for a cigarette and lit it carefully with a Zippo. His thumb near covered the "1968."

Each angel is terrible

(Rilke)

Heading for Mexico and aiming specifically for Acapulco was a tropical depression. Very soon, as it gathered force, ferocity and momentum, it would be upgraded to hurricane status and, of course, named. As usual, despite the feminists, it would be called Pauline. They were sure going to remember her.

The Mexican President, Ernesto Zedillo, was assured it was not a serious storm and yes, go ahead with his trip to Germany.

He did.

It would be a tragedy of huge human loss but also bring about a major political crisis.

Fenton boarded his plane and felt he should at the very least have one of those hats so beloved of British resorts, with the logo: "KISS ME QUICK."

He remembered an awful Elvis movie with Ann-Margret or one of those Elvis-type movie women... lush bodied... Now what the hell is the name of it?

As the seat belt sign flashed in preparation for take off, it came to him and he muttered, "Yeah, *Fun in Acapulco*."

Now try to get the damn tune out of his head as it lodged there like stale muesli.

Brown is the new Black

(London fashion guide)

Nancy D'Agostino didn't want her assignment. Like sure, nurse-maiding some English bobby. He'd probably smoke a pipe and wear one of those London Fog godawful raincoats. She looked like Nancy Allen. Remember her? A real cutesy who'd been married to John Carpenter before he lost the run of himself and donated his talent to Wes Craven. She'd been at her prettiest in *Carrie* and her slide began post *Philadelphia Experience*.

Nancy held a placard — "D S BRANT LONDON" — and figured even an English cop could detect this.

As Brant emerged from Immigration, he spotted Nancy and saw her smile. He thought, "Jaysus, I'm going to get a jump on this side of the Atlantic too."

He was wearing the Aran sweater and blue serge trousers. Nancy thought, "Oh my God, one of the Clancy Brothers."

Brant looked round. "Jaysus, it's busy."

Nancy produced her ID. "I'm Sergeant D'Agostini with the New York City Police Department. I'll be your guide and facilitator while you're here."

"Facil-i-what?"

She took a deep breath and before she could speak, he slapped her thigh, said, "Lighten up, woman. Where's the bar?" And he produced a cigarette.

She put out her hands. "This is a NO SMOKING zone."

He eyeballed her and cranked a worn Zippo. "Are we cops or what?"

"Well yes, but…"

"So fuck 'em. Let's get a brewski."

The bar at JFK is a good intro to New York. The staff are

rude

busy

hostile.

After Brant and Nancy had waited for five minutes, she said, "Let's head into Manhattan, we'll get you a cold one at your hotel."

Brant gave his satanic smile, roared, "Hey Elvis, before Labour Day, all right?"

Nancy had to suppress a smile – he sounded so Noo Yawk. The barman asked, "What'll it be?"

"Coupla beers."

"Domestic or imported?"

Brant leant on the counter, still smiling, right in the guy's face. "Forgot the floss eh? … Bring us two strong beers and bring 'em now."

Nancy asked, "This isn't your first time in America?"

He reached in his pocket, showed her a small book:

Asshole's Guide To New York – How To Be Ruder Than The Natives.

(By P Catherine Kennedy)

Brant asked, "You want a glass?" And he chugged his from the bottle.

She said, "Like I have a choice."

He ruffled her carefully brushed hair. "I think you're my kinda chick."

Children's program

Deep down in an area beyond definition, Falls struggled to wake. She knew consciousness was reachable but she couldn't make the first step. The plans for the baby, how they'd curl up together on the couch and watch TV... If she could recall the names of the Teletubbies, she felt she'd crash to the surface. Tinky-Winky. OK. Got one. That's the blue colour, and... Dipsy. Oh yeah. On a roll now. The yellow one – what was the little shit's name? ... Da-da? ... No, but close. ... La-La! Yes! Just the fourth to go. The small red fella... with the simplest name of all. She was that near and then it began to slip. With stark terror she forgot what she was trying to remember, saw a black meteorite come hurtling and tried to shout...

Dougal... Magic Roun...

And her mind shut down.

A radio was playing softly in the hospital ward. Rosie prayed that Falls couldn't hear the particular song now playing – Toni Braxton with Kenny G – "An Angel Broke My Heart."

Jesus.

She sat by her friend's side holding her hand. The nurse came, did nurse-like things like fluffing the pillow, checking her watch, sighing.

Rosie asked, "Will she wake up?"

"You'd have to speak to her doctor."

"What can I do?"

"Talk to her."

"Can she hear me? ... Or have I to speak to her doctor?"

The nurse gave her trained smile, alight with:
understanding
tolerance
and the tiniest hint of contempt .
"Just chat like you would ordinarily."
After the nurse left, Rosie muttered, "Cow," then cleared her throat self-consciously, as if she were recording. Hesitantly she began, "So hon... Good grief, I nearly asked how you were."
She glanced round to check if her faux pas had been clocked, then, "Where was I? ... I never got to tell you about my trip to Goa. Oh yeah, Jack was always on about the sanitation and he couldn't see any evidence of pipes. Me? ... All I need to know is it works, like pur-leeze, spare me the mechanics. But then someone said, "Notice all the pigs?" They were everywhere and very well fed." (Rosie gave a small shriek) — You've guessed it! Isn't it too awful? I'll never eat a bacon butty again."
Then Rosie felt a pang of hunger. She was on yet another diet, the "T" model.
T for torture.
She could murder an obscenely over-buttered thick wedge of toast, coat the lot in marmalade and eat it without dignity so the juice ran down her chin ... and she'd wash the lot down with sugared tea.
Ah!
Yet again she felt tears for Falls, for herself, for carbohydrated freedom. Then she straightened her back, said, "Hon, I have a confession to make. I'd never have told you, but I fancied the pants off yer fella. Not that I'd ever have... you know, but he sure had something. That cute bum... but it was those staring eyes. I thought he could see into my soul. Isn't that daft? He made me feel so exposed I had to look away."
Falls stirred and Rosie jumped. But it was only a reflex and she settled back into the void. Rosie continued to hold her hand.

Roberts was beginning to wear out a space in front of the Super's desk. As usual, he was getting a bollocking. The Super tore into him about the usual fuck ups, then asked, "What's the story on the ducks?"

For an insane moment, Roberts thought he said, "What's the story on the ducks," and wondered if the radiation was softening his brain. He answered, "Excuse me?"

"The ducks in Hyde Park, some nutter beheaded five of them."

Roberts was sore tempted to try, "Not our side of the pond,' but went with, "How is it our concern, sir?"

"How? I'll tell you flamin' how... the heads were put through the letter box of the Chief Constable at his place in Old Town Clapham. What do you say to that?"

Again the demons urged – "*Duck!*" – but without waiting for a reply, the Super was thundering further. "As for the WPC... Forbes..."

"Falls, sir."

"Eh?"

"Her name, sir, it's Falls."

"Don't get impertinent laddie. Do we have any hope of apprehending them or have they joined the migration to America?"

Roberts thought that was quite witty and probably true but he said, "We're following a definite line of inquiry."

The Super was out of his chair, shouting, "In other words, we haven't the foggiest."

But Roberts did have a definite lead. Following the oldest police hunch of all, he got back to the beginning. Roberts had checked with Croydon CID. Sure enough the suspect had bolted for home. That anyone would flee to Croydon was a measure of how desperate he was. The buzz had hit the station that his whereabouts were known. Eager constables flocked to Roberts hoping to be part of the team. He was having none of it. Outside the station, a Volvo was waiting, engine turning, door open. Roberts peered in. "You're keen, I'll give you that."

The driver, a blond haired man in his twenties smiled, asked, "Croydon?"

Roberts got in. "What's yer name sonny?"

"McDonald, Guv."

"Oh wonderful, a bloody Scot. Spare me the Billy Connolly shite, OK?"

McDonald put the car in gear, asked blankly, "Billy who?"

"Good lad, you'll go far."

Elgin Lane is that rarity in this part of London. It's got trees and grass verges and a large Greek presence. No connection to them marbles.

McDonald parked and Roberts said, "Number nine."

They got out and walked casually to the house. A line of bells, reading: Zacharopolous/ Ohrtanopolous Yoganopolous.

Like that.

Except for one blank bell, indicating the ground floor. Roberts said, "Use all yer police training and guess which one is our man."

The door was ajar and in they went, scrutinised the ground floor flat. Roberts said, "Tut tut, no dead bolt, just yer basic Yale... what do you weigh, son?"

"Weigh?"

"It's not a difficult question."

"Fourteen stone."

"Well son, the door won't come to us."

"Oh."

"Right."

McDonald braced himself against the far wall and before he launched, a young woman came down the stairs, gave Roberts a dazzling smile and said, "Kalimera."

Roberts answered,"Whatever," and after she left, added, "The Greeks have a word for it all right... OK son, are you going to hang about all day?"

He wasn't and took the whole jam of the door in his onslaught.

Roberts gave a low whistle. "What are they feeding them?" And followed in.

The police piled down a small corridor, which translates as Sweeney tactics. Roar like bulls, pound them boots, and put the shite crossways in all and sundry.

The suspect was crashed out on a double bed, entangled in a sheet. He was arse naked. A dense cloud of "hash-over' near made him invisible. Despite the noise, he didn't stir.

Roberts asked, "What is that smell?"

"Dope, sir."

"And there's the biggest dope of all. Go get a jug of cold water – *very* cold water."

"Yes, sir."

McDonald returned with a large basin, it made a clinking sound. "On the rocks."

"Perfect, the Chief Constable will be looking over his shoulder."

McDonald already knew that. "Shall I?"

"Give it yer best, lad."

McDonald swung the basin in a wide arc and on the upward tilt, he let the contents fly.

Whoosh!

A ferocious roar came from the bed and the suspect leapt up, crying, "What's happening, man?"

Roberts said, "Wakey, wakey,' and nodded to McDonald. He moved quickly and catching the sus by the hair, flipped him over and handcuffed him, hands behind the back. He considered, then open handed he gave the sus an almighty slap on the arse.

Roberts gave a low laugh and the sus tilted his head round. If he was cowed, he wasn't showing it. "Hey, where's the black cunt – ain't she doing house calls no more?"

McDonald raised his hand but Roberts signalled no. Emboldened, the sus taunted, "What is this anyway? I haven't got a TV licence... that it?"

Roberts glanced at the TV, then casually tipped it over. "No TV either. OK... let's go."

McDonald dragged the sus to his feet, wrapped a blanket round him and pushed him forward.

The sus shouted, "Ey! Lemme get the Tamogotchi!"

Roberts was puzzled. "You want a takeaway now?"

McDonald stifled a laugh. "It's a toy, sir, a cyber pet."

The sus looked at McDonald almost warmly as if he'd found an ally, said, "Yeah mate, I'm going for the record. I've kept it alive for twenty days already."

Roberts asked, "Where is it?"

The sus was animated now. "Under the pillow, man, you got

to keep it near – it gets lonely."

Roberts looked at McDonald, said, "Well, Constable, you know what to do."

McDonald got the pet and glanced briefly at it. The sus said, "Give it here, dude."

McDonald dropped it, then lifted his foot and crushed it with his heel.

A howl of anguish went up.

Roberts felt he might have found a replacement for Brant.

"One of the most disturbing facts that
came out in the Eichman trial was that
a psychiatrist examined him and
pronounced him perfectly sane. We
equate sanity with a sense of justice,
with humanness, with the capacity to
love and understand people. We rely on
the sane people of the world. And now
it begins to dawn on us that it is
precisely the sane ones who are the
most dangerous."

Thomas Merton.

Fenton liked Mexico. Well, he liked Acapulco in so far as it was hot and sleazy. And boy was it hot, was it ever? From early morning that heat just rolled up and smacked you in the face.

A sucker punch.

He was staying at El Acapulco and, wow, how did they come up with that? El?

Lounging by the pool, he signalled a waiter.

"Si, Senor?"

This was great, like being in a John Wayne movie. Fenton had, like tops, ten Spanish words and decided to spend a few now.

Tried: "Donde esta la Rio Grande?"

"Senor?"

"Just pulling yer chain mate." He held up two fingers and said, "Dos Don Equis."

"Si, Senor."

Fenton stretched and then read what he'd so far composed.

SILHOUETTES
So Sharp the budding hope – a flicker
lone your face
this night a past remember
can you some the dread took on
this silhouetted this justified alone...

That's it. That's what he had.

Once he'd heard David Bowie interviewed. What the spider-man did was, write all the lines down, then cut them up with a scissors and let 'em scatter on the floor. Then he'd pick them up haphazardly and that'd be the shape.

The beers came, silver tray 'n' all. The waiter was about to pour when Fenton shouted, "Jeez, Jose, don't do that! Yah friggin wet-back, don't yah know shit, yah spic bastard?"

Fenton had seen the change from glasses to bottles. No one used a glass no more. Just took that beer by the neck, chugged it cool.

Posing.

Oh sure, but what the fuck – he could nod towards cool. Plus, he really liked the way the moisture drops slid down the bottle, like pity.

He looked at the waiter who was standing perplexed and said, "Yo, Jose, get with the game, vamoos caballero," and laughed. He was having a high old time. The waiter, whose name was Gomez, went back to the bar and said, "That animal needs taming."

If you'd leant on the precise translation, you'd get the exact sense of "gringo" to suggest "Alien."

Hurricane Pauline was building, moving closer.

My kind of town

(Ol' Blue Eyes)

Nancy D'Agostino had arranged accommodation in Kips Bay on East 33rd for Brant. He looked at her. "Run the name by me again."

"East 33rd?"

"Jaysus... the other bit."

"Oh... Kips Bay."

"Screw that babe, I'm for The Village."

"But it's been arranged by the Department."

Brant gave her his full smile, said, "Fuck 'em, eh? I want to stay in a 'Y' in The Village."

She looked for an exit on the ramp and thought, "Could be worse – he might have had a hard-on for The Bronx, and then what?"

Brant watched her drive and asked, "This is an automatic?"

"Yes."

"Stick-shift?"

"What?"

"Four wheel drive?"

She glanced at him and he slapped her knee. "Just winding yah up, babe."

Gritting her teeth, she said, "I'm a sergeant in Homicide... do you have any idea of what it takes to make detective, to get my shield?"

Brant said, "It takes a babe... am I right?"

The Band-Aider, Josie O'Brien as she was now officially identified, was being held in the psycho ward. "Why?" asked Brant.

Nancy gave the department answer. "Suicide watch."

Brant gave an ugly snort. "She kills other people – not a snow-ball's chance of her hurting herself."

Nancy agreed but continued, "She saw her boyfriend shot in the face and had to beg for her own life... she could slip into depression."

Brant shook his head, then asked, "So... can I see her?"

Incarceration had suited Josie. Being off the streets, a bath, nutrition, had transformed her. Her dirty blond hair was now shining and looked high-lighted. The previously scabbed, worn face was now scrubbed clean and her eyes had a sparkle.

As Brant prepared to enter the room, he turned to Nancy. "Where are you going?"

"I'm to be present. It's..."

"Department Regulations. Christ, will yah learn a new tune? Look, I'll buy yah dinner if yah fuck off for ten minutes."

Nancy, who thought she'd gotten some sort of handle on Brant, asked, "Ever hear of Popeye Doyle?"

"Nope."

"That figures. Get it straight, I'm with you all the way."

Brant decided to roll with it, said, "Yah dirty article."

When Brant walked into the room, Josie appeared almost shy. On their previous meeting, her partner had sunk a knife in Brant's back. She said, "Hiya."

He didn't answer, took the chair on the other side of the table. The hospital guard gave Nancy an expectant look, like, *what's going down?*

She had no idea.

Brant reached in his pocket and everybody jumped. He took out his Weights and Zippo, placed them on the table.

The guard said, "This is a NO SMOKING ZONE," as if noticing him for the first time.

Brant gave him a brief glance. "Fuck off."

Nancy signalled to the guard – "Cool it." He tried.

Brant tapped the cigs. "Want one?"

"Oh, yes please."

He shook two free and Josie took one. As he cranked the Zippo, he seized her wrist, the flame in her face, asked,

"Why'd ya kill the young copper?"

If Josie was spooked, she stifled it. "Gis a cup o' tea, cunt."

Brant let her go and asked, "What's she on?"

Nancy looked to the guard, "The methadone program."

Brant shrugged, asked Josie, "Why'd you want to go back?"

"I'm homesick."

He laughed out loud and she added, "I'm going to be in a mini-series, maybe Winona Ryder will play me. I'd let Brad Pitt play Sean."

Brant played along, "Gonna be famous, that it?"

"I've got an agent."

"You've got a hell of an imagination. You're going to Holloway, not Hollywood. The only stars you'll see are when the bull dykes ram yer head against the bars."

Josie looked to Nancy, panic writ large. "Tell him to shut his mouth!"

Brant stood up. "When can I have her?"

Nancy consulted the paperwork. "She's waived all extradition, so the day after tomorrow, I guess."

Brant looked at Josie. "How's that, eh? Wanna take a ride with me?"

Josie was pulling it back, spat, "I've ridden worse."

He was delighted. "I believe you... do I ever!"

Back in the squad room, Nancy checked her desk for messages.

Brant asked, "Can I use the phone?"

"Sure."

It took a time but eventually he was connected to Roberts. The squad room fell silent as Brant's London accent rang loud and entrancing. To them, he sounded *sooo* English.

"Guv, that you?"

"Yes."

"It's Brant, I'm in New York."

"And like it, do you?"

"I met with the Band-Aider, she's a piece of work."

"Any problems?"

"Naw. What news of The Alien?"

Roberts knew he had to proceed carefully. He hedged, and as he did, a radio kicked into loud, sudden life with "Don't Blame It On Me" by Stevie Nicks. Nancy went to turn it down.

Roberts said, "Fenton's ex-wife has been murdered."

Deep intake of breath, then Brant said, "He bloody dun it... jeez!"

"Well, he's long gone, vanished without trace."

"Yeah."

"Falls went after that arsonist."

"On her lonesome?"

"I'm afraid so."

"Is she OK?"

Time to lie... "Yes."

A moment as Brant tasted the answer, decided it could suffice, then asked, "Did you get the fuck?"

To the assembled detectives it sounded like — "Did yah get the fok?" — and they loved it. In cop bars all over Manhattan, it had a brief shelf-life as the catch-phrase of the moment.

Roberts decided to play it a little humble and answered, "We got him."

"Who, exactly?"

"Ahm... McDonald."

Brant gave a bitter laugh. "You'll get the credit, I suppose?"

Refute that.

Before Roberts knew how to answer, Brant said, "Well, some of us have a job to do."

And rang off.

Nancy took Brant to Choc Full O' Nuts. She asked for: "Double decaffeinated latte," and looked to Brant.

He said, "Jaysus, I'd settle for a coffee."

The waitress and Nancy exchanged a look that read: "*English... right!*" At least he hadn't asked for tea.

Brant reached for his best Hollywood accent, said, "I'll need your shield and weapon."

"What?"

"Gis a look."

Suspicious, she took out the blue and gold shield.

He said, "It looks like tin."

"It is tin."

"All we have is a warrant card... it doesn't quite have the same effect. Show me your weapon." This with a leer.

She exclaimed, "I can't figure you!"

"Don't bother. So, what are you carrying? Some dinky .22 with a mother of pearl handle?" The coffee came and Brant stared at the double latte. "Looks like cappuccino with an inflated ego."

She took a sip, went, "*Mmmmm...* I carry a .38."

Brant had moved on, asked, "What's yer full name?"

"Jesus H. Christ, you jump all over the place. It's D'Agostino."

He tasted the word then asked, "Are you connected?"

"You're kidding."

"What are ye calling it now... mob ... family ... crime syndicate?"

Nancy shook her head. The man was beyond help. She tried for a total shift, said, "I have a list here, look... it's the places you'll probably want to see."

The list:

Empire State

UN Building

Chrysler Building

Statue of Liberty

Macys.

He looked at it. "What's this shit?"

"It's the sights."

"Spare me the tourist crap. I want to see the Dakota building and the Chelsea Hotel."

"Why?"

"Where John Lennon lived and then where Sid and Nancy crashed. Plus, Bob Dylan wrote "Sad-Eyed of the Lowlands" in the Chelsea."

Nancy was intrigued. "Did you know they used the Dakota in *Rosemary's Baby*?"

"Who gives a fuck?"

Nancy followed after him trying not to feel crushed, when he suddenly turned. "You know what the best sight would be?"

"I have no idea."

"You... without a stitch on."

Nancy D'Agostino's husband had been killed in an auto smash.

His bad luck.

Nancy had survived. She called that her bad luck.

The sole passion of Brant's life had been his Ed McBain collection. He'd had the early green Penguin editions at 2/6 a throw. On through the author's outings as Evan Hunter and the Matthew Hope series. Of the nigh eighty titles produced by McBain, he had close to the full collection.

For some reason, the police procedures struck a chord with Brant. As if the boys of the 87th came closest to what in his heart he believed a cop should be. When Nancy asked him, "Is there *anything* you value?" he nearly told her.

But the Band-Aiders – Josie and Sean O'Brien – had broken into Brant's flat, trashed it and his book collection. Thus had begun his pursuit of them which ended in the death of a young policeman and Brant's own narrow escape.

It crossed Brant's mind that the whole story might get him a sympathetic fuck, but he decided to forego the telling.

For his last night in New York, Nancy had taken him to the restaurant on top of the World Trade Centre. On the elevator up, he'd bitched about the SMOKE FREE ZONE As they were seated, Nancy said, "Some view, huh?"

"Better through a nicotine haze."

Nancy ordered seafood chowder and Brant ordered steak. Rare and bleeding.

Nancy said, "That man you bumped into on the way in... it was Ed McBain."

She couldn't believe his reaction, as if he'd had a prod in the ass. "What? Are you serious? ... Oh *shit*! ... Is he gone?"

Like that.

When he finally calmed, he shook his head, muttering, "Ed McBain... Jesus!"

Nancy took a sip of her Tom Collins. "It was him or Elmore

Leonard... I always get them crime writers confused."

Brant was beyond comment; took out his Weights, lit one and exhaled: "*Ah...*"

Naturally, the Maitre d' came scurrying over but Nancy flashed the tin. He wasn't impressed. "There are rules."

Brant smiled and said, "Hey pal, want to step outside and discuss procedure?"

He didn't.

After, they stood outside and Nancy wondered *what now?* Brant flagged a cab and held the door for her. Yet again, he'd taken her off balance. Manners were the very last thing she'd anticipated. He said to the cabbie, "Take the lady home,' and they were peeling rubber. She looked back through the window to wave, or... But Brant was staring up at the World Trade.

Applicant

Bill was interviewing killers. Well, would-be or wannabe ones. As usual, he held court in the end section of The Greyhound. Situated at The Oval, it's a bar that restores pride in the business, and for as long as Bill had been kingpin in south-east London, he'd treated it as his office.

What to look for in a potential hit man.

1. Patience
2. Cool
3. Absolute ruthlessness

A hard man who'd never have to shout the odds. You didn't ask about his rep, it had already reached you. Word was out that Fenton, The Alien, had lost it or gone to the US. Which amounted to the same thing if you clubbed in Clapham. (No, not night discos but crash-yer-skull clubs.)

Bill had already seen four guys. All young and all bananas. They wanted to be on the front page of the tabloids. Trainee psychos and apprentice sociopaths. They'd call attention. Sipping from a Ballygowan, Bill said to one of his minders, "I miss the old days."

"Guv?"

"Get the motor, we'll call it a day."

"Call it what, Guv?"

He sighed. With the Russian villains making in-roads, maybe it was time to head for the Costa and listen to Phil Collins albums. Or album. Seeing how he simply recorded the same one each time.

The minder said, "Guv, there's one other bloke."

"Yeah?"

"That's him by the cider pump."

Bill saw a guy in his early twenties, leather jacket, faded jeans, trainers. The urban uniform. There were half a million right outside the door. Nothing to distinguish him, which was a huge plus.

Bill said, "Send him over."

The guy moved easily, no wasted energy.

Bill nodded, said, "Take a stool."

"Yes, sir."

Another plus. The last time Bill had heard "sir" was in an Elvis interview. He offered a drink, got, "No, sir."

"Shit," thought Bill. "This kid could *surprise* a bloke to death." He asked, "You got a name, son?"

"Collie. It's Collie, sir."

"What, cos you like dogs, is it?" And got to see the kid's eyes. Dark eyes that were ever so slightly out of alignment. They gave the sense of relief that you weren't their focus. Nor would you ever want to be.

Now the kid smiled, almost shyly. "Something that happened when I was young."

Bill smiled, like the kid had to be all of twenty three. "Tell me." Not a request.

"Our neighbour had a dog; every time you passed he threw himself against the gate. People got a fright regular as clockwork. Like, one minute there wasn't a sign of him, then as you passed, he'd jump snarling and barking." Bill didn't comment, so the kid continued. "The dog got off on it."

"What?"

"Yes, he got his jollies from it." He pronounced the word "yollies." giving it a resonance of distance and disease.

Bill had to ask – "How did you know that?"

Now the kid gave a shrug, said, "I looked into his eyes."

"Oh."

"Yeah, before I strangled him, I took a good look."

Bill decided to ask the important question. "What is it you want, son?"

"To work for you, sir."

"And what do you want, to be famous, get yourself a rep?"

Now the kid looked irritated, said, "I'm not stupid, sir."

"Done time, 'ave you?"

"Once. I won't be going back."

Bill believed him. "OK... I'll give you a trial." Now he reached in his jacket, took out a black and white photo, pushed it across the table. "Know him?"

"No, sir."

It showed Brant, resplendent in his Aran sweater as he boarded a flight. His face to the camera, he looked like he hadn't a care in the world. Bill stared at it for a while then, back to biz, said, "That's Detective Sergeant Brant. Due back from America any day." The kid waited. "Your predecessor, The Alien, was supposed to put some pressure on the man, persuade him to drop his interest in me. But... he fucked it up. And Brant not only *didn't* lose interest, he paid me a visit." Bill's face was bright red. Famous for his cool, he was close to losing it. "What I want is to hit him where it hurts. Not *him* – too much attention if he's damaged personally. But if something he cared for got nobbled..." He stopped, asked, "Do you follow me, son?"

"Yes, sir. Damage where he'll feel it."

"That's it. Think you can handle it?"

"Yes, sir."

Bill reached again in his pocket, took out a thin wedge. It had the glow of fifties. He nudged it across the table. "To get you started; a bit of walking round money."

The kid didn't touch it. "I haven't earned it yet."

"That's what you think."

Something in the way
she moves

Falls finally crashed through the surface and immediately wished she hadn't. As soon as she opened her eyes she knew the baby was gone.

Then the event of the pool hall returned and her whole body shook. She knew if she called, a gaggle of help would arrive. Instead, she cried silently... and as the tears coursed down her face she remembered the fourth Teletubby.

Po.

The very name raised her to new heights of anguish. Finally, she stirred and sat up. Looking down to the IV, she tore it from her arm and pulled the needle from the monitor. A wave of nausea engulfed her, but she weathered it. Got her feet on the floor and felt the room heave.

A nurse came rushing. "What on earth are you doing?"

Falls slowly raised her head and tried to focus. She gave a sad bitter laugh, answered, "Now, isn't that a good question?"

At almost the same time, an impromptu party had begun in the police canteen. Roberts was being toasted with beer and cider.

The duty sergeant raised a glass. "Let's hear it for DI Roberts... hip, hip!"

Roberts acknowledged the toast and then indicated McDonald. "I had help."

More cheers. More booze.

The Super dropped in for a moment, gave Roberts a gruff nod.

"Well done, laddie." Which was rich, him being five years younger. As these events go, it was tame – muted, even – due to Falls still being in hospital.

The duty sergeant, by way of conversation, said to Roberts, "You'll 'ave heard about the new Mickey Finn the buggers are using?"

He hadn't, said, "I haven't."

"Aye, they meet a young girl in the pub or a club and buy her a drink, slip Rohypnol into it and the poor lass blacks out. Comes to next day after five of them have raped her."

"Jesus!"

"Aye, that too."

Roberts wondered if anything like that had happened with his daughter. Fear and rage crept along his spine. Finishing a pale ale, he resolved to turn everything round. He'd go home, say to the missus, "Listen honey, let's have a fresh start. I have skin cancer, I'm skint too (a little humour), and let's talk about our daughter. Who banged her up?" It would need work but it was nearly there. He had the drive home to polish it...

With his career now having a shot of adrenalin, he felt down-right optimistic. Parked the car and stood for a moment outside his house, thought: "OK, we're mortgaged to the bloody hilt but we've still got it. Hell, *I've* still got it."

Thus emboldened, he went in, shouted, "Yo... I'm home."

No answer.

Never-no-mind – he'd grab a bite from the kitchen and begin the new life. He began to hum the truly horrendous "Begin The Beguine." He hummed mainly cos he didn't know the words. Opened the fridge. It was bare, like, completely empty, save for a note taped to a sorry lump of cheese. He read:

"WE'VE GONE TO MY MOTHER'S. THAT'S IF YOU EVER GET HOME TO NOTICE'.

That was it.

He held on to the handle of the fridge, then muttered, "Now, that's one cold note."

Montezuma's Revenge

The Alien admired his growing tan, thought: *Yah handsome
devil!*

The thing about foreign holidays was you could do all the
asshole things you'd always ridiculed. Such as:

1. Wear Bermudas
2. Perch shades on yer hair
3. Carry a bum bag

Reg Fenton was many things – ruthless, determined, and
uncompromising. What he had never been was given to flights of
fancy. He had no truck with superstitions, omens, any of that. He
believed in what was in front of him. Sitting at the bar, he was
drinking tequila with all the trimmings. Salt on the hand, slices of
lemon and sure, it gave the rush. He suspected all the ritual was a
crock, but what the hell. He said originally.... "When in Mex!"

A tape was playing Dire Straits' "Ticket to Heaven." a song
that proves, yeah, them guys did have something. Glancing out
the window, he saw Stella and dropped his glass. The waiter, startled: "Que pasa?"

Fenton looked at him, then back to the window, she was gone.
He moved to the waiter, grabbed his arm, shouted, "Did you see
her...? Jesus H. Christ... it was her!"

"No comprende, Senor!"

Fenton let him go, tried to rein in his emotions, then staggered
over to a table and sat heavily. The waiter approached, nervous as
a rat. "Senor would like something?"

"Yeah, get outta my face, arsewipe... no... hey... get me a
tequila. Shit, bring the whole bottle."

As the waiter got this from the bar, he put his finger to his forehead, made circular motions, whispered, "Mucho loco."

The barman nodded. Tourists, gringos, Americanos... he'd seen all their shit.

I have a need

Demian in "Exorcist III'

Collie was euphoric. He felt the wedge of cash in his hip pocket and thought: *I'm on my way... To step right into the big time.* But he'd need to get heeled, get a shooter. On the Isle of Wight, he'd celled with a Yardie, one of the Jamaican gangs who terrorised North London. His name was Jamal. Out now, he kept a low profile and kept it in Brixton; the busy end of Railton Road. He had the bottom half of a terraced house. Upstairs was a fortune teller. Collie could smell the weed halfway down the street. He knocked three times like the horrendous song from the seventies.

A white woman answered, aged about thirty. Her eyes were lost, but she had an attitude. "What?"

"Tell Jamal it's Collie."

A black arm reached out and pulled her aside. Jamal, bare chested, gave a golden tooth grin. "Me mon!"

Which is like "Hi' ... sorta.

He gave Collie a hug and then they did the series of high-fives and palm slapping.

Buddy stuff.

Inside, Dubstar were laying down a cloud and Jamal said, "Yo bitch, y'all git some tea fo' my bro." He gave another illuminating smile. "She from rich white folk."

"Yeah?"

"Yeah, de bitch be into Marxism and Jamal be in ho ass and trust fund."

"How'd you find her?"

"She be sellin' de *Big Issue*... I bought de lot, bought ho back mo crib. That be Tuesday... what day is dis, mon?"

"Ahm... Tuesday."

Jamal looked perplexed, then said, "Must be some other Tuesday. So, bro, wanna *Big Issue*?"

And they laughed together. Just two bros, hanging in the hood.

The woman brought mint tea in glasses and four cakes on a brass tray. Jamal said, "De tea be Julep like de cats in Marrakesh and de cakes be hash brownies... mo hash than cake... yo cool?"

He was.

In addition, Jamal rolled the Camberwell Carrot made famous by *Withnail And I*. Jamal had an added ingredient: he lightly sprinkled angel dust on the paper. It didn't quite blast yer head off but it sure put you in orbit.

As Collie felt the countdown to oblivion he forced himself to concentrate on biz. "I need something."

"Sure, mon, whatcha be needin'?"

"A shooter."

"My mon, I no do dat sheet no mo."

Collie waited, skipped his turn on the tote, nibbled on a cake. Finally, Jamal said, "Less I gives mo own piece... mah personal protection. How dat be?"

"I'd hate to leave you... defenceless."

Big Jamal grin. "Sheet, I git by somehows." He stood up, said, "Gis a mo."

"Sure."

The woman hunched down on the floor, lotus style. Collie could see her knickers, and more, he could see she saw. Then she raised a brownie to her mouth began to nibble...

gnaw ... gnaw ... gnaw.

She asked, "See something you like?"

"Nope."

"Are you queer?"

The dust was popping along his brain and tiny colours were exploding on the edge of his vision. He didn't answer, tried to focus on the brightness. In Stephen King's novel *It,* the clown says, "Come into my bright lights." Then it shows rotten razored teeth. Collie looked at the woman, half expecting her to do likewise.

The trance was broken by the return of Jamal. He carried an oil clothed bundle, sat and unravelled it. A gleaming gun slid onto the table. Collie whistled. "A bloody cannon."

Jamal gave the big grin. "It's a Ruger six speed, see what's on de barrel there?"

It read "Magnum."

Jamal put a closed fist down alongside the gun, said, "Here de icing on de cake!" And opened his hand. Six dum dum bullets rolled out. "They puts a fat hole in de target."

"How much?" Jamal held up five fingers. Collie shook his head. For the next ten minutes they haggled, giggled, fingered. Eventually, they settled on three. The dope had kicked in and with full ferocity. It took Collie ages to count out the price, but finally it got done.

The woman glared at them. If dope is meant to mellow you, no one had told her. And she was sufficiently out of it not to disguise her aversion. Collie looked at her, then laid a five spot on the pile. "Buy sweets for the child." Set them off again.

Jamal pulled his zipper down, said, "Git some o dis mama." She didn't move so he added, "I ain't *axin* you, bitch." He picked up the Ruger, put a dum dum in.

Collie said, "Hey Jam... don't handle *my* weapon!"

They were off again, huge hilarity. Just ebony and ivory crackin' up, having a walk on the wild side. The woman approached, hunkered down and took Jamal in her mouth. Collie closed his eyes. This he didn't need to see. Loud groans followed.

"*Sheeet, arghh... fuck it...*"

When Collie opened his eyes, Jamal said, "I need a cigarette."

The woman was wiping her mouth, a brightness in her eyes as if to say: *Top that.*

Collie got to his feet, said, or tried to say: "Time to rock 'n'roll."

Jamal asked, "Yo bro, ya wans a BJ?"

Collie looked at the woman who was now smirking.

"Thanks, but I already ate."

Jamal's laughter followed him out into the street.

Collie had tucked the gun in the waistband of his jeans. At the back, of course.

Fist

"How d'ya feel about blood sports?"

McDonald was taken aback by Roberts' question. He'd earned some kudos, he didn't want to blow them. "You mean like coursing, fox hunting?"

"No, I mean pugilism."

"Ahm..."

"It's bare fisted boxing, like Harry S. Corbett, Diamond Jim... There's a bout at The Elephant tonight."

"And we're going to bust 'em?"

Roberts laughed, said "There'll be over two hundred punters gathered. Hard asses. We're going to have a wager."

"But Guv – isn't it illegal?"

"Course it is, why d'ya think it's exciting?"

As Roberts predicted, there were at least two hundred gathered. All men, and as per, the very air bristled with unspoken aggression and excitement. The "bout" was to take place at the sheltered car park to the rear of the Elephant.

When they got there, Roberts said, "Back in a mo."

McDonald was wearing a black leather jacket and jeans, felt he smelt of cop.

A punter said, "Wanna drink, John?"

And offered a flask.

"Sure." Best to blend. He took a swig and near choked, felt molten lava run down his throat, burning all in its path. He gasped, asked, "*What... was... that?*"

"Surg and chicken soup." Surg as in surgical spirits. The infamous White Lady of south-east London drinking schools. He could only hope to fuck that the guy was kidding.

When Roberts returned, he collided with a young guy.

There was a moment it hung there, then Roberts said, "Excuse me." And Collie nodded.

The fighters emerged to a mix of cheers, catcalls, whistles.

Roberts said, "The big guy, he's from Liverpool and evens favourite. The other is a London boy."

Both men were bare-chested, wearing only shorts and trainers. No frills. The London boy was runtish but he had a wiry look. In contrast, the Liverpudlian was a brick shithouse. His muscles had muscle and he exuded confidence.

Roberts said, "Best get yer wager on."

"What?"

"Don't tell me you're not going to have a go."

"Oh... right... ahm."

"See the guy in the black suit? He's the bookie."

"OK... how much... I mean... would five be enough?"

Roberts scoffed, "Don't be so Scottish... have a decent go. I've already dun Liverpool, so you take 'the boy'."

"But he's the underdog."

"All the better. Hurry up, now."

A bell sounded and the bout began. Each round was approximately five minutes but it wasn't rigid – the third round lasted ten.

McDonald had grown up in Glasgow and as a copper he was accustomed to violence. But this spectacle sickened him. It was the crunch of bare knuckles on bone. Real and stereophonic. He asked, "What are the rules?"

"There aren't... sometimes biting isn't allowed."

"*Sometimes?*"

"Shut up and watch... I think your boy's in trouble."

He was.

Bleeding from his eye and mouth, he looked for escape. None available.

Then all of a sudden he seemed to be electric, and headbutted Lou who staggered back. Like a terrier, the boy went after him, and with three blows to the head, Lou was down.

The boy walked round him then kicked him in the back of the head.

All she wrote.

McDonald said, "I won!"

Roberts said, "*We* won."

"I thought you backed the favourite?"

"Yeah… for *us*. Like you did… for *us*. Hurry up before yer bookie legs it."

When McDonald collected his winnings he half considered legging it himself. Reluctantly, he handed a wedge to Roberts who said, "Lucky I made you get a bet on eh?"

"Yeah… lucky."

In the pub, Roberts said, "Get 'em in, lad, nobody likes a tight-fisted winner. I'll have a brandy."

When McDonald had followed the Morse series on TV, he'd felt it was unreal. Now he was reconsidering. Roberts took his drink and asked, "What's that you're drinking?"

"Snakebite."

"Eh?"

"It's lager and white cider."

"Time to grow up son… get us a couple of scotches, eh?"

I had a dream

(ABBA)

When Falls was discharged from hospital, it was AHA – not the Scandinavian pop group, but Against Hospital Advice. Like she could care.

The doctor said, "Would you consider counselling?"

"Which would do what for me exactly?"

"Ahm... help you get over your... trauma."

"I lost my baby, it's not a trauma... and no, I don't want to 'get over' that. And I don't expect to."

The doctor, flustered, said, "I've taken the liberty of prescribing some medication... I..."

"No thanks."

"Might I suggest you reconsider?"

"No."

Falls took a cab home. The driver droned on about a range of topics. She neither heard nor answered him as they drove along Balham High Road. She said, "Here... drop me here."

The driver saw the off licence and thought *Uh-oh*, said: "Mother's little helper, eh?"

The words lashed her but she managed to keep control and asked, "How much?" She fumbled a rush of coins and pushed them at him.

Like his brethren, he wasn't to be hurried. "You've given me too much, darlin'."

"Alas, the same can't be said for you."

But he'd triggered something and she bought a bottle of gin. The sales assistant asked, "A mixer?"

"No thanks."

She thought gin 'n' pain would mix enough. Her father hadn't drank gin. He drank everything else, including water from the toilet bowl, but alcoholically maintained: "Gin makes me ill."

He drank for no reason.

She had a reason.

Perhaps she'd uncovered a dual motive.

Entering her home was nigh unbearable. In her wardrobe were the baby things. She got a cup from the kitchen, sat, uncapped the bottle and poured. Said: "Here's to Po," and drank.

Two hours later she put the baby stuff in the garbage.

The following morning she was as sick as a dog, but she dragged herself to the shower and readied her energies, knowing she was going to need them.

Arriving at the station, the desk sergeant exclaimed, "Good God!" Then tried for composure. What was he to offer – sympathy, encouragement... what? He did the procedural thing – he passed the buck. "I'll let the Super know you're here... ahm... take a seat."

Like Joe Public.

Various colleagues passed and seemed embarrassed. No one knew how to respond.

The Sergeant said, "The Super will see you now." He gave a dog smile as if he'd done a good turn. She felt her stomach somersault.

She wasn't invited to sit by the Super. He asked, "How are you doing?"

"Not too bad, sir, fit for duty."

He frowned, looked down at his hands, then, "Perhaps it would be best if you took some time... the criminals will still be here, eh?"

He gave a police manual laugh. This has absolutely no relation to humour. Rather, it's the signal for shafting. Falls waited and eventually he said, "Take a month, eh? Catch up on the ironing."

Even he realised this was hardly PC, but she answered, "Thank you, sir, but I'd like to get back."

Now he cleared his throat. "I'm afraid that won't be possible... there may be an enquiry."

Falls was astonished. "Why?"

"There's a question of... recklessness... Going after a villain alone... the powers that be..." (here he paused to let her know: *hey, this is not my idea*), "frown on... mavericks."

She was going to argue but knew it was useless.

He said, "You're suspended on half-pay pending an enquiry."

She considered for only a moment, then said, "I don't think so."

"I beg your pardon?"

"I resign."

"I don't think..."

She got out her warrant card, laid it on the desk and turned to go.

He blustered, "I'm not quite through WPC."

And she gave a tiny smile. "But I am... all through."

Twenty minutes later she was home with a fresh bottle of gin. No mixer.

Taming the Alien

Fenton could hear Celine Dion with "You Are The Reason' and wasn't sure was it real or a memory.

He stared intently at the almost empty tequila bottle. No worm at the bottom.

The Alien had followed Stella into the poor part of town. At least he thought it was her. He'd yet to catch up on her, see her full face. She was always an elusive ten yards away. Gradually, he'd been lured into the shanty area. All the evidence of dire poverty escaped him. Spotting the sign "CANTINA," he'd stumbled into a shack. Now he shouted to the bartender, "Where's my worm?"

"Que?"

"I can't see him! Jesus... unless I ate the fucker... Can yah eat them?"

The barman shrugged his shoulders. He was about to close as the wind was up and howling. The Alien had a mess of dollars before him. The barman pocketed them, shoved a bottle of mescal into Fenton's arms then got him outside. "Go, Senor, the hurricane ees here."

"Fuck off."

Fenton slumped down against the shack, opened the mescal, drank deep and shuddered. Then he closed his eyes.

When the hurricane hit, the poorer areas took the brunt.

The tourist hotels, resort and apartments escaped.

Down in the shanty the Cantina was practically demolished.

It took a long time for the rescue teams to find Fenton, and by the time they got him to hospital, it was too late to save his legs.

Run for home

(Lindisfarne)

Brant was finishing his first doughnut. A second, heavily sugared, sat expectant.

Nancy said, "I hate to rush you."

"You won't, don't worry."

She looked at her watch. "You wouldn't want to be late."

He bit into the remaining cake and Nancy added, "You'd slide right into the NYPD."

"Think so?"

Nervously, she produced a package. "It's for you."

"A present?"

"Well, to remind you of your trip."

"This travel lark is a blast – people keep giving me stuff."

Without finesse, he tore open the package. Inside was a Macys tag and a hat. He said, "It's a hat."

"Like Popeye Doyle."

"Who?"

"In the movie 'French Connection'."

Then she saw him laughing and she blustered, "I didn't know what you'd wear – a fedora, a Trilby, a derby…?"

"But you knew I'd wear it well."

For one awful moment she thought he was going to sing.

He stood up, said, "I hate to rush you."

As they drove to Kennedy, she didn't know whether she would be relieved or sad at his going.

Brant thought: "The hat'll be a nice surprise for Roberts…"

A room had been set aside for the transfer of the prisoner. As

Brant and Nancy waited, he signed the ton of paperwork. Then he took out his Weights and checked the wall. Yup, right there: SMOKE FREE ZONE.

He lit up. Nancy ignored him.

As he fingered the Zippo, he suddenly acted on impulse, said, "Here, it was my Dad's."

Nancy looked at the offered lighter, said "Oh, I couldn't."

"OK." And he put it back in his pocket.

The door opened and Josie was let through. In chains. a belt round her waist joined manacles from her wrists to her ankles. Naturally, it impeded movement and she had to shuffle pigeon-toed. Four guards with her. Brant said, "For fucksake!"

Josie gave a rueful smile, said, "I'll never get through the metal detector."

As the handover was done, all the chains were removed and then a new long handcuff was placed on her right wrist, the other cuff offered to Brant.

Before he could respond, Nancy said, "It's regulations."

"It's bloody nonsense."

But he took the cuff. Josie said, "Like we're engaged."

Nancy said, "We accompany you to the aircraft, then it's all your show."

They were boarded before the other passengers and right at the rear of the plane. Two rows ahead would be kept empty.

Nancy said, "You better not smoke."

"Me?"

The guards left and Nancy had a word with the Chief Steward, then she stood before Brant. "I guess it's been fun."

"Don't let me keep you, D'Agostino."

She turned and was half way down the aisle when he shouted, "Yer a good un, Nance."

Not sure what that meant, she decided it was complimentary, and hugged it thus.

Josie asked, "Did yah ride her?"

"Watch yer lip."

Brant reached over, unlocked the cuffs. She massaged her wrist. "Thanks."

"Any messin', I'll break yer nose, OK?"

Josie gave him a long look. "I could give you a blow job."

He laughed in spite of himself. What was amazing to him was she was kind of likable. In a twisted, selfish fashion, he felt almost protective. He tried to dissipate that with: "You'll get some reception in prison – you being a police killer."

She nodded. "Least I'll get a decent cup o' tea."

"You'll get a hell of a lot more than tea, me girl."

She looked out the window. "I'm afraid."

"You have good reason, lass."

"No, I mean… of flying."

Brant nearly laughed again, said "Jaysus, you'd be better off if we crashed."

"Can I hold yer hand for take-off?"

Brant shook his head and then she left a piece of paper on his knee. He asked, "What?" And uncrumbled it to find a five dollar bill. Soiled, worn, torn, but hanging in there.

She said, "I'll buy the drinks."

"How did you hide it?"

She gave a slow smile. "Them yanks isn't all they're cracked up to be."

As the plane took off, he saw the sweat on her forehead. He placed his hand on hers and she nodded.

Once airborne, the hostess asked, "Like a drink? It has to be a soft one for your… companion."

"A Coke for her and two large Bacardis."

"Ahm…"

Brant stared at her, defying her to question him. She let it go. Josie said nothing.

When the drinks came, he measured them evenly and indicated Josie to take one. She said, "I love rum 'n' coke."

"Well drink it then."

She did.

The in-flight movie commenced and Josie said, "I love the pictures."

Shooting

Collie watched the funeral with a sense of awe. All the taxi drivers of south-east London had turned out for their murdered colleague. Each cab had a black ribbon tied to its antennae and they fluttered in the light breeze.

"I caused this. They're here cos of *me*."

It was a heady sensation. Collie had figured he needed a dry run with the gun, to see if he had the balls. He did.

Kept it lethal and simple. Hailed a cab at The Oval, blew the guy's head off at Stockwell. Then walked away. He couldn't believe the rush. He hadn't touched the takings – he was a professional, not a bloody thief.

The few days previous, he'd done his Brant research. All that required was hanging in the cop pubs. To say they were loose tongued was to put it mildly – numerous times he heard of Brant travelling home with a woman. Next he rang the station and, in his best TV voice said, "This is Chief Inspector Ryan of Serious Crimes at the Yard. We need the assistance of Sergeant Brant."

Mention of the Yard did all the work. He was told the time and terminal of arrival. Now, on the day, he put on a black suit and dog collar, checked himself in the mirror and said, "Reverend....? You looking at me?"

At The Oval, he bought a ticket for Heathrow and *The Big Issue* to pass the journey. As he settled into his seat, the gun was only slightly uncomfortable in the small of his back.

A woman offered him a piece of chocolate and he said, "God bless you my child."

At the airport, he checked the arrivals board and settled down to wait.

Over Heathrow, the plane was preparing to land. Brant said, "We've got to cuff up."

"I like bin chained to yah."

"Jaysus, girl!"

Then she lowered her head. "I'm sorry."

"What?"

"For yer trouble."

"Yeah...well..."

In truth, he didn't know what to say. Being sorry hardly cut it, but... He said, "Leastways you'll get a decent cup o' tea."

"Two sugars?"

"Sure, why not?"

As Brant and Josie emerged into arrivals, he slung his jacket to hide the cuff. Collie saw them and thought: *Holding hands. How sweet.*

He moved up to the barrier, Brant vaguely clocked a priest and looked away. The gun was out and Collie put two rounds in Josie's chest. The impact threw her back, pulling Brant along. Collie was moving fast and away, the gun back in his waistband.

Brant leant over Josie, saw the holes pumped by the dum dums and shouted, "Oh God!"

Collie was at the taxi rank and his collar allowed him to jump the queue. That, plus cheek.

"Central London," he said.

His elation and adrenalin was clouded by what he'd seen. A handcuff? How could that be?

Then he realised the driver was talking... incessantly. Collie touched the gun and smiled.

Acts ending
if not concluding

When Bill heard of the airport shooting he shouted "What the bloody blue fuck is the matter with everyone? Can't anybody do a blasted thing right?"

His minder didn't know, said, "I dunno."

"Course you don't bloody know, yah thick fuck."

What Bill knew was the shit was about to hit the fan – and hard.

He headed home and his daughter Chelsea was waiting. She said, "I love you, Dad."

Bill had recently caught a BBC documentary on Down's syndrome. The children had been titled "the gentle prophets." He wasn't entirely sure what it meant but he liked it.

Picking up Chelsea, he asked, "Want to go on a trip with yer Dad?"

"Oh yes!"

"Good girl."

"Where, Dad?"

"Somewhere far and till things cool off."

"Can we go tomorrow Dad?"

"Darlin', we're going today."

Roberts was once again before the Super. A very agitated Super, who asked, "What the bloody hell is going on?"

"Sir?"

"Don't "sir" me, Roberts... the fiasco at the airport... Who on earth would shoot the woman?"

"They say it was a priest."

The Super displayed a rare moment of wit, said "Lapsed Catholic, was she?"

Roberts gave the polite smile, about one inch wide.

The Super snapped, "It's hardly a joking matter! Could it have been Brant he was after?"

"It seems to have been a very definite hit, sir."

"Where's Brant now?"

"Still at Heathrow – Special Branch are de-briefing him."

The Super stood up, began pacing. Not a good sign. He was muttering, "God only knows what the Yanks will make of this."

A knock at the door and a woman looked in. "Ready for your tea, and biccy, sir?"

He exploded, "Tea? I don't want bloody tea, I want results!"

She fled.

The Super leant on the desk. "You'll have to have a word with WPC Fell."

"Falls, sir."

"What, like the present continuous of the verb "to fall," not the past tense? You're giving me an English lesson?"

"No, sir... I..."

"The damn woman has resigned. I mean, her being black... you know... *Minority Policing* and all that horseshit... Get her back." Before Roberts could reply, the Super was off again, "Well don't hang about, eh?"

"Yes, sir."

Roberts had reached the door when the Super said, "Send in me tea."

Brief debriefing

We'd like you to go through it one more time, Sergeant."
Brant lit up a Weight, took a deep drag, exhaled.
"You're trying to learn it by heart, that it?"
The two men conducting the interview wore suits. One had a black worsted, the other a tweed Oxford. Black said, patiently, "There may be some detail you've forgotten."

"It's on tape, yer mate in the Oxfam job had a recorder."

Oxford said, "We're anxious to let you get home."

Brant sat back, said, "We arrived at Heathrow, I re-cuff us–"

"Re-cuff?"

"Is there an echo?"

"Let me understand this, Sergeant. The woman was *uncuffed* during the flight?"

"You catch on quick, boyo."

The men exchanged a glance, then: "Please continue."

"We got off the plane and I covered the cuffs with me jacket..."

Another exchanged look.

"Then we came out and a priest shot her."

"What makes you think he was a priest?"

"Was he was a good shot? What d'ya think, he looked like Bing Crosby?"

Now Oxford allowed his skepticism to show, said "He was hardly a priest."

"Are you catholic?"

"No, but I hardly see..."

"If you were a catholic, you'd not be surprised what priests are capable of."

Black decided to take control – cut the shit, cut to the chase. "*You* won't be shedding any tears, will you Sergeant?"

"What's that mean?"

"Well, I mean… like someone did you a favour, eh? She tried to murder you once, killed one of your colleagues… how much can you be hurting?"

Brant was up. "Enough of this charade, I'm off."

Oxford moved to block the door and Brant smiled. "'Scuse me."

Oxford stepped aside. Brant opened the door, paused, said: "I may need to talk to you two again. Don't leave town."

J is for Judgement

(Sue Grafton)

Roberts met with Brant in The Cricketers. He'd parked his car near The Oval, said to *The Big Issue* vendor, "Keep an eye, eh?" and indicated the motor.

The vendor said, "Play fair, Guv, they'd steal yer eye."

Brant was at the back of the pub, a tepid coffee before him. Roberts put out his hand. "Good to see you, Tom,' and meant it. Then, "Don't you want a real drink?"

"With all me soul but I was afraid to start."

"Start now."

"I will."

They did. Whiskey chasers.

No conversation, let the scotch fill the spaces. Then Brant rummaged in his jacket and produced a squashed hat, said, "Got yah a present."

"Oh."

"It's a bit battered. I fell on it."

Roberts tentatively touched it, then took it in both hands. "I dunno what to say."

"Give it some time, it will bounce back."

"Like us, eh?"

Brant gave him a look as if he were only now really seeing him, asked, "You were sick?"

At last thought Roberts, I can finally share. "Naw, nothing worth mentioning." Then he added, "Falls is out."

"Out where?"

"The force, she resigned."

Brant was animated, life returning. "She can't do that!"

"Word is you lent her the dosh to bury her father."

"*Me?*"

"Did yah?"

"C'mon Guv, am I a soft touch?"

"What d'ya say we finish up, go round to see her?"

"Like now?"

"You have other plans?"

"Naw."

They finished their drinks, got ready to go. Brant asked, "Out of vague interest, how much am I supposed to have given her?"

"Two large."

Brant didn't answer, just gave a low whistle. The figure was twice that, but then...

Who was counting?

In Balham, as they approached Falls' home, Roberts asked, "How d'ya want to play this?"

"Let's make it up as we go along."

"Good plan."

They banged on the door and no reply. Roberts said, "Could be she's out."

"Naw, she's home, there's a light." Brant took out his keys, said, "Pretend you don't see this," and he fidgeted with the lock, pushed the door in.

They were cops accustomed to nigh on any reception.

Neither of them could have forecast a skinhead. All of fourteen years old and wielding an iron bar. He shouted, "Fuck off outta it."

"*Wot?*" in chorus.

The skin made a swipe with the bar, said: "I'll do ye."

Brant turned his back shrugged, then spun back, clouting the skin on the side of the skull. Flipped him, knelt on his back, said, "What's yer game, laddie? Where's the woman?"

"Play fair, mate... jeez!"

Roberts had gone searching, shouted, "She's here... in the bathroom."

"Is she OK?"

"Debatable."

Brant stood up, put a lock on the skin's neck, gave him two open-handed slaps. "Whatcha do to her?"

"Didn't do nuffink! I'm protecting her!"

"*Wot?*" Again, in chorus.

Now the skin went bright red with a glow of injured dignity. "She gave me a quid one time, so when I seen her 'elpless like, staggerin' home, leavin' the door open, I said I'd mind her till she got her act back. Know what I mean?"

They did, sorta.

Roberts took out his wallet, said "Yah did good, now here's somefin' for yer trouble."

"I don't need paying... she's like... a mate."

Brant looked at Roberts, then. "All right, then, you ever get in a spot o' bother ask for DI Roberts or DS Brant, we'll see you right...OK?"

"OK."

"Take off then, that's a good lad."

He did.

Roberts said, "I've seen it all, a skin protecting a copper."

"A black copper."

"Yeah... go figure."

They couldn't.

Together they hoisted Falls into the shower, kept her there till she came round. She came to, to retch, to curse and struggle. Then they dried her and got her into a dressing gown.

Brant rooted in his wallet, took out two pills and forced them into Falls' mouth. Roberts raised an eyebrow and Brant said, "Tranqs... heavy duty sedation."

Falls said, "Don't want help."

"Too bad – it's underway."

Brant and Roberts took it in shifts over the next 48 hours, washing her, feeding her, holding her. Times they got some chicken soup down her, times she threw up all over them.

When the horrors came, as come they do, Brant held her tight, wiped the spittle from her mouth. When the sweats coursed down her body, Roberts changed the bed linen, got her a fresh T-shirt.

❖

DAY 3:

Brant's shift. Falls had slept for eight hours. She woke, her eyes focused, asked, "Can I have a cup of tea?"

"Toast?"

"OK... I think."

She could. Two slices, lightly marged. Then she got outta bed, didn't stagger, said, "I could murder a large gin."

"Darlin', it's near murdered you."

"I know... and yet...?"

Brant went and found a drop in one of the pile of bottles, said, "There's a taste in this, enough to fuel you to the off licence." He held out the drink. "What's it gonna be, darlin'?"

Perspiration lined her forehead, a tremor hit her body, she said, "I ache for it."

He didn't speak.

Then she shut her eyes, tight like a child before a surprise. "Sling it."

He did.

Later, after another shower, she asked, "Why?"

"Why what?"

"You and the Guv... helped me."

"Well, they say you owe me three large, I'm protecting me cash."

"I've resigned."

Brant stood up, said, "Don't be stupid, I'll see you at the station. Be on time, WPC."

"Which party would you
like to be invited to?"
'The one', I said, "least
likely to involve
gunfire."

('Midnight In The Garden Of Good and Evil'
John Berendt)

Collie was having a party for one. It's not difficult to prepare such an event. You buy enough booze for six and don't invite anyone. He'd laid out on his coffee table:

4   Bottles of Wild Turkey
2   Six Packs of Bud.
1   Cheese Dip and
        The gun.

The gun isn't always a prerequisite, it depends who's after you.

Music.

Verve with "Lucky Man", over and over.

To complete the festivities, he'd put down four lines of coke.

Ready to party.

When the phone rang, he picked up the receiver, breathed, "Yeah?" Lots of muscle in it.

A pause at the other end, then, "So you're home."

Collie recognised Bill straight off, answered, "Yes, sir."

"You screwed up."

"Wasn't my fault, sir, I thought she was his bit of gear."

"Didn't the handcuffs signify something else?"

"I didn't see them, sir... I thought they was holding hands... I can fix it, though."

"How?"

"I'll do Brant."

"And you call that fixing it?"

"I dunno, sir... tell me and I'll do it... I done the taxi driver good, didn't I?"

A long pause, a sigh, then: "You did the taxi driver?"

"Yes, sir, one shot, clean as anything."

"OK. Stay home, don't go out... Can you do that?"

"Yes, sir."

"Good."

When Brant got home, there was an envelope under his door. No stamp. Inside was a single sheet of paper. It read:

"THE AIRPORT SHOOTER LIVES AT:

FLAT 4, 102 VINE STREET,

CLAPHAM JUNCTION."

Brant picked up the phone, dialled, then heard Falls say, "Hello?"

"It's Brant. Wanna be a hero?"

There's a hospital on the outskirts of Acapulco called La Madonna D'Esperanza.

The Virgin of Hope.

It's a mental hospital, and hope is pretty scarce.

Pan along Corridor C, turn left towards the windows and there's a man in a wheelchair. He's silent because he's learnt she won't appear if he speaks. His hands rest on the rug covering his lower torso.

If he keeps his eyes glued to the panes, she'll eventually come, and then he'll whisper:

Stell.

Stella.

The McDead

Kick off

"Am I dying?"

Answer that. Do you lie big and say, like in the movies, "Naw, it's just a scratch,"? Or, clutch his hand real tight and say, "I ain't letting you go, bro',"?

Chief Inspector Roberts was a professional; a professional liar, among other things. It didn't teach you that in the police manual. No, that came with promotion. He considered all the lines he could use. What he said was, "You're dying."

Roberts had got the call at three in the morning. The hour of death. Coming reluctantly out of sleep, he muttered, "This better be bloody good." And heard, "James!"

No one used his christian name, not even his wife. He said, "Tony... Good Lord... where are you? D'ya know what time it is?" And heard a sad laugh.

Then: "I didn't ring to ask the time. I'm hurt... I'm hurt pretty bad."

He sounded hurt, his speech was coming through slow and laboured. Eventually, Roberts pinned down an address, said, "Don't move, I'm on me way."

Again, the sad laugh, "I won't move, I can guarantee it." Roberts dressed quickly. His wife was asleep in another room. Yeah, like that.

"Would it fuck." Roberts said aloud, "God, I haven't much called on you... I know... but maybe this would be a good place to start."

He'd learned from his sergeant, a dubious example of catholicism, that it was a bartering thing. You did something for God, He did something for you. Like the Masons really.

He wasn't sure what he had to trade and said, "I'll... ah... do good works." What that entailed he'd no idea. Perhaps buy *The Big Issue* more regularly and not wait for change.

Yeah, it was a place to start. He waited, then tried the ignition again.

Nope

Nada

Zilch

He glanced briefly upwards, said:

"It's about what I figured."

A mini-cab later and he arrived in Stockwell, where the pitbulls travelled in twos. Ludlow Road is near the tube station, a short mugging away. At that hour the streets were littered with

the undead,

the lost, and

the frozen.

The building was a warren of bedsits. No lock on the front door. A wino was spread in the hall, his head came up wheezed: "Is it Tuesday?"

"No."

"Are you sure?"

Roberts wondered if the guy even knew the year but hey... he was going to argue? He said, "It's Thursday... OK?"

"Ah, good. I play golf on Tuesdays."

Of course.

Flat six had a cleaner door than most. It was ajar. Roberts entered slowly. Entered devastation-ville. The place had been thrashed, cushions slit open, TV smashed, broken chairs and crockery, and his broken brother lying in the bathroom. He was a mess of blood and bruising. From the angle of his legs, Roberts knew they were gone. He opened his eyes, well, half opened one. The other was shut down. By a hammer it seemed.

He said, "James, can I get you something?"

And Roberts tried not to smile, bent down said:

"I called an ambulance."

His brother seemed to have lost consciousness, then said: "Oh good, is it a weekender?"

A south-east London maxim. You called one on a weekday,

could expect it on Saturday. Roberts didn't know what to do, said: "I dunno what to do."

That's when Tony asked if he was dying. He tried to cradle his brother's head, there was blood everywhere, asked, "Who did this, Tone?"

"Tommy Logan."

Before he could ask more, his brother convulsed, then let his head back, and died. When the medics arrived and scene of crime boyos, Roberts was led outside to the ruined sitting room. As they moved the body, a mobile fell to the floor. The officer in charge said, "I'm sorry, guv, but I have to ask some questions, you understand."

"Yeah."

"Did he say anything?"

"No."

The officer tried to proceed delicately, asked, "He called you?"

"Yeah."

"And he didn't give any indication of what had happened?"

"He said he was hurt and could I come."

"Yes?"

"I came."

"Right... was he... ah... conscious... when you got here?"

"No."

The officer looked round, said, "I see." But he didn't. Went another direction, asked, "Were you close , guv?"

"Close?"

"You know, like regular contact?"

Roberts focused, then said, "I spoke to him ten years ago... maybe eleven."

"Ah, so you weren't, then?"

Roberts turned his full look on the officer, said, "No wonder you're a detective."

Living next door to Alice

(Smokie)

WPC Falls was standing in front of the Superintendent. He was drinking tea and drinking it noisily. It's a very difficult task to chew tea but he appeared to have mastered it.

Gnaw

gnaw

gnaw

Like an anorexic rodent. He'd get it down but that didn't mean he had to like it. Worse. A biscuit, a club milk. He slid open the wrapper, then carefully peeled back the silver paper, said, "They're well protected."

Did he mean the public, criminals, tax dodgers? So, she just said, "Yes, sir." Which is about as unthreatening an answer as you can get.

WPC Falls was black and pretty or, as they said in the canteen, "She's pretty black." Argue the toss. Recently, she'd fucked up spectacularly in both her personal and professional life. She'd been pregnant and had gone after an arsonist alone. Nearly killed, she'd lost the baby and almost her job.

DS Brant had forced her along to arrest a hit man. It had saved her job and restored some of her confidence. Not all, but definitely in the neighbourhood. After, he'd said, "You know Falls, you're getting a mean look."

"What?"

"Yeah, a nastiness around the eyes."

She couldn't resist, said, "Like you, sergeant?"

He laughed, answered, "See what I mean? Yeah... like me and, if you're real smart, you'll work on it."

Surprised, she asked, "Will it go away?"

"Fuck no, you'll get meaner."

The Super put the biscuit to the side, said, "Gratification postponed is gratification doubled."

Falls had a flurry of thoughts – *Thank Christ he didn't start on the biscuit. Yer pompous fart* – all hedging on the insubordinate. She cautioned herself. Chill to chill out. Now the prize prick was flicking through her file adding sighs, tut-tuts, teeth clicking, every few pages. Finally, he sat back, said, "A checkered career to date."

"Yes sir."

Now he was tapping a pen against his teeth, exclaimed, "And such promise, you have the potential. Oh yes."

Falls thought, Yeah, I'm black and a woman.

He closed the file then, as if only now was the idea crystallising, said, "I'm going to take a chance on you Falls, eh."

"Thank you, sir."

"No doubt you're familiar with the Clapham Rapist?"

Who wasn't? A serial, he'd attacked six women, six black women. The lefties were kicking up a stink. Phrases such as "selective policing" were surfacing.

He continued: "You'll be living in a bedsit in Clapham, going to pubs, clubs, all the places this johnnie hunts."

She tried to restrain herself but couldn't, said, "A decoy?"

He gave a tolerant smile, said, "Not a term we're keen on my girl, smacks of entrapment. We'll have you covered all the way." Sure. "So, are you up to the job? I've picked you especially."

"Yes, sir."

Thank you sir. Won't let you down sir, etc.

Brown-nosing to screaming point.

"Good, the desk sergeant has the details. PC McDonald will be assisting you... that's all."

She was just closing the door when he pounced on the club milk. Could hear him wolfing it as she moved away, muttered, "Hope it bloody chokes him."

As Brant had said, "Getting meaner by the minute."

The Greeks have a word for it

There's a narrow street connecting the Walworth Road to the east entrance of The Elephant and Castle shopping centre. It has second-hand furniture shops, a bookies, a boarded-up off licence and a taverna. The taverna is called The Spirit of Athens. It's a dump. But it does OK, and has a minor reputation for its bacon sarnies. A hint of kebab is added to the mix and the locals like it. Gives a taste of the exotic and disguises the bacon.

Culinary delight indeed.

The owner is named Spiro Zacharopoulos. He's a snitch and, more to the point, he's DS Brant's snitch. Brant looked like a thug and he was real proud of that. The Metropolitan Police *believed* he was a thug and were deeply ashamed of him. He'd had some major fuck-ups in his career which ensured he'd not rise above the rank of sergeant. But a number of last moment high profile case solutions had saved his career. It was always thus, thin ice to the promised land.

A mix of ruthlessness and the luck of the Irish kept him in the game. Snitches were the lifeblood of police work. Brant knew this better than most. Now sitting at a table, he said to Spiro, "Jaysus, would it hurt to give the place a sweep?"

"Ah Meester Brant, help is so... how you say... diskolo... difficult to get."

"By the look of this joint, it's downright impossible. Couldn't you get a brush?"

Spiro spoke perfect English but it was useful to play it down.

Gave him the edge. He said, "Ah Meester Brant, you make a joke."

Brant reached into his jacket, got a pack of Weights and a battered Zippo, lit up, exhaled, said, "When I make a joke boyo, you won't be in any doubt about it."

Spiro, playing the anxious-to-please role, went and got an ashtray. Written along the side was Ouzo-12. Brant looked at it, flicked his ash on the floor, said, "That's going to make all the difference, eh? What's the twelve for?"

Now Spiro could be the true Greek, hospitable friendly sly, said, "Ouziko Dodika."

"Which tells me what exactly? Doesn't tell me shit pal."

"Wait... wait one moment." He got up, crossed to the bar and busied himself. Five minutes on he's back with glasses, a bottle, snacks on plates and a jug of water, says, "Let me demonstrate." Pours the ouzo, adds water and it becomes the colour of window cleaner, nods to the snacks, explains, "These are meze, we eat, we drink, like we're in Greece."

The "snacks" consisted of

two Ritz crackers,

two slices of "rubber,"

two thin wedges of cheese.

Brant stared, then: "Jaysus, you broke the bank with all this grub... what's the rubber bits?"

"Octopu."

"I can only hope you're kidding. Tell you what, I'll feast on the others – you have the condoms."

He took his glass and before he drank, Spiro said, "*Aspro pato.*"

"Whatever." Knocked it back, gasped and said, "Paint off a fucking gate..."

"You like?"

Brant wiped his mouth, bit on a stale cracker, said, "Let's cut the crap, boyo, and drop the Greek lesson... OK? You came to me pal offering yer help if I could help you with some problems. I delivered, you haven't been shut down so, let's hear it. You're a snitch, so snitch."

Now Spiro was the offended party, whined, "Meester Brant, ah... I thought we were friends. Friends do each other a *leetle* favour."

He was into it now and would have built to operatic outrage but Brant leant over, gave him an almighty wallop to the side of the head, said:

"You're not paying attention, Costos."

"It's Spiro."

"See, now you're listening. Who's the main player these days?"

The main player had been Bill Preston. He was on sabbatical and various villains were vying for position. Spiro glanced round the empty restaurant, then said, "Tommy Logan. Like you, he is Irish, I think, but he has the mind of a Colombian."

"What's that mean?"

"Without mercy, no... how you say...? boundaries... is why he is top because he will do anything."

"Well now, I'd like to meet the bold Logan."

"Mister Brant, be careful, this man is crazy. He has no respect for police or for anybody."

Brant poured some ouzo, said, "Let's have some more turpentine, drink to Tommy Logan."

"Ah, you begin to like the ouzo."

Brant leant over and Spiro cowered, but the sergeant only put his arm round the Greek's shoulder, squeezed, said, "I like you Costis, you and yer shit-hole caff."

Song for Guy

A handful of mourners at Tony Roberts' funeral. The Chief Inspector, Brant, Falls, McDonald, and a wino who looked vaguely familiar, but Roberts couldn't quite recall where from.

The vicar read, "Man is full of misery and has but a short time to live…"

Brant nudged him, none too gently, said, "Jaysus, padre, something less depressing."

The vicar said, "I say, do leave this to the proper authority. There are set rules and services."

Brant gave him the look, asked, "Wanna be first in the hole?"

The padre looked for help but none was forthcoming, so he read an up tempo passage on light and salvation. Brant liked it fine.

A persistent drizzle was coming down, not an outright soaking but a steady wetting. As if it hadn't the balls to just pour on bloody down. When the body had been lowered, Brant moved near to Roberts, asked, "All right, guv?"

"What… oh yes… thanks… listen, I, ahm… don't they usually have sandwiches for people after…?"

Brant smiled gently, a rare to rarest event, said, "I put a few quid behind the bar at The Roebuck, they do a lovely spread."

"Oh, do they?"

"Well the owner's a mick, knows about wakes. He'll do us grand. I'll leave you a moment, guv."

Roberts turned, asked, "What will I say? I dunno what to say."

"Tell him goodbye, guv… oh… and that you'll fix the fuck what done him… OK?"

Only Roberts and the wino remained. Then it came to him –
the wino outside Tony's door. The man said, "Sorry for your
trouble, he was a gent he was. Gave me a few quid now and
again."

Roberts reached for his wallet and the man was horrified. "I
didn't come here for beggin'."

"I know, I appreciate that, but for a last one with... Tony...
would you humour me?"

The wino was indignant but not stupid, took the cash, said,
"So long's you know I didn't come cos o' that."

Roberts nodded, stood alone for a moment then whispered,
"Goodbye Tony, I'll fix the fuck what done you... OK, lad?"

Top dog

There's a new boot on the market. Heavy, thick-soled, menacing and highly impressive, called *Wehrmacht*. And, yeah, they pronounce it with a V and a tone. So, OK, it's not actually called the Third Reich, but it's implied. Could they give a fuck. Selling like designer sunglasses. Tommy Logan had a pair and he adored them. For good measure, he had the toes reinforced with steel. Kept them spit-shined and did those mothers gleam?

His real name was Tommy Nash but that was before. In the Scrubs, he'd drowned a guy in a toilet. Not an easy task. You have to truly want to kill somebody. Tommy did.

That evening in the recreation room, Johnny Logan won the Eurovision for the third time. The cons were allowed to watch. To be in the Eurovision three times is some awful sentence but to win it three times, that's diabolical. One of the lifers said, "Hey Tommy, you know what?"

"Yeah?" Lots of hard in his answer fresh from the afternoon kill, he was bullet-proof.

"You look like that guy – that winner."

Tommy checked round, see if it was a piss-take. No. Lots of con heads nodding. Yeah, they could see it. Tommy heard the word WINNER. It sang to him.

Johnny Logan was tall, dark hair, and the face of a cherub. He sang like a tenor angel. Tommy was short with mousy hair and a baby face. But the fit was in.

Next day Tommy got a prison make-over. Had one of the cissies dye his hair black using polish and gel. Got it sleek and raven. After, he let the cissy go down and came quickly. A few minutes later he beat the cissy to pulp, shouting, "I hate fucking queers, man I just fucking hate 'em."

On Tommy's release he didn't go back to north London. He headed south-east and became Tommy Logan, adopted a half-assed Irish accent and thought it passed for humour. To complete the transition, he got a heavy gold Claddagh ring and ordered bottles of Guinness in public. It worked for Daniel Day Lewis. His music of choice was Sinead O'Connor. He believed her to be openly psychotic. Her songs sang to him of

violence

pay-back

fuck you-all.

The current favourite was Troy, where her Dublin accent lashed full and lethal. Jaysus, he couldn't get enough of it. To hear Tommy sing the chorus with Sinead was to understand Armageddon. When she grew her hair again, he was a tad disappointed. To complete his Irish accreditation, his weapon of choice was a hurley. The national sport in Ireland, apart from talking, is hurling. A cross between hockey and homicide.

A hurley is made from ash and about the length of a baseball bat. Twice as lethal as it's much handier to swing. You get one in your hands, you want to swing like a lunatic.

Every year the All Ireland Final was broadcast to London and Tommy relished every murderous minute. He'd spotted a poster of the Mayo team at an Irish dance and had it away. The team looked like a hardened bunch. Tommy imagined getting them behind you in the yard at Wormwood Scrubs and shouting "Up yah, boy."

Jeez, what a rush. During the televised final, regardless of who the teams actually were, Tommy would shout, "C'mon Mayo."

While this would have been much appreciated in Mayo, it tended to confuse elsewhere. Tommy made his pile with crack cocaine. Got right into the very bases and wielded intimidation from the off. Knowing no limits, he grew into major league.

Bill Preston had been top of the south-east for a decade and when he took off, Tommy was next in line. His motto was:

The only good witness is a dead witness.

And his lack of jail time proved it. On the climb up, Tommy

learned about care, caution, planning, and the best solicitors.

Front everything.

Hide

Hide

Hide

Start a company daily and muddle your tracks. A high profile led to heat and Tommy was beginning to appreciate the value of stealth. His one major weakness was his temper. He hadn't yet learned to control it. Tony Roberts was proof of that.

Wake up

The Roebuck had, as Brant predicted, laid on a "grand spread." Mountains of sandwiches. Cocktail sausages, nicely burnt. Lashings of tea, soup and, of course, plenty of booze.

Roberts was holding a cup of tea; he hadn't tasted it. Falls prepared a plate of food, brought it over. He shook his head, she urged, "They're very good, sir, try one of those lads."

"No... thank you."

Brant came over, nodded to Falls, and she backed off. Brant took the tea from Roberts, put a glass there instead, said, "It's Irish, kick like a bastard."

"OK, Tom."

The others looked round.

Tom!

It never occurred to them Brant had a Christian name. His expression told them they best forget it. PC McDonald was a tall blond Scot. Falls might have felt an attraction if he wasn't so... smug. He was wolfing down food and she asked, "Missed breakfast?"

He gave her a glorious smile. It was a winner, he'd been told and often made women weak at the knees. She said, "You're the rising star."

Now he was modest, toned down the smile wattage, said, "I got lucky."

"Word has it you'll get Brant's stripes."

"Oh I dunno, would I be up to his rep'?"

Now Falls treated him to *her* smile. All teeth and absolutely no warmth, said, "You've got that right."

He grabbed a napkin, carefully wiped his mouth, and she thought, Uh-oh, all the moves.

He touched her arm, said, "When we're done here, I wonder would you like to come back to my place?"

"When we're *done* here – you mean scoffed the food, then we'll scarper?" He decided to play, prove he could be a fun guy, said, "Yeah... sound good?"

She moved his hand away, asked, "And back there we'd do what exactly?" The full smile now.

"Oh, something will come up, eh?"

She looked full at his crotch, said, "If we waited for that to come up, we'd be here all week." And moved away.

McDonald considered following but then grabbed another sandwich, muttered, "Cold cunt."

Brant and Roberts had moved to a table, a line of empty shot glasses on the counter. Roberts said, "God, that's a strong drink."

"Aye, takes the edge off."

They laughed at that notion. The drink hasn't been invented that *keeps* the edge off. Still, they'd enjoy the reprise.

Brant asked, "What the medical examiner say, guv?"

Roberts had to shake himself, focus on where he was, said, "That he'd been beaten with a stick... maybe a club, broke every bone in his body. A systematic beating was how he described it. Took a while. Took a while."

They digested that, then Roberts asked, "What d'ya think, a baseball job?"

"Could be a hurley, guv."

Roberts nodded, then, "I know who did it."

"Jesus, guv, are you serious?"

"Tony told me before he died."

"And you haven't told anybody."

Roberts raised an eyebrow, said, "I'm telling you." And he did.

When he was finished, Brant whistled, said, "This is what they call synchronicity, I think."

"What?"

"Sting had a song about it... well he would, wouldn't he? You know, like coincidence."

Roberts was lost, said, "I'm lost."

Brant was almost excited. "Guv, I've a new informant and guess who he says is the new kid on the block?"

Now Roberts gave a bleak smile. "Mr. Logan?"

"Bingo!"

Roberts stood up, swayed and Brant asked, "We're going to get him now?"

"Oh no, that's something I want to do properly. I want to savour it. I'm going to get some more of that Irish."

Brant sat back, said, "That's the spirit, guv."

Private investigation

Rosie, a WPC, was Falls' best friend. When she heard of
Falls' new assignment, she snorted:
"They had me on that."
"What?" Rosie laughed.
"Did the Super tell you he'd picked you specially."
Falls was mortified, considered lying but thought, What the
hell? Said, "Yeah, he gave me that whole crock."
"Set you up in Clapham?"
"Uh-oh."
"Girl, they're shitting you, when there were three victims, they
weren't sure he specifically targeted black women, so they put my
white ass on the line. I hung out in clubs, pubs till my Jack said
he'd get a divorce."
"Did you talk to the victims?"
"Honey, they're black... are they gonna open up to a white
girl – a white *po-lees* girl? Sure, where you been girl?"
As she spoke, she realised, and tried to counter, "Oh gawd, I
mean... I'm a stupid cow, I'm sorry."
"It's OK. Anything else?"
"Well, they got in a profiler... just like the telly. He said the
attacker was a white male in his thirties and that the violence
would escalate. It has. He used the knife last time almost as if he
were working up to a kill."
She shuddered and said, "Don't do it girl, say you're not
completely recovered."
Falls gave her the look and Rosie said, "Please be extra
careful."
"I will, I promise, so there."

"You know that rape is about hate, not sex."

"I read the report."

"Oh... and here's you lettin' me prattle on. Then you know about the garlic."

"What?"

"All the victims mentioned his breath stank of it."

"Gee, that should narrow it down. We can eliminate all young males with fresh breath."

"Of which, in the whole of London, there's probably five."

"Five percent?"

"No, just five."

Falls thought about Brant, then asked, "Do I look different to you Rosie?"

"You mean... since?"

"Yeah."

"A little quieter."

"Do I look... mean?"

Rosie hugged her, said, "You always looked mean."

L⊙dgⓔd

McDonald was summoned to the Super's office. When he got inside, the Super came to shake his hand, did the Masonic bit. The Super sat and said, "Take a pew son."

"Thank you, sir."

"You set for bigger things?"

"Yes, sir."

"But we must be seen to go through the motions. Are you with me?"

"Absolutely, sir, one hundred per cent."

"That's the ticket. Did you know Scots are the back-bone of the force?"

He didn't, said, "No, sir."

"Oh yes. Now the Irish are... what's the word, too..."

"Rough?"

"Well yes, actually I was going to say Celtic."

Time for some brass humour. He said, "Naturally you'd be a Rangers man."

"Rugby League, sir."

And they took a moment to savour their wee pleasantries. Then, "You'll be watching out for the black woman, when she's on decoy."

"Of course, sir."

"No need to over-do it, we don't expect a result. Keep her outta mischief eh?"

"Very good, sir."

Now, time for the real bones. The Super leant over the desk, said, "DS Brant continues to be an embarrassment."

McDonald waited.

"If you were to perhaps, notice some infringement… you'd be doing your duty to… let me know."

"I'd be honoured, sir."

"Good man, capital… see you anon."

When McDonald got outside, he took a moment to gather himself. Near jumped when a finger touched his shoulder.

Brant. Who said, "Bit edgy boyo."

Edgy, he was stunned, tried to recover, said feebly, "Oh you know how it is when you get a roasting."

Brant was eyeballing him, said, "Oh? Got a bollockin' did ya?"

"Yes, sarge… yes I did."

Brant slapped him on the shoulder, said, "Well, keep you outta mischief."

"What?"

"Good man, capital, see you anon."

Check up

Roberts had been diagnosed with skin cancer. For eighteen months, he'd undergone radiation therapy. The treatment left him bone weary and with a mega thirst. Being a policeman had the same effect. Now, he was in the doctor's surgery awaiting results of a check-up.

The doctor was at his desk doing medical stuff and looking grim. Which told him zilch. Finally, the doctor asked, "Do you smoke?"

"What?"

"It's not a difficult question."

Roberts thought, Oh ch-err-ist, what have I now?

"No I don't."

"Good man. Don't start."

"What?"

The doctor smiled, not a pretty sight, said, "Though on this occasion, you might indulge in a small celebratory cigar."

"I'm OK?"

"Yes, you are and, with care, there's no reason you shouldn't live another six months."

When he saw Roberts face, he said, "Just kidding, a little medical levity. How often do I get to deliver good news?"

Roberts couldn't quite take it in, had lived with bad luck, bad news, for so long, asked again, "And I'm OK?"

"Just stay outta the sun."

"In England... a tall order." Now they both laughed. A weather joke always broke the ice.

On his way out, Roberts said, "Thank you. I'll do my damnest now to stop the malpractice suit."

"What?"

"Just kidding, doc."

After Roberts had left, the doctor lit a cigarette and hoped to hell it was a joke. You never could tell with cops.

Roberts said to Brant, "Let me get those, I'd some good news today."

"Sure thing, guv, though I'd 'ave 'ad a sarnie if I'd known you were paying."

Roberts took the drinks, said, "Good news, not magnificent news."

Brant looked longingly at the food cabinet, said, "They sure are tempting."

They took a corner table at the back of the pub. A police position, to see and not be seen.

Brant said, "Your boy, the Scot, is hoping to shaft me."

"McDonald?"

"Yeah, him."

"You're getting paranoid, Sarge, he's all right."

"I heard the Super tell him."

Roberts took a sip, then, "Oh sure what did you do... bug his office?"

"Yes."

It took a moment to sink in. Then incredulity, "No... not even you would be that crazy!"

"The Super says I'm too Celtic."

Roberts took his drink in a gulp, shook his head. Brant said, "Over on the Tottenham Court Road there's a shop called Total Surveillance. A Spy Supermarket."

Roberts put up his hand, "Tell me no more. Good God, they'll hang you out to dry."

"That's what they want to do, guv, this way, I'm a jump ahead."

"You're a flaming lunatic is what you are."

Brant signalled to the barman. Then he roared, "Same again... before the holidays."

The drinks came and Brant said, "He's paying. He's had good news."

The barman didn't appear too pleased but said, "How nice."

"And I'll have one of them sarnie jobs. Pop it in the toaster, let it near burn."

The barman said, with dripping sarcasm, "Would there be any other jobs?"

"Naw, you're doing too much as it is."

Roberts sulked till Brant asked, "Wanna know what they said about you?"

"No I bloody don't."

Then a few minutes later, "Go on then."

"That you're out on yer ass."

"Never."

"Would I lie? It's on tape."

"Bastards, keep buggin' 'em."

Profile

Barry Lewis was thirty-two-years-old. Tall, with a slight stoop, he had blond hair in a buzz cut. Even features that missed being good looking. He was in shape due to two sessions weekly at the gym. Barry burned with hate. He'd recently lost his job "cooking" at McDonald's. Prior to that, he'd been with

Burger King,

Pizza Hut,

Pret a Manger.

A brief stint with British Rail was hardly worth mentioning. He never did.

All his supervisors had been black and female. Each time he'd start out well. He had it all:

Punctuality,

Cleanliness,

Friendliness.

He knew how to fit, he just didn't know how to fit continuously. Slowly, the supervisors would all begin to notice, snap, "Wotcha always got yo' eyes on me, white boy?"

As if he'd look at the bitches. So OK, once or twice he'd sneak a peek. Imagine that black flesh under his hand, all that heat. He swore out loud: "I never touched that cow at Burger King."

Like that. He knew they wanted it.

Or that woman at Pizza Hut who'd asked, "Yo Barry, nice boy like you, how come you no got yourself a girlfriend?"

Putting him down. Making him go red and howling, "See, seed a white boy blushing."

Packing his gear at British Rail, the knife was just lying there.

It gleamed. Long black bone handle and the shining blade. Took it in his hand, it felt good. No... it felt right, and he mimicked his tormentors, said, "Ah-rite."

Slipped it in his jacket. He'd had no plan, no outline strategy. One evening he'd gone out, had a few beers, loosened up. A trendy pub off Clapham Common, Whitney Houston on the speakers. Jeez, he'd like to do it to her. Yeah, kick fuck outta Bobby Brown first. The woman just drifted into his line of vision.

She was with friends, head back laughing. Yeah, he saw the bitch touching the men on the knees, getting them hot. Followed her out and she said goodbye to the group. Headed off *alone* in London at night? Had to be begging for it.

Next thing he had the knife to her throat, shouting obscenities in her ear. After, he wanted to kill her. The following weeks, the need grew and he went hunting. He wasn't even sure how many. Only six had gone to the cops.

He was famous. When he read the papers and they'd said, "Reign of Terror," he'd felt omnipotent.

Now who was staring? Who was fucking blushing, eh?

Barry liked to cook. Had an Italian recipe book and was working through it. Regardless of ingredients, he always used garlic and would laugh out loud, thinking, Keep the vamps at bay. It never failed to amuse him.

He went into the new wine bar, had a glass of white. Not bad. Then he saw her. Felt the rush, oh yeah, she was next. Fit all the points,
Pretty
Black
Confident.

It was an added high because he knew he'd kill this one. On her way out, she bumped his back and he said, "My fault." Falls gave him her best smile.

Rosie had answered a routine call. Disturbance on the ground floor of a high-rise. Probably nothing, but she was sent to check anyway.

All quiet when Rosie got there, she banged on the door. A

young woman answered, about twenty-two, her eyes had seen it all and none of it pretty. Launched into it. "It's Jimmy, he's back on smack, beat me when I said I'd no money."

Rosie stepped in, asked, "Where's Jimmy now?"

"He's nodding off in the bedroom."

Rosie smiled, said, "I'll have a word, eh."

"Tell him I've no money, he won't believe me."

Rosie went to the bedroom. The curtains were drawn and she tried the light. Nope. A figure was hunched on the bed, long hair hanging down. Rosie said, "Jimmy?" No response. She moved over and put out her hand to touch him.

His hand came up and he sank his teeth in her hand, bit down. Rosie heard the woman scream, "Don't let 'im touch yah, he's got AIDS."

Brant was standing at the Oval. Roberts was due to pick him up. A guy had been clocking him, sussing him out. Brant was aware without being concerned. He knew it would be a hustle, he figured he'd heard them all. Finally, the guy approached, asked, "In the market for a good watch, mate?"

"Sure."

The guy looked round, said, "I'm not talking yer Bangkok monkeys. None of that rubbish. This is prime."

"Let's have a look."

"It's a Tag."

When Brant didn't react, the guy said, "Like Tag Hever, man, top of the heap."

Brant sighed, said, "Are you going to produce it or just keep yapping."

Brant could see it in the guy's eyes – "a hook... gotcha."

Out came the watch and Brant took it, said, "It's a fake."

The guy was stunned. "It's no fake."

Then Brant took out his warrant card and the guy rolled his eyes. Taking off his own watch, Brant tried on the Tag, said, "So's you don't go away empty handed, I'm going to give you this original."

The guy took it said, "It's a Lorus!"

"A real Lorus, not a copy."

"Lorus is a piece of shit, worth a fiver tops."

Brant said, "Here's my lift, gotta go."

He got in and as Roberts moved into traffic, he looked back. The guy was still staring at the Lorus.

Brant adjusted the watch and Roberts asked, "That a Tag?"

"Yup."

"A fake though."

"No, it's the biz. I'm as amazed as you are."

As they proceeded, Brant continued to sneak glances at it. He was well pleased.

Roberts said, "Mr. Logan has an office at Camberwell Green."

"Yeah, and what's he floggin'?"

"Real estate."

"Figures."

They parked in Denmark Hill, walked down.

Brant said, "Like in the movies, good cop, bad cop."

"I hate that crap."

"Me too... so can I be the good guy?"

The office was busy. Three phones going in the outer. A receptionist asked, "Can I help?"

Brant showed the warrant card, said, "We need a moment of Mr. Logan's time."

She sighed, truly pissed and said, "I dunno, we're frightfully busy."

Roberts said, "No prob. We'll go and get *more* police and come barging back. How'd that be?"

She glared at Roberts, like she hated him, said, "Let me see." And strode into the back office.

Brant was looking at brochures, asked, "You live in Dulwich, guv?"

"Yeah, me 'n' Maggie Thatcher."

Brant looked at the prices, whistled, said, "Jaysus, you can't be hurting."

The receptionist came back, said, "Mr. Logan can spare you five minutes."

Tommy rose to greet them. They both clocked the hurleys

crossed above his desk. Brant flashed his card, said, "I'm DS Brant and this is my chief inspector."

Tommy was affable, said, "Gentlemen... please... have a seat... some tea... coffee?"

"No thanks."

They didn't sit. Brant asked, "Ever know a Tony Roberts?"

Tommy put his hand to his chin, like he was trying, said, "I remember a Tony Roberts in the early Woody Allen films."

He pronounced it "fill-ums" like an Irish broadcaster. Continued, "but I think he fell out with the Woodster and ended up in one of the Poltergeist things."

He gave a little laugh, said, "I suppose you don't mean him eh?"

Brant smiled, said to Roberts, "See all the stuff they learn in the nick, guv, all that time to kill?"

Tommy lost his affability. "Was there something else?"

Roberts was about to lose it when the door burst open. A woman was shouting, "Tommy, you asshole, you put a block on my account." Then saw he wasn't alone, muttered, "Oh."

Tommy did a little bow, said, "Gentlemen, my wife, Tina."

She was five-foot-four-inches tall, thereabouts. A face almost too pretty. You got to thinking... What's she like when all the make-up's off? Still. A lush body and she knew it. Playing men was her best act.

She turned to face Roberts and went, "Oh my-God-sweet-Jesus!"

Tommy didn't know what was happening, but it wasn't good. He said, "So Teen, I'll catch you later, here's some cash, eh."

Roberts played a hunch, asked, "What is it, I remind you of someone... that it? Do I look like Tony... Tony Roberts, my brother?"

Tommy couldn't help it, said, "Yer brother? Yah never said."

Brant smiled.

Tina said, "No, it's a dizzy spell. I don't know who you mean."

Roberts pressed on. "You know what they did to him Tina? Took a stick."

He spun round, pointed at the hurleys, continued, "Like one

of those and systematically broke every bone in his body."

Tina sobbed, "Leave me alone."

Tommy went to grab Roberts arm, shouting "That's it."

Roberts turned and grabbed him by the shirt, ripping buttons and pushed him over the desk, said, "Don't put yer hands on me, yah piece of shit."

Brant said, "Guv."

Roberts straightened up, took a deep breath, said, "I'll frigging have you."

Tommy tried to fix his suit, looked at the shirt, whined "Yah tore it. Eighty nicker and he rips it."

Now he spoke to Brant, "I have juice... oh yeah... you don't mess with Tommy Logan. I have connections."

Brant said, "You're going to need 'em pal."

On their departure, Roberts said to Tina, "He's going down, be smart and don't go with him."

Tommy slammed the door. He moved over to Tina, raising his fist, said, "Yah stupid cow."

The ringing of the phones in the outer office couldn't disguise the sound of the beating.

At their car, Roberts put a hand against the door, took a few deep breaths.

Brant said, "Just one question, guv."

"Yeah?"

"Were you the good or bad cop back there?"

Fear to fear
itself unfolding

Rosie couldn't stop sobbing. Falls had her arm round her, didn't know what to say, said, "I dunno what to say." "Tell me I'll be OK."

"You'll be OK."

Rosie gasped, said, "Jeez, put a bit of conviction in it. Lie to me for heaven's sake."

"I'm a bad liar."

Rosie held up her heavily bandaged hand, said, "It hurts so bad."

"Didn't they give you anything?"

"Two aspirin."

"Oh shit."

Rosie went quiet, said, "He's eighteen! God, I have shoes older than him!"

"Maybe he isn't HIV."

"It's the waiting. The doctor said it could lie dormant for years. How am I gonna tell Jack?"

"I said a dog did it. A mad dog... It was true, though, wasn't it? I won't be able to make love to Jack, I mean I couldn't."

Falls felt lost, tried "Maybe if a third-party told him? He's a good man, he'll support you."

"No... later he'd start to hate me. Think I should have been more careful."

She started to cry again.

Falls hugged her, said, "You have to hang in here, it will be all right."

Both wondered how on earth it could ever be that.

Evening song

Falls was on her eighth night of trawling. Jeez, she thought, this life of single bars and clubbin is boring. Every guy in south-east London with the same prized line: "Grab yer coat, you've pulled."

At least the women had variety – "Lemme apply yer lip gloss" through "Same old pricks, hon, try something feminine." Like that. Earlier she'd vented on McDonald, "I hope you're watching my back."

"Don't you fret doll, you're not supposed to see me."

"Well, I haven't, not once."

"I'm there, count on it." But she didn't.

Asked Brant, "Is McDonald reliable?"

"No."

"Sarge?"

"What?"

"Gimme some encouragement."

He handed her a canister, said, "Take CS gas, it's encouraging."

"Isn't it illegal?"

"I doubt yer attacker will report it... though, nowadays..."

Brant was quiet, then asked, "Would you carry a shooter?"

"You're joking... aren't you?" He gave her the look.

She took the CS gas.

Rosie was at home. Jack was working nights. She lined up twelve sleeping pills, all in a neat line. Took another hefty swig of the rum, the litre bottle going down. She was gently singing, "I like sailors 'cos sailors like rum and it sure does warm my tummy, tum, tum."

Dressed in a worn pink dressing gown, it made her feel domestic, said, "Now to pop two of those lads, there yah go."

It was the best she'd felt in weeks, thought, Oh God, the note... the police hate it when there's no note.

She got one of her special notelets, a Christmas present from Falls. They had a rose motif and along the top it read "Because Rose Cares." She carefully cut that off. Then wrote the note quickly.

The bath was nearly full and she turned the tap off. It sure smelled wonderful. She'd put in patchouli oil and mandalay scent. The steam had obliterated the mirror. Not that she'd have looked. Considered very briefly as she popped more pills what the verdict would be. How many times had she heard "death by misadventure"? Well, she was a Mrs. ... could they put Mrs Adventure.

She had been so careful with the pills. Christ, the last thing she wanted was to throw up. The rum she'd mixed with blackcurrant cos it was her favourite. The bottle was empty. "Oh" she said, "I'm a greedy guts." No more pills either. A half remembered ditty from her childhood:

> "Now I lay me down to sleep
> I ask The Lord
> My hair to keep."

No, that wasn't right. She could feel her mind shutting down and took off the robe. Just before she got in the bath, she left the plastic bag on the side. The water was divine and she gave a shudder of pleasure, said, "Please remember, don't forget." Reached for the plastic bag, "never leave the bathroom wet, Nor leave the soap still in the watta, That's a thing you never oughta."

Pan back from the bathroom and there, at the door, are her fluffy slippers, Snoopy dogs on the front. Pan further back into the living room and there's the note. Reads:

"I'm so sorry Jack.

I love you."

❖

As Rose ebbed away, Falls was leaving a club in Clapham,
thought, This isn't working, and walked quickly past a dark alley.
Then stopped. It was a short cut but you'd never dream of taking
it. Not at night. Thought, Girl, you have to start moving like a
victim.

The alley looked extremely forbidding. She checked for the CS
cannister in her pocket, took a deep breath, muttered, "Oh shit,
let's go."

Turned in.

Barry Lewis had nearly given up on this one. She'd always
stuck to the bright side of the street. Was about to turn for home
when the victim stopped. He couldn't believe it! Was she going to
risk the short cut? The endless stupidity of women! She took her
time, debating. Under his breath, he urged, "Go on, go on yah
black bitch, daddy's waiting."

It worked!

He began to quicken his pace, the adrenalin building to hyper.

Back at the club, McDonald clocked Falls leaving. He had just
scored with a neat little number from Peckham and was comfortable. The girl said, "I'd love a Harvey Wallbanger."

He'd been about to leave, shrugged and figured what could
five minutes hurt. Turned to the girl, his smile electric said, "Yah
go for wallbanging, eh?"

Falls was about half way down the alley when Lewis hit her. She
barely heard the footsteps when a shoulder crashed into her, send
her sprawling. Then he was kneeling on her back, tearing at her
tights, muttering, "Gonna give it to yah doggy-style and then I'm
going to turn you over, cut yer fucking throat."

His weight was overwhelming. Falls tried to function... where
was the gas? Then the weight was gone and she heard a crash. As
she turned, Brant's voice asked, "You OK, love?"

Lewis was hunched over, groaning.

Falls got shakily to her feet, asked, "How?"

"Gotta watch out for our own."

"McDonald?"

"No doubt keeping it warm."

Brant picked up the knife, moved over to Lewis, said, "Let's see what we got here."

Lewis was recovering fast, said, "Big deal, you can't prove nothing."

Held out his gloved hands, added, "Can't even prove the knife is mine."

Brant said, "Me too."

Showed his gloves. It confused Lewis and Falls. Brant was tapping the knife against his palm, said, "Worst scenario, you'd get two years, be out in six months. That how you figure?"

Lewis was nodding, looking at Brant, said, "Yeah, and then guess who I'll come looking for."

Brant said, "Wrong pal."

Moved fast in front of Falls. She saw Brant's hand go out, grab Lewis, pull him forward. A grunt, then a smothered scream. Brant pulled back and Lewis was on his knees, the knife embedded. Brant walked behind him, said, "Whoops, watch yer step," and kicked him full in the back.

Lewis went forward.

Falls said, "Oh sweet Jesus."

Brant took out his Weights, lit one.

Falls noticed his hands were as steady as a rock. He bent down, checked for pulse. None.

Falls said, "I don't believe this, you'll never get away with it."

Footsteps and McDonald came running, stopped, tried to assess the scene, asked, "What happened?"

Brant answered, "It's the rapist. Fell on his knife during the struggle with Falls."

"Is he dead?"

"As a doornail."

Brant started to walk away, said, "You'd better call it in, I mean you are on this case."

McDonald turned to Falls, asked, "Are you OK? I got delayed... I..."

She spat in his face.

Fall out

Tina Logan emerged from the hairdressers.
By sweeping her hair up and to the side, the bruising was mostly hidden. Her heart sank when she saw Roberts. He was leaning against his car.

"Go away."

"Tina, Tina... give me five minutes."

She pushed back her hair, said, "Look."

"Jesus!"

"Yeah, so please... he'll kill me."

"I just want to know about Tony, that's all."

She sighed, said, "Five minutes?"

"Guaranteed, the clock's already ticking."

Got in the car. He asked, "Wanna go someplace, get a drink?

"No, I want to get away from you."

Reached in her bag, took out a pack of Marlboro Lights, said, "Jeez... Lights! If Tommy sees me, I won't be worrying about cancer. They should put a health warning on men."

She lit up, said, "I suppose this is a 'smoke free zone'?"

"Don't worry about it."

She gave him a full look, said, "Oh I won't, you can be sure of that."

Roberts had a hundred questions, didn't know where to begin.

She did: "It was so corny. I dropped some packages and he helped me. Our eyes locked over a crushed M&S bag. I didn't tell him who I was."

"Tommy was on his way up and, being more crazy than usual, I started to meet Tony twice a week. He was gentle and where I'm coming from, that's unheard of."

"Funny too. I didn't know men could get you laughing. Then when Tommy began to suspect, I tried to call it off."

"But not really."

"I couldn't give him up. He was like... the beat of my heart. The rest you know. If your're thinking would I ever say that in a court, forget it."

"What was Tony to me? He made me feel special. Like, if I was reading *The Sun*, he wouldn't look down his nose. Oh yeah, he loved Smokie."

"Smoking?"

She laughed, said, "No, Smokie, a pop group from the '70s who kept on playing. Tony said they were the purest pop band... 'Living Next Door To Alice'?"

Roberts shook his head and she seemed disappointed, said, "You probably listen to classical stuff. Tony said I was his Alice... corny eh?"

She was crying now, said, "Ah jeez, me eye make-up is ruined. They tell you it doesn't run. Believe me, everything runs. Can I go?"

Roberts nodded, said, "Tina, I'll get him."

"You probably believe that, but I doubt if you ever will." And she was gone.

When Falls met Brant at the station, she said, "We have to talk."

"Naw, I don't think so. You did all right – got a commendation. McDonald's too smart to probe. He knows *he* was lucky."

"But it's wrong."

"Gee, that's a pity." And he strode off.

A few minutes later, the desk sergeant called her, said, "Phone, down the hall."

She picked it up, said, "Hello?"

"It's Jack."

"Oh Jack, I am so sorry, I..."

"Yes, undoubtedly..."

"She was my best mate, Jack."

A pause.

"She expressed a certain fondness for you too. I would like you to do something for me."

Perturbed by his tone, she was off balance, said, "Anything."

"Please inform your colleagues that we want no police at the funeral. No wreaths or vulgar flowers shaped like a helmet."

"OK, Jack, but her friends can surely attend as private mourners, I mean…"

"I most expressly forbid it."

"Oh… well, you're upset."

"Don't counsel me, lassie."

"I didn't mean…"

"Good day to you." And he hung up.

Dazed, she stood with the phone in her hand, then thought, It's good, good he can focus his grief, vent it and get it out.

Then she thought, The self-righteous prick. I'll send the most vulgar display he's ever seen… Yeah, fuck you too.

Powerful

Tommy Logan had gathered his men. He began, "Now lads..." You could cut the Irish brogue with a shillelagh. He could have been speaking Swahili for all they cared. They were on a roll and cash was steaming in. Plus, they knew he was the last man on earth to fuck with.

He continued, "Ye'll be familiar with informants. Or snitches, as they call them in this country. It seems the police have somebody doing the dirty on us."

Raised his voice, "Play fair I say."

It received the required laugh. "So now, I'll put five large into the hand of the fellah who finds the snitch."

An animated murmur. They liked the deal.

"OK, then... go get 'im... oh, one more thing..."

They paused.

"Be careful out there."

More polite laughter. Ol' Tommy, he was a big kidder.

Then he got on the phone. His solicitor, chosen well.

"Harry... it's Tommy Logan."

"Tommy how are you?"

"I've a wee bit o' bother."

"Oh dear, maybe we can help."

Harry was a Mason, knew where help was located.

"There's two policemen, a DI Roberts and his sergeant, a guy named Brant. They've begun to harass me, upset the missus, that sort of thing."

"We can't have that."

"I knew you'd understand."

"Leave it to me Tommy, it's already being processed."

"Thanks Harry."

"We must have that game of golf soon."

"Of course... ta-ra then."

"Bye."

Unless Tommy took his hurley to the links, there was as much chance of nine holes as Brant being promoted.

The *South London Press* had a photo of Falls on the front page and the headline:

"SHY HEROINE STOPS CLAPHAM RAPIST"

Shy because she refused an interview.

McDonald got a brief line as her partner. He wasn't complaining. Brant's version of the event had been accepted and if he got a little glory, all the better.

Rosie's death had prevented a deeper investigation. It was known that a keg of scandal could be opened, so the authorities let it be.

Falls tried to talk to Roberts, cornered him in the canteen. He said, "I'm sorry about Rosie, I liked her a lot."

"Thanks, guv."

She indicated his cup, offered, "More tea?"

"No, I'm about finished." Which, roughly translated meant, "Spit it out."

She tried. "It's about the rapist, sir..."

"Oh yeah. Congratulations, you did well... bloody well."

"Sir, it's about his death."

"Good riddance I say."

"Sir, on moral grounds..."

He put up his hand, "Whoa, we're coppers – morality has no place in it."

"But, sir—'

He quoted, "If a mere code of ethics could keep it legal, there'd be no need of us. I don't give advice but lemme say this... *Leave it alone.*"

"I don't know if I can, sir."

He stood up, said, "You've no choice. If there's anything to be resolved here, it's why you don't appreciate the sergeant who saved *your* life."

Walked away.

"So he knows… God, why am I surprised?"

Roberts got the call to the Super's office. No invitation to sit down, right to it.

"You're to lay off Tommy Logan."

"*What?*"

"There's a highly sensitive investigation underway. You'd only jeopardise months of work."

"Are you aware that he killed my brother?"

"Are *you* aware I'm your superior officer and to be addressed as 'sir'?"

Roberts felt reckless, dangerously so, said, "I don't get it, Logan's not a Mason."

The Super was up, spitting, "I don't think I like your inference, you'd be wise to proceed with great care."

Roberts didn't even hear him, was trying to put it together, then, "Wait a mo! It's his bloody solicitor, that scumbag Harry Something. Christ yeah, he's definitely in the lodge."

"That will be all Chief Inspector. I'm going to overlook your outburst, put it down to your grief. You can go."

Roberts pulled himself together, prepared to leave. The Super added, "It would be a conflict of interest to have you on a family case."

"With all due respect, that's bollocks… sir."

Moving on

Sarah Cohen was Rosie's replacement. On her arrival at the station, the desk sergeant said, "Cohen? A bloody Yid." She now knew what to expect. With curly brown hair, brown eyes and a snub nose, she was half-ways pretty. Like any new person, the voice in her head roared:

Run

    Get

        The

            Fuck

                Out

                    Now

                        Before...

Burning with zeal, she had done a year of Social Science. That burnt out. On a whim, she'd applied to the police. Here she was, scared witless. The desk sergeant asked, "What would you like to do today?"

She'd been about to respond, "A little light traffic to start and home early."

The desk sergeant was grinning, said, "How does the North Peckham Estate sound?"

Sounded awful is what. Before she made a total fool of herself, a voice said, "Lay off her, Dennis."

Brant. He nodded at Dennis, said, "He likes to fuck with new people. I need a WPC... let's go." And he was already moving.

The desk sergeant offered, "Outta the frying pan..."

Sarah had hoped for a nice cup of tea to begin. She was up all night pressing her uniform. Brant was climbing into a battered Volvo, asked, "Wanna drive?"

"Ahm, no thank you."

A huge smile and he said, "I love fuckin' manners."

Falls was getting obsessed with Brant and didn't try to fight that. It stopped her thinking of Rosie which she couldn't get a handle on.

In the pub one time, they'd all been celebrating. A little tipsy, she asked him, "How come you've never come on to me?"

"What?"

He was mid-Cornish pasty and stared.

"You've never hit on me. All the times we've been thrown together. Am I not yer type?"

He looked at the pie, said, "Ever notice with these things, you start off cold. Lulls you into a false sense of security and then the middle is burning, leaps to the roof of yer mouth and clings?"

She laughed, asked, "Is that a metaphor?"

He dumped the remains on the floor, said, "Naw, it's just a pasty. But naw, yer not my type."

More bothered than she would have anticipated, she got silly, said, "Is it a *black* thing?"

"I like black fine as long as they're bimbos."

"Oh come on sarge, I don't buy that."

He grabbed a pint, drank half, belched, said "I have no problem with women talking. Hell, it punctuates the time. What I hate is women thinking they've something to say."

She was horrified, let it show, then, "That's the most chauvinistic thing I've ever heard."

He drained the glass, said, "I've got a question…"

"Go ahead."

"When this shindig's over, will you let me jump you?"

She physically drew back. "How *dare* you!"

"See… you're a good cop, Falls, and not bad looking. But yer not a babe. You'd want to talk after we'd done it. Me, I want me kip, so I'm off, grab a bimbo, whisper sweet shite, then wham, bam, and lock the door on yer way out."

Then he was gone. For the first time in her life she lamented not being a babe.

Sarah Cohen and Brant pulled to a stop outside McDonald's on the Walworth Road. The radio was squawking gibberish. Brant seemed to comprehend it, said, "We're on it."

Turned to Sarah, said, "It's a couple of drunks, my only suggestion is, don't get too close."

Sarah didn't answer. She intended getting a hands-on approach from day one – being a real police person.

To the left, as you enter McDonald's, there's a children's area. With toadstools for seats and other such furnishings to put the children at ease. On the wall is a portrait of Ronald McDonald, the spit of John Gacy. Not so much a haven for little people as a creation by little-minded people. A man and a woman were holed up there, shouting obscenities and hurling burgers at the staff.

Brant said, "Pissed as parrots."

Sarah asked, "What's the strategy, sir?"

"I'm gonna get some doughnuts, want one?" And he headed for the counter.

Sarah felt this was her window, began to approach the couple, said, "I say."

Thought – "Oh God, I sound like a school girl. Get some street in there."

The woman had been nodding, almost out of it, then her head snapped up, spotted Sarah, called, "C'mere love."

Sarah did. The woman struggled to her feet and threw up over Sarah.

Brant came with coffee and doughnuts, asked, "Jelly or sugared?"

Took a look at her, said, "Now, that's sick."

Peered closer, added "I spot pepperoni, it's a bastard to keep down, here hold these."

Then he walked to the side, pulled the fire extinguisher from its bracket, strolled back, muttering "Point the noozle where?" Opened it up, shouting "Go on, get outta it." Drenching the couple and literally spraying them to the street. A round of applause from the staff. He nodded to Sarah, said, "That's about it I'd say."

And walked out.

Sarah followed, trying to unsuccessfully clean the uniform with wafer thin napkins. She looked at the soaked couple, asked Brant, "Aren't we taking them in?"

"Do you want to put them in the car?"

She got in beside Brant and he said, "Open the window love, vomit will linger." And he put the car in gear.

Back at the station, she rushed to the bathroom, was attempting to clean up when Falls walked in. She'd heard about the black WPC, said, "I'm new."

"Oh really?"

She looked in the mirror, wanted to bawl. Falls looked at the soiled tunic said, "You've already met DS Brant."

Sarah smiled, felt it was an overture, went for it. "I'm sorry about your friend."

"Why... did you know her?"

"No... but..."

"Then ration your grief, you'll be getting plenty."

Sarah couldn't help it, babbled on: "I mean, I know I can never replace her and..."

Falls cut it short, said, "You got that right."

And left her.

When she emerged from the bathroom, Brant was waiting. Sarah felt she already hated him. "There you are love, c'mon I'll get a tea." And she warmed to him again.

In the canteen, he said, "Get us a tea, two sugars, I'll grab a table."

Sarah looked round, every table was vacant. She got the teas and the canteen lady said, "You're the new girl?"

Oh, Jesus.

"Never you mind, pet, the teas are on me."

Not a grand gesture, just a moment of kindness and Sarah wanted to hug her. The woman nodded at Brant, said, "Watch that 'un, he's an animal."

Brought the teas over and Brant asked, "No biccies?"

"Oh."

"Never mind but you'll know next time. I'm partial to the club milks."

She said, "Could I ask you something?"

"As long as it's not for cash, it's a bit early."

"Oh Good Lord no. It's about my predecessor."

"Rosie?"

"Yes. I know I've no right but... what was she like?"

"A loser."

She was shocked and maybe a tad relieved. Brant finished his tea, said, "Yeah, she got to pull the ultimate sulk you know – na-na-na-na-na – you can't catch me, like never. Everybody gets to feel guilty and she's outta here."

Sarah thought a defence of some calibre should be shown, said, "But if her state of mind was disturbed?"

He stood up, his closing words, "She was a cop, yer mind is always disturbed, otherwise we'd be social workers."

The Super's wife was a dowager. Leastways, she looked like one. She was never young but, when she got seriously aged, she'd be Barbara Cartland, or Windsor, or both.

Her home was in Streatham Vale but she was a Belgravia wannabe and managed to mention said place in every conversation. Her car broke down near the Oval and she had to abandon it. Walking down towards the cricket ground, she was in fear of her life. Her husband *did* bring his work home.

She saw a black cab. Oh merciful God! A man stepped up beside her and grabbed her arm, pinned it under his and neatly removed her Cartier watch, shoved her back, said, "You can 'av this piece o' shit, and slung a Lorus at her."

Brant, on being told by Roberts, said, "I love it."

"The Super's on some warpath."

"Even better, I know how to solve it."

"You're kidding, unless..."

"What?"

"*You* mugged her!"

"Close, but no. So, who do we want to do well?"

"Let's give it to the new kid, see how she cooks."

"The Yid it is."

Brant caught up with Sarah later in the day. He said, "Apprehend me."

"What?" She hoped it wasn't sexual.

"During your training, didn't they show you how to arrest someone?"

"Yes."

"OK, then. Picture this. I'm a suspect standing at... let's say, the Oval station... OK?"

"OK."

"So arrest me."

"What have you done? Oh, I'm sorry, what have you *allegedly* done."

"For Christ's sake, what does it matter?"

"I want to be prepared."

"Oh, I get it, you're a method police person."

She nearly laughed but stuck to her guns... "Sarge, it's the degree of force. I don't want to club you to the ground if it's only a parking ticket."

Brant smiled. "Good point, though personally I prefer the clubbing method regardless. Let's say I'm a mugger."

"A what?"

"Christ, a bloody..." And next thing he knew he was flat on his face, his hands held behind him.

She said, "See, I distracted you."

"I'm impressed... where'd you learn that."

"Girls' boarding school."

"My favourite. You can let me up now, I think you've got the hang of it."

Brant *was* impressed. The girl had some moves and would be worth cultivating. She and Brant drove to the Oval the next day. Parked opposite the entrance, she asked, "Why are we here?"

"You'll see."

After an hour, the man appeared, took up his habitual position. Brant said, "See 'im?"

"Yes."

"Go get him."

"Arrest him?"

"As if you meant it."

Brant watched her go. The kid was a definite comer and not bad looking. Nice legs. He saw her approach the man, then bingo, she had his arm behind his back, marched him to the car. Brant got the door open and pulled him in the back, said to Sarah, "You drive." The man was protesting... "I didn't do nuffink... hey... wait a mo'... *I know you!*"

Brant grabbed the man's testicles, squeezed, said, "Repeat please: *I never saw you before.*"

He repeated.

When they got to the station, Brant said to Sarah, "When you're bookin' him, check his arms."

"For tracks?"

"Not exactly."

Coup

S arah was the heroine of the hour. To such an unprecedented extent that the Super emerged from his office and addressed those gathered.

"Today we have reason to be proud. A rookie applied the tried and tested methods of policing and got a result."

He flourished the Cartier in all its gleaming glory, continued "If this is an indication of the standard of new blood entering the service, then I say the Met has very little reason for concern for the future."

Cheers, congratulations, and cameraderie filled the station. Quite overcome, Sarah retreated to the ladies. Falls already there, said, "You've arrived in style."

"Beginner's luck."

"Or the hand of Brant, perhaps."

Sarah was tempted to ask, "Touch of the sour grapes?"

Falls looked directly at Sarah, said, "Is he fucking you?"

"My God, of course not."

"Yeah, he's doing it to you one way or another, he puts it to everyone."

Now Sarah went for it, "Don't worry, no one's moving in on your manor."

Falls laughed, "Well, you've got spunk, I'll give you that."

Sarah eased up, said, "Maybe we can have a drink sometime."

"I doubt that."

And was gone.

Brant and Roberts were in the pub. Drinking vodka because it doesn't smell of desperation, leastways, not for a while. Roberts said, "I've been warned off."

"I know."

"What?"

"I told you, I've got it taped."

"Was it the Masons?"

"Yup."

"Fuckers."

"What now, guv?"

"I dunno."

"But you're not like… giving up?"

For an answer, Roberts just looked at him and Brant said, "Good, I'd hate to chase him on me lonesome."

Roberts laughed. Of such moments are the best friendships sealed. They ordered some more vodka and Roberts said, "Shouldn't we eat something?"

"I suppose."

"Want something?"

"Naw."

"Me neither."

Let the silence build a while and allow the booze to do its number. Then Brant said, "The woman's the key."

"His missus?"

"Yeah, get 'im through her."

Roberts was uneasy, said, "I kinda like her. I wouldn't want her to get hurt."

"There's always fall-out, guv."

Roberts chewed on that. Then, in an exact imitation of Brant, said, "You're right, fuck her."

Despite the best efforts of the vodka, they didn't get any further along. Then, as is the wont of alcohol, it flipped sides and Roberts thought about Smokie, thought, At least Brant won't have heard of them either.

Aloud, he said, "Don't suppose you've heard of Smokie?"

"The group?"

"Yeah."

"Sure, 'Living Next Door To Alice'."

"You know that, too?"

Brant looked almost happy. "They were like a cross between the Small Faces and The Hollies. Their lead singer got killed a time back, I was sorry."

And he looked it.

The past

Next morning, Brant was sick as forty pigs. That's real bad. Dragging himself to the shower he swore, "Never again."

Yeah. Fragments of the night returned.

How when the pub closed, that's when they got hungry.

Off to the Chinese where they drank bamboo wine... Could that be right?

Leaning against the toilet bowl, Brant begged, "Please let me not have had the curry."

As he threw up, he thought, "Damn, I had the curry."

Afterwards, they'd come back to Brant's place and played neo-whine songs. All the great torches. Barbara Streisand, "You Don't Bring Me Flowers"; Celine Dion, "Theme from Titanic"; Bonnie Tyler, "Lost in France"; Meatloaf, "Two Outta Three Ain't Bad."

And if the debris in his living room was any indication, they'd drank:

Beer,

More vodka

and

Cooking sherry.

"Jaysus... please, not cooking sherry."

Threw up again. Yup, the sherry.

Got in the shower and blitzkreiged.

Coming out he felt marginally better. Then to the living room, muttered, "Fuck," as he surveyed the carnage. How many cigarettes, exactly, had he smoked? Shuddered to think, and he needed one now. Took a stubbie from an ashtray, lit up.

Rough.

Once he got past the coughing jag, the bile and nausea bit, it wasn't too bad. Said aloud, "Hey, it's not as if I *had* to have a drink."

Got his clothes on and checked out the mirror. Mmmm... least he hadn't slept in them. Still, looked like somebody slept *on* him.

In the kitchen, made the coffee, two heaped spoons. Jolt himself into the day. Added a ton of sugar and then surveyed it, said, "I am not, repeat not, drinking that shit," and slung it down the sink. Then he physically shook himself and left.

A few minutes later he was back, walked across the room, picked up an open vodka bottle, chugged the final hit. Waited.

It stayed down.

He said, "Now yer cookin."

And went to fight the day.

At the station, the duty sergeant said, "A woman called you."

"Called me what?"

"Said she was yer wife."

Jesus!

When Brant didn't say anything, the uniformed sergeant added, "Wanted yer number but of course I said I couldn't do that. So she gave me her number."

Passed the piece of paper to Brant, then said, "I didn't know you had a wife."

"I don't." Not any more.

Mary had left him over ten years ago. Hadn't heard a dicky-bird since.

Called the number and when a woman answered, said, "It's Brant."

"Oh Tom, thank you for calling me back, I wasn't sure you would."

"What do you want?"

"No hellos or how are you?"

"You rang to see how I am?"

"Well, not completely but…"

"So get on with it."

He heard the click of a lighter, the inhale of smoke, nearly said, "You smoke?" But then, what was it to him? She could mainline heroin, what did he care?

Then:

"My husband, Paul… I married again five years ago… he's in trouble."

"What kind?"

"He was accused of shoplifting at M&S, at their flagship store."

"Their what?"

"The big one at Marble Arch."

"What did he nick?"

"Oh Tom, he didn't… the store detective stopped him outside, said he didn't pay for a tin of beans. He'd over thirty pounds of shopping. Would he steal a tin?"

"Would he?"

"Course not. Can you help?"

"I'll try."

"Thank you Tom, I've been so worried."

"What's the name?"

"Silly me, it's Watson, he's the security officer on food."

"*Your* name, your married name."

"Oh."

"It would be useful if I had your husband's name."

"Johnson… Paul Johnson, he's…" Brant hung up.

What he most wanted to know was why he was so reluctant to use the word "husband."

Kebabed

Spiro the snitch was having a bad morning. The VAT crew had been on the phone and promised a visit soon. Plus the health inspectors he'd managed to twice defer. But, he knew he couldn't do that indefinitely. He'd have to get Brant to do it for him.

Aloud he said, "Mallakas" – or seeing as he was born and reared in Shepherd's Bush, he could have simply said, "Wankers."

He had a few words of Greek but rationed them carefully. He was attempting to clean the spit for the kebab meat. Standing vertical, usually it was shrouded in meat and he carved accordingly. Now, it was bare and red hot. It gleamed with heat and hygiene. About to turn if off when there was a loud knock. A voice said, "Police."

"Now what?" he fumed as he went to get it.

Tommy Logan and two of his men.

Spiro said, "You're not police."

"We lied."

With a dismal record in the Eurovision, the Greeks were familiar with the winners. Spiro stared at Tommy, asked, "Are you...?"

"Trouble? Yes I am, let's take it inside."

They bundled Spiro back into the taverna.

Tommy said, "Spring cleaning or should that be spit cleaning?"

Spiro said, "I'll turn it off and perhaps I can get you gentlemen a drink."

"No, leave it on, gives the room a cosy atmosphere."

Tommy stared at Spiro, said, "Let's do this quick and easy.

You've been telling tales to the Old Bill, haven't you? No lies or I'll make you lick the spit."

Spiro was close to emptying his bowels, and yet his mind registered how awful a dye job Tommy had.

He put out his hands in the universal plea of surrender, said, "On my mother's grave, I didn't."

Tommy grabbed Spiro's hands, said, "Hold him."

The men did, then dragged Spiro over to the spit. Tommy said, "You're a hands-on kind of guy, I can tell." And slapped Spiro's hands to the hot metal.

His screams were ferocious and Tommy screamed right along with him. Then he let go and Spiro fell to the floor, whimpering.

Tommy said, "Next it's your tongue, then yer dick. We'll kebab till the early hours. Or would you prefer to talk?"

He talked. Tommy listened, then said, "Spiro... it is Spiro, am I right?"

Nod.

"Do you know me?"

Shake.

"So why are you making trouble? What should I do now? Do you feel up to a solid beating?"

"No... please..."

"OK."

Spiro was too terrified to hope. Then Tommy said, "You've cost me an arm and a leg so let's break one of each... you choose."

It got a bit messy and they had to break both arms and his left leg.

Tommy said, "You've a fine pair of lungs on yah."

As they were leaving, Tommy asked one of his men, "You eat that Greek food?"

"Me... naw, I like Chinese."

Tommy shook his head, said, "Irish stew is hard to top... Give the polliss a call, say their Greek takeaway is ready."

Shopping

Brant went to "records," gave Shelley his best smile. She wasn't buying, least not right away, said, "You want something?"

"To take you dancing."

"Yeah... sure."

"Honest, the Galtimore on a Saturday night, all of Ireland and oceans of sweat and porter."

"How could a girl resist... whatcha want?"

"A security guard with Marks and Spencer, name of Watson. He's at their flagship. You know what that is?"

"Sure, Marble Arch."

"Jeez, everyone knows it, eh?"

"Do you want the straight CV, or do I dig?"

"Dig please."

While he was waiting he lit a cigarette. Shelley looked at the profusion of NO SMOKING notices but said nothing. Ten minutes later, she said, "Gotcha."

Got a printout, showed it to Brant. He said, "Looks OK."

"Take a look at 1985."

"Ah."

"That's it."

"Thanks, Shelley, I'll remember you in my prayers."

"Is that a threat or a promise?"

Brant enjoyed his excursions to the West End. To be in a part of England no longer English... pity the parking was such a bitch. Finally he got a space off the Tottenham Court Road end of

Oxford Street and hiked to Marble Arch. His hangover was crying out to be fed but he decided to wait. The crankiness might help his endeavour.

At the entrance to M&S was, as luck would have it, a security guard. Tan uniform, tan teeth. Brant flashed the warrant card, asked, "Where might I find Mr. Watson?"

"He'll be in the basement, foodstuffs are his manor."

"All right is he?"

The guy looked at Brant, the look that yells, "Do me a favour pal," but said, "He's a supervisor."

"All right as a supervisor is he?"

"I couldn't say, I only know him on a professional basis."

Brant had an overwhelming desire to kick the guy in the balls, but said, "Don't give much away do ya, boyo?"

The guard put a hand on Brant's arm, moved him slightly to the left, said, "You're impeding free access."

"God forbid I should do that. Tell you what though, do you have a good friend?"

"What?"

"Cos if you put a hand on me again you'll need a good friend to extract it from yer hole. No carry on, no slouching."

In the basement, Brant clocked him instantly. No uniform but eyes that never saw civilians. He was standing near the fire door. Brant let him see his approach. Nice and easy, loose, asked, "Mr. Watson?"

"Yeah."

Oh lots of hard. This was a guy who doled *out* the shit, always. But Brant knew they were mostly cop wanna-be's, so he flashed the card, said, "Could I have a moment of yer time?"

Deep sigh. Like, not really but for a brother in arms, only don't lean on it. Said, "Come to my office in back."

It was a broom closet but if he wanted to call it that, be my guest. There was one swivel chair and a small desk. He sat, put his feet up, said, "Shoot."

You knew he'd rehearsed it a thousand times. Brant could play, said, "You got a guy on shoplifting a few weeks back."

Watson sneered "Buddy, I get hundreds every week."

"Of course, this was literally a tin o' beans."

Now Watson's eyes lit up, "Yeah, he freakin' cried, can yah believe it? Big baby."

Brant let him savour, then, "Can you let it slide?"

Guffaw.

"In yer dreams, buddy."

Brant was peaking, couldn't believe his good fortune. Who could have prophesied such a horse's ass? Decided to let the rope out a few more inches, said, "As a brother officer, I'm asking for a bit o' slack. Doesn't hurt to have a friend in The Met."

Watson was off on it, power to full octane, said, "No way, José."

Brant hung his head, and Watson, flying, said, "Don't do the crime if…"

Before he could finish, Brant was roaring:

"Shudd-up, yah asshole, and get yer feet off the desk…"

Brant leant over, nose to nose, said, "I tried to do it the easy way. But, oh no, Mister Bust-Yer-Chops gets all hot."

Watson blustered, tried to get the reins back, "You've got nothing on me."

"Does M&S employ criminals?"

"What… of course not!"

Brant took the paper from his jacket, slapped it on the table, said, "I draw yer attention to 1985."

Watson looked, then, "You've no right to that, it's not on my application form."

Realising what he said, he shut down.

Brant read:

"1985 – Watson – D&D – Suspended. They see this, they'll bump yer ass from here to the dole queue."

Watson said, "If I could… make it right with the other thing, you'll go away?"

"Well, I'll call in now and again, see you're not slacking."

Resigned, Watson said, "The perp's name again?"

"Perp?"

"You know… the perpetrator…" He looked up, anxious to please, said, "The alleged… now cleared… person's name?"

"Paul Johnson."

Brant threw his eyes round the closet, turned to leave.

Watson offered, "I was only doing my job."

"Naw... you're a vicious little shit. Stay outta south-east London."

Whining now, "Me old Mum lives there."

"Move her."

Brant rang Mary, said, "It's Brant."

"Oh hello, Tom."

"It's done."

"What? Oh my God, Paul... Paul will want to thank you."

"No need."

"Tom, maybe we could all meet, have a meal, our treat?"

"C'mon Mary."

"Oh."

"Goodbye then."

"Tom... Tom if ever we can..."

But Brant had rung off.

Mary knew she should be elated but what she felt was a sense of let-down, a whisper of sadness.

The Coroner's verdict on the Clapham Rapist was "Accidental Death." Falls and McDonald sat on opposite sides of the hearing. Twice he'd tried to approach her, trying, "Can we move on?"

"No."

Then: "If we're going to have to work together at least..."

"Fuck off."

He'd let it be.

In an unusual development, the Coroner praised the police for the conclusion of a fraught and dangerous episode. Falls squirmed.

Outside, she managed to dodge most of the reporters. A woman came up to her and asked, "May I shake your hand?"

"Ahm?"

She took Falls by the hand and said, "I want to thank you for ending the nightmare. I was number six. That piece of scum, I hope he rots in hell."

The violence of the words and the ferocity of her manner pushed Falls backwards. She tried, "There is counselling available."

A bitter laugh, "Oh you were all the counselling I needed." And then she was gone.

McDonald called, "Yo' Sarah!"

"Yeah."

He caught up with her, said, "I don't think I congratulated you on yer success."

"Thank you."

She found it the easiest answer. She gave him a fast appraisal and thought, "Doesn't half fancy himself."

He held out his hand, "I'm McDonald."

"Weren't you the…"

"Involved in the Clapham Rapist? I played a very minor role."

"Oh, I'm sure you're being modest."

He gave her the full heat of his smile, turned it up to full dazzler. "Listen, whatcha say about a drink later?"

"Ahm, I don't know…"

"Hey, no strings… we work together so it's no big deal."

"OK… why not?"

After he walked off she felt it was a bad idea. But hey, maybe they could be mates and keep it at that. She wasn't convinced, not at all.

"What do you know
about scenery?
Or beauty? Or any of
the things
that really make life
worth living?
You're just an
Animal,
Coarse,
Muscled,
Barbaric."

"You keep right on
talking honey.
I like the way you run
me down like that."

Barrie Chase and Robert
Mitchum in "Cape Fear."

In the modern world

Roberts went into a record shop. The last record he'd bought had been by the Dave Clark Five. He was stunned by the shop. The sheer volume of the noise deafened him. Everybody looked like a drug dealer. Worse, he felt like a pensioner. Mainly he wanted to flee. But gathering his resources he marched up to a counter. An assistant, a girl who looked about twelve, said, "Yeah."

"Ahm... I'm looking for... a... Smokie..."

"CD or cassette?"

"I think you can take it that if the customer is over forty, it's a cassette."

"Is it hip-hop, dance, techno...?"'

"Whoa, wait a moment... they're a pop group from the '70s."

"Then you'll want retro."

Eventually, he was led to the cassette section and, no luck.

No Smokie.

They offered to order it, saying, "Seventies... cool."

He declined.

Roberts sole passion was film *noir* of the forties and fifties. Now he resolved to re-bury himself in the genre. It was what he knew.

Lesson

Brant found Sarah in the canteen. She was about to have a tea and a danish.

He said, "Wanna see another side of policing?"

She gave the danish a look of longing.

He added, "I mean now."

Grabbing her bag, she got up and Brant leant across, grabbed the danish, said, "Don't want to waste that."

The Volvo was outside and between bites, Brant said, "You drive."

She got the car in gear and he said, "St. Thomas's... mmm... this is delicious, must have been fresh in."

Sarah was cautious in her driving, conscious of him watching. He was.

He asked, "What's this?"

"Excuse me?"

"Yer driving like a civilian, put the bloody pedal to the metal."

They found a space to park and walked back to the hospital. Brant said, "I frigging hate hospitals."

"Who are we seeing?"

"A snitch, well probably an ex-snitch."

Sarah wasn't sure how to answer so she said, "Oh."

Spiro was in an open ward on the third floor. He seemed to be covered in casts and bandages. His leg was suspended.

When he saw Brant, his eyes went huge with fear.

Brant smiled, said, "Spiro!"

Spiro's eyes darted to Sarah and Brant said, "It's OK, she's a good 'un."

He took a long look at the injuries, then asked, "Who did it?"

"I dunno Mr. Brant, I was attacked from behind."

"Sure you were."

Spiro's eyes pleaded to Sarah and he said, "I am very tired, I must sleep."

Brant moved closer, said, "I don't need you to say a dicky-bird. I'm going to mention a name and if it's correct, just nod. That's all and we're gone."

Sarah felt useless, gave Spiro a small smile.

Brant said, "Tommy Logan."

For a few moments nothing; Spiro had closed his eyes. Then, a small nod.

Brant said, "OK, you need anything?"

Head shake.

Brant turned to Sarah, said, "Let's go."

They were on the ground floor before Sarah got to ask, "Who's Tommy Logan?"

"A murderin' bastard is who."

"Things are entirely
what they appear
to be and behind them
there is nothing."

(Sartre)

Falls was shopping. With an air of total abstraction, her eyes kept wandering to the booze counter. The bottles called out, "Come and get us, ple-eze."

She sure wanted to. Just crawl into a bottle and shout "Sayonara, suckers."

Block out everything.

The Rapist,

Brant,

McDonald,

…And especially Rosie.

But she wasn't certain she'd return. Her father had climbed in and never emerged. Without awareness, she was shredding a head of cabbage. A voice said, "I don't think it will improve."

She looked up. A man in his late-forties was smiling at her. He indicated the cabbage, said, "Like life, it doesn't get better with the peeling away."

Jeez, she thought, He is one attractive guy.

His hair was snow white and he had a three day beard, which was dark brown. Then the eyes, deeper, holding brown. They held her.

He said, "According to the experts, shopping is the best way to meet members of the opposite sex."

She didn't think such gibberish deserved an answer so she said nothing. If it bothered him, he hid it well, said, "My Mother believed you should go out the door you came in."

"Which means what, exactly?"

"That I'm backing off; sorry to have interrupted your shredding." Then he turned and walked off.

Falls said quietly, "Oh that's great, frighten him right off."

Her eyes turned again to the booze and she made her decision, shouted, "Hey!"

He stopped, and when she caught up, she said, "Tell me more about yer old Mum."

Brant was going against his instincts but, hell, he felt reckless. As he and Sarah returned to the station, he asked casually, "What's yer plan for this evening?"

She took it easy, answered, "I'm going out with friends."

"Have a good time, eh?"

"I'll try."

After she'd gone, he sat in the car and tried to figure out what he was feeling. Took out a cigarette and lit it. As the nicotine hit, he tried not to admit that he was disappointed. Then he looked up to see Sarah and McDonald leaving the station.

Her head was thrown back, laughing.

Brant said, "Fuck."

Tommy Logan was hyper, roared, "See what happens to those who fuck with me."

His men grunted in agreement. What they mainly hoped was he'd be brief.

More: "Not even the cops can come at us. I had a chief inspector try, eh... Where is he now?

"His DS, the hard case Brant, what had he to offer? Bloody zero, that's what. I'm throwing a party on Friday, the biggest fuckin' bash in south-east London. This is just the beginning."

Flushed, he wiped his brow and waited for applause. Applause wasn't really in their vocabulary but they knew a response was required. A few hip-hips were produced and it had to suffice. Tommy turned to his right-hand man, said, "Get the invitations out. Let it be known it's *the* event."

"Sure, guv."

He was the only one Tommy trusted. The rest he knew would sell him for a pony.

Ideally, Tommy would have loved to get Johnny Logan singing for the party, but he'd found out he was lost in cabaret in Western Australia. Still, he might do a song himself, it depended on the crowd.

The party invitations went out. Harry, the solicitor's name went on the invites. Thus, a broad cross-section of people could be invited. Including the Super.

The Super rang Harry, "Harry, it's Superintendent Brown."

"Superintendent, how are you?"

"Fine, fine. Thank you for the invite."

"A pleasure. Will you and your lady wife be able to attend?"

"Wouldn't miss it."

"Splendid, the theme is law and order."

"Highly commendable."

"The Lodge will be there."

"Better and better, Harry. Any help I can give?"

Harry paused, gave it the momentary respect, then, "Any chance some of your lads might assist with security?"

"They'd be delighted to."

"Well, that's a load off my mind. See you at the party, then."

"Absolutely, thanks again." The call concluded.

Both men felt they'd done pretty damn fine.

Drinking
lights
out

"I don't think I've had piña coladas before." Sarah had two empty glasses in front of her, working on a third. It was unlikely she'd had a drink of such calibre before. McDonald knew the barman and had signalled, "doubles." on each round. What used to be called a Mickey Finn but now was simply referred to as "loaded." McDonald was drinking scotch – singles – and watching Sarah go down.

Feeling the alcohol, she said, "My Mum would forgive a man anything if he was handsome."

McDonald posed the obvious, "Would she have forgiven me?"

Sarah gave him a shy look, said, "You know the answer to that."

He gave a modest nod which came across as smarmy. She said, "My father could dance on the side of a saucer."

She pronounced it "soo-sir' as the coladas kicked in.

McDonald gave the obligatory chuckle, asked, "Fancy one for the road?"

Emboldened, she asked, "One what?"

Music to his ears.

Another drink and it would be Ride City.

Band

" **O**wn Us" were an up and coming band. A cross twixt Oasis and Verve, they were still hungry. Word of mouth was beginning to repeat their name and a record deal was in the air. When approached to do Tommy Logan's party, they didn't hesitate a moment, said, "No." Relayed back to Tommy, he said, "Fuck 'em."

Then, "Burn 'em."

Tommy's right-hand man proposed he have a chat with them. Tommy asked, "Why, Mick?"

"'Cos they'll get us lots of press."

"OK, have a shot but if nothing's doing, screw 'em."

"They'll agree, I guarantee it."

The lead singer was named Matt Wilde (sic). He had acquired the mandatory mid-Atlantic drawl for rock stars. Plus, he scratched a lot. Mick found them rehearsing in a warehouse at the Elephant. He listened to their set and thought, Christ, they're bad.

Matt called a break and signalled to Mick. Being summoned by a nineteen-year-old pup was energising. The star was scratching his neck, asked, "What's yer bag man?"

"I'd like you to reconsider doing the Law 'n' Order party gig."

"No can do man, never gonna happen. It hasn't got, like, cred. You hear what I'm saying?"

Mick shrugged, asked, "Do any Vince Gill?"

"What?"

"You have a mobile?"

"Course."

"Tell you what, give Kate a buzz."

"Kate?"

"Is there an echo in here? ...Yeah, Kate, yer model girlfriend."

Matt was less sure of himself, took up his mobile and, as required, dialled. "Kate?"

"Matthew, hi."

Mick said, "Ask her if there's a blue Datsun parked outside."

He asked... waited, then, "There is... OK."

Mick nodded, said, "There's a bloke sitting here, he's got an acid container... need I paint a picture."

Matt jumped at him and got an almighty blow to the solar plexus. The band members murmured but didn't move.

Mick said, "Copyright infringement but we've got it sorted... haven't we, Matt?"

Matt, still on his knees said, "I'll go to the cops."

Mick hunkered down beside him, said, "That would be very silly. Where would Kate get a new face, eh? You have a little think about it."

Mick stood up, patted Matt's head, said, "I think coffee break's over."

> "There's no such thing as unconditional love. You just find a person with the same set of conditions as yourself."
>
> (Mark Kennedy)

Falls wasn't sure what to wear. She had been through her wardrobe, rejected it all. He'd said, "Let's have a drink, see how we go?"

Out loud she said, "Meaning, if I don't bore the arse offa him, we'll move to level two." And instantly chided herself.

If she was to get out of the mire, she'd need to change her attitude. Decided to go down-home-folks, pulled on tight worn 501's and a UCLA sweatshirt. Pair of red baseball shoes and she was Miss Selfridge.

"What do I call you?" she'd asked.

He thought about it, then, "Ryan."

"Like Ryan O'Neal?"

He smiled, "Not really."

They'd arranged to meet at The Cricketers. When she arrived he got out of a car, said, "You're on time."

"Oh, was it a test?"

He stopped, said, "You've some mouth on you." But he was smiling so she let it slide.

Inside, the pub was hopping and he explained, "Darts night."

"Oh."

She'd made a commitment that come what may, she'd tell the truth. Even if he asked what she did. Most times, say you're a cop, they'd say, "You're never!"

What hung there was not a woman being a cop but a bogey, a *black* woman. Most legged it. So she'd tell the truth, all down the line.

Okay.

He asked, "To drink?"

"Bacardi and coke."

Got a table away from the dart players. He came with the drinks, scotch and water chaser, said, "Cheers."

"Cheers, Ryan."

A tight smile as his drink hit, then he asked, "What do I call you?"

"Yvette."

First lie.

"Nice, I like it."

"Do you work?"

"Customer services."

Second lie.

She crossed her fingers, a third lie was outright wicked so she asked, "Are you married?"

"That's fairly direct, does it matter?"

"If we're planning an engagement."

He traced his finger on the rim of the glass, said, "I'm married with two kids, I'm not planning on leaving her."

Falls was taken aback. At the very least, he could have whinged that his wife didn't understand him.

She said, "Yet..."

"What?"

"You're not planning on leaving her *yet*."

He gave an uncertain smile and she added, "Give a girl a bit of hope."

"Oh."

Jeez, she thought, is he going to be as thick as two planks.

Then he said, "I don't like lying."

"You must have an amazing wife... shit, I mean life."

He finished his drink, grimaced, then: "I said I don't like it, not that I don't do it."

The music got louder and Falls asked, "Like this?"

"Yeah, I do, but I don't know it."

"It's Ocean Colour Scene."

"I believe you."

"Called "Beautiful Thing' with PP Arnold on there."

"You like music?"

"C'mon Ryan, what colour am I?"

"Sorry... look Yvette, could you cut me some slack here. I'm nervous and it cuts my banter into shit."

She felt her heart jump, touched his hand, said, "Nervous is good."

Later, they drove up the Edgware Road for bagels and lox. You have to know someone real well or not at all. Plus, it helps if they like lox. She did.

That night, after they'd made loud, sweaty, exhilarating love, she said, "Is it just me, or does lox sound slightly obscene?"

Crying time

Falls was bubbling. She bounced into the canteen and wanted to shout, "Oh yeah!"

She saw Sarah sitting alone. Head down, the picture of misery. Walking over, she said, "The star's a little dimmed."

Sarah looked up, said nothing. The skin above her left eye was bruised.

Falls sat, asked, "What happened?"

"Why, do you care?"

Falls touched her hand, said, "Wise up, I'm here."

Sarah mumbled, "Thanks."

"Listen, we could do like in *Cagney and Lacey*."

"Go to the Women's Room?"

"No... cry."

Falls stood up, went and got some tea and danish. On the way back she put four sugars in the tea, plonked it on the table, said, "Here."

"Oh I couldn't."

"It's for the sugar rush but it won't last, nothing does. You can tell me on the upswing."

Come the upsurge, came the story.

Like this: "I was having a drink with... with McDonald. He was getting me piña coladas. I've had them before but not like this. By the time we left, I was near legless. Next thing I know, we're in the front seat of his car and he's trying to push... his... thing in my mouth. I hit my eye against the door and then I vomited all over his... his, lower part. He got so angry, he pushed me outta the car. I was lying on the pavement, and this I do remember, he leaned over to shut the door and said, "Yah useless slag." Then he drove off.

"I dunno how I got home. Can I have some more tea, it was lovely?"

Falls got the tea, then asked, "What ya going to do?"

"I dunno. Will you tell me?"

Falls took a deep breath, then, "You could charge him."

"Oh God."

"God won't help and neither will the brass. They'll drag you through it and make it impossible to stay in the job. You might – big *might* – make some trouble for him but they'll massacre you."

Sarah looked set to cry again, said, "So, he gets away with it?"

Falls grabbed her wrist, said, "I never said to let it go, I just told you about the official method."

Hope now in Sarah's eyes, "There's another way?"

Falls gave a smile that Brant would have understood, said, "Course there is."

Once we were worriers

Brant was drinking a Sauza Sunrise. A close relation of The Eagles' "Tequila S", it consists of two Shots of Sauza Tequila, and...

lightly carbonated orange juice.

Brant was able to tell this to Roberts with some expertise mainly because the barman had just told him. There's a tapas bar on the corner where Kennington Road hits Kennington Park Road. Brant had arranged to meet Roberts there.

"Why?" asked Roberts.

"'Cos I'm feeling Spanish."

"You are a weird person, sergeant but, why not?"

Brant got there first. A barman in near flamenco gear, said, "Hi."

Brant said, "*Buenas Tardes.*"

"*Senor, habla espanol?*"

"Naw, that's it, I do have another word but I'd like to ration it."

The barman, not sure if this was humour, smiled. He was sure Brant was *el polica*. He'd be *mucho* cautious.

Brant said, "I dunno all this stuff from shit. What d'ya recommend?" And thus he was enjoying his second.

Later, he told the barman he'd try taco, enchillados, cerveza, if he could stand up.

"*Bueno,*" said a very nervous barkeep. The waitress was in her late ambitious thirties. Her mileage showed but she'd made the best of it. A raw sexuality danced in her eyes. She said to the barman, nodding at Brant, "Now, there is a bull of a man, a real *el toro.*"

The barman sighed. He was going to apply for income support.

Roberts tasted his drink, said, "You could get a liking."

"Good man, that's the spirit."

Roberts, the only person who ever got to use Brant's first name, said, "Tom, I hate to worry you but…"

Brant was shaking his head, "I don't worry."

Roberts stood back from the bar, said, "My mistake. You're a warrior, yeah."

Brant had the grace to look ashamed, said, "Oh gawd, do I sound like a horse's ass?"

"Yes."

"OK… What's worrying you?"

"A new sergeant being transferred to us. Starts Monday."

Brant shrugged. "I know."

"Do you? Oh shit, you're still bugging the office."

"Course… might I add, they dislike me."

"That's true."

"I hadn't finished, but they outright hate you."

"Jesus!"

"Yeah. The new guy's named Porter Nash."

"All together?"

"And he's a good cop."

Roberts asked for a beer. The barman got it, said, "*Una Cerveza.*"

Brant lit up. "Ah, that's beer."

"It's Don Miguel, *senor, mucho gusto.*"

"Yeah… later Juan."

Roberts asked, "Are we gonna eat?"

"Let's get a bit pissed, then we won't care what we eat."

"That's your plan?"

"For the moment. Anyway Porter Nash ain't going no further than sergeant, despite having a degree in criminology."

"Christ, you're well informed. What's the matter with Porter Nash?"

Brant smiled. "His dance card's not full."

"What?"

"He's a poofter, an arse bandit."

Roberts took a nervous look round, said, "Jeez, sarge, keep it down."

English graffiti

"They're Spaniards, they hate pillow-biters."
They went quiet for a while, get some concentrated drink down, then Brant asked, "Any ideas on how to get Tommy Logan?"

"Nothing feasible yet."

"We could shoot him."

"If it were anyone else but you, sergeant, I'd think that was a joke."

Brant raised his hand, shouted, "José... food please... *arriba*... don't worry, guv, I got the lingo covered and I think I'll get to ride the waitress."

Porter Nash was finishing up the Sunday papers. Reading about Peter Ackroyd, he noted:

"There was only the game of living
and the reality of writing."

"Hmmmph," he said and substituted "policing" for "living" and "homosexuality" for "writing." Not bad but it would be somewhat awkward to slide into conversation. The phone rang.

He lifted the receiver, said, "Yes?"

"Faggots aren't welcome in Kennington."

Nash said, "Thanking you for your interest."

And hung up.

He stood up and stretched. He looked a little like Michael York with edge. He was tall with blond hair and that fresh-faced

English look that's often mistaken for weakness. Yet again he wondered why he had asked for a transfer. It wasn't as if he expected some amazing tolerance in the south-east. But he'd been going stale and ceasing to care. Whatever else happened, he wanted to care.

Monday morning when he entered the canteen, it went completely quiet. Packed to capacity before the week's mayhem began. He went to the counter and got a tea. They knew he knew the toilets of both sexes had been written on… saying:

SERGEANT PORTER NASH

SUCKS ANY DICK

Even the tea lady knew. He avoided her eyes but unlike most of the ill-mannered buggers in there, he said, "please" when he asked for things, and "thank you" when he got them.

As he walked away, she said to the cashier. "Well, say what you like about him, he has great manners."

"They do, always."

He walked back down the length of the canteen, then took a sip of tea, put the cup down. As he headed out, conversation began to buzz but he stopped, turned and said, "I'm not arguing the basic truth of the toilet graffiti." And then he raised his voice, "But I do take exception to the word *any*. Even I draw the line at Sergeant Brant."

Then he was gone.

A moment later, huge applause erupted. By evening, not a trace of the graffiti remained. Later, when he and Falls had become friends, she asked, "Did you ever find out who wrote the graffiti?"

"Oh yes."

"Who?"

"I did it myself."

Falls would rarely be as impressed again.

Some friendships take a lot of work, others just develop, due to geography and environment. Then, now and again, you get the instant variety.

Even before they got to know each other, the friendship was cemented. Not love at first sight, but out of the same stable. Thus it was for Falls and Porter Nash. A near riot was sizzling in the DSS at the Elephant. Nash and Falls took the call.

Outside the station, he asked, "You want to drive?"

"You're the rank, I'll follow orders,"

He could see the spirit in her eyes. He said, "I order myself to drive." She liked that.

As he drove, he felt her examination, asked, "See anything you like?"

"I was thinking you got a rough reception."

"Honest in its way."

"Is that how you see it?"

"You want me to call them rednecks and bigots?"

"I do."

He considered, then, "That's because you're black."

It hung there till she said, "As I'm painted."

"Touché."

Approaching the DSS, she asked, "How are you going to tackle this?"

"Badly."

"Uh-uh, should we ask for back-up?"

"We should get guns but what the hell, let's make it up as we go along."

They could hear the disturbance and it sounded bad. He said, "Of course there's always the master plan."

"Yeah?"

"Run."

"That's my favourite."

Nash strode into the middle of the DSS office. Four or five different fights were happening on the left. Staff were cowering behind protective glass. A chair bounced off it. Falls tried to keep up with Nash. He stopped in the centre, roared, "*Who wants money – now?*"

A chorus of:

"What?"

"Eh?"

"Who's 'e then?"

"Wanker!"

He continued: "Those who want their money, please gather to the right; those wishing to fight, please await the riot police."

A stocky figure emerged from the crowd, asked, "Who the fuck are you?"

"I'm the man giving the money."

People began to move to the right and Nash said to Falls, "Get the staff moving."

She did.

The stocky guy marched up to Nash, asked, "Wotcha gonna do tomorrow?"

"Eh?"

"When I start another fight, will you give me more money."

"What's your name?"

"Les."

Nash moved closer, said quietly, "Can I give you fifty quid?"

"You what?"

"Tomorrow, it won't be my problem but I need to look good today... know what I mean?"

Les considered, then, "Is that fifty on top of my dole?"

"Of course."

"OK."

"Let's step outside, keep it discreet."

Falls watched the two men leave. They seemed almost friendly. With Les out, the riot fizzled away. The DSS manager approached, said, "Thank you, it could have turned nasty."

Falls nodded, and the manager, anxious to please, asked, "Any suggestion on how to proceed now?"

"Yes, try treating them with a little respect."

She went to find Nash. He was sitting in the car, no sign of Les. She asked, "Where did he go?"

"To pastures greener... or Peckham."

Then she saw his knuckles were raw and bleeding and he said, "Hands-on policing."

"Oh."

He moved to the passenger seat, asked, "Will you drive?"

She did.

No words for a while, then she said, "I have a question."

"OK."

"What is it with Barbara Streisand and you lot?"

He laughed out loud, said, "Only if you answer a question too."

"Sure."

"What is it with the baseball caps?"

Making Amends

McDonald was anxious. He'd yet to see Sarah and he was fearful of her reaction.

He wasn't sure if:

A She'd physically attack him,
B She'd verbally attack him,
C A *and* B.

Or, worse, report him.

He was playing these various scenes when she appeared in the corridor and… she was smiling! Jeez, he thought, has she a knife? His experience linked women's smiles to violence.

"Hi," she said.

"Oh right… listen, about last night… I…" She waved him quiet, said, "I'm the one who needs to apologise. I blacked out after the pub, you must have taken me home."

"Ahm… yeah… I did… you don't remember?"

"I am mortified. Please let me make it up to you."

"What?"

"Dinner at my place, Friday… eight o' clock… do you eat curry?"

"Curry… sure, that's great… I'll bring some wine."

She gave a shy smile, "Just mineral water for me. I want to remember this night."

"Sparkling?"

"I'm lit up already."

"What about the hotel
where I was asked, do I
want the double bed or the
comfortable bed?"
I thought, "This is a
quiz I am not up to"

(Janet Street-Porter)

B rant stirred, thought, Oh no, not again.
But OK... he wasn't dying. Went to stretch and his left
hand touched a face.
"Jesus!" he roared, sitting straight up.
Took a quick look:
A woman... thank God.
Then he looked again: the Spanish woman.
Yahoo, he'd scored... way to go, Brant!
For one horrible moment a movie flashed through his head.
Jane Fonda comes out of a blackout to find a corpse beside her.
If he could just remember her name. Weren't all these Spanish
women called the same?
His hangover, though not a killer, was jamming his mental
faculties. *Isabella!* Yeah, didn't they even have a queen with the
name?
He went to get some tea and clothes. Took another peek at
her, not bad at all. Made the tea and dry swallowed aspirin.

Rough.

Got some toast done then took it back to the bedroom. Thought it was a shame to wake her, because then she'd start to talk. Touched her arm, said, "Isabella?"

No movement.

Poked harder.

"*Que?*"

"*Buenos tardes*, Isabella."

She took a moment to focus, landed, asked, "*Que es* Isabella... who is this... is evening?"

"No, it's morning."

She sat up, none of the modest grabbing for sheets.

Let it show.

"You said, *Buenos tardes*."

"It's kinda all I got."

She tasted the tea, went, "*Caramba!*"

And leapt out of bed, said, "This is no good, I'll make us Spanish coffee."

"But I don't have anything from Spain."

She put her hands on her hips, asked, "And what am I?"

"Oh... right."

She disappeared into the kitchen with a shopping bag. Time on, she's back with coffee and baked or heated toast – sorta. Brant tasted the coffee, said, "It tastes like... vanilla..."

"*Bueno*, now eat, and then you'll make fiery love to your woman."

Brant was less sure about the last bit. Mornings were not a passionate time for him. He asked, "So what, you carry mini meals around with you just in case?"

"It's my shopping and I didn't get home."

He thought the coffee wasn't half bad. Could vanilla taste bitter? This did.

Took some toast and said, "I never ate sweet toast, like it's got edge."

"Now we make love."

He stood up, time to take charge.

Went and got her a T-shirt, said, "You go and shower, I've got to go to work."

She put on the T-shirt and it reached her knees. On its front were the words:

I AM A NATURAL BLOND

PLEASE TALK SLOWLY

It amused him all over again. He gave her a slap on the arse, said, "Let's move it, toots."

As he headed for work, she said, "My name is Concheta."

For one bizarre moment, he thought she said, "Cochise".

He said nothing and she added, "Those close to me call me Cheta."

"OK."

"Please, one time, say it."

"What... oh... all right... Cheta."

"*A muy buena*, you are *mucho simpatico*."

He looked at his watch, said, "I'm bloody late is what I am."

That evening, Brant was saying to Roberts, "I swear, guv, she stayed the night."

"I don't believe it."

"Straight up, guv – and mad for it. Got to go."

Roberts was impressed and envious, said, "You always land on yer feet."

Brant gave his lucky smile, answered, "Always."

Outside the station, the rain was lashing down. To Brant's amazement, he saw two white teenagers about to break into his Volvo. If not exactly broad daylight, it was brazen.

"Oi!" he shouted and came running.

Grabbed one by the neck. A long steel bar slipped from the kid's hands, clattered on the kerb. Brant was about to launch forth when an incredible pain wound up his insides, sweat poured down his face.

He dropped to one knee, near doubled in agony.

The first kid asked, "What's with 'im?"

The other kid, marvelling at their deliverance, said, "Bugger's sick he is."

Brant pushed out his left hand to grab the car for support.
The second kid said, "Jeez, look at the watch, it's a Tag."
"What?"
"Take the bleeding thing."
The first kid was dubious, "Is it a fake?"
Through his pain, Brant tried to say yes but it emerged as a grunt. The second kid moved forward, grabbed Brant's wrist and took the watch, said, "Let's go… quick."
Brant lay on the pavement, rain caressing his face.

Brant threw up and that made him a little better. He managed to get to his feet and, after four attempts, he got the door open. Fell in behind the wheel and let his head rest. Every inch of him was soaked. He almost passed out, then came to. Weak as a kitten but better. Put the car in gear and drove slowly home.

He didn't intend reporting this. Him, mugged by kids. He'd lose his rep. The Tag he'd get back, by Christ, see if he didn't. But his rep, he couldn't jeopardise that. Like luck it was near impossible to recapture. At home he fell on the bed, damp clothes an' all and slept for ten hours.

Ice Cream

Roberts, as per deal, bought a copy of the *Big Issue* every week. His vendor knew he was a cop and seemed unfazed. He was eating from a tub of Haagen Dazs ice-cream.

Roberts said, "Bit cold for it, isn't it?"

The vendor moved aside, said, "Look."

Behind him was a large box with maybe another dozen tubs.

Roberts asked, "You also sell ice-cream?"

The vendor laughed, "A while ago a Daimler pulled up at the kerb. The window rolls down and a woman said, 'You there, come here'."

He mimicked the posh to perfection, continued, "I thought it was Liz, come to give me an MBE."

Roberts laughed.

"'Ere, I'm serious, guv... they gave one to a traffic warden last year. So, I goes over, took me cap off and this woman, leans out, asks, "Are you one of the homeless chappies?"

"I said, 'We sell THE *Big Issue* for the homeless, yes Ma'am'."

"She says, "Righty ho, my driver has something for you people." Then she tapped the glass partition for the driver and shuts the window on me.

"The driver gets out and he's in all the gear, peaked cap and boots. Like a nazi!"

The vendor stopped and sold two copies to two girls and gave them a tub each. They were delighted.

He winked at Roberts, said, "Like loyalty cards, a little bonus for my regulars. Any road, the nazi opens the boot and takes out the ice-cream. I asked, "What am I supposed to do with that?" He gave me the look, said, "Try eating it."

The vendor took another taste, said, "It's not bad if you put a touch o' lager in it."

Roberts took out his change, had only a fiver... The vendor said, "We take all the major credit cards."

Roberts gave him the five, got change, then waited a moment... no tub. Roberts said, "Well, see you next week."

Dejected, he was walking away when the vendor shouted, "Oi, you forgot yer Haagen Dazs."

"The only actress on the
planet who can play a
woman whose child has been
killed by wild Australian
dogs and can actually have
you rooting for the
dingoes."

(Joe Queenan on Meryl Streep.)

Falls smiled as she recalled Ryan's reaction to *A Cry in the Dark* when she put on the video.

They'd planned an evening at home, her home, where they'd:

Make love
Eat
Make love
Watch a video.

He cried, "Oh Jesus, no, not Streep again. C'mon darlin', I watched *Out of Africa* with you, but I swear, I can't go another session with her."

They watched *The Untouchables* instead.

She'd been seeing Ryan for two weeks, twice he'd stayed over.

On the video nights. Little did he realise, she'd planned on the whole Streep catalogue. Most days she felt:

Queasy

Exhilarated

Nervous

Giddy

Had no appetite

Phone fixated.

And realising, said, "Oh shit, I love him."

She was acting like a schoolgirl, trying out his name, projecting babies, wanting to talk about him incessantly. Tried to burst her own balloon with:

He's married,

Kids,

Said he won't leave.

But no, that balloon of hope just climbed on up there.

He'd said, "You look good in red." Changed her whole wardrobe. Oh yeah.

She turned on the telly, got local news, *London Tonight*.

The top story was:

RETURN OF THE CLAPHAM RAPIST

She felt dizzy. Another attack had taken place, the details were the same: a black woman, a knife, an alleyway.

"It can't be!" she cried.

A local councillor followed demanding an inquiry into police methods. And then he asked, "Who was the man killed in a police decoy operation?"

The phone rang. She picked it up, heard, "You and McDonald in the Super's office at nine sharp."

"Yes, sir."

She rang Brant. He sounded groggy and she told him the news. He didn't reply for a moment, then, "It's a copycat."

"But what about the guy who attacked me?"

Deep intake of breath and he snarled back, "When a guy jumps you in a dark alley, and puts a knife to yer throat, he's up to no good, believe me."

"But maybe he wasn't *the* Clapham Rapist."

"Well he was some bloody area's rapist and good friggin' riddance."

He slammed down the phone. She started to cry… wanted to drink, then rang Ryan.

He answered, "Yeah?"

"Help me."

"I'm on my way."

She tried to compose herself. Decided she'd only tell him a little.

When he arrived, he put his arms round her and she told him the lot. He'd made her a cup of sweet tea and held it while she drank. When she'd finished her story, he said, "I'd never have took you for a copper."

"Because I'm black."

"'Cos you're beautiful."

Fright night

Neville Smith was doing good. A stockbroker, he had a house in Dulwich, two kids at boarding school, and his new car. An Audi. As he gazed at it he said, "*Vorsprung Techniquo.*"

It was that and more.

Neville liked to drive fast and just a tad recklessly. He truly believed that ninety percent of drivers had no right to be there. They all had the look of National Assistance. He liked to cut them up and take the road. Austin Micras, Ka's, Datsuns, "all garbage," he said.

There'd been a diversion so he found himself heading for the Elephant roundabout. If he could make the light, he'd gain time. He swerved in front of a Rover almost touching the fender. He definitely took paint and made the light. He could see the driver and his passenger shouting at him. The adrenalin rush made him near euphoric and he put up the two fingers.

Through the lights and he accelerated, shouted, "Morons!"

The Rover pulled in near the park and Tommy Logan asked, "You got the number?"

"Sure did, guv."

"Good man, I want to know who he is by lunchtime."

The driver was speed dialling, said, "I'm on it."

Two days later, Neville was relaxing over a gin and tonic. His wife asked, "How about sushi?"

He took his cue, followed with the expected line, "If you knew sushi like I know sushi..."

They both laughed, not so much humour as the ease of familiarity.

"Will you open the wine darling while I prepare the table?"

"Of course."

He'd done that and was about to glance at the news when the door bell rang.

He said, "I'll go."

Opening the door, he saw two heavy set men. One asked, "Do you own an Audi?" And gave the registration.

"Yes I do... why?"

The first said, "You've got dirt on the side."

"What?"

Then he was pushed backwards and the men followed him in closing the door. The first man began to slap Neville across the face. His wife came running, started to scream.

Tommy Logan kicked her in the stomach, said, "Don't start."

Now Tommy moved over to Neville and spun him round, face down on the stairs. Tore Neville's pants down and said, "Do yah want it, eh? Want some of this?"

Tommy stood back, asked, "Have I got yer attention?"

"Yes."

"Do you know who I am?"

"No."

Tommy lashed out with his fist, roaring "I'm the guy you cut up in traffic."

Another blow and, "And gave the two fingers to."

"Oh God, I'm sorry."

"You're sorry now, sorry we caught you."

Neville was blubbering, "Let me make it up to you... money..."

"Shaddup!" Tommy said. And, as if he'd just thought of it, "Course, the car's to blame."

Neville, sensing a tiny shimmer of hope, said, "You're right... one gets carried away."

Tommy smiled said, "It must be punished... bad car."

Tommy pushed Neville out to the garage.

Took a look round then said, "My man has just the ticket."

Mick came in, dragging the woman and carrying a hurley,

handed it to Tommy, who took it and gave a slow swing. Asked, "Isn't it a beauty?"

Handed the hurley to Neville, said, "Go on... won't bite you."

For a moment, as he held it, a fire touched his eyes.

Tommy laughed, "Don't even think about it or I'll make you eat it."

"What do you want me to do?"

"Punish the car, beat the living daylights outta it and keep saying 'bad car'."

Tommy looked over at Neville's wife, said, "If you don't, my man there is going to fuck her all over this garage. Trust me, he's an animal."

Neville lifted the hurley, said, "Bad car."

Say cheese

Brant was sitting in his armchair, smoking and thinking. In his career, he'd broken two major cases with a hunch. He'd acted on them when all the evidence pointed elsewhere. He'd play what he knew, then let it settle, add in the possibilities and bingo, he'd get an answer.

Now he sat bolt upright in his chair, said, "Jesus." Then he got on the phone, said, "It's Brant."

"Sergeant, how are you? Did the bugging device work?"

"Like a dream."

"Good, do you need something?"

"A hidden camera."

"No problem, where is it to go?"

"In a kitchen."

"Mmm, tricky to install."

"It's my own kitchen."

"Right... when?"

"Now."

"Gimme yer address, I'll be there in an hour."

Brant gave it, said, "I appreciate it."

"A pleasure."

"I'll watch for you."

The man laughed, said, "Sergeant, leave the surveillance to us, it's what we do."

That evening when Cheta arrived, she was carrying bags of groceries. First off she gave him a swallowing kiss, then pushed him off, with "*Hombre...* my *caballero*, first we eat."

Needling, he said, "Let's go out."

No way. She indicated the bags of stuff.

"This is especial, now... you relax, the kitchen is mine... no *hombres* allowed."

He made as if to follow, "That's not very liberated."

She threw her hands, mock horror, said, "I am Spanish."

"OK... what's on the menu?"

"Paella... with the recipe of Andalucia, *gorelax*."

He opened a beer but barely touched it, gave her forty-five minutes, then, "Honey, I've got to go."

She came storming out, "How? I hear no phone."

"My mobile, very discreet but it's urgent."

"But the dinner... is ready... have *pocito*, taste."

He was already at the door, "I'll make it up to you tomorrow."

"Will I wait?"

"No, it's an all nighter."

He waited outside in the Volvo. He figured she was cunning but none too smart. They rarely got to be both. After half-an-hour, a cab pulled up, she came out, gave her destination, never looked round. She lived in Streatham, back of the swimming pool. A row of terraces in the passageway, she went into the second.

As he drove away, he phoned Roberts, asked, "Like to see a video?"

"What now?"

"It's a one-off, you'll recognise the star."

"Do I bring anything."

"Handcuffs, probably."

The picture was quality, none of that grainy effect. If Brant thought it was strange to watch her in his own kitchen, he didn't show it. Just smoked a lot of Weights. They could see her put the paella on the plates then go to her bag, extract a small bottle and douse one plate.

Brant said, "Guess who that's for."

Then she was gone.

Brant explained, "It's me telling her I'm off."

Back she came and they could see her rage as she scraped the dishes into the bin.

Roberts asked, "You have the bin?"

"Oh yeah."

Next she tidied up, washed all the gear, even wiped the floor. Roberts said, "Good little housekeeper though."

Brant smiled, answered, "Deadly."

The lab test showed liquid arsenic.

Roberts asked, "Wanna come when we give her a tug?"

"No... I'll pass I think."

Later, Roberts said, "Buy you a drink?"

"Yeah great, but a pub with no barmaids."

"Right."

After they'd had a few, Roberts asked, "Wanna hear about it?"

"Sure."

"She had a reason."

"Oh good, that makes it all right then."

Roberts signalled for another round, said, "She claims she never intended to kill, just to sicken you as it is men always sickened her."

Brant took a belt of scotch, said, "A nutter eh?"

"Barking."

Roberts felt he should offer some support or even solace. But, all he could give was, "Don't let it put you off women."

Brant gave a huge belch, said, "It sure as hell put me off paella."

Benediction moon

"I'm a spiritual person" the man said to Porter Nash. It was a rite of passage at any new station, you got the loopy cases. This was certainly that.

The man had been attacked by a pimp and a hooker. They'd given him a sound thrashing. Nash asked, "How did you happen to ah... meet these people?"

The man sighed, he didn't suffer fools gladly.

"I go to professional ladies and to demonstrate their baseness to them, I pay them in a similar coinage."

"You're not a priest, are you?"

Tolerant smile, "I'm a deacon of the flesh."

Nash read the charge sheet again. He was getting a migraine. He said, "You gave the *lady* two forged fifties."

"It's debauchery, paid for by deceit."

Nash asked, "Where do you get the funny money?"

"A chap in an ale house had a bag of them, a British Homes Store brand... yes, I'm sure of that."

Nash said, "You'll go down for... something."

The man stood up, "I'll embrace the penitentiary."

"Believe me, they'll help you."

As they took him away, he shouted, "I see auras."

"Course you do."

"And yours, sir, is blue."

Nash had to ask, "That good?"

"'Ish."

He went to the canteen and the tea lady was delighted anew with his manners. Ordered tea and got two slices of toast he hadn't ordered, said, "I didn't order toast."

She gave a full silver toothed smile, "It's my little treat."

"Gosh... how wonderful."

Thinking, if he got five minutes with a novel, he'd better meet the day. Had a round of toast drenched and dripping in butter, then opened his book.

"Can I join you?"

Falls.

He thought, Ah, shag off, is it too much to ask for a few minutes?

He said, "Please do."

She asked, "Wotcha reading?"

"It's Jane Smiley's *A Thousand Acres*."

"I dunno her."

He wanted to roar, "Quelle surprise!", but said, "She won the Pulitzer."

"That's good?"

"It's not bad."

"Is it good?"

"Well, I'm only on the third acre but it's boring the pants off me."

She laughed, said, "Thanks for not treating me like an ignoramus."

He offered the toast, saying, "It's heaven."

She took it, asked, "How'd you get toast like this?"

He only smiled, so she said, "I think we're mates."

Nod.

"So, can I ask your opinion."

He gave her the final slice, a true sacrifice and said, "I'm a good choice 'cos I tell people what they want to hear."

"Oh God, don't do that."

"OK."

"There's a man..."

"I hear you."

She glanced around, she sure as hell didn't want anyone to hear, asked, "How do I know if it's... you know... love?"

This Nash could do. He smiled said, "A few questions will answer that."

"Oh."

"Do you wanna go for it?"

"Ahm... OK, I think."

"Do you think of him [here Nash did an American accent] like all the time?"

"Yes."

"Have you got the runs?"

She laughed and nodded. "Is your appetite screwed? Do songs seem to be directed specifically at you? Do you want to do nothing but stare out the window?"

"Yes, yes, yes."

"Now for the biggie, the litmus test."

Falls felt nervous, said, "I feel nervous."

"So you should, here goes."

He went American again.

"Would you, like, just *die* if you saw him with somebody else?"

"Oh yes."

"Then I must inform you, WPC Falls, that you are completely and irrevocably in love, and may God have mercy on your soul."

Later, rearranging his CDs, he pulled out "Benediction Moon." Its mix of keening loss, awareness, and wonder were the articulation of a heart on fire.

Let's party

A warehouse near The Elephant had been transformed. A crowd had gathered outside to see the party-goers arrive. When Tommy Logan got there he gave two fingers to the crowd. That they understood. Gave him a rousing cheer. "My people" he said.

As fixed, security was provided by off duty cops. McDonald was on the door, he said to Tommy: "Good evening, sir."

Tommy palmed him a ten, said, "Keep up the good work."

Inside the band were tuning up. Tommy said to Mick, "Who are they?"

"The band you requested."

"Can they play?"

"They're a spit from being famous, guv."

The warehouse had lived many lives. At one stage it had been a cinema and a balcony ran along the back. The projection room was still intact. A flight of stairs led from it to the street. Mick moved up to the band, said to the surly Matt, "Get started."

"We're artists man, we don't just *start*."

Mick hopped lightly on to the stage, went nose-to-nose, said, "You're history if you don't and never, like fuckin' *never* call me *man*, get it?"

He got it.

They kicked off with a cover of The Verve's "Bittersweet Symphony," the extended one.

Tommy said, "Sounds like the Rolling Stones."

Mick was clued, said, "Based on 'The Last Time'!"

"It's good, they're OK."

Mick said, "They're keen as mustard, chuffed to play for you."

A stir at the door as the Super arrived. Harry the solicitor behind. Their wives were interchangeable. Like models of Mrs. Thatcher. Tommy moved to greet them, signalling to a waiter for champagne. Outside, to the left of the crowd, Brant was leaning on his car, cigarette going. Roberts drove up, rolled down his window, said, "You're not supposed to be here."

"You neither."

"You going to gatecrash?"

"If you're game."

Roberts smiled, said, "Lemme park, I'll get back to you."

Brant flicked the cig away, said, "I'll be here."

When McDonald saw them approach, he went, "Oh, shit."

Worse, they were smiling at him. Inside, the band were attempting "Working Class Hero" as a touch of contempt.

But as usual, those who least understood the song were the ones who most appreciated it. Roberts said, "Bit of moonlighting, McDonald?"

"Sir."

They made to enter and he stepped in front of them, said, "Guv, I'll have to see yer invites."

Brant said, "Gee, we left them in the car."

McDonald didn't move and Roberts said, "S'cuse me son."

He moved.

The first person they met was Tommy's wife, Tina. She said, "I can't believe you got invited."

Roberts looked at her, said, "Wouldn't miss it for the world."

The Super glared at them across the hall. Brant waved. More people arrived and the place was becoming crowded. Brant asked Tina to dance, she said, "Get real."

Tommy said to Mick, "I want them outta here."

"There'd be a scene."

"Are you saying let 'em be?"

"For now."

"Fuckers!"

Food was served and Brant was first in line. Got double helpings. His plate overflowing, he moved back to Roberts, said, "The grub is good, guv, wanna try some?"

Roberts looked at it in disgust, said, "It would choke me."

"Food dunno from shit, guv… it's like money."
"You're getting very philosophical."
"Naw, just hungry."

Like all shindigs worth the name, there was a raffle. Cops love them. Brant had a fistful of tickets, said to Roberts, "Do you feel lucky?"
"Gimme a break!" And he moved off.
First prize of a music centre went to Harry the solicitor.
Good humoured shouts of "*Fix! Fix!*" punctuated his acceptance of the prize. Tommy was doing the presentation. His face was shining, his triumph assured. He said, "Second prize of my own personal favourite, a Waterford crystal bowl, goes to a green ticket Number 93."
When he saw who'd won, his face dropped. Brant. When Brant got to the stage, he gave Tommy a huge hug, whispered, "Ya wanker." Then stepped back as Tommy handed over the prize.
Brant took it, looked down at the crowd, then let go. The crystal shattered in a thousand pieces. Brant said, "Oops!"
On Brant's way down the hall, he came face to face with The Super who said, "My office, nine of clock sharp."
Brant smiled, said, "Wouldn't miss it for the world."
The band launched into a frenzied version of "Let's Dance."
Brant spotted Tina, asked, "Wanna quickstep?"
"You've got to be kidding."
"Yeah, you're too fat for it all right."

Tommy was checking his speech. Before the party finished, he'd say a few words.
He said to Mick, "There's no jokes, it needs humour." Mick thought, You're the fuckin' joke, but said, "Maybe it's best to play it straight."
"You think?"
"Yeah, more dignity, know what I mean?"
"I can do dignified."

When the time came, all the lights went out. A lone spotlight lit the stage. Tommy strode out. Looking down the hall, he was blinded and could see nowt. He began, "Officers and ladies…"

A single shot rang and a small hole appeared over his right eye. He gave a tiny "Ah," and fell backward.

Who shot TL?

The suspects were:
Brant
Roberts
Tina Logan
gang rival(s).

Brant and Roberts had received a bollocking from the Super and he let them know they were high on the suspect list. Now, over coffee, Brant said, "Well, guv, I know I didn't shoot him, did you?"

"No… but I'm shedding no tears."

"Who do you think?"

"I strongly suspect you."

Brant laughed. "What about Tina, his wife?"

"She could have got somebody to do it. Who'd blame her. He sure needed shooting."

Brant stretched, said, "It was a great party, I really enjoyed it."

"God forbid you shouldn't be happy."

The desk sergeant appeared, said, "Brant, there's a call for you, a Paul Johnson."

"I'm not here."

"He says it's urgent."

"Tough."

The sergeant went away muttering.

Roberts asked, "Who's Paul Johnson?"

"My ex-wife's husband."

"Oh!"

"Oh is bloody right."

❖

McDonald was in the Super's office. No Masonic hand-shit this trip. It was ball-busting and vehement.

The Super said, "For heaven's sake, you were on the door and you didn't see the shooter?"

"It was pandemonium, sir. People were panicked and stampeding. Plus, there's a fire escape leading from the projection booth to the street."

"The papers are having a field day. We've got to find the shooter and fast."

McDonald had thought it over and decided to go for broke, said, "I think I know who it is."

"What? Spit it out man."

"DS Brant, sir."

The Super's eyes bulged.

"Are you mad?"

"Sir, he'd do anything for DI Roberts. He was there and he is without conscience. It has to be him."

"Can you prove it."

"I will, sir. I guarantee it."

Now he was way out on a limb. If he was wrong, he'd be out on his ass.

The Super said, "OK, keep it under your hat. I don't need to spell it out if you're right *or* if Brant gets wind of your claim."

"I'll be discreet, sir."

"You better be."

Outside the office, McDonald wiped his brow. Sarah was coming along the corridor, asked, "Are we set for this evening?"

"What?"

"My place, I'm cooking dinner for you."

"Oh yeah... right... sure."

He thought "a leg over' was exactly what he needed. Calm him down and let him focus on frying Brant's ass.

Falls was in the canteen, listening to the various stories on the party. People were poring over the tabloids. Falls asked, "Can I see the paper?"

One came sailing over to land on the table. The front page had a large photo of Tommy Logan, stretched on the stage. A man was bending over him and there was something about the tilt of his head. She muttered, "Oh no."

She got up, ran from the canteen, the paper in her hand. Near collided with Roberts who said, "Whoa, where's the fire?"

She pushed the paper at Roberts, cried, "Who's that?"

"Tommy Logan – the late Tommy Logan."

She tried to control her hysteria, said, "Not him, the other one."

"That's Mick Ryan, his lieutenant, the next in line."

"Ryan?"

"Yes, do you know him."

She gazed at the paper before answering, "No, no, I don't know him at all."

When McDonald knocked on Sarah's door, he was carrying flowers and chocolates. On heat, he was anticipating the ride of his life. That she was a snotty little cow only fuelled his excitement. She opened the door, wearing a white silk kimono. Her breasts were tantalisingly on display. He moved inside, pushed her against the wall, began to grope. A few minutes and he'd have popped.

Pushing him away, she said, "Let's whet out appetites."

A glass of whiskey was already poured. She asked, "Is Glenfiddich OK?"

"Aye, lass."

Truth to tell, he'd never had it. So if it tasted a tad off, he wouldn't know. Put mustiness down to quality.

"You sit here." And she manoeuvred him into an armchair.

"More?" she asked, coming with the bottle. As he held out his glass, he had to loosen his shirt, said, "Jeez, it's hot in here."

She smiled, poured, said, "Animal heat."

The room was tilting and he thought, "I'm legless, how can I be so pissed."

As he sank back into the armchair, he tried to focus on Sarah but he was seeing double. Odd thing was, he could have sworn that half of Sarah was Falls. What? He closed his eyes.

The doctor said, "I don't quite know how you managed it but your penis is Super-Glued to your testicles."

McDonald didn't know what to say. He wanted to howl. He'd come to in his car with a bastard of a headache. Nothing of the evening could he remember. Bursting for a piss, he found his dick wouldn't budge. Thus the doctor and his absolute mortification.

He strongly suspected the doctor was smirking. Worse, he had a nurse who was outright laughing. The doctor said, "Here's what we'll do to... ahm... release you, but I won't lie, it's going to be painful."

It was.

McDonald howled for all he was worth.

Smoking

Brant was standing outside the station with Roberts. He was lighting one cigarette with the stub of another. Roberts said, "Those will kill you."

Brant nodded but didn't speak. A young constable came down the steps, said, "Sarge, there's a call for you."

"Who is it?"

"Ahm, oh yeah, Paul Johnson."

"I'm not here."

"What."

"Are yah deaf, I'm not available."

"Oh... right."

A car pulled up at the kerb and Porter Nash got out. Both men watched him closely. He came right up to Brant, said, "I have something for you."

"For me?"

"I caught two teenagers breaking into a car yesterday. They offered me a watch to let them slide."

Here, Nash put his hand in his pocket, produced the Tag, continued, "I persuaded them to tell me where they got it." Brant looked at Nash and the moment hung. Then Nash said, "Seems they saw you drop it."

Brant let out a deep breath, took the watch, said, "I owe you one."

"Glad to help."

After Nash had gone, Roberts asked, "What just happened?" But Brant was raging, spat "I fuckin' hate that."

"What?"

"Him. You know, owing him a favour."

"I thought you'd be glad to get the Tag."

"They never forget, you know."

"Who?"

"Queers... they hold it over you..."

Roberts sighed, said, "You are a very twisted man... very."

Mick Ryan knocked on Falls door. She opened it, said, "What do you want?"

"To talk."

"I'm surprised you have time, I mean aren't you supposed to be running a crime empire."

He looked round, said, "Please."

She had been expecting a rage of homicidal proportions. But all she felt now was sad and tired, said, "Come in."

For a moment they simply watched each other. He tried, "I dunno where to begin."

"The truth would be nice."

"I'm not going to apologise for who I am. But I'm truly sorry if you've been hurt."

"If!"

"I'm getting out... like all the rest, I'll go to the Costa."

"How nice."

"Come with me."

She gave a bitter laugh, asked, "As what, yer au pair?"

"You can have your own villa... it could work."

Falls sat down, said, "I'm in deep shit over the rapist and you're offering me a shag in Spain. No thanks."

Ryan went to touch her but let his hand fall away, said, "Watch the papers on Saturday, it's the least I can do."

"Oh, you've sold your story."

He moved to the door, said, "Take care."

She said nothing at all.

Brant was heading for the pub, asked Roberts, "Wanna pint, guv?"

"Naw, I'm knackered."

The Cricketers was quiet and Brant ordered a Stella. He was getting on the good side of that when a man came into the bar, looked around and headed his way.

He said, "DS Brant?"

Brant gave the man a hard look, asked, "Why?"

"I went to the station and they said I might find you here."

"Helpful bastards, aren't they?"

The man put out his hand, said, "I'm Paul Johnson."

Brant ignored the hand, said, "And that's supposed to tell me what?"

"I'm married to your ex-wife."

"Oh."

"I wanted to thank you for extricating me from the shop-lifting charge."

Brant turned away. "No big deal, you needn't have wasted the trip."

But the man didn't go and Brant let his testiness show, barked, "What?"

"I think I can help you."

"Help me? And how the fuck could you help me?"

"The Tommy Logan killing. I know who did it."

Brant moved off his stool, took the man's arm, said, "Let's park it at the back."

Moved to a table at the rear, Brant said, "Let's hear it."

"A few weeks back, a man named Neville Smith cut up Tommy Logan in traffic. Later, Logan came to Smith's house, terrorised him and his wife. Then, to complete the humiliation, Tommy Logan invited them to his party. Neville Smith is ex-army and a very proud man. His wife told Mary..."

Brant wasn't sure what to say, tried a gruff, "Thanks."

It had to suffice. That evening Brant rang Roberts, laid out the story. Roberts listened without comment and Brant asked, "What will you do, guv?"

"Nothing."

Two days later, Roberts got a package in the mail. No note or

message, just a cassette tape. He read the title with a tight smile –
Smokie's Greatest Hits.

When Falls woke late on the Saturday morning, she went to get
the paper before anything else. It was on Page four, a half column:

*"Man found naked and chained to a tree on Clapham
Common. A notice round his neck read: 'I AM THE COPYCAT
RAPIST'. Police were issuing no statement until a full investi-
gation could be launched."*

Falls looked up into a clear blue sky. Saw the trail of a plane,
and didn't expect it was heading for the Costa... But... you never
could tell.